FORTUNATE
MONSTERS

T0006950

A Novel by
Manuel Luis Martinez

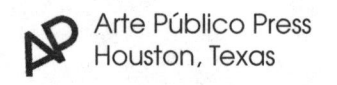
Arte Público Press
Houston, Texas

Fortunate Monsters is funded in part by a grant from the National Endowments for the Arts and the Texas Commission on the Arts. We are thankful for their support.

Recovering the past, creating the future

Arte Público Press
University of Houston
4902 Gulf Fwy, Bldg 19, Rm 100
Houston, Texas 77204-2004

Cover art and design by William Denton Ray
Author photo by Molly S. Martinez

Library of Congress Control Number: 2023943403

♾ The paper used in this publication meets the requirements of the American National Standard for Information Sciences—Permanence of Paper for Printed Library Materials, ANSI Z39.48-1984.

23 24 25   4 3 2 1

For my daughters, Cora and Hannah

Contents

The vast majority of macro mutations can only be viewed as disastrous—called monsters. But every once in a while, a macro mutation might, by sheer good fortune, adapt an organism to a new mode of life, a "hopeful monster."

Richard Goldschmidt, *The Material Basis of Evolution*

It is true, we shall be monsters, cut off from all the world; but on that account shall we be more attached to one another.

Mary Shelley, *Frankenstein*

CHAPTER 1
Real Father

Virginia didn't remember much about him at all. Not even his name. A visit once when she was only four, her mother telling her that she was going to meet her *real* father, a terrible fight, a stuffed dog. The toy dog was still around somewhere. At some point, its eyes had gone missing, first the right, then the left, after a couple of years of her dragging it around everywhere she went.

The visit was mostly a memory of a memory implanted by her mother before the man who raised her, who insisted on calling himself her father, a trucker named Benny-Boy Lopez, came on the scene. Benny-Boy was terrible jealous and he didn't want the ex-husband's name mentioned in his house. He'd even objected to the stuffed animal when he'd found out its source. That suited her mother just fine, and so she'd taken it from the little girl and "put it away," telling Virginia she could play with it when Daddy, that is, Benny-Boy, wasn't home.

That didn't mean her mom *never* brought up Virginia's real father. When Celia got to feeling lonely and angry, she'd tell Virginia that men were for shit. Benny-Boy was no kind of man, but he was better than the sack of shit her real father was. That's what she called him, her *real father,* as if using his

1

given name was beneath contempt. She'd say, "your real father was nothing but a no-account druggie, wife-sluggin', whore-mongerin', sonuvabitchin' jailbird. And if he'd had been able to just keep his nose clean for ten minutes, the two of us wouldn't be beholden to Benny-Boy Lopez."

Her mom wanted Virginia to know that all failure, all suffering, could and should be attributed to Real Father. But to young Virginia, Real Father was a godsend. A powerful, mysterious figure who would have rescued her from her horrible life if only he'd known she was suffering. He'd have taken her away from her indifferent and bitter mother, who looked the other way when Benny-Boy graduated from hugging her a bit too tightly as she started to develop her formidable *chichis* to coming into her bedroom at night and doing way worse. She loathed him so much that nightly in the mirror in her room she looked fearfully for any subtle resemblances that might have possibly asserted themselves not through genetics, but through some horrible osmotic exposure.

Benny-Boy would wake her in the middle of the night, dragging her from sleep, the one place of refuge in her miserable teen life, and tell her that she needed to 'preciate just how much old Benny-Boy had done for her. She was a little ungrateful bitch. He'd sit there, recounting how hard he worked and how bad his ass hurt from all the driving, and how his shoulders cramped all over on the countless thousand miles he had to drive, and nobody waiting at home to give Benny-Boy Lopez the small favor of a goddamned shoulder rub, and wasn't she goddamned ashamed of how she was turning out like that bitch of a mother of hers? Well, where was that bitch of a mother of hers, anyway? Out on the town with a horde of other no-account bitch mothers who should've had the goddamned decency to be home giving their husbands a goddamned shoulder rub, that's where!

It went on like that for years, until one night when Benny-Boy came into the room, drunk and rubbing his crotch, Virginia clubbed his staggering ass with a souvenir bowling pin that Benny-Boy had won at the Holy Ghost Creole Festival that past November. He went down like a sack of potatoes rolled off the back of a pickup truck. But that didn't stop Virginia by a long shot. She wanted to hurt Benny-Boy bad. Maybe even kill him. She beat on his head like Moses beating the rock at Horeb. She wanted to see the bastard leak. And leak he did. He lay there moaning and blubbering, trying to get the strength to pull his hands up to his bruised, bloody scalp. Virginia grabbed him by the ankles and, using all the leverage she could muster, pulled him down the hallway, facedown, blood and slobber trailing as he muttered and pleaded and cursed. She tried to kick him down the stairs, but lying as he was, prostrate and compact, it proved too difficult. She left him on the stairs, his head a mass of lumps, leaning awkwardly on the top step, his feet pointed towards the bottom, his pants drenched in cold piss. Virginia looked at him, one of his boots in her hands, having come loose as she dragged him. She spat on it and tossed the boot downstairs so her drunken mother would have a path to follow. And then Virginia got the hell out and headed for her best friend Carmen's house. She stayed a month.

When she came home, making sure Benny-Boy's rig was gone, her mother told her that he was gone for good. As Celia wept on her shoulder, Virginia started to laugh and not gently or in an embarrassed, muffled way. The laugh was from the belly, and it shook her body so that her shoulders convulsed and Celia was knocked from the drunken, self-pitying embrace.

She stared at her daughter and finally said, wiping the tears away, "Just what's so funny? What's so funny!" She yelled when Virginia couldn't find the breath to answer. "Huh? What's so funny?"

It took all Virginia could muster to halt the laughter and ask an even more important question. "Am I yours? Maybe you stole me from a truck stop. Tell me you stole me from a grocery store when my real parents were looking at a box of cereal or somethin'."

At this, Celia took a drunken slug at her daughter, but Virginia dodged it easily. She'd developed a talent for dodging things.

Virginia walked out and got drunk with Carmen, her only friend. She told her, "Boy, Virginia, you're lucky, so lucky that at least Benny-Boy Lopez isn't your flesh and blood. Try living with my pop!"

"I don't care how long it takes, I'm gonna find my real father."

The two best friends were sitting on a stone bench at the little shit-assed park in their shit-assed neighborhood on the shit-assed outskirts of shit-assed Opelousas, Louisiana, drinking the cheap wine Virginia had taken from the fridge, the last thing Benny-Boy Lopez was ever to provide her.

Afterward, she went back home. There wasn't anywhere to run. Her mother had fallen down the rabbithole long ago and didn't give a damn about what she did or where she went. Celia finally broke down but she'd been looking for a reason to break down all her life. Virginia didn't blame her much. She'd learned that people are meant to break down. Some of them last longer than others, and Celia had spent a lifetime trying to find somewhere to lie down and get it over with. Thank God for food stamps and Walmart, where Virginia got a job as soon as she was allowed and brought in just enough to keep the lights on and water running.

For the next two years, she found out what she could about her real father. She didn't expect a ton. All he had to be was the guy who'd cared enough to bring her a stuffed dog that one time. At most, maybe he could explain things and give her the answers she needed.

Having no help from her mother, Virginia became a sleuth, looking through her mother's things, her drawers, her clothes, trying to find the secret place, some place where she might have hidden things from Benny-Boy: money, pictures, a letter or two, maybe even a diary. But she found nothing. Her mom wasn't the type to keep a diary. She was more the type to blubber it out in fits and starts while she sank into her grimy chair, looking as if she wanted to be swallowed by it, as she pitied herself and finally got to the juicy parts, the parts that Virginia might be able to use to find Real Father.

When Celia was drunk enough to mention him, she'd manage to catch herself, almost as if it were a game, and clam up. "It's for your own good," she'd tell her. "I haven't been much of a momma to you, but at least I can keep you from more heartbreak." She'd say this as if more heartbreak weren't the soup du jour.

She kept getting fatter and fatter, as if she were feeding on all that heartache, supping on her dark little secrets, the choice ones, the meaty ones, the cheese-stuffed crust of her dark secrets.

One night, she was drunk as usual, calling Virginia all sorts of names, telling her how she was going to wind up just like her, pregnant from a sonuvabitch like Saturnino. Virginia didn't say anything. Her heart was racing because now she had a name, *his* name. Real Father's name wasn't Joe or Juan or Carlos or Bob. It was the stately *Saturnino*. The sound of it was a hell of a lot more intoxicating than a bottle of Benny-Boy's cheap wine. Four bountiful, insistent syllables, Sa-tur-ni-no, like a name out of a history book. The name of an ancient god. Maybe like a writer or philosopher. Or a soldier, a general in a foreign army. Maybe Saturnino was out there waiting for her to break out and come join him. That's all she could think about. She googled his name.

She read the mythology of the Roman god, the lord of renewal and liberation. His pagan festival became Christmas, with its gift-giving, merriment, revelry, feasting and celebration of peace and plenty. This wasn't a man who would stop at a stuffed dog. Not with a name like that. Something or someone had chased him away or lied to him!

The day before Virginia turned eighteen, Celia finally got out of Opelousas. She took a couple of handfuls of some pills she used to fall asleep, pills she picked up from some shit-ass at the bar she practically lived at. Virginia found her in the afternoon, shrouded in dirty sheets, her hair streaked with oily, yellow vomit.

The ambulance came. The Fire Department too. It was a mess she'd left. The cops asked some questions, took some notes. All the while the EMS and coroner were taking vitals and pronouncing her dead and taking some pictures for what only God knew. They took her in a gurney, pulling a yellow body bag over her huge carcass. They didn't pull a white sheet over the body like they did on TV. Just hoisted her away like a bag of garbage.

A cop, a muscle-head with a mustache, asked her, "You got kin? Anybody we can call? How old are you anyway?"

"I'm eighteen." The number sounded strange because it was new.

The cop told her he could call child services, but she said she had an aunt in Baton Rouge who'd come down and get her. The cop looked a little uneasy about that, but he let it go. Just as quickly as the house had got crowded, it was empty. Nobody but her in the house, her and the stink her mother had left behind. There was no denying it, *the stink*. Her sweaty bedclothes, her dirty bed sheets in which she'd taken her last shit when the sleeping pills had kicked in.

Virginia moved like a zombie, moving outside her control, not herky-jerky like a movie zombie, but like a slowed-
down robot, kind of retarded-like. She went into her mom's
room and stripped off the shitty sheets and wrapped up her
gown and slippers in it and then grabbed all Celia's personal
things, her cheap perfume and Walmart makeup, her pink
acrylic hairbrush with the clear, plastic bristles tangled in a
nest of black-dyed strands. She tried to count the items for
some reason, the smell of her mother's shampoo and hair-
spray radiating a vague, mild nostalgia.

Virginia swept it all into a pillowcase and wrapped the
ball up in the shitty sheets. Then she dragged the bundle into
the garbage can outside. It wouldn't fit, so she packed it in the
broke-down '98 Grand Am they'd shared and drove the stinking bundle to the Walmart distribution center backlot to chuck
it into one of the enormous, green dumpsters.

She was trying to chunk the stuff into the dumpster, but
the side of the bin was so high that she had to get some real
momentum going to get the bundle over it. She was swing-
ing the shitbag back and forth, each swing getting higher and
higher, and just as she let the thing go, one of those cop spot-
lights went on, and she turned right into its blinding glare.
The bundle, not having been thrown high enough, hit the
edge of the dumpster, and its contents came raining down.
She couldn't make out a thing until a shadow came through
the light, walking up slowly, taking its time to look in the car
to see if there was anyone else in there. The guard got up to
the window, and it was then Virginia noticed he was just a
skinny kid.

He knew she worked there because of the parking decal
on the back of the car. "Dumping stuff here will get you fired,
you know."

That's when she broke out crying. It was the first time she'd cried since finding her mother in her shitty bedclothes, her slobber still wet and clingy.

The kid thought she was crying because she'd been caught. He wasn't a tough guy. He liked to come off tough because he was so lanky and he hated being lanky. When he saw her tears, he rushed back to his car and shut the spotlight off. He came back and apologized to Virginia.

"Hey, look, I'm not going to bust you," he said, trying to make her quit crying. But she only cried harder. "It's just you're not supposed to be dumping stuff here. Jesus don't sweat it. I'm not going to turn you in. Look, I'll help you get the stuff together."

This decency only made Virginia sob louder. He put his hand on her shoulder, and she told him about finding her dead mother.

He kept saying, "Jesus. You all right, you all right? Jesus."

~~~

Daniel spent thirty days at the VA substance and alcohol in-patient program after Cristina called him a "limp-dick fag" and pushed him down a flight of stairs. If he'd been sober, he probably would have kept himself from going ass over teakettle, but he wasn't. He'd been soused and high on painkillers. Cristina was small, but he being shit-faced went over easy-peasy. He'd laid at the bottom, groaning and laughing at the same time, his collarbone broken.

She kept up the barrage. "You fuckin' momma's boy faggot."

Really, there was nothing funny about the situation, and so why was he laughing? He had just enough time to think before Cristina heaved his packed duffle from the top of the stairs landing squarely on his nuts.

"You aren't running away from this fight, motherfucker!" she screamed. "You don't just get to disappear!"

Daniel kept laughing and groaning.

Now, thirty days later, living in his mother's converted garage, he stood in front of the mirror, getting ready to shave off the weak mustache he'd grown during rehab. Fonzo, his buddy from the war, sat on Daniel's bed, a shoebox of meds in his lap, casually picking up prescription bottles, reading the labels, plucking a couple of pills when he encountered something tasty.

They were both out of the Army now. Fonzo had jacked-up knees that had been replaced twice after a mortar shell went off in his vicinity and the explosion blew him into a weird backflip that had him land on his feet with his knees all sorts of wrong. He moved around gingerly, now, would for the rest of his life, looking like a man walking on broken glass. That injury had gotten him a full pension along with too many surgeries, including one that had implanted an electric thingamajig in his spine to quell the pain. It hadn't even numbed the pain. He sold used cars because he had two exes to support and other complications.

Daniel loved Fonzo. He was a little dude, but he'd been solid in the desert. Saved Daniel's ass a couple of times, in fact. At first, Daniel had figured him for a shitbird. But Fonzo had proven him wrong. One thing you learned over there was you couldn't tell who was going to show up just by their looks.

"You just better watch yourself, have an extraction point worked out," Fonzo said, squinting at a label. "You ain't got kids, Danny Boy, and that's good. Kids, pal, kids. I've got two baby mommas, lots of bills, no wife and the constant hustle. It's a bitch, brother."

"Roger that," Daniel said.

He rarely used military speak unless he got around Fonzo, and then it came natural. They'd been best buddies since they used to douse themselves with the same bottle of cologne when they got liberty and went out barhopping in Lejeune. Their unit saw action in Fallujah, where an F-2 fighter jet sent their pal, Scotty, thrashing into the big dark.

"Listen," Fonzo said suddenly, "why don't we hit a titty bar or something. Your mom's garage is depressing as shit."

Daniel turned from the mirror. "I'm not in the mood. If you wanna drink, I got a bottle of Goose under the bed."

Daniel popped three oxys, swallowed them dry. He stepped out of the bathroom, not having shaved.

"You mind if I grab a few pills out of your stash?" Fonzo asked.

"Nah," Daniel said and lay down on the bed and closed his eyes, vodka and oxys making him feel warm and sleepy.

"Look," Fonzo said, "just 'cause you've retreated don't mean the war is lost."

"Listen, pal," Daniel said, "I'm wiped. I'm gonna hit the rack."

"Yeah, man, of course. Now that you're back, we'll have lotsa chances to reconvene."

Daniel smiled and said, "Sure."

Fonzo made his way out the back door that connected the garage and the house.

Daniel closed his eyes. He saw Pumpkin. They were going to name him after her father, but when Pumpkin died, she named him after Daniel. He took two more swigs of the Goose, but it was too late. He felt it coming on.

Shaking is for Jell-O, Daniel reflected, as he sat on the john, dreading the onset of a panic attack. They'd come on after Fallujah. It wasn't fear exactly. He'd always associated fear with a direct threat, something material, menacing, even if faceless. But the shakes came from somewhere inside, not from anything external. Sometimes he woke up sweating like an old man in the grips of Parkinson's disease. His grandfather had been afflicted so. He had lain in his bed, night and day, trembling from head to toe, especially his arms and hands, like an infant being tickled or a mad conductor at the head of an invisible orchestra. That shit wasn't funny, but when Daniel was a kid, he and Alena would mimic the old man, giggling. It wasn't mocking, it was more out of the unexplained mystery of it. His mom would say, "'Buelito is sick." Only he didn't seem sick so much as possessed by an old-fashioned malfunctioning alarm-clock, quaking like a motherfucker.

Sometimes the shakes came on because of something direct. Sometimes they came on for no apparent reason. There wasn't a particular trigger. It was not like he felt panic when he heard from an Army buddy or saw something on the news or the Internet. It was often a response to everyday shit, like a loud sound, or too much silence, or the heat, or maybe the sight of kids in the hood hanging around outside a house or shitty apartment. Sometimes it was when he closed his eyes and saw Pumpkin.

He told the Army shrink that when he felt an attack coming on, he had to hunker down, get out of sight because he looked like a spaz, a crazy person, like Wile E. Coyote after he takes Acme earthquake pills. If it came on while he was driving, God forbid, he had to pull over.

"I'm liable to fucking pancake a goddamn soccer mom if I'm at the wheel, Doc. Medicate my ass."

But the shrink told him to quit trying to control the spasms. "Go with it."

"They'd put me in a rubber room."

"It's not remotely connected to insanity or madness," the shrink told him. "It's your body remembering trauma. It's not even really connected to your being conscious of what is causing the distress."

"I never got 'distressed' in the field, Doc. Tired, pissed, scuffed up and mostly plain old scared. Point is, never got the shakes in the Sandbox. We took pride in giving the Muj the shakes."

The shrink smiled at Daniel's bravado. He saw it all the time. It was a defense mechanism, but he refrained from telling his patients that.

In the end, the shrink told him he should just shake like a willow tree on a windy day. Let his limbs loose, breathe deep, let his body shake the trauma out. "Think of it as cleansing your psyche and your body. You don't even need to understand it. Just give yourself permission to feel it."

It was painfully embarrassing to Daniel to "go with it." He preferred controlling the episodes with oxy and vodka. He had to stupefy himself to calm it. Not just the shakes, but the face of the Iraqi woman, her slow heaving breath, the baby dying inside her as surely as she was dying on that floor. Goldfish. A suffocating goldfish. A broken fishbowl and a dying goldfish. The image would grow and grow until it was more real than the fucking ceiling he stared at. And then the shakes. Then, four or five oxys followed by three or four slugs of vodka. And still the shakes.

He often dreamt that the Muj fighter he strangled was watching him with glazed eyes while the dying mother breathed her last. Only her belly still moved, ever so slightly, but undeniably. The tiny goldfish in her womb, unknowing, but not unfeeling, still kicking in its death throes. Shaking its last, just like Daniel shaking his last.

"I'm not going to understand my way out of this," Daniel told the shrink. "Just ain't, Doc. Maybe it's my whatchamacallit, my cross to bear."

"Don't think about it that much then. . . . Just fucking shake!"

So shake Daniel did.

He had three mantras for the shakes: 1. It's all my fucking fault. 2. Oh Jesus, oh Jesus. 3. A low guttural moan that came from a pinpoint deep, deep inside, so potent that it drowned him in hopelessness. Sometimes he used all three. Sometimes just one. It all depended on how he felt: 1. Guilty. 2. Terrified. 3. No words. An abyss. Hell without the hellfire.

Most often it was number one: "It's all my fucking fault." This one came on when he was relatively sober in the late evening, say midnight or so. He'd get to thinking about Pumpkin and how Pumpkin never stood a chance, how Cristina was right about him. How he couldn't protect even himself, let alone his unborn son, his vulnerable depressed wife, his tortured mother, his unhappy sister, his innocent niece. The world was too much for Daniel Lomos, decorated grunt, bonafide war hero, manly man. Inside he was a scared, confused, messed-up sonuvabitch. No match for the terrorism of modern life. IEDs littered his path, always threatening to detonate at the vibration of one hesitant step. PTSD was like that. You never left the desert, never stopped humping the road with its hidden mines. "It's all my fucking fault," he'd whisper out loud, as he shook on the can, always fully clothed, always until he was exhausted, always followed by the oxys and a glass of vodka. Oblivion. Like a goddamn perverse orgasm.

That was the loop he was caught up in, round and round. It was easy enough to see it, recognize it even as it entangled him. There just wasn't anyway to cut it, so it seemed. It's not that he wished he'd never been born. Nothing melodramatic like that. He could've offed himself a long time ago, if that's what he wanted. Sure, it was an option. But who'd clean up his mess? He didn't like the idea of that. Of course, if need be, he could always drive to Corpus Christi and walk into the ocean, go back to sleep, not have to worry about waking up anymore. But, honestly, most of the time it just felt like too much damn work. Better to numb down, find the bottom of that pool deep down where the oxys took him, and just be miserable in those dark brown, almond eyes of the dying woman, the fading light that was so poignant, so irrevocable. Slow, labored breathing growing more and more shallow, then strangled, then terribly silent. A woman destined not to bear forth a new tiny life, but rather to quietly surrender to death.

~~~

Daniel's mom, Teresa, danced in front of the television for hours every day. The video it played was homemade. She had taken her old video camera and set it up in the church, front and center, to record her daughter Alena's Christian dance troupe that performed each Sunday. Teresa's goal was to make the A-team and perform the quasi-Jewish dances in the long black skirts with the gilded hems. She wanted to earn the tambourine with the long, flowing silver streamers. At home, she practiced with a paper plate decorated with silver Christmas tree icicles glued to the edges. Alena, whom Daniel's mother called daily for clarifications on particular dance moves, refused to put her in the top dance squad. Daniel often watched Teresa dance. He thought she was pretty good. He figured Alena didn't want to be accused of nepotism by the other ladies.

The church, El Testimonio Cristiano, was located in the heart of the westside of San Antonio. It was hundred percent Spanish-speaking, and the pastor, Brother Alfred, was on a hardcore Jewish kick. He claimed that Latinos were long-lost Jews from Spain—Sephardic Jews, he called them. He'd been to Madrid the past summer to research the whole thing.

Daniel was skeptical, but Teresa and Alena believed the narrative wholesale. They planned to go on the Holy Land tour that the church was planning for the summer. The church and its parishioners were saving up for the trip. There was a video, Jerusalem 360°, that they showed from time to time to fire everyone up. They held fundraisers every week to help subsidize the poorer members. Daniel contributed by buying a taco plate after church on Sundays.

On Sundays, he drove Teresa to church in the Nissan pickup her dead husband, Tino, had left her, the only thing he had owned. All he had was his back, his legs and his heart. Tino's legs had given out long before his heart did. The church people could hardly believe that Tino, of Tino and Teresa, one of the central believers, was gone. They embraced Teresa after Tino's death, mindful that Teresa was lost without him.

Tino Fuentes had resembled a sixteenth-century conquistador: short and squat with thick legs, a pointed French nose and sunken passionless blue eyes that squinted when he was getting ready to lose his cool. All he lacked was a metal helmet to complete the conquistador bearing. He hadn't been much of a talker, so when he spoke up, you listened. He told stories about his long-past drug days as a heroin addict and dealer, the drug rap that had put him in the penitentiary for almost a decade, the head-on collision that ruined his legs by splintering them in a dozen places, his come-to-Jesus moment when his doctors told him he'd never walk. But he'd walked again, crooked and painfully, long white tube socks covering his tortured shins. He'd walked. When he testified at El Testimonio Cristiano, holding out the long steel rods that had held his fractured bones together, everyone leaned forward and listened.

Ironically, Tino had loved to dance. At their tenth anniversary party, an old friend of his had told Daniel, "Your stepdad, God, he was one for *cumbias*. I remember him back in the old days at the Cuco Lounge. He'd dance all night long. He'd ask every girl in the bar, *gorditas*, las skinnies, *las feas*, the beauties, *las cochinas*, *las virgencitas*, *las prietas*, *las güeras*, *las pobres*, *las ricas*, single, married and in-between."

Before Teresa would marry Tino, she told him, "*No más.*" No more dancing, no more beer, no more anything that would remind him of those dark days out in the world.

"Out in the world" was what the good brothers and sisters called the time before you knew Jesus. Outcast, unsaved, an orphan.

"What do I need to dance for," he'd told her, and they got married.

He told Daniel later, "What was I giving up? I can barely walk."

Now that the man was dead, Daniel's mother couldn't stop dancing.

Tino had liked Cristina, Daniel's ex-wife. She was petite and demure, a charmer. She'd cut Tino's hair when they visited. Teresa detested her son's ex-wife. She'd warned him not to marry Cristina, saying, "She'll cause you nothing but misery."

He was now trying to be philosophical about the breakup. His time in the alcohol treatment center had revealed a central reality. Everybody was sick and just barely hanging on. It was clear that the key to a successful relationship was a matter of meshing mental diseases. It wasn't the alcohol or drugs that were the problem, it was hanging on to things.

After they'd lost the baby and Daniel was discharged, Cristina became desperate to get pregnant again. Daniel made it clear that he was not onboard. She didn't care. When it didn't happen after two feckless months, off to the fertility clinics they went. The endless blood tests for her, including a procedure where they inserted a camera in her to see what the problem was. And for him it was semen tests in the clinic's man cave, a jerk-off room with a big comfy leather chair, an HDTV and a porn DVD titled, "Help! My Ass is on Fire." Afterward, he'd fill out the form checking the box, "Masturbation." Then they'd sit in the office while the doc critiqued his jizz point by point, as exacting and detailed as any briefing he'd sat through in the Sandbox: the numbers were good, the motility so-so, the shape above average.

Did he miss her? Sometimes. Mostly he didn't. Not her asking him if he was going to go to church or if he'd joined Promise Keepers like he'd promised, pretending like he was praying alongside her night after night asking Jesus for a pregnancy. But most of all, he didn't miss her hounding him to go to the baby's grave every week.

The night it broke, he finally just told her he wasn't going to do it anymore. He didn't want a kid. She wanted to know why. He couldn't tell her that he didn't much want to wake up in the morning anymore. Didn't want to piss off God more than he already had. It was a blood grudge, and everyone knew God always won blood grudges.

He was working on a full glass of bourbon, just like about every night since he'd gotten back. She followed him down the hall where he was trying to escape to the john. He stood in front of the sink, looking into the mirror, watching the man in the frame: unshaved, saggy drunken eyes, taking another big swig of bourbon. She stood outside the door crying, yelling, desperation growing, as she banged her knuckles raw, and Daniel watching himself watching that fucked up man drink.

Glass empty, the pounding on the door having stopped, his wife's exhausted crying dropping in volume, he felt it was clear to go downstairs so he could be more alone. She was there waiting when he opened the door. She looked up at him, tear-stained face momentarily lit with a dim hope that darkened, as he stepped around her heading for the stairs. He stopped at the top of the stairs as Cristina told him, "Just who do you think you are, you fucking bastard?" As he turned to take that first step, she caught up with him and gave him a shove. It wasn't a heavy shove, more of an angry nudge. As he fell, he'd tried harder to save the glass than to catch himself, and that's when he went ass over teakettle and broke his collarbone.

On her way out the door, she'd stepped over him. "I don't know why the hell I ever thought you could ever be a real father!"

~~~

Easter was still two months away, but the church was on it. El Testimonio Cristiano was going to put on a Resurrection gala. There'd be dancing aplenty starting with the children's group, followed by the B-teamers and then the A-team led by Alena. The A-team was going to get new outfits for the occasion, white gowns with swirling glittery teal capes that hung down to the waist. The pastor was going to do his patented chalk drawing where he used fluorescent chalks on black paper under black lights that turned on at the final moment to illuminate the picture dramatically: Jesus bursting forth from the tomb in all his glory. There'd be a picnic afterwards at the campsite where all the families would turn up with their kids carrying around huge Easter baskets that held dozens of *cascarones*, eggshells decorated beautifully and filled with confetti that would be cracked on unsuspecting adult heads. The men would barbecue. The women would fix all the rest. There would be a softball game in which an out-of-shape someone would sprain his ankle pretty badly and then, an hour before dusk, the congregation would head to the stream, and the pastor would baptize anyone needing certainty that they were heaven-bound.

Alena told Daniel about the importance of staging. "It's very complicated. Lighting, spacing, sound, picking the perfect music." She'd attended a number of Christian dance conferences, picking up new routines, cutting-edge stuff with dramatic lighting and emotive, sharp moves. At home, Teresa pumped Daniel about the A-team routine. She wanted Daniel to pressure Alena into putting her on the squad. She went on and on about the new outfits, about what a blessing it would be to dance with her daughter, about how hard she'd been practicing the basic moves, the half-twirls, the half-kicks, the full turns, the jump-jump-step forward-twirl-shake-tambourine.

"Did you tell her how hard I've practiced," she asked Daniel.

"She knows."

"But did you tell her?"

"No, Mom, but if you want, I will."

"You tell her that if she doesn't let me on the A-team, you won't come to the play."

≈≈≈

Teresa didn't talk much about Daniel's "situation." She was satisfied with telling him that everything would be fine. She wanted him to know that he could stay for as long as he wanted, longer even. Tino's truck needed a tune-up and an oil change. The lawn needed weeding and mowing. The paint throughout the house was grungy, and the carpet had to be pulled and replaced. She knew he was glad to do those things, things she didn't ask for directly, so that he wouldn't feel like he was just lying around thinking all the time.

Teresa didn't like talking about Tino. However, Alena and her church friends wanted to talk about Tino. It didn't do her any good, but they didn't understand this. Daniel never mentioned Tino, maybe because he understood loss so well. While Tino lay dying, Daniel had come to keep watch with Teresa. He'd stayed another week after the funeral until Cristina made Daniel go back home. She needed him, too, after he'd been gone so long for the war.

After they left, Teresa couldn't be alone in the house, so she invited Alena to come. She brought little Tonia, and they slept with her in the same bed. She would tell Alena, "Please get closer to me, I have to feel someone next to me."

Either way, it was terrible. The warmth of another body made her miss Tino all the more. A cold bed made her realize profoundly that Tino was gone. It didn't help that she was always cold, even in the summer when the heat got bad. She didn't like thinking about Tino. It made her angry, although she didn't admit this to her children. Tino should have listened to her. But he was *muy macho*. Last year and the year before, when she was going through her heart scare, she'd have him take her to the emergency room when she felt chest pain, which was often. He'd wait with her while they ran an EKG. The hospitals admitted you fast when you told them you were having chest pains.

She'd tried to convince Tino to get his heart checked.

He just wouldn't listen. He'd say, "Don't I have enough trouble with your heart?" He'd say it in a way that Teresa knew he meant the case was closed. No more talking about that or anything once he made such a pronouncement. Not that Tino was stubborn. He wasn't. He cared about what Teresa thought. He always tried to please her. Even before they'd married, he'd done everything he could to make her happy.

Now, Teresa didn't want to think about Tino. And yet, when she talked about him, she'd give examples of his goodness, his basic kindness; he never cared if she wore her house dress to the grocery store. Never. He might say, "Teresa, comb your hair before you go out. *Te miras como la hija de la mera luna.*" But he'd say it with a smile, and Teresa would pretend to be insulted.

Tino never needed to be told to comb his hair. He was fastidious that way. Up at five in the morning. A cup of coffee with his friend, Menríquez, the old widower from across the street. They'd talk about what was going on in the neighborhood, what little fucker was causing trouble, selling drugs or breaking into houses. Then he'd take his walk. Then back to the house to take his shower, shave, trim his mustache and comb his hair, running his Brylcreem through it and getting it just so. Wranglers, always pressed with a crease. His shined boots when he wanted to dress up for church or dinner out at the Red Lobster. He couldn't wear his boots very long, though, because his legs were always in pain. Around the house he wore jean cutoffs and his tennies with long tube socks to cover his ruined legs. It made Teresa so sad to remember them. She didn't like to think about Tino.

He'd been washing his truck. It was still new. He'd wanted a pickup for so long, and Alena co-signed for him because they wouldn't give it to him with just his disability checks. He washed it two or three times a week.

Menríquez came banging on the door that Friday afternoon. Teresa had just gotten out of the shower. She remembered being so scared at the banging at the door, knowing that something was very wrong even before she answered it. "Call the 911," Menríquez said, and Teresa could see how scared he was.

"What's wrong, what's wrong?" she asked instead of running for the phone.

Teresa stepped outside in a panic, and there was her poor Tino, crumpled on the driveway. She thought, "He's fallen, he's cracked his head."

It was worse than that. "A widow-maker," the doctor called it. He'd lasted a week or so, but there was too much damage.

Only the dancing was left now. Teresa knew that this might sound cruel because she loved her children and her granddaughter more than she loved herself. But that's how she felt inside. The dancing. The A-Team. Just enough to keep her hoping for something. That's why she practiced every day for hours and hours. Just to get her chance.

#1

Danny is used to intense heat. Fact is, the heat is better in the Sandbox because it's dry and at night it gets cold. Not like south Texas where the heat is humid and eternal, seeming to emanate from every direction, from your own skin even. But at least you can breathe. The air in the Sandbox is mostly dust, flour-like, on everything, in everything. The grunts call it moondust. Within minutes Danny is covered in the silty stuff—fatigues, boots, face, arms, neck, nostrils, mouth, his rucksack, helmet and, soon enough, on and in all his belongings. His lungs ache as if he's been smoking two packs a day for years. "Might as well light up," Scotty tells him. "Your lungs are gonna be for shit the duration of this little vacation. At least get the nicotine." Danny's unit is deployed down-range to a forward operating base. They are expected to get into the shit ASAP. The Muj have taken over Anbar, have made a show of hanging and mutilating four Americans who were contracted there. All of them ex-military who knew the rules. But knowing don't mean shit because they are dead as hell. Dragged down the streets, hanged off a bridge like sides of beef, all fucked-up, bloated, kicked to shit, the Haji motherfuckers mocking the corpses, taking a giant shit on them for all the world to see. It looks like the Sunnis aren't going to take a backseat after all. There isn't any mission accomplished as far as Danny can see.

Back in boot camp, he watched the video of Nicholas Berg getting his head sawed off, slow, gurgling butchery. It was the most horrible thing Danny had ever seen. At least till then. "It's on now, motherfuckers," their drill told them after the video. He was right. The honeymoon is over and the shit is getting intensely nasty. Danny is hyped, glad to be fighting bad guys, really bad, bad guys. People who work nonstop figuring out how to do the worst things they can imagine to other people because of Allah or something. Still, though, landing in the Sandbox is an awakening. It crosses his mind, as he gets his gear and makes his way to a Humvee, that Dubya has made a big mistake getting them involved in this place. This is going to be like fighting on the Moon. Foreign, unknown, godforsaken and alienating.

Scotty tells the newbies, "Drink your water, grunt. You'll keel over faster than greasy goose shit if you don't hydrate. This place is hotter than two rats fucking a wall socket."

"Got that right, Sarge," a corporal with a smirk and a clipboard says.

Sgt. Scotty has survived two tours in Iraq, fought in Mosul, fought in Muqdadiyah, where he took two AK rounds to his left arm from a Mahdi militiaman. He could have gone home, but he insisted on going back to the Sandbox to continue to lead his squad. They are his brothers. The only family he has, the way he sees it. He grew up in Buttfuck, Georgia, population 79, joined the Army as soon as he could to get away from his asshole father, his tweaker buddies, desperate girls and the meth-head culture. He got a GED, signed up, did an outstanding job during basic, caught the attention of his Drill as high speed, proved himself a deadeye dick and volunteered to get into the shit fast. One tour was all it took for him to make fire team leader as a corporal. Second tour, when he took the two rounds, he kept firing like a beast, kept yelling orders to his team, and they managed to waste a dozen

Muj motherfuckers, all foreign fighters, all true-believers. He's come back from recovery a sergeant and taking over Alpha squad. His boys respect him, know he has their backs. In a jam, he is going to get them out, even with Haji rounds ringed in blood, he is the Motherfucking Man. It is just like that, immediately. Danny feels it. Danny and Fonzo are both assigned to Alpha, right into the goddamn war. You join the infantry to see action. FOB shit. This doesn't mean they aren't scared and discombobulated when they hit the desert. Three weeks in, a massive firefight in Diyala has turned them into veterans. This is largely due to Scotty, who leads by ex-ample. He doesn't make any excuses or take any. He is straight out Hooah, but not an asshole. What inspires his squad is that the dude is there to fight. If there is a high-risk assignment, he does it. So when he tells you to do something, you are ready to take it on, shit-task or not. You want to bleed for this guy.

Just before the big fight, on patrol on yet another hot fucking day, they stop for a short one. Smokes and water. Squad leaders and Scotty huddling in the shade.

"Listen, I ain't complaining about dis here shit," Scotty says. "I'm here to get it done for my men and for the coun-try. Duty and all that."

"Duly noted," says Danny.

"But, what kinda buggyfuck bullshit is this? Why are we fighting in the world's biggest monkeyfuck? What the fuck is there to win out here? Lookee, man," he exaggerates look-ing about goggle-eyed, waving his hands around in futility. "This here, now, this here, all this here? Is bullshit."

"Not very hospitable," Danny says.

"Fuck that," Scotty says, pausing for a drink from his camelback. "I can take the heat, bruh. I'm just blusterfucked as to why this wasteland? Whoever pulled this one out his ass, he never saw this place or even read about it. Otherwise, we wouldn't be here. This is like building a city on the fucking Moon."

"Moon dust all the way up my ass," Danny says disapprovingly.

"Further up than that, bruh," Scotty says, getting ready to get the men on the move again. "Less get up, grunts. We got a shitload of clicks to walk. This sand's not gonna blow itself."

Then in Fallujah, less than a day into the fight, he runs through an open patch kill zone, gets caught in the coils of electric wire that litter the field between houses. He's gone in to cut free one of his boys who's caught a bullet in the throat. Jaworwski is KIA, but Scotty isn't going to let one of his soldiers die alone. Hell, you never know who is going to make it. Jaws is a tough fucker. As he tries to cut Jaworski free, he catches a bullet just below his helmet line that blows his brains out the back of his head. It is over in a second. Danny has to restrain Fonzo, who is the grenadier, from running pellmell into the kill zone. Instead, they sit tight in the small house they've secured. Scotty was charged with moving Alpha out of there to clear three houses directly across a bald field when Jaws was ambushed.

"Jesus. What the fuck now?" Fonzo asks Danny.

Danny peers through the night vision goggles, focusing on which of the houses is directing the fire. There is at least one bad-ass sniper out there waiting for another soldier to cross his line of fire.

"That motherfucker has got a clean shot at anyone going through that field. I'm not letting anyone go out there."

"What the fuck?" Fonzo says. "We might be able to save them."

"They're dead," Danny says. He hands the goggles to Fonzo. "They're gone."

Fonzo looks through the greenish haze at the bodies, Scotty and Jaws, deader than hell, motionless, Scotty lying on top of Jaws in a heap like two spent wrestlers too tired to keep struggling against each other.

"Well, looks like you're fire team leader, Danny. What do we do?"

Danny focuses. He can't think about Scotty or Jaws. He has to calm down, remember his training, his experience, get his team out of the house and through that field and smoke that sniper's ass. He can't depend on the other fire team to do more than offer cover fire. They are pinned down too.

CHAPTER 2
Godismosly a fuckinaccounant

The house was already haunted, the Moon having dropped, Celia's ghost there, angry, waiting for Virginia. She hadn't thought about Celia's response to her dumping her things. Virginia had only been thinking about getting rid of all traces of her mother, the misery, the stink of her sad, fatal indifference.

The Walmart boy-cop, Rick, had given her a ride home and walked her to the door, shining his light through the windows because she was scared to walk into the house so dark.

He told her, "It's okay. I'm right here and, besides, there ain't no such thing as haunts."

Virginia felt silly holding tight to his arm, behind him like a small girl. She couldn't shake the image of a ghostly white malevolent Celia floating into the hallway to drown her in all that sad stink.

The boy-cop, sensing her dread, went on. "Hell, my granny sold haunt wash back in Cypress swamp. Wadn't nothing but shine with a pinch of Spanish moss that'd give you straight up dook butt if you were crazy enough to drink it. Some people was, though, cuz granny kept making it."

Virginia didn't loosen her grip, so he offered her a place for the night. "I gotta be on the job till the sun come up anyway, so you'll be by yourself with no one to bother you. I even got a bottle or two of granny's haunt wash if you need it. Be warned though, it'll get you peelayed."

Virginia smiled at that.

"I'll get my things," she said and didn't wait for him to shine his torch at her bedroom door. For some reason they hadn't turned the lights on.

She felt something warm for the boy-cop. In the light, in his apartment, she looked him in the face and recognized him as a quiet one, the type no one needs to notice. Rick wasn't tall, or muscled, or anything like that, but he had a sweet face, reddened from too much sun, a little pockmarked. Virginia figured he wasn't the type to ever hurt anyone, at least not on purpose.

The funeral was cheap as could be, with only a handful of people, a neighbor or two. They put her in a rented casket, gray and worn from a dozen previous funerals. There weren't enough men to carry the body to the hearse, so Rick and his friend helped carry Celia to her final ride. They cremated her. Virginia never did claim the remains.

Rick brought Virginia things to eat and didn't judge her. He only listened and hardly slept because he now worked two shifts: one at the Walmart and the other at his apartment keeping watch over Virginia, who could only sleep when he was home. Virginia didn't leave Rick's apartment until he told her he wanted her to go to the Crabstravaganza down in Grand Chenier. It was a pretty good time, deep blue skies and dirt roads lined with silverbell trees, plenty of crab and good music.

It was that night, when they got back, that Virginia wanted to thank him. She took a shower and got ready. Then she led him back to the bedroom. He had a quizzical look on his face, like he knew what was happening only couldn't believe his luck. He kept quiet except for saying, "Virginia," as if he wanted to give her a chance to change her mind.

Rick was the first one that felt real, that felt good. She'd been with other boys, even recently. It was a fuck-you-very-much to her mom. It was some kind of wanting a man of her own. But all she'd found was lots of horny boys. The novelty wore off quickly about the time she realized she'd become a run-of-the-mill Opelousas slut.

With the boy-cop it was good. Not good in a passionate way, but good in that it meant not being afraid or sad or worried for a spell. Virginia could tell she made him happy and that he was grateful. It was after they lay in bed a while that she asked him if he'd help her find the secret place her mother was sure to have kept.

Rick used his Walmart cop instincts in searching every nook and cranny, going places that Virginia hadn't dared search when Celia was alive. They found a silver key under the mattress that fit the lock of a wooden box Celia had kept in her closet with a towel thrown over it on which she had set her three pairs of shoes. The box had always been in plain sight so you wouldn't think it held anything important. Rick laid it on the bed. The box weighed nothing at all. That was the saddest thing for Virginia.

Rick turned the key, and the lid came open. A faint smell of a perfume Virginia didn't recognize emerged. It wasn't one Celia'd worn for Benny-Boy. It was like a perfume from a long time ago, from Celia's days as a young woman before she got the sad-stink.

There was a stack of yellowed letters, stiff, like no one had unfolded them since they were put in the box. Rick pulled out a purple bottle, a French name on it in fancy hand-lettering that read *Désirée*. It smelled like lilac and cinnamon, but the bottle was long empty. There was a matchbook, one of those made for a restaurant. It had been ripped up, and all you could read was part of the name, *Tropical*. There was an old bus ticket to Houston from when Virginia was still a kid. And then, there was a picture of Saturnino. Young, tall, deep-set eyes that held a hint of a smile, his lips, thin, not smiling. He stood next to Celia. Saturnino wore a loose black suit and a skinny black tie. Celia, still slim, smiling, head tilted into Saturnino, clearly in love, pretty, not yet angry, not yet doomed. They were young. Virginia recognized the blue eyes, the nose and the lips immediately. She'd been seeing them in the mirror all her life. On the back, it said, "Saturnino Loves You Always, Con Safos, 1987, Houston."

~~~

"Once you take that drink, it's going to happen like it always happens," Daniel told himself. A glass of vodka in his hand, he channeled the doctor at the clinic. "Just one drink. Then one more. Then fuck it. You know this," the doc would say in group. It was his mantra. Everyone agreed, nodding, knowing that the doc was exactly fucking right and nonetheless dying for a drink and for the doc, a good guy, a solid Army guy minus the hooah bullshit, to shut the fuck up and let them have their drink in peace.

Everyone in the program was service. Some had been deployed, others not. There were sailors, airmen, soldiers and Marines. Young and old. They were there to own up to the "real problem." The thing that made you want to not think. "Here you think," the doc, thinning dark hair, black army issue glasses half down his nose, said. "Out there in the field, you're drilled to follow the training, not think, but act."

Everyone agreed that this wasn't the best course of action in the real world. Daniel knew that people liked reasons and explanations. They wanted to be sure, reassured, certain, before they did mostly anything.

And all the pointy-head wanted was for him to walk down that long dark hallway of his mind, pushing doors open, looking inside, contemplating. He'd rather drink, pop a pill, watch Mom dance with a distant bemused smile and not think.

"How am I supposed to keep my shit together," said Otis, a big Appalachian cracker with a burned, withered arm that'd taken a bunch of white phosphorous during Anaconda at Takur Ghar.

He'd been shooting Afghani tar into that scarred mess since. The doc couldn't answer that question convincingly, so Otis, and most everyone else, Daniel included, figured shine that motherfucker on and stop listening to the cake eater.

Listening was always going to be a waste of time. Daniel did the thirty days, got out, moved in with his mom. The Army gave him a disability ticket related to PTSD. Cristina had given him walking papers related to him not wanting to take a crack at a new baby to replace the dead baby.

"What you donunnerstanis," he slurred as he tried to explain to her just before she'd pushed him off the landing, "God ismosly a fuckinaccounant, right? And he isn't done with me. Yougitit! Goddamnit!"

Daniel's mother wasn't around when he got up that afternoon. She'd gone to clean a house. She and Alena did a couple a week. "Americanos," his mother called the house-owners on the north side of San Antonio who kept their houses immaculate and only wanted dusting and some other light cleaning and paid a fair wage. She always let the owner know her son was a veteran of the Iraq War. They smiled politely. They didn't seem to remember there was a war going on.

It was good to have the house to himself. He downed a couple of oxys with the vodka, felt better, cleaned up and walked to the library to check his email. He'd also look for a DVD to bring home. His mom liked the classics.

The neighborhood had grown even more shitty than when he was a kid. In his childhood the hood had been blocks of shabby, cramped row houses for working-class folk, with tiny yards, chain-link fences, framed by a huge stinking drainage canal and populated by a million fire ant mounds. Now it was straight up barrio. Nothing but dry grass and weeds sun-burned a permanent brown. A couple of check cashing places, a pawn shop, a liquor store that would cash a check with a hand still attached to it.

The air was as humid as his ball sack in tighty-whities, he thought as he walked the half mile to the library. The old-time grunts liked to talk about the jungle rot in Nam. The desert had its own challenges, though. Dust always in your face, sand in your fatigues, eyes burned dry, your shit always baking in the heat. No fucking shade, not ever.

While he'd been in Iraq, the city of San Antonio had built a large block of public housing just across the drainage canal from his mother's house. That meant scores of young kids with nothing better to do than tag everything in sight, in-cluding abandoned houses, sidewalks, bus stops, anything with a surface the little fuckers could reach. Daniel tried to read the tags on the way to the library, but they were in-scrutable. Nothing but coded threats and boasts that only bangers understood.

When he'd been growing up, there were gangs, but they weren't quite visible. There were fights and bullies, lots of trouble if you wanted it, but not bonafide gangsters like now. In Westwood Village, with the Section 8s and the public housing, the abandoned dwellings, the disappearance of de-cent work, it had gotten so that you couldn't go out at night, maybe not much during the day, either. Three times since Tino had died, someone had broken into Teresa's house and ransacked the place, emptying everything onto the floor, breaking things when they found nothing of any value other than the TV. A kid had been shot in front of his mother's house just the year before. Tino had told Daniel all about it. He'd stand out in the front yard and point out all the houses that were dealing drugs, the houses where *tecatos* lived, where someone was beating a wife or kids, where someone was running ass. It was as bad as any war-torn, gangster-run spot in Iraq—well, almost. A unit of grunts could have cleared it out easy.

The city had widened Military Drive, which connected the five air bases in San Antonio. Military Drive crossed through the neighborhood obnoxiously in only the way a street called Military Drive can. People flew through the wide lanes like they were on the highway, and every once in a while, a kid got flattened trying to cross one of the intersections. And more often than not, there was a floral of dried dog guts on the pavement.

The one nice thing was the local library that the city had put up five years earlier. It was done in a kind of Spanish modernist motif, with strange angles and festive Mexican red, yellow and green-painted steel sheets that made for a disjointed visual in the midst of the barrio's dreary palette. There were nice women who worked there and a decent collection of literature. There was a computer bank with enough machines to satisfy the kids and the few adults scattered there in the afternoon. Most people came to escape the heat. It was only late April, but it was already into the nineties on some days.

Being at the library allowed Daniel to feel like he was doing something akin to a job, at the very least a routine that wasn't entirely comprised of sleeping until two, taking an oxy/vodka cocktail, reading a bit, sleeping some more, and repeat until nighttime and the blessed release of more sleep. Alena suggested that he was depressed, but he didn't feel depressed. He felt numb. This was fine with him.

Alicia, the younger of the librarians, a chubby, cheerful Latina of about fifty on whose nose sat an enormous black mole, greeted him.

"Hello, Daniel, I think there's a computer open."

He smiled and said, "How are you, Leesh? I think I'll be checking some things out today." He liked being known by name at the library.

He checked his email every couple of days. All he ever found were invites from a local veteran's group and harangues from Cristina. There was a pattern to her missives. They generally began in a cold, studied way, in which she expressed hope that his mother was well, in which she alerted him that she prayed that he was getting the time and help he needed to realize the dimensions of his failure as a husband, son and brother. After the general charges, she would work herself into a towering rage of accusation from which she let him know that it was the worst mistake of her life marrying him, trusting him, caring about him. "You wouldn't even give me a baby!" He added the weight of her anguish to the weight he carried.

Those accusatory emails were better than the sad ones, the ones where Cristina would beg him to come back, try one more time, forget the past, find a way of making it work and making her happy. In those emails she didn't blame him. She blamed the war and the Army for sending him off to do horrible things, see things he couldn't blot out even with the drinking and drugs. Jesus could help him, she could help him, if only he'd give them a chance. Those emails made him mad because, fuck her and, Jesus, they didn't know shit.

"I was awake all night thinking about Pumpkin and how we are cursed. How I am cursed. What did I do to deserve all this pain and death? Do you know? Do you?!!"

Daniel did know. He'd passed on his curse to her and his unborn son, like a virus or STD. When an IED went off in the streets of Baghdad, the targeted patrol lost men to heinous injury or death. And there was always collateral damage. Some kid getting her eardrums blown out, shrapnel flying into people's faces. Sometimes more serious injuries. The day after Daniel got into the war, his platoon rendered aid to a Marine squad that had been hit while on patrol. The IED had been a big one, detonated from across the street by a Haji sumbitch. Two Marines had been killed. So, too, had an old man, a merchant selling fruit, and two women who'd had the misfortune of being at the wrong place at exactly the wrong time. The gore had been thick, pieces of meat and bone all over the street, the walls, in the garbage-filled gutters. It fell to them to make sure the roving packs of dogs didn't get to the dead before the bodies were cleared out.

You could call it bad luck. Terrible, in fact. But it wasn't personal, not for the civs, anyway. They weren't the targets. Bad luck was this cosmic cloud of toxins. Like a rancid fart in an elevator that you walked into not knowing any better. It didn't have a center of gravity, nor did it have anything to do with fate. Daniel's theory was that this cosmic cloud of toxins just *was*. And if you walked through it, you were going to inhale it, take it into your very being. You were poisoned and you carried that stench to others. He couldn't tell Cristina this. He deleted the email without responding. What could he say? It was a curse, just not hers, but hers all the same.

Daniel surfed a while trying to find out where his old unit was, checking the temperature in the desert, reading the empty bullshit about progress and finishing the mission. Nothing any of the politicians said matched what was going on. It was all platitudes and misdirection. Nobody wanted to read about scared skinny kids in the towns, dead Hajis in the decimated buildings, grit-covered gore on the streets and walls after a firefight.

And then there was the desert so hot he couldn't muster a piss during the day, the heat making his skin crawl, water from canteens always hot as tea, face battered to shit by the sand in the wind, everything so faded nothing stood out after a while. Night was worse: cold, dark, too quiet, too much time to think about who he missed. It got to where he was happier on patrol than lying in his cot, body fatigued but unable to turn off his mind.

Now he sat in front of the computer, a pointless attempt at distraction, Daniel surfing and surfing, no matter how far afield, always winding up somewhere in the desert, a little goldfish mother squirming to death on the edge of a broken glass bowl, him looking on, nothing to do about it. Cursed.

~~~

Tonia had the sniffles and Alena's mother wanted her to take Tonia to the hospital. She'd called Alena four times and demanded to know if she'd checked her temperature. She wanted to know why she'd sent her to school if she wasn't feeling well. "If I did that, Mother, she would never go to school."

Adding to this annoyance, Alena was not speaking to Richard. He'd made a mess of things as usual. Nothing major to the untrained eye, but Alena's eye was trained. Richard's problem was that he just didn't care very much about much. He was easygoing and all that. This had been attractive in the beginning when they met in high school. He played football. She didn't have many friends, and to have him, a popular boy, pay attention to her? He wasn't a Christian back then, but he made the concession to go to church and even pretended to get saved.

He took her to the prom in his '76 Malibu Classic, which was *muy* tricked out. The car had a superb stereo and even though he insisted on his *rancheras* and *cumbias*, it was a privilege to ride with him. He would pick her up at 7:30 every morning, rain or shine, always with an easy smile and always willing to listen. No one had ever listened to her before. Certainly not her mother, and Daniel was always involved with other things, although he treated her well and took her to the movies when he had money.

Richard didn't promise her much, and that much he delivered. That sounded mean, but it was true. Richard drove a truck for Coke, worked hard, brought home his money, tossed his stinky clothes in the hamper, cooked dinner occasionally and didn't ask for much more than to watch the Spurs play. But he didn't know much about love. He was no *romántico*. It wasn't in his DNA. The Latin lover myth didn't apply to Richard. But if you loved someone, shouldn't you want to have sex once in a while? She'd read somewhere that men hit their sexual peaks at the age of eighteen. She could attest to that. Richard's sex drive had been sold off with his Malibu ten years ago.

Or was it when she'd had the baby? Okay, she'd gained some weight. But was it her fault? Women gained weight when they had children. What did he think, that it was easy? The stretch marks and stitches, the veins that grew thick and turned blue overnight. What was she supposed to do about that? Part of the reason she'd started to dance at the church was to take some of the weight off, to make herself more attractive for him.

She'd never look like one of the Spurs cheerleaders with their big *chichis* and their skinny white rumps shaking like they had an earthquake somewhere in their vulvas. It made her sick. She canceled HBO and Showtime. Who needed the competition? She'd even bought a book about making romantic life sexier. The ideas were degrading, but she tried a couple of the ones that allowed for a semblance of dignity.

After a couple of candlelit dinners and shelling out twenty dollars for a sitter, she gave up not on the wanting of it, but on the begging for it.

It was their anniversary, their ninth, and she'd had to bring up the date after hinting all through dinner. Richard, his stupid mouth full of *carne guisada* and beans, was looking at the television with one eye, completely uninterested in what she was saying.

"You know, it's coming up," she said.

"Um—hum," he said in a way that let her know he had no clue. He was good at playing stupid. She tried again.

"Nine years." That was more than a clue. It was a shovel across the head. But still nothing.

"Yes, nine," he said, taking another bite of tortilla.

"What are we going to do?" she finally asked him.

"Hmmm," he said chewing deliberately while he gave himself time to come up with something that would make sense. "Well, anything you want, baby."

That's when she blew up. "Anything I want? Anything? Well, how about you start with figuring out what we're talking about, Richard."

He chuckled at this, like it was a joke, a gag. That was it for her. She got up and went to the bedroom. He tried to make it up to her later. It took him a while to figure out what she'd been talking about in the first place.

"Our anniversary," he said. "Sorry. It's not like I forgot. It's still a couple of weeks away, baby. I'm tired today. It's been tough at work. Carlos is giving me all of Beto's stops till he gets back from his broken leg. I'm putting in overtime. What say I give you some dough from that and you go get yourself fixed up, hairstyle, nails, makeup, the works. And then you tell me what you want, and I'll make it happen."

That was not what Alena wanted to hear. The truth was, she didn't know what she wanted to hear. Maybe she didn't want to hear anything. She got to the point where there didn't seem to be anything left, and she didn't want to hear any more baloney. It got easier to not want to make it up. She lived like this, and it became a pattern. She wasn't one of those disgruntled women who listened to Oprah. She hated those women, always complaining and feeling sorry for themselves. "Ohhh, look at me with my unhappy marriage and my butterball ass and my lonely life," Alena thought scornfully. When she thought that maybe she was one of those women, it made her feel like throwing up. She wanted to break the mirrors in the house. She wanted Richard to get home so that she could look at him and blame someone besides herself.

That sounded horrible, but it was the truth. And then the phone rang for the fifth time. The answering machine clicked on.

"Alena, this is Mom. Pick up the phone if you're there. Pick it up, Alena. Hello. Hellooo. Helloooooooooo. Pick up, pick up, pick up, pick up, pick . . ."

"Hello, Mother."

"*M'ija*, how is Tonia? Don't give her a bath today if she has a fever. Does she have a fever?"

"No, Mother, she doesn't have a fever."

"Did you get her from school early?"

"No."

"How do you know she doesn't have a fever?"

"Mother, I'm in the middle of washing clothes. Let me call you back."

"Well, okay, but before I let you go, I was watching the video from last Sunday and I want to know about one of the moves. Sister Gutiérrez and Sister Alicia didn't do it the same way. Did you notice?"

"No."

"You should watch it again."

"I haven't watched it the first time, Mother."

"Well, do, and then call me back and tell me which is the right way. And check Tonia's temperature when you finally get her home. Remember, honey and lemon if her throat hurts."

It took all Alena's self-control not to hang up on her. And then the phone rang again. It was Daniel, the only person in the world in worse shape than her. He sounded depressed, maybe bored, but lately that's the way he always sounded. He invited himself over for dinner. Alena thought this was good. It would give her someone to talk to since she wasn't speaking to Richard. She told him to come over early.

Daniel was waiting when she got home after picking up Tonia. He was sitting on the porch looking into the yard, lost in thought. Her brother was a mess, or as Tino would have put it, *todo perdido*. Tonia, who was feeling just fine, jumped out of the car and ran up to him.

"Tío Daniel, Tío Daniel."

She loved him and he paid attention to her, now that he'd moved back with her grandmother. He would take her to Dairy Queen and the bookstore. She always came back with one or two new books. Daniel had always been very considerate with children. Alena knew that from experience. He would have made a wonderful father before he went off to war.

Maybe one of these days when he met the right girl . . . There was plenty of good in him if only he'd pull his head out and look around. He'd wasted too much time with that woman who only wanted to harp on him and make his life miserable. If you asked her, it was Cristina who'd really screwed him up, even more than the war. She was a hard case, and with a woman like that you had to take a decisive hand. Alena didn't like thinking this way, but this was her brother. And she told him many a time, "Daniel, you've got to put your foot down with that woman. Plenty of women lose a baby. They move on. It's not your fault."

Daniel stood up and gave Tonia a hug as he walked up to the door. He smiled in a way that let Alena know it had been a bad day, a bad day in a long stretch of bad days. She kissed his cheek, and they walked into the house. It was a nice house. Small, but big enough for the three of them. Richard was good at doing things, this much Alena would admit.

When they moved in, the place was a wreck. A woman and five cats had lived there and finally lost the place. The cats had torn it up good. It smelled of ammonia and cat shit, the bathtub looked like it had been used to bathe goats, and the paint both outside and inside was peeling in coats. But they only paid twenty thousand dollars and, with a few months of hard work, they fixed it up. They were happy then, Richard and her.

"What happened today?" she asked Daniel.

"What do you mean?"

"Well, you look like something is bothering you. Cristina?"

"Nah. Nothing special."

"So you didn't hear from the witch?"

"No, no."

"Well, is *that* the problem?" she asked him. "That she didn't write you an abusive email? Are you that in love with feeling guilty all the time?"

"C'mon," he said, turning on the set. "I'm just tired, alright?"

"Daniel, Daniel," she chided. "Big brother, you seem dead set on punishing yourself. And when you're not punishing yourself, *she's* always waiting in the wings to do it for you. If you're that hungry for it, go log on and reread some of the old hate mail from her. I'm sure you've saved it."

He laughed.

"You haven't!" she said. "You have! Good God, Daniel! Sometimes I think you're beyond help."

He didn't answer the charge, ignoring her as he looked at a picture Tonia had drawn at school that day. "Pretty cool cat," he told her. "Let me take this one home. I'll put it on the fridge so all the world can see."

"I made it for you!" Tonia said, delighted at her uncle's appraisal.

While Tonia took her bath, Daniel followed Alena to the kitchen. Daniel was a good cook.

Alena watched him take some things out of the refrigerator. "What are you going to make?" she asked, smiling.

"I dunno. Some sort of pasta thing," he said.

He'd brought a bottle of wine, which Alena didn't much like, but in his state, she didn't complain. He opened it and poured himself a glass.

"Want some?" he asked.

Alena wrinkled her nose. "Nooo." She thought about asking him what his AA buddies would say about him drinking, but she stopped short.

"Suit yourself." He went back to cutting the chicken.

"Mother's driving me crazy," Alena said.

"What now?"

"Tonia, dancing, you know, just being Mother."

"You're too hard on her."

"*I'm* too hard on *her*? Oh, brother, brother."

"Okay," he said, "you're too hard on each other. Relax. The war's over. You both win or lose or whatever."

"I'm willing if she's willing, but she's not," Alena said. "Maybe you can broker a peace deal."

He shook his head as he pulled a frying pan down and poured olive oil on the minced garlic and basil.

"Not me, sis. I still remember the high school years. How many times did I have to run into the hallway when you two fought, still in my goddamned underwear? It seemed like every morning."

"Not my fault," she said. "And language, please. My daughter is home, and I don't want her to hear her beloved uncle blaspheming."

"What's the deal with Richard?"

"Richard?"

"Yeah, you know, the guy who sleeps with you."

"Nothing. Who told you there's a problem?"

"Mom says you and Richard were out of sorts on Sunday."

"I don't even know where to begin."

"Try," Daniel said, stirring the chicken into the frying pan.

She'd been waiting for the cue and started with the anniversary, the lame "I'm-tired" routine, the insulting proposition that she go "fix herself up."

"C'mon," Daniel said, "that's silly stuff. Richard works his tail off. Sure, he's tired."

This response irked Alena. Not because Richard didn't deserve a defense. He did. She wasn't so unfair as to recognize that. But Daniel was always playing devil's advocate. She was always ready to take a shit on Cristina for his sake. He should be loyal enough to do the same for her. All she wanted was to vent and feel like someone was on her side and understood.

After a few minutes, Tonia came out of the bath, but Alena sent her to do homework so she and Daniel could keep talking. Richard would be home soon, and then it'd be sports talk and silly boy jokes. Daniel liked Richard.

"So, he forgot your anniversary. It happens," Daniel said. He added peppers to the mix in the frying pan.

"I knew you'd say that," Alena told him. "But it's not just forgetting our anniversary, although he's had nine chances now to get the date down. Sometimes I think I ought to sew a patch on his uniform with the date on it right next to his name."

Daniel laughed.

"It's a metaphor, Daniel. Forgetting the anniversary is an episode in the life of our dreary marriage. Sometimes I think you're lucky and don't even know it."

"Some luck," Daniel said.

"I'm sorry," she said. "I didn't mean it."

"It's cool," Daniel said re-filling his empty wine glass.

"No, it's not," she said, taking a tiny sip of his wine. "It's that sometimes I forget. You're so quiet about it all. You never complain. How do you never complain?"

"Grunts don't complain," he said as he put the pasta in the boiling water. "Hooa."

Alena knew this was not true. Plenty of complaining sonsofbitches got exactly what they wanted. "Hmph," she said.

Just then, Richard came through the door. He looked tired and he stank from the hot day. He smiled at Daniel and said, "What's up, bro?" and then looked over at Alena with a glimmer of hope in his eye.

She pursed up her lips and said, "Hi, Bear," gave him a kiss and sent him off to take a shower before dinner.

#2

Although Danny joined with a college degree, he shunned officer training. He is here to learn to be a man, prove his manhood to himself. The infantry is where you prove yourself. Fonzo and Scotty think this amusing, call him Danny College, but respect the fact that he isn't a wannabe, a rear echelon motherfucker dreaming of a little chest salad.

Over the past year, they've learned to trust each other with their lives. They've crawled through shit-filled trenches, breathed the same dust-heavy air, kicked in hundreds of doors, secured as many houses, killed a few bad guys, eaten, puked, shit, fought and bled together. In the field, there is a code. You maintain your front, your tough-guy act, even when you're unsure or scared or plain homesick. You are all tough guys relying on gallows humor as your only sanctioned relief. In the Sandbox, everyone is unsure, scared, homesick and beat up. No use being a bitch about it.

Danny calls Cristina when he can. He keeps his mouth shut about the conditions, the danger, lets her talk about the pregnancy, how she's heard their child's heartbeat that makes a sound like a distant steam engine pummeling the air, as it beats its way up a mountain. It cheers him up, takes him outside his dusty head for a minute. Once the call ends, though, he heads for the mess or his barracks, and he is nowhere else but in Iraq. In Diyala, an Abrams shoots a MICLIC, a string of concussion bombs that wipes out a whole block, a street full of insurgent holdouts. The string of bombs essentially levels the tangle of houses. The bodies of fighters and civilians alike litter the street, rotting chunks of meat cooking in the hot rubble. Bodies turned inside out, lying in confused violent shapes never meant for the human body to make. The twisted bodies are burned into his head, burrowed deep, never to be unseen. Until then the war has seemed artificial, existing outside his grasp, even though he's already been shot at. The dust-covered gore and wide-eyed dead change that for him. After that, the war is one hundred percent here and fucking now.

The day before Fallujah, at dusk, before Scotty bit it, after the men had loaded up the Bradleys, they were sitting in small groups, bullshitting, smoking, proclaiming their brotherhood, forgiving each other for petty grievances, the things they didn't want weighing them down like overstuffed rucksacks. They took pictures, trying in vain to memorialize themselves and their buddies before the shit came down. Some of them would not come back. They knew this. There were thousands of Muj waiting for them, hardened fighters, true-believers, martyrs, crazy fuckers who knew what they were doing. So, take a picture while you can. Except for Scotty. He didn't go in for superstition. Of course, refusing to have his photo taken was itself superstitious, but Danny refrained from telling him so. He was busy enough making sure his fire team was ready. As it grew darker, the men grew quiet, not whispering quiet, but no more jostling or joking. They were ready to move out. The waiting was the worst part. Too much time to think, the nervous energy too much to keep buried.

Now, a few hours later under cover of night, with Scotty dead, Fonzo and the SAW gunner, Fuentes, look to Danny for a plan.

"Fuentes, give us cover. Fire short bursts. That raghead is gonna show his ass. Fonzo and I will move around the perimeter and express-mail his ass to Allah when he shows his balls." He looks over at Fonzo. "You stay on my wing. Don't fucking fire till we're close enough for a killshot. Keep steady, man."

They move out, using the goggles to scan the field and the houses. Danny looks for a telltale rifle barrel or any movement. Fuentes begins firing. A short five-round burst, a tracer leaving a red beeline across the field like a supersonic, pissed-off firefly. No return fire. No movement. Danny becomes acutely aware of the silence. Then the sounds of ricocheting bullets and whumping mortars in the distance. A Bradley's heavy-motor echoing from a street close by.

"You hear that?" Fonzo whispers sharply.

"What?"

"A moan, goddamnit."

Their circuit has taken them to within fifty feet of Jaws and Scotty's prostrate bodies.

"I don't hear shit," Danny whispers.

"One of them is still kicking," Fonzo says.

Danny peers through the goggles at the bodies. "Nah, man. You imagined it." He prays he is right. "We can't render aid till we get that fucking Muj sniper. Push on."

Fonzo nods as he squints at the two bodies piled on each other, his former friends, still, silent. Dead.

Then there is another burst from Fuentes' SAW. Then the crack of the sniper's rifle. Then another and another. Danny pinpoints the muzzle flash. The sniping is coming from two directions. Crossfire, a kill zone. Scotty and Jaws never had a chance of making it through.

"We're gonna get to that house. If I go down, do not render aid. Keep moving. Let's get these motherfuckers."

They slide through the darkness. It is moonless, cold, as the two men duck low, walking at a steady crouch, all eyes and ears. The field is mostly mud. Both Danny and Fonzo are already covered in slick stink. Another crack of one of the sniper's rifles, this one closer than before. One of them has eyes on Danny and Fonzo. The two drop to a crawl, a low hazy fog giving them some cover. They move as quickly as they can. Pushing the panic aside, Danny grows lightheaded. He feels unmoored, not scared, but definitely in danger of losing his bearings. He fights through feeling lost, in a dream-like haze. He re-focuses.

"The house closest to us," he whispers to Fonzo.

Another burst from Fuentes' SAW. Finally, at the periphery of the house, darkened and foreboding, a ghostly white in the dark. Fonzo and Daniel move to the front door. Daniel readies himself.

"Gonna kick this fucker down. You come in firing. We gotta get up the stairs double-fucking-time. Let's go," he says taking a deep breath before smashing his boot just below the doorknob, the door jamb giving way in a sudden whoosh, pungent, wretched hot air hitting him in the face.

"Move, move," he says as Fonzo rushes in unloading a barrage of rounds into the dark room.

The tracers bounce around like Star Wars, the red streaks surreal and beautiful. Both men rush the stairs. They know the snipers will be nested upstairs at a window or on the flat roof of the house.

"Fire an RPG through that doorway," Danny orders Fonzo.

Whoosh, then thump, then a loud blast deafening in the confines. It feels as if the stairwell is lifted and dropped instantly, with Danny hanging onto the splintered railing. Splinters and dust pour from the doorway. Fonzo catches some nasty shrapnel to the face. Daniel can see the blood streaming down his cheek, pooling around his collar.

"Let's go," he says, and the two enter the wrecked second floor.

More firing, more splinters, more dust, more shrapnel. But there's nothing else up there. They hit the roof, clear it, and move cautiously to the balustrade of the small parapet outside.

"Fucker must've cleared out from here," Fonzo says.

The nearest house also has a balcony. The sniper either jumped or used a ladder to bridge the six feet of space between the houses. He hasn't waited around, either. They discover a tunnel in the second house, which allowed the sniper to escape. The second fire team, having finished a firefight down the street, picks up Fuentes and sets off to meet up with Fonzo and Danny. The second house has a commanding view of the field and is high enough to give them a good position. The two squads recon.

"Fuck," Fuentes yells. "Fuck, man. Fuck."

There isn't much more to say. Nothing exists that can be said to express the rage the seven men feel at losing Scotty and Jaws. It not only hurts, it is a fucking omen.

"You got a nasty one on your forehead, Fonzo," Danny says.

Fonzo puts a wad of Red Man in his mouth and spits. "I'm good."

The squad spends the next hour on the roof, each man thinking, readying.

"Those Haji motherfuckers have to be close, man," Fonzo says.

Danny radios for a Bradley to give support. "Soon as that track gets here, we'll move out. We clear houses till we find them."

Just before dawn, the Bradley providing cover, Alpha moves up the block, kicking in doors, where there are doors, bashing through half-destroyed houses, mostly finding nothing but splintered furniture and dusty pieces of concrete and plaster. At the third house, still preserved mostly, Danny stops the team from moving in. He catches a whiff of propane and moves from bull-rushing to caution.

"This fucker is booby-trapped," he tells Fonzo. "We start firing in here or trip on something, we're likely to go fucking boom."

They enter slowly, methodically, and find a dozen barrels of propane waiting to be triggered.

"This house is one big IED," Fonzo says.

Clearing a house is supposed to be quick work, blast, bash and whip through. Element of surprise. Get the jump on the Muj positioned inside. But the booby trap changes things considerably. Now they have to move slowly, keep their eyes on the ground, look for fuses and wires. It makes the whole thing more dangerous, the men in danger of a horrible surprise. The floor of the house is littered with burnt furniture, broken glass, clothes left behind.

"Keep on my wing," Danny orders. "Don't fucking fire unless you see a live Haji."

On the second floor, they find more of the same. More propane barrels, the windows bricked over, no exit, guaranteed to blast anyone in that room into shreds of roasted grunt. After making sure there aren't any enemy soldiers, they go back outside the house.

"Unload on that fucking house," Danny orders the gunner in the Bradley. "Blast it before some other team gets blown to shit."

The blast and the heat of the massive, blackened flames destroy a threat, giving the men sight of the rage they feel. The fire is supposed to burn away the helplessness they felt as they witnessed the killing of Jaws and Scotty. It isn't over, has in fact hardly just begun. Danny, Fonzo, Fuentes, the others want to bring the pain to the Muj who shot their buddies. If they can't find that Muj, any Muj will do. A Muj is a Muj is a Muj.

The sun has come up on Fallujah. Both Jaws and Scotty have been bagged. The squad has been ordered to clear more houses. "Take it slow, but don't drag it out" is the instruction. Three houses in, Danny's team takes fire from a rooftop. There are at least three Muj shooting from on high.

"Blast that fucking roof," Danny orders.

The Bradley shoots every round in its track. The team wants to find nothing but meat soup when they go in. The blasts bullwhip the men waiting to move in. Danny and Fonzo move into position at the gaping hole which was the front entry. The heavy gate hangs uncertainly from a battered hinge. As soon as they enter, they take fire. At least two of the bastards have entered the stairwell and are shooting. Danny and Fonzo duck behind ruined furniture and a giant roof beam which has fallen on one side. They return a few rounds and retreat to the Abrams.

"Shoot a Javelin missile in that goddamned hole," Danny orders. It's over the top, but Danny is too angry to contemplate anything else.

The missile courses upward and then dives directly into what is left of the roof. The blast knocks both Danny and Fonzo into the air and onto the moondust street. Debris explodes from the windows and holes in the wall. The heat blast scorches the men's faces as they watch.

"Let's go," Danny orders his team.

As they enter the house, Danny sees her. She is covered in dust so thoroughly; she almost looks like a sculpture that got knocked over. Until his eyes adjust, and he sees the growing slimy pools that cover her legs and torso. Her face and neck show streams of dust-thickened blood coming from her mouth and nose. She has wet red burns all over her hands and her exposed skin. When she moves one of those burned hands to her belly, Danny realizes she is breathing. He moves toward her.

"Careful, Danny Boy," calls Fonzo. "She could be wearing a vest. She's trying to get to something on her belly."

Danny ignores Fonzo's caution because he's seen something. He kneels at her side, putting down his rifle. It is not a vest she's reaching for. Her burned hand has begun to slowly, painfully stroke her belly. She is pregnant. Big pregnant. The blood pouring from between her legs is profuse, inundating the gray dust from the blast that coats her clothing. The blood and dust make for a muddy color, different from the blood coming from her mouth and nose. She strokes her belly softly, mustering the only strength she has left. Her eyes are on Danny's face.

Fuentes and Sky enter the house. They say something to Danny, but he is not listening. They go about their business, Fuentes covering Fonzo as he makes his way up rickety stairs, Sky looking for blind spots, triggers, weapons, anything or anyone hidden in the dark recesses of the blown-to-shit house.

"There's another body over here," Sky announces.

Danny doesn't say anything. He is on his knees, listening now, the woman's scorched lungs wheezing as she tries to breathe. Each breath brings forth more streaming blood and speckled pieces of lung tissue.

Danny doesn't turn from the woman, whose breathing is growing more rapid and shallow, her burned paper lungs rasping like tearing paper. Her lips move. Their eyes lock. She is pleading with Allah to save her child.

"Hey, Danny," Sky repeats himself. "Hey, Danny, there's a dead kid over here."

The woman coughs, spraying blood into the air, onto Danny's face in tiny red droplets. She is done. Danny turns his eyes to her belly in which a baby is turning blue, suffocating like a tiny goldfish on the edge of a broken fishbowl. There is a convulsion, as if the unborn has kicked its last, a tiny, frantic protest doomed to be noticed by only a still-dazed soldier kneeling helplessly next to its broken and burned vessel.

"It's a boy, probably six or seven," Sky says hardly loud enough for anyone but himself to hear.

The boy's neck is broken, his ragged feet bloody and torn and blackened. He is probably the woman's son. Maybe one of the Muj shooters is his father, these three his family.

Danny picks up his rifle, still looking at the dead woman on the floor, and stands up. He walks over to Sky, who is standing over the boy's body.

"What the fuck they doing here? Didn't those Haji fucks know what was going down?" Sky says nonplussed. This is his first dead kid.

"Move up there," Danny directs Sky, "Give Fuentes and Fonzo cover."

There is no need for cover. As in the previous house, the fighters have slipped away. All that's left are the bodies of the woman and the boy. Other than the dust on his body, the boy looks unscathed. His eyes are closed. He could be sleeping, except for the terrible, sharp angle of his neck. Danny gets on one knee and places his heavily gloved hand on the boy's chest. He is confused as to whether he wants to apologize or pray for the boy. Danny hasn't prayed in a long time and he doesn't remember how. Instead, he says, "Jesus, fuck," as his men cluster behind him.

CHAPTER 3
Con Safos, 1987

Looking at the picture from behind her shoulder, Rick saw the resemblance right away. "Is that your father?" he asked her.

Virginia couldn't take her eyes off the picture. "Yeah, that's my father."

"That the only picture your mom kept of him?"

"It's the first time I've ever seen him. That is, knowing he's my father." She gazed at his face, trying to make out his eyes, but they were obscured in the grainy image.

"You going to let him know about your mom?"

"Got to find him first," she said, still trying to make out his eyes. Were they kind? Loving? Did they hold any answers?

All Virginia took from the house was her clothes and Celia's box. It was her box now. It had been the coffin of her mother's dead hope, but she could use it to revive her dream. A *real father*, a new self, a new life. It was intoxicating, thrilling.

She told Rick she was leaving to find Saturnino. He was sad that she'd be leaving but didn't say anything to convince her to stay. She had already bought a twelve-dollar bus ticket to Houston. She had the matchbook with the name of the restaurant, La Tropical, and a second letter's postmark pointing her to Houston's Magnolia Park, Magnolia, a barrio close to the ship channel. And that was it: she was gone.

On the bus, Virginia felt a bit of kinship with Celia. Taking the Greyhound was to identify, if only for a short while, with the mother who had held a ticket to Houston so many years earlier.

La Tropical was no longer in business, but the sign was still there on a storefront on Canal Street, the windows busted out behind the iron burglar bars, the door covered in graffiti and faded flyers. All of the neon letters were shattered, but their faded images remained on the background of the sign.

Virginia invented a narrative in which Saturnino had run the mean streets until he'd met Celia, perhaps right in this restaurant. She'd been his waitress, and one day he'd gone in there and told her to quit because he was going to marry her, and no wife of his was going to work as a two-bit waitress. She'd gone into the manager's office and told him, "I quit," and the manager got angry and told her that she'd be back when that worthless *cabrón* left her high and dry. In this scenario, the manager had also been in love with the young, still pretty Celia. She'd laughed in his face, but with mirth, not the ugly cynicism Virginia had always heard in her mother's laughter. And then she'd left with her *real father*, on his arm, still laughing, happy and in love.

That's why Saturnino had chosen La Tropical for their reunion all those years later. When he didn't show, Celia grabbed the matchbook as a tragic memento, a token of betrayal.

Virginia walked the streets of the neighborhood knowing that her mother and father's story, her story too, was written on those streets, those sidewalks, on the house and storefronts she was looking at.

She remembered that Benny-Boy had often talked about getting his mechanical training at a shop in Magnolia. He liked to brag that he didn't need to drive no goddamned truck, that he was once the best mechanic at Pedro's Car Shop. Virginia found it in the phone book and went there the next morning. There was a young boy who didn't remember any Benny Lopez, but when Virginia said, "How about Benny-Boy," an old man sitting in the little office said, "Who wants to know about Benny-Boy?"

He was bald and skinny, with yellow teeth from smoking too much. There was a picture of a bare-breasted girl holding a big steel wrench on the wall. The old man looked Virginia over in a way that made her feel dirty, but he told her that he remembered Benny-Boy.

"Does he owe you money?" He laughed a smoker's laugh.

Virginia told him that Benny-Boy's wife was dead, and the old man sobered up some. He stopped leering and stroked his chin pensively. "He's got family around here. I think he's got a cousin living over on Beltran, by the EZ-Mart, in front of the old washateria, so far as I can recall. I used to go over there with him and have a few beers." The old man didn't remember Benny-Boy's cousin's name.

Virginia found Benny-Boy's cousin who, after quizzing her as to why she was asking so many questions, directed her to her mother's cousin still living in the neighborhood. She went there next and found an older woman, Ester, who insisted on giving the girl something to eat. She was a diabetic, an amputee sitting in a cheap wheelchair, orange rust showing through the dull aluminum.

Ester said, "I knew Benny-Boy wouldn't do anything for her but make her miserable. Saturnino was no prize, but he was better quality than that."

She explained how Benny-Boy hooked up with her mother after Saturnino had been sent to prison on a short stint.

"We never were sure who the father was, Benny-Boy or Saturnino. We never got a look at you. He would have known you weren't his just by your eyes. He was wild. In and out of jail. Running around with drugs. He'd be all over Magnolia dancing with the girls. Believe it or not, I was once young and pretty like you, and I loved dancing, too. Saturnino was a dancer like no other. He got all the girls on the floor.

"But you know Mexicans, there'd always be one who didn't like Saturnino and his pomaded hair, with his after-shave and his shiny Stacys. *Envidia*, girl, pure jealousy, and if your father had had a few too many, which he always did by the end of the night, there was no backing down. The Lizard Lounge was his, and the bouncer always threw out the instigator. There's more I could tell, lots more, but you should get it from the horse's mouth."

"Do you think he knew before he went to prison?"

"About you?" Ester asked. "I don't know. He came look-ing for Celia right after he got out the first time, but he never mentioned a daughter, and none of us were willing to add fuel to his search. He mistreated your poor momma. He was mean, jealous, always with ugly *fantasías* about your mom cheating on him. But your mom didn't cheat on him.

"It was him who'd disappear for days, always coming back with excuses about his work, his druggie work. I'm sorry to have to tell you this, but you should know why your momma left with you in her belly when Saturnino landed in jail again."

"Why Benny-Boy?"

"He was around. He gave her attention. And Celia needed attention. Why am I telling you? You must know! Course, he was nothing but trash. He was even more jealous than Sa-

turnino. He dragged Celia out of that very chair you're sitting
in one night when she came looking for some cheer from her
cousin. She was big with you, too. He was a good-for-nothing."
Saturnino came looking for Celia after he got out. He'd
gone to her house, but no one wanted to open the door.
"Where's my wife," he yelled from the yard.
Ester yelled back, "We don't know, Saturnino, we don't
know."
He wouldn't listen until her poor old aunt, half-blind,
came to the door and walked right up to him and said, "She's
gone, m'ijo. And you got no one to blame but yourself."
Saturnino got this look like he knew she was right. He
shrugged it off and left.
He came around a few more times asking if they'd heard
anything. After a while, he didn't come around anymore.
Celia's cousin, Velma, heard from someone he'd been in a
bad accident and almost been killed.
Ester told Virginia about Saturnino's brothers. It took her
some time, but she finally found Leo, the eldest: "You can
go find him, if you want to find out some more."
It was during her days in Houston that Virginia learned
she was pregnant.

~~~

Teresa was going to take Daniel to Jim's Coffee Shop
after church. She liked the hamburgers and, more than that,
it was where Tino had proposed to her. As usual she would try
to sit in the same booth from that long-ago early summer
evening when Tino had asked her if she'd ever marry a guy
like him. It was as sentimental as Teresa got.
Daniel had tried to beg off of going to church. He'd gotten up with a terrible headache, a desert-sun headache, the
kind that swells so much your helmet feels like a vise, the

bright light brutalizes your dusty eyes and every step jolts you from neck to crown. He'd had some sort of dream, one he couldn't remember, but he sensed it had been ugly, dark, violent.

The headache was no excuse. Teresa wouldn't let him off the hook. "I'll take you to Jim's after," she said in a singsong voice full of sweetness but tinged with a steeliness he understood all too well.

He was fucking going to church.

Daniel swallowed a couple of oxys and got himself dressed. At Teresa's church, at the very least you wore dress pants and dress shirt. No shorts, no tees. The services were two and a half hours long. There was sure to be a dire warning about hell and damnation. And it was sure to end with a loud, lengthy series of prayers shouted into a microphone and then the awful laying on of hands, a sweaty undertaking of holy violation.

If Teresa felt the urge, she would drag Daniel forward for prayer.

"Jesus, Jesus! Give our brother peace of mind and heart," the pastor would scream into his ear.

In short, it was a combination of the worst possible conditions for a goddamn hangover.

Fortunately for Daniel, that Sunday no one offered to pray for him. He made no eye contact, shook no one's hand. He made a beeline for the car and waited for his mom. Teresa played the piano for the morning service, which always put her in a good mood.

As they waited for the booth at Jim's to be available, Daniel sat uncomfortably in his too tight dress shoes. The humping in full pack for two years had flattened out his feet, and he now wore a full-size bigger shoe. Teresa jabbered on about someone or other at church and their family travails.

"We're at war, Daniel, at war with a spirit that won't rest until it's taken as many to hell as it can. You've seen war, *m'ijo*. You know what it's like! But we're all at war."

Teresa held his hand. The grip was soft and warm. His mother had comforting hands. She always had. As a kid, when he had debilitating headaches, she'd put her hands on his forehead and soothe his aching scalp.

Usually, he managed the shakes privately, since they mostly occurred after sunset. But not that afternoon, looking straight ahead, he winced as he felt them coming on. A shudder, a sense of oncoming panic jittering from just under his ribs and spreading down his gut. His mother sipped gingerly on a complimentary cup of tea they'd brought her while they waited. Daniel could feel his fingers jingling with uncontrollable energy. He had to get to the bathroom before the Shakes hit him like a thudding mortar shell. He pulled his hand free and half-ran to the john like he had a case of the squirts. Pulling the handicap stall door open, he plopped down on the piss-speckled toilet seat, trying hard not to hyperventilate. He had to focus on the shaking as his fucking shrink had instructed. He shook and shook and moaned and moaned and didn't notice a man's hasty retreat from the next stall.

He stayed on the pot, shaking, focusing, trying not to break down. He was in there for a long while, so long that Teresa had ordered for them both and their food had already come.

"Are you okay?" she asked him with concern. "I was about to send the waiter in there to see if you were okay!"

Daniel nodded and took a drink of the decaf his mom had waiting for him. "Fine, Mom," he said.

Teresa nagged him to talk to Brother Alfred. "Just talk to him. He's a good man, a godly man."

He'd always refused. It was a joke, really. The small, coiffed preacher, sincere but completely clueless, just like every other

civvy joker who didn't know shit. He thought hell was somewhere in Middle Earth, with flames, demons, pitchforks. . . .
Daniel knew hell. He'd been there and had brought it back with
him. It didn't have anything to do with God or a devil.

Teresa was persistent. She waylaid Daniel the next Sunday after service, Brother Alfred in tow. "You two talk!"

Brother Alfred gave a weak smile, embarrassed to be out
of his depth, but still game. "Your mother's offered to pay
for our lunch," he said with a playful shrug. "How about it?"

Daniel was high, coasting, feeling light, guard down.
"Sure, Pastor."

They'd gone around the corner to the Tica Taco.

Brother Alfred opened with his admiration for Teresa and
how she was handling Tino's death. "Good man, your stepfather. Hard life, hard answers, kind and pliant heart."

Daniel thought that an excellent description of Tino.

"Your mom is a godly woman too. She prays for you. She
worries about you."

"Yeah," Daniel said. "God loves her."

"God loves you, too."

"Yeah, well thanks for all the care you've given her,"
Daniel said. He was grateful for Alfred's support of his
mother, but right then, he badly needed the pastor to eat his
tacos, maybe move on to the Spurs or some other light bullshit.

"How long has it been that you've been back home
now?"

"Almost a year."

"About the time Tino went," Alfred said, dousing his taco
with picante.

"Yup."

"Been tough for you," Alfred said, fixing Daniel with a
steady, deep gaze.

"Sure," Daniel said, hoping the admission would avoid the "very concerned" talk Alfred was getting ready to unload. "But I deal." He smiled decisively, hoping that would end the conversation.

"What is it that is bothering you the most?" Alfred asked. This took Daniel aback. No one had asked him directly since he'd returned.

"The war? Your wife?"

"Ex-wife," Daniel said. "Ex-wife, Brother."

Alfred nodded sympathetically.

"Pastor, I appreciate what you've done for Mom, really, I do. But there isn't much I need you to do for me."

"Not me," Alfred challenged. "Jesus, Son, Jesus."

"Okay, so Jesus," Daniel said. "But you don't know, can't know the load of shit . . . I don't want to talk about it, really. But just to cut to the chase, it's too much for Jesus to sort out."

"That can't be true," Alfred said. "There's nothing too much for the loving power of Jesus. Will you let me pray for you, Son?"

Daniel did not care to be prayed for in the least. It made his stomach turn. What was there to pray for? He'd done enough praying in the Sandbox, and it hadn't done a goddamn bit of good. But the good pastor wasn't really asking. He intended to lay hands on the wounded soldier, like it or not.

"Sure, Brother," Daniel said, putting the last bite of taco back on the plate. "But let me hit the head first."

Brother Alfred nodded sympathetically. "Of course. I'll be right here."

Daniel stood up and headed for the back of the restaurant. There was a small window in the bathroom, just large enough to hoist himself and squeeze through, which he did posthaste. It was either that or freak out. The thought of Alfred holding his hand and praying in front of the diners nudged Daniel towards panic. He hit the ground upside down, absorbing the jump with his hands. It was a slow-motion fall, and he rolled onto his back. Watching him was a surprised older couple on their way out to their car. Daniel nodded politely and broke into a slow jog.

Pastor Alfred watched him through the dining room window, a comically confused look on his face. As Daniel picked up the pace, the pastor muttered a prayer for the young man, anyway.

~~~

Teresa was in bad shape. She was upset that Alena didn't care about her.

"I'm just a drag on her," she confessed to Daniel. "How else can you explain the way she treats me? She won't listen to anything I have to say about Tonia. She was sick this weekend, and Alena knew it, but just to spite me, she didn't do anything about it. Do you know that she sent that poor baby to school yesterday? It breaks my heart."

"I was there, Mom, and Tonia is just fine. No sickness. She was bouncing all over the place all night. You worry too much about her. Alena is a good mother. She learned from the best," Daniel said, trying to make his point and compliment his mother at the same time.

"Did you talk about the Easter Pageant?"

"A little, but not much. You were right about her and Richard being out of sorts. Nothing serious. Miscommunication about their anniversary. He forgot, and I don't know what else. It seems to be over for now."

"Hmph. I don't know what gets into that girl's head. Tino and I never did anything special for our anniversary. We'd go out and get something to eat. He'd buy me a new sweater for church, and I'd get him a package of tube socks, the kind he liked from Montgomery Ward. I didn't need any fancy flowers or love notes. Who needs all that? It's ridiculous. Flowers make me feel like it's my funeral. Women are too spoiled today, and that's what led to all this *bribonada*. Take care of your husband and he'll take care of you. Leave all phony baloney romance for the *telenovelas*. I bet Cristina is thinking the same thing right now. You bet."

"I don't know about that," he said, trying to change the subject.

"Well, I know."

She moved to the kitchen to get her practice tambourine, the one made from a Styrofoam plate and Christmas tree silver strands. When she returned, she headed for the television and put on the tape of the A-team dancing the past Sunday. She practiced for about two minutes and then shut the set off.

"I don't know why I'm even bothering," she said, sitting down, the Styrofoam tambourine in her left hand, the strands dragging on the carpet. "Alena is right. I'm no good. No good for anything. Not as a mother, a grandmother and certainly not for dancing."

"C'mon, Mom," Daniel said. "I'd be living on the street if it weren't for you. You're just going through a bad spot. Everyone goes through a bad spot. With Tino dying and you trying to get used to a new life. . . ."

"Some new life," she said. "I'm an old woman. That's all there is to that. I might as well get used to it. No one needs old women. I could just sit here alone and stop going anywhere and no one would notice."

"C'mon, Mom, everyone at church would notice. You practically hold the place together."

"Well, Alena certainly wouldn't notice. She'd probably be happy if I didn't show up for church anymore. It would make it easier for her to avoid telling me I stink."

"You keep practicing, and I'm sure you'll make the team," he told her.

Actually, he had brought up the dancing to Alena. But Alena was stubborn when she perceived someone moving into her territory. She got the same scary tone of voice that Teresa got when one had gone too far.

"I have a responsibility," Alena had said, "not to Mother, but to God, the church and Pastor Alfred. I can't just let Mother on the A-team. This isn't amateur hour, Daniel. Besides, if I let her on just because she's my mom, how would that look? Then I'd have to let anyone who wanted on the A-team."

"You let Pastor Alfred's wife onto the A-team. She's way worse than Mom. I've seen drunks with better coordination." She knew Daniel was right on the pastor's wife, so she didn't address it. "I have to evaluate people by their ability, and that's what I'm going to do. If and when Mother is ready, she'll get on the team." And that was that.

When Daniel got back to his mother, he wasn't about to tell her what Alena had said. He encouraged Teresa the best he could and then offered, "Let's take the afternoon off. We'll go out for lunch and then the used bookstore."

Teresa cheered up at that. She spent all her time in the self-help section looking at books with titles like, *Being the Best You, You Can Love*, or *God's Strategy for Eating Healthy the New Testament Way*. She'd pick up a pile of them and bring them to a chair, where she read like a fiend until the store closed.

That afternoon after performing her ritual at the bookstore, she told Daniel, "I'll take this one."

"Just the one? You have about ten books there."

"Well, I liked this other one, too."

"Let's take both then," he told her.

"Can you afford them?"

"Mom, they're just a few bucks. I think I can cover that." She was all smiles.

They made their purchases and went home.

~~~

Daniel needed a job. Richard offered to try to get him on
at Coca-Cola. It was tough work, back-breaking, and the heat
was brutal at the plant.

"But if I can get you on my truck as an assistant, once we
get on the road, we're on our own."

It sounded as good as any job. Part-time, only a couple of
days a week. It sounded fine to Daniel because it'd spare him
having to fill out multiple applications at the mall for a min-
imum-wage job. He didn't want much responsibility. In fact,
he wanted the minimum amount of responsibility. He needed
just enough to pay his credit card bill, the one he'd agreed to
take over from the marriage. It was a ten-thousand-dollar
debt. Cristina had taken the two smaller cards, Pier 1 and Target, with less than a thousand combined. Guilt had led Daniel
to volunteer to pay the big one.

Within a week, he was loading crates of Coke onto
Richard's truck. Daniel marveled at the sheer volume of the
beverage consumed in just one town. Thousands and thousands of cases, filled with tens of thousands of bottles, two
liters, three liters, sixteen-ounce bottles and twelve-ounce
cans. It was no wonder everyone in the country was fat as
shit and coked to the gills. Everyone at the distribution center was hooked. Coke was free, so no one drank the coffee,
which cost 50 cents. Richard drank what appeared to be
twenty gallons of Diet Coke a day. By the end of his first
shift, Daniel had drunk a gallon himself.

The work was simple, but hot. You loaded up the cases on
the truck and unloaded them at the grocery stores and stocked
them. It was a racket. The various soda companies competed
for the best shelf space. They wanted to make sure that the

customers couldn't miss the fifty-thousand, three-liter bottles of Coke, so the drivers made gigantic pyramids of the bottles. They also lobbied to shelve the drinks to be as easy to reach as possible. Americans don't want to bend over to pick up a four-pound bottle of sugar water.

Daniel enjoyed Richard's company. His brother-in-law liked to talk. It was a constant stream of invectives about his coworkers, especially the foreman, Carlos, who Richard called "bumblefuck" because he wielded just enough power to make life miserable for his workers. He was constantly on everyone's back, talking shit about moving merchandise and picking up the pace. He had an office, but Daniel had yet to see him in it. He was always on the loading docks or pacing the warehouse floors. "If this was Nam, he'd have been fragged by now," Daniel admitted.

Daniel was paid ten dollars an hour, chump-change for the heavy work, but he wasn't complaining. He hoped Richard made a good deal more. Richard told him about the grocery store managers and how picky they were about stacking drinks, about how they lorded it over you that they made the decisions about where things were to be merchandised.

"You've got to watch out. The Pepsi guys are always trying to get the primo spots, and if you lose that battle, believe me, it shows up quickly. You wouldn't think so, but people buy less if it's not right up in their grill."

"So, what are you going to do for your anniversary?" Daniel asked.

"I don't know. I have to come up with something good. Alena's been kind of worked up about it. I was thinking I'd get her this mirror she's been wanting at Target. It's the kind with the lights on it, and you flip it and it magnifies your face so you can pluck whiskers and pop the blackheads."

"Hmmm," Daniel said dubiously, "that sounds like a plan, but maybe you should think about something more romantic."

"You think?" he said. "I mean, that isn't all I'm going to do. I was going to take her and the kid to a nice place, maybe Spaghetti Warehouse."

"Hmmm . . . the Warehouse doesn't have that romantic zing you're shooting for, don't you think? Maybe you should pawn the kid off on Mom and take her somewhere a little quieter. How about that joint up on the northeast side, out towards the hill country. That's where I popped the question to Cristina. It's got outdoor dining, and they've got a nice garden patio with mesquite trees and whatnot. On the weekend, they've got a little jazz trio. You might even buy her some flowers. Forget the mirror, bro. It's a bad idea."

"Yeah, maybe you're right."

"Course I'm right. You have to think about messages. Now, what kind of message does a whisker-spotting, zit-magnifying mirror send out? That she's got zits and whiskers? . . . What kind of message is that?"

"Okay, okay, I see where you're going with this."

"Right," Daniel said. "Let *her* get the mirror. You get her the flowers and the romantic dinner. Write her a nice card. You know, put on the charm. You know how to do that. You got her to marry you, right?"

"I'm not good with the poet stuff. Never have been." He looked over at Daniel, snapping his fingers. "Hey, maybe you could help me out? You know the kinds of things women like to hear."

"Listen, pal, I don't know how you figure that, but how about you buy one of those Hallmark cards, one that leaves space for you to write in. Then you come up with something, and I'll look it over before you write it into the card."

"You've got a deal," Richard said, smiling.

By the time Daniel got home, he was always bone-tired. He hadn't done anything physical in a long time. His first paycheck, just less than three hundred dollars for thirty hours of work, felt like he'd really earned it. There was sweat in that paycheck. Of course, he couldn't *live* on it, not even at full time. There was no way he could afford an apartment and a car. Forget food. He'd have to live on Diet Coke and cat food. There might be honor in physical work, but there was definitely sweat, and there wasn't room for anything else.

Although, there was something about being bone-tired, coming home, dropping a couple of oxys, taking a shower and feeling that warmth riding over tired muscles. It made him feel like he'd gotten something done instead of just sitting around fretting about everything. Hell, the work even helped keep the shakes at bay.

〜〜〜

She didn't know what happened to Richard, but he'd actually done a good job on their anniversary. Maybe it was the silent treatment, but she didn't think so. It had never worked before. Usually, he moped around until she felt sorry for him, and then everything would go back to normal. But this time, he'd got it right. He bought her a very nice bouquet of flowers; tiger lilies like in their wedding. That was a sweet touch. He took her to dinner at the Grey Moss Inn and even arranged for her mother to watch Tonia. Even the card he'd given her was perfect. He'd written some very sweet things. At dinner, they ordered a couple of glasses of wine. What the heck, Alena figured, it was a special occasion and, anyway, whose business was it? It wasn't as if Pastor Alfred was hiding in the salad ready to recriminate them for drinking.

On their way home, Alena asked Richard, "Aren't we going to pick up Tonia?"

"I asked your mom if it was okay if she spent the night."

〜〜〜

Alena was working on the pageant. It had to be good. Pastor Alfred had put a lot of money into the new costumes and he was expecting something big. It had to be moving, entertaining and original. That was a tall order. She wished Daniel would help her. He'd always been so good at that stuff. She remembered him acting on the stage in high school and college. She knew she had sufficient talent, at least for the dancing, but what about the presentation? It was staging that mattered. People didn't notice the tiny details of the actual performance. They noticed how things glittered, how the backdrop looked, the music and lights. She could choreograph the moves and make sure that her ladies lined up right and executed the steps and turns. But she needed a story too. And she didn't want to do the usual passion story. Everyone did that. Pastor Alfred always drew his Passion of the Christ glow-in-the-dark portrait live and onstage before Easter altar call. She didn't want to simply replicate. It had to be about innovation and power. She had to think.

She imagined that Jesus would probably scoff at the idea of pageantry and pomp, but she realized this wasn't about pleasing Jesus. Images floated in her head: the lamb, the cross, the palms—yes, palms were a must. The girls would hold palms instead of tambourines. That was good. She liked that. There was also the issue of the stigmata, the stone being rolled away, Jesus rising from the dead, the witnesses being turned away by the angels—"He whom you seek is not here!" How could she put these together in a new way? The music was important. There were the classics, of course, and then there were the contemporary Christian songs. But they got used every year in every church, by every dance group. Daniel made an interesting suggestion. He thought she should use classical music, something by Brahms. Alena liked that idea, but how did one choreograph to that?

It would be a challenge, and she liked a good challenge. Yet, she worried that people would think the troupe was putting on airs. Perhaps the audience would be bored. Admittedly, she was not much for classical music. It put her to sleep, and if it put her to sleep, what would it do to Sister Gutiérrez or Pastor Alfred?

One day when Tonia really was sick and running a fever, Alena kept her home. She didn't dare call her mother with this news because she knew that Teresa would blame her. "I told you she wasn't feeling well last week. You should have held her back then," she'd undoubtedly say.

In any case, she wished she could do something to help her mother. Something to distract her. Not the dancing. That was out of the question. She had to stick to her principles and the fairness of things. But something else. She'd told Teresa that she could train the children's dance class, but she didn't want to do that. Teresa thought it was a trick, little more than a sop, and Alena guessed that it was.

The problem was that Teresa was obsessed with only two things: Tonia and dancing. She wouldn't admit it, but she missed Tino immensely. He was the quiet, calm strength that Teresa needed. Without him, she was a ball of nerves, jittery, unhappy, obsessed with imaginary ailments. Alena didn't want to be unkind or insensitive. She loved her mother, but Teresa had to take some responsibility for things. With Daniel around, it made it easier. Alena knew it went further than paying her bills on time or keeping appointments. It was about *life*.

Her mother wasn't really that old. She was only sixty-three. When Alena was a child, she remembered both her grandmothers as *old* at that age. They wore their hair in buns and didn't color their gray. Her *abuelitas* would have had a conniption if someone suggested they dye their hair. That was something only prostitutes and actresses did, and for her grandmothers, there was no real difference. They grew old without seeming to mind it much. There were health issues, yes, but as far as feeling resigned or even saddened by old age, there was no hint of it.

How times had changed. Even at the church, the women her mother's age were doing things to keep themselves in tip-top shape. They exercised, they dressed well, they did their nails and colored their hair. They wore lipstick and eyeliner. They went to lunch with each other and gossiped. They were not living in a dark house waving paper plate tambourines. It frustrated Alena when she thought about it. It was too much pressure. It wasn't fair. She had loved Tino very much, but she sometimes had gotten angry with him for not taking better care of himself. He shouldn't have let himself die. He shouldn't have left her mother alone.

Alena hadn't much liked Tino at first. She was just a kid, not much older than Tonia was now. Her father had been gone for a while. She didn't have any real memories of him being around. Maybe a vague birthday but not much more than that. So it wasn't that she'd been jealous for her biological father. Teresa had told her enough so that she knew he was a loser. It was that Tino wasn't part of the picture and it didn't seem right that he should just waltz into the family. It disturbed her equilibrium because his good fortune was *unearned*. Her mother was impatient with Alena because she didn't welcome him like Daniel did. Daniel never said much about anything. He didn't complain even when he should. And Tino hadn't been the easiest guy to live with. He was always around, always watching, like an off-duty security guard who didn't take his uniform off at home. He didn't say much, but he was always ready to give her a look that said, "I know what you're up to." And he was always throwing things away. You couldn't put a piece of paper down for two minutes before he was tossing it into the trash. You couldn't imagine how many letters, notes and homework assignments disappeared after Tino moved in. It drove Alena crazy that he wouldn't admit it either.

The worst was when she started dating and he got to chasing boys away. Once she'd invited a boy from school over to do homework, and Tino wasn't pleased. So when their tomcat wandered into the house, Tino took the opportunity to kill two birds with one stone. While Alena watched in horror, Tino picked Cat up by the scruff of his neck and threw him out into the front yard from halfway inside the living room. Cat went screeching though the air like he'd been launched out of a cannon and landed ass over teakettle thirty feet away.

"That's what you do with a tomcat," Tino said when Alena came out yelling at him. But he hadn't said it to her, he said it to the boy. It was one of his more subtle messages.

And yet, when Alena moved out for college, Tino acted like she was moving to the moon. He was so sad, trying hard to hide his feelings. He moved her into the dorm single-handedly, even with his bad legs. Anytime she needed anything, he was there. She'd come home and he'd wash her car and fill it with gas before she knew what he was doing. When she graduated, he was there with a dozen roses and tears in his eyes.

After Tonia was born, he went completely gaga. He'd volunteer to babysit at the drop of a hat and always he had a dollar for Tonia's snack after church. Little things like that she remembered. She wondered if Tonia would have any memories of him. Probably as vague and gauzy as Alena's memories of her father.

That was why the Easter pageant was so important. One had to remember things. If you didn't, they went dim. The pageant was a way to keep your focus, to remember the past. It was fine, all this talk about forgiveness and salvation and grace and faith. But what did it mean? They were just words, abstract principles and concepts. Humans needed things that they could see and touch and hear so that things might become real. That's why Richard's forgetting of their anniversaries was so frustrating. You could say I love you a hundred times a day, but what did it mean, what did it feel like? She would love a pageant for her marriage. Wouldn't that be nice? She wondered what it would look like, but she couldn't even imagine Richard in a pageant of any kind. He'd have scoffed at the whole idea. She'd become used to the reality of a humdrum marriage. No magic there to see. Alena had once found Richard's macho sensibility alluring. Not so much anymore. Now it was just indifferent and boorish.

The card he'd given her read, "I don't always do the right thing, but the best, most right thing I ever did was to marry you."

That was sweet. Not the most passionate thing she'd ever read, but sincere. That was probably the best way to describe Richard, if she thought about it. She'd like the two things combined. That was a good way of thinking about the pageant: sincere and passionate. She'd use that as her theme. Daniel could help her with that. She'd supply the passion, and he could supply the sincerity.

≈≈≈

When Teresa needed to think something through, she made a list. She put all the good things on one side and all the bad things on the other. She learned that from a Dr. Phil book. It helped some people to see things. She'd given Daniel that tip. She thought that he was trying to decide whether or not to go back to Cristina. He was always thinking about Cristina, although he wouldn't say much about her. Teresa thought he should make a list. For her, it wouldn't have been much of a list. On one side it would say, *Ya No Más* and on the other side, *Ya Por Fin*. But she couldn't tell him that. It wouldn't be right. He had to make his own decision about his life. Although she wouldn't mind if he'd stay with her forever. What did he need a selfish *vieja* giving him trouble for anyway? From what Teresa could see, he was getting along just fine without a woman pestering him all the time. He got awful headaches too. Daniel was like her when it came to stress. They couldn't take much.

That's why a list would help. When Teresa met Tino, she'd made lists and lists before deciding to marry him.

NO—
1. I do not want to marry another *malcriado* (once is enough).
2. He's an ex-*borracho*, ex-con, ex-drug addict, ex-*sinvergüenza*.
3. Quiet.
4. Bad legs (it has to be said).
5. Occasionally says bad words.
6. He doesn't play a musical instrument.
7. Alena doesn't like him.

YES—
1. He is strong,
2. quiet,
3. *cristiano,*
4. nice mustache and he's *güerito*.
5. Daniel likes him.
6. He doesn't like to argue.

There were other lists too. Lists about how she felt. Lists comparing him to the first husband. Lists about how they conversed and argued. Teresa knew that arguing was important. You spend a good amount of time in marriage arguing,

more so than making love. One should consider it very carefully before committing to another for life.

Perhaps she made too many lists. It got confusing sometimes. In the end, she had to make a list of lists. How many
of the lists were net positive, how many net negative? It
turned out to be 50/50, so she had finally gone with her heart.
For her it always came down to the heart, but lists helped to
feel good about it. Her advice: make no more than three lists.
After that, it gets to be too much.

Tino and his brothers all looked the same. There were
seven and one sister. Tino was the youngest. They each took
turns dying young. First Conrado, next Agapito, followed by
Mateo, and then just a year later, Francisco. All of them from
heart problems. She was only around for the last two funerals. Each time she looked down into the casket and saw a man
wearing her husband's face. It was too terrible. She got a
gnawing in her heart that she couldn't stop feeling even after
they got back home. Not even prayers could soothe her
nerves. She'd wake up, Tino next to her, not snoring because
the man didn't snore, his eyes closed, sunken, in a deep sleep,
looking the same as the body she'd just seen in the coffin.
She'd panic, shaking him until he opened those pale blue
eyes. "¿Qué, Teresa?" And she'd hug him, hug him tight like
she didn't during the day. It hadn't mattered. God had taken
him, or maybe the devil, whoever's job it was to take good
men for no good reason.

Tino had grown up in Houston by the ship channel. Don
Agustín, his father, was a merchant marine when he was
young, a drunken lout when older. His way was to drink and
then dive into a fury and take his anger out on his sons. Tino,
being the youngest boy, often got the worst of it after the older
ones had left as soon as they were able. Don Agustín was a
tough man among the toughest men. With no woman to soften
him up, there was no one to stop him from drinking all day

long. No one dared speak or make noise and risk his ire. And the boys did not make it easy on themselves. Left to their own devices, they got into all kinds of trouble: arrests, drugs, their own wild drinking. The oldest son went to prison, the second joined the Army and went to Vietnam to avoid prison. The other, not yet thirty-five, died of a heart attack from living wild. Tino would tell Teresa of the nights when Don Agustín—the only way Tino referred to his dead father— would call him to the kitchen where he sat drinking. He would demand that Tino account for himself, for his troubles and weakness. Tino, ten-years-old at most, had to stand there and take the slaps and punches without cowering. Crying was out of the question. To cry was to prolong the beating and the verbal assault. Tino would run away for days at a time.

"I had to leave," he told Teresa more than once. "If I'd stayed any longer, I would have killed him. I carried a kitchen knife to bed and, to fall asleep, thought about how I would do it. I'd wait for him to slap my face or punch the back of my head. I'd spin on him and drive the blade through his veiny, thick neck. I went to sleep with those visions playing in my head like a horror movie. Only in dreams could I feel safe. Only in my dreams would the old monster finally die."

He told Teresa how he slept under bridges, because finding shelter with one of his brothers was impossible. They were either in jail, homeless or in cantinas.

"They learned to be mean and vicious from Don Agustín. I took a helluva lot of beating at their hands as bad as anything Don Agustín dished out." Tino would laugh when he told her things like this, as if he was amused by the horrible memories.

He told Teresa how he started to deliver packages for men who sold drugs to other men who sold drugs. They gave him money and sometimes a place to sleep. Before long, he wanted to know what it felt like, these drugs that he delivered. Only eleven, he started to sample them, and it wasn't long before he found himself under bridges injecting himself with heroin.

He was caught delivering drugs or using them several times. Each time, he was sent to a juvenile camp, and after the sentence was complete, he was back home, where Don Agustín would execute his own dreadful sentence. Tino would say, "In the camps, you only had to be tough. I had brothers whose reputations preceded me, so I was left alone for the most part." That meant nothing to Don Agustín, who welcomed Tino home by hitting him on the head with a wrench, ripping part of his ear from his scalp.

After Tino left home for good, he became even wilder: jail, needles, fights, drunkenness, blackouts, two failed marriages and things worse than Teresa could even imagine. When it came to why he had spent seven years in Huntsville Federal Prison, Tino was not so forthcoming. He never told Teresa the full details about a drug deal gone bad, only mentioning someone cheating his boss out of a piddling sum. Tino never divulged that someone had been shot. Those seven years cost him his wife; a woman named Celia. Later, it cost him much more. No one ever pressed Tino on the exact details, and Teresa was more concerned with his drinking, drugging and mistreatment of Celia.

He'd been a terrible husband, a cheater, a drunkard, a criminal with a terrible temper. He'd taken to following Celia around, even to slapping her when she denied his accusations. After an arrest, and six months in county lock-up, Celia disappeared. "It was her chance to escape," he told Teresa.

Tino tortured himself over Celia. There were stories that Celia had left with a child. He acknowledged her fate was his fault, and he imagined the worst. Celia didn't seem so blameless to Teresa, and it seemed to her that it was pointless for Tino to torture himself for his old misdeeds. After he got out of prison, he tried to find out what had happened to Celia and the child, but no one wanted to help him.

"What did you do?" Teresa asked him.

"I drank more, did more drugs, put myself into as shit-faced a condition as I could manage. I decided to kill myself slow, just like my brothers."

He showed Teresa his old driver's license from those days. It wasn't Tino in that picture. His eyes were red and ragged, the pale blue of them grown so dull that they almost had no color. There was a mean, brittle look in them and in the way his mouth was drawn tight, his cheeks hollow as if he'd had everything soft and giving sucked out of him. There was a haunting deathliness in that face, a man dangerous and unpredictable, too scary to look in the eyes. It was a terrible thing to see, frightening. It was all Teresa needed to see to know that his stories were true.

It was the accident that gave him a new life. Still drunk from a previous night's binge, he fell asleep at the wheel of his car, went off the road and rolled over two or three times. Tino claimed that the doctors told him that he'd died and come back to life. He saw Hell. It was dark and filled with moaning and shrieking. He knew he belonged there, but what terrified him the most, he would say, was that he knew Don Agustín was lying in wait for him in the depths like a wolf hidden in the brush, red eyes gleaming.

When he came to in the hospital, he was told that his legs had been shattered into pieces like broken candy canes. They wanted to amputate them, but he wouldn't allow it. He told them he'd walk again, even if they didn't believe it. Leo, his oldest brother, took him in. Leo had married a Mexican woman who treated him well. Tino got better there. He would tell how when his brother and sister-in-law were at work, he would get out of his wheelchair and try to walk. The pain was terrible, like bones being re-broken, like the screws and pins were splintering shins and femurs. He would collapse and drag himself back to his chair. He did this for months until he could take a few steps. The doctors credited his immense will power. But Tino knew that there was something else at work. He'd seen Hell and didn't want to go back there. He knew he had to atone for his sins.

The doctors gave him braces and canes, and performed more operations, inserting more pins, more screws, more steel rods. There was always the temptation to ease the pain of his legs and his soul by going back to heroin. But then he'd think of Hell and how he'd lost Celia and the child.

One day, he met a man who told him he'd been a junkie too. He'd been raised in the same neighborhood close to the ship channel. He recounted how his life had been changed by Jesus. Tino was willing to try almost anything but Jesus. "Jesus was for women and *pendejos*. But this man was no *pendejo*, so I listened."

The day Tino walked into the men's mission was the beginning of a new life. They put him to work, put him on a disciplined schedule, taught him things he'd never learned about taking care of himself and his surroundings, taught him to feel responsible for his brother. None of those things would have meant shit if they hadn't been held together by the deep fear that death was lurking close by. He could feel its stinking breath on his neck.

Tino was never good at reading and writing, but the mission nevertheless sent him to study at the Spanish seminary in San Antonio, the very same one Teresa's father had attended as a young man. Teresa met Tino when, as a student, he was sent to testify at El Testimonio Cristiano. All cleaned up, full of the holy spirit, he had one hell of a wild testimony.

CHAPTER 4
A Grain of Rice

Plus. +. Positive. Virginia was pregnant. It was the boy-cop's baby. No way she was going back to fucking Opelousas. She'd get rid of it. She googled Planned Parenthood as she sat on the dingy toilet in a Motel 8. There was one close to where she was staying near the bus station downtown. She didn't know exactly what they did to terminate the pregnancy, but only about a month in, she figured it couldn't be too bad. She googled it. One quarter inch long. The baby didn't even have a heart yet. It was a grain of rice. As shocked as she was, there was a part of her that thrilled at the idea that there was something inside her that left alone would become a full-blown human being. But not this time, right?

This was Celia's script, not hers. What was she supposed to do, carry it, birth it, marry a fucker like Benny-Boy and tell the kid that he was not her real daddy? Stupid, stupid, stupid. What kind of father was she likely to attract anyway? A loser, that's who. Not someone who would molest the kid, though. Never that. Celia hadn't given a fuck. Sitting on that dingy toilet at the Motel 8 in downtown Houston, she saw it developing in front of her, like a silent horror movie. Benny-Boy, liquored up, breath stinking, his fat lips mumbling, his harsh, scabby fingers working their way up and down her body as she pretended to sleep.

The first time, she told Celia the next morning. She remembered Celia shaking more and more violently, her face red, eyes growing wild, big, angry. Celia pressing her back into a corner and then slapping her hard. Again, and again. Three times in all, each slap a head-ringer. Celia warning that if Virginia ever lied about Benny-Boy again, she'd get way worse. "Way worse," she remembered those words. "Way worse," like there was a way worse.

Virginia needed to throw up, then and now. She managed to get off the pot just in time to spew a soup of bitter vomit into the toilet. She flushed and flushed. She cried in anger. Stupid, stupid, stupid!

The next morning, she walked to the Planned Parenthood. She was afraid there'd be a mob of self-righteous Christian pricks waving signs and screaming "slut!" But it wasn't like that. Just a glass-encased building just south of downtown. She walked in, and there was a reception area like in any kind of clinic. The woman at the desk was nice enough, asked her why she was there. Virginia told her, half-expecting the lady to give her the once-over and show disapproval in her eyes. But it wasn't like that. She didn't need insurance. There were a couple of other women waiting. A half-hour later, a nurse called her in. Virginia told her the situation.

"Are you here to terminate?" the nurse asked her.

It was strange, this white woman, in her thirties, just coming right out with it.

"I don't know," Virginia said.

"Well, let's make sure you're pregnant first of all," she said. Another test. Another positive. +.

"If you're not sure what you want to do yet, that's okay," she told Virginia. "Do you have someone, a friend, a mom, someone to talk over your options with?"

It was a simple enough question, but it caught Virginia off guard. No, no she didn't. Not a single person. Her best friend was in Opelousas, and Virginia wasn't going back there.

"What about the father?" the nurse asked the question displayed on her wrinkled brow.

"No," Virginia said. "Nobody."

"Where are you living?" the nurse asked next. "There are resources if you are homeless. You can get a little help before you decide what you want to do."

"If I was going to keep it, what should I be doing?" Virginia asked.

"There's diet, prenatal vitamins, checkups, things we supply here. Are you a drug user? I have to ask."

"No."

"Good. Smoking? Drinking?"

"No, not really."

"Good. Why don't we talk to our social worker. She's very helpful. She can help you sort things out. Make sure you're on solid ground before you make your choice."

Virginia sat on the examining table. The nurse told her to dress and go to the waiting room. She'd set up a talk with the social worker. Virginia nodded. She dressed and slipped out the front door without saying a word to anyone. What she needed was to complete her mission. Find Saturnino. He was her real father and he'd help her, pregnant or not. If she found him, the context of her predicament, her history, would be so very different from what it was in that space full of helpful strangers. It was only a grain of rice right now. She'd know what to do with it when the things she needed to make clear were clear.

~~~

Fonzo needed a break from dealing with two carping baby mommas and the used car lot where he worked as a broke-assed, chiseling salesman, so he talked Daniel into a weekend in Vegas.

They booked a room in the seen-better-days Riviera. The Elvis Suite was cheap enough, and the bar featured nude dancers.

"Danny Boy," Fonzo shouted over stripper music, "it's like you want to live in a haunted house forever. You got ghosts, bro. Not me. I got enough with trying to deal with the living. My marriage lasted three years while I was in Iraq. And then I fucked up bad by coming home. Things got weird fast. I started looking for tail anywhere I could find it. Mostly anonymous ass, but I slipped up and started cheating on wifey with this chick at the sales office.

"This girl wasn't the smartest, but she was irresistible hot, and we started banging. Well, that's when I really got caught slipping because I wound up knocking both Rachel and this chick up at the same time. When I found out Rachel was pregnant, I was like—whoa!—I got to stop with *la otra*. But you know how that goes. I wanted to let her down easy. We'd been going at it for a couple of months. So a couple of weeks later—two fucking weeks!—she tells me, 'I'm going to have your baby.' Just like that. 'Your baby.' In other words, no mistakes about it. It's your bun in my oven. I still had to ask her, 'You sure it's mine?' Of course, she was insulted. Chick goes ballistic and tells me, 'You think just because I'm seeing you, I'm a whore?' The short answer, yes, but I can't tell her that. I'm a gentleman.

"I could tell there was no use asking her if she was going to get an abortion. I could see in her eyes that this was a production, and she was working her way up to 'What are you going to do about this?' I know you don't got kids, Danny Boy, but let me tell you, when your girl tells you she's having a baby, it's a clarifying moment. Either you're happy or you're not. When Rachel told me, I was glad even though I knew I was playing around and had all these complaints in my head about her. But when Chick told me she was knocked up, my soul dropped out my asshole. And now, I was looking at her like you look at re-enlistment papers you signed after its too goddamned late.

"I was a nervous wreck for nine months. Just wrecked. I had to keep Rachel happy, knowing the whole time that if she found about *la otra* she'd kick me out so fast my pants would be looking for me for a week. And Chick, you can imagine. Always whining, always on my ass, always halfway threatening to spill the beans. I won't lie, I had to make her promises to keep her quiet. It was shitty. I felt like a *culo*. But what was I supposed to do? Tell Rachel, 'Hey honey, I know you're pregnant and everything, but I have another pregnant *ruca* on the side and I have to go take her to her doctor today.' So finally, it all came out.

"Rachel showed up at work just when I was having this dramatic conversation with Chick, and Rachel wanted to know, what the fuck, because Rachel is like that, and Chick tells her, both of them standing out in the sun on the lot with broken down wrecks, both with matching baby bumps, and me figuring out which car I should make a getaway in! I don't even want to tell you about the next week. Rachel is the type who calls friends and family and my reserves officer, homie, and she lets it all hang out. I got it from every angle, crossfire, from on top and from down below. I was the World's Biggest Asshole. Long story short, I'm paying child support for two kids, neither looks like me, and both moms hate my guts. I'm living in a hole and driving a car so beat up, even the janitor at the office has a nicer ride. They even took my PTSD money!"

Daniel listened casually. He knew the story. Fonzo enjoyed repeating it. They were drinking in the Riviera bar. There was a burlesque with topless girls, exotic dance music, expensive drinks. The two buddies were already loaded from the free alcohol they were comped on the casino floor.

"My point, Danny Boy, is you aren't too far gone. You can still pull it together. And I don't mean in a goody-goody way. You do you! But relax, man. We're a long way from the Sandbox. You're permanent Ft. Livingroom. New rules here. Gotta recognize."

Fonzo raised his glass. "To titties," he said and downed a double Goose. He made a large O with his mouth, exhaling sharply, as if he were expelling a demon.

"Who you hearing from?" Daniel asked, wanting to change the trajectory of the conversation.

"Funny you should mention it. Heard from Fuentes a couple of months ago. He's living like the Unabomber. Off the radar, using that Army training. Somewhere in Idaho. His old lady took one look at the new setup and the prospect of eating venison for the rest of her life and said bye-bye, fucker. He told me that Sky got hitched and is a full-time drunk. Cantu took his re-up bonus and bought into a steakhouse that went tits up. How you going to open a steakhouse in Eugene? Nothing but hippie-vegan snowflakes out there. I ain't got nothing against meat, brother."

"That's what I always thought," Daniel said.

"Yeah, man. Fuck yeah! To meat!" He raised another double Goose, expelling another demon. "For real, though, my boy Ezzat, dude was a SAW gunner in my squad after you split. He got this cushy gig driving a limp-dick fobbit colonel around the Sandpit. The good colonel, limp dick and all, hooked him up as an attaché. Thought Ezzat was a funny motherfucker. Went to work for him after his tour was up. Made a grip skimming whatever the good colonel didn't gobble first. Anyhoo, homie is kicking it in Vegas. Dude's got some sort of membership like in an orgy club. I let him know some grunts we're in town. Wants us to come over. Top-looking girls. No hags is what he says."

Before Daniel could sneeze, there was a black stretch limo at the curb.

"That's the way we kick it in Vegas, hooah!" Fonzo said, hanging his arm around Daniel's shoulder.

They got in. They had brought along a fresh pint of Goose and they took turns hitting it. By the time they landed at the place, Daniel's head was spinning. The lights of the city were long gone. They were in the desert, enormous house after enormous house drifting across the limo's windows. It reminded Daniel of the palaces that Saddam's ministers and corrupt oil barons owned up and down the Euphrates, only there wasn't any water here.

He wasn't looking for action, but Fonzo being occupied with tail meant he didn't have to talk about Cristina or their dead baby, how the baby had been born premature with his lungs too undeveloped and how he had suffocated like a tiny fish gasping on the floor next to a broken fishbowl.

They arrived at the house, a modernist three-story compound, all straight lines and windows. All the lights blazing.

"All right," Fonzo said. "Les get strange like in the old days."

They walked in. No passwords or other skullduggery. If you were there, you belonged. It seemed the only rule was get naked.

Fonzo looked around for Ezzat, but there was no sign of him.

"Probably getting boned in one of the rooms," Fonzo said.

There was a bar. The two headed that way. There were about forty or fifty people chatting and smiling coyly. Mostly old guys with hairless, tanning-bed orange skin. Some wore towels, others didn't. More than a few were sporting hard-ons. There were two large bowls of viagra on the long bar, like peanuts. The women were younger, mostly blonde, most sporting naval rings and long manicured fingernails. Proba-bly strippers. But apparently, even at an orgy, you had to do small talk to get laid.

Predictably, Fonzo nodded at a petite blonde with long, blue-streaked hair. She was hot until you looked at her close and saw the bloodshot eyes and caked mascara.

"On like Donkey Kong," Fonzo said smiling. "I'll see you when I see you. Just don't go funny and fuck me in the ass in one of these orgy dens. Hooah!"

After a while, a girl sat down next to Daniel. She had on lingerie, red, of course. He could smell the shampoo ema-nating from her long, straight brunette hair. She was petite like Cristina, but prettier in a club kid way. She said her name was Marissa. He could smell the vodka on her breath. She needed to booze up to do this grind.

"What's your name?" she asked him after she got a drink.

"Daniel," he said.

"You look like a kid at the zoo for the first time, Daniel," she said sipping on a vodka tonic. "I haven't seen you here before."

"Newbie," he said.

"You be a newbie?" she said.

"That's what I be," Daniel said. "Pure as the driven sand."

"You wanna go talk somewhere quiet?"

"I'm just here with a buddy," Daniel said.

"He seems to have found something better to do."

Daniel hadn't been laid in over a year. He took her into one of the rooms and fucked her. At one point some geezer came in with a girl young enough to be his granddaughter. Daniel didn't want any part of watching a saggy-balled leech screw. He gave Marissa a thank you kiss on the cheek and headed for the toilet to wash his cock in the sink.

She was still waiting when he came out. She was still naked. The old man and younger girl were gone.

"Hiya," he said stupidly.

"Did you like that, cowboy," she said. "We can go again. I'll give you a two-fer. But I do accept tips."

It dawned on Daniel that a service had been rendered and that he needed cash. "Oh," he said. "I thought this was something different."

"Yeah, no," she said. "We girls are all working tonight."

"Sure, I gotta find my buddy. He has the cash. High roller."

The girl's look hardened mostly imperceptibly, except for a slightly less generous smile. Daniel opened the door to the bedroom and looked over at the bar. No sign of Fonzo. He ducked back in.

"He must still be occupied. We can hang out at the bar till he's done."

As the two made their way to the bar, Daniel took a closer look at the set up. Old men, evil-looking, leering sweaty ogres, and the young flesh. The booze had worn off, and he felt empty as a spent shell.

After a while, Fonzo reappeared. "That was hardly worth taking my zipper down for, bro. Where to next? C'mon, some mission focus here."

Daniel told him the bad news.

"Ah shit," Fonzo said. "You got any money?"

"I don't have what this girl is asking for."

"Let's break, then," Fonzo said. "No one's gonna button-hole us here."

"What about your friend?"

"Haven't seen that sumbitch all night."

There was no need to run for it or even sneak out. They just walked out the front. One of the goons even held the door open.

"Must be on the cooze honor system," Fonzo said.

There was no limo to take them back. So they took an Uber to a liquor store just off the strip. While Fonzo was in the store, Daniel took a leak in the alley. He threw the empty bottle of vodka at the piss stain. Glass shrapnel everywhere.

Fonzo came out and poked his head in the alley. "Let's un-ass, soldier."

Back at the Riviera, they rode the elevator in silence except for Fonzo's "yup, yup" every few seconds. Fonzo didn't like silence much. Back in the room, he stripped to his skivvies and poured them some more drink.

"Remember how that Bradley tore that house up after Scotty? We really had it in for that house. Gomez shot every single round he had on his track. There wasn't shit left."

Only there had been. The boy and his mother. The kid dead, the woman pregnant, still breathing.

"You ever think about the girl?" Daniel asked him.

"I think about a lot of things," Fonzo said. "Scotty for one. But, yeah. Fuck yeah." They raised a glass to Scotty. "Hey, you can't let that clusterfuck direct your current situation."

"Nah," Daniel said, "it's just that sometimes I think that if I could've done something for her, she'd have made it."

"She was a gonner," Fonzo said. "No Sonny Jesus nor Big Poppa God was going to resurrect her."

"Yeah, sure," Daniel said.

"Listen, man, it wasn't your fault you weren't there when your kid died either. Nothing you could do but try to get back with your head still on your shoulders. Scotty and a lot of other good guys couldn't manage it."

Daniel wanted another drink.

"Listen, you're as good a guy as there is, brother."

"I'm a bastard."

"Well, yeah," Fonzo said. "But we're all bastards now. Look," he said, "just cause you're retreating don't mean the war is lost."

"I'm gonna hit the rack," Daniel said suddenly.

He went into the bathroom and shook and shook, but there was no relief to be had. He dry-swallowed two oxys, and with Fonzo drunk asleep, he ended up in the lobby watching the gamblers. Only the diehards were still at it. He began to nod off. In the haze, he thought about calling Cristina. He got to remembering how she looked when he got to her after the baby was gone. Or was he dreaming?

He'd taken a taxi home from the airport. He thought she'd be in bed, but she was waiting for him in the kitchen. She cried when he came through the door. She showed him a picture of the baby. He held the photo in his hand. The baby was a cardinal red with umpteen tubes and wires hooked into him, as if he'd been tangled in the mess just like poor Scotty. He'd lasted a few hours, lungs too undeveloped. The kid had never had a chance, as if he'd been born to suffocate for Daniel's sins. There was no grave, just a memorial spot with a plaque and a small cement bench. She'd had him cremated.

Daniel was home for six days before he went back. He could've stayed longer, but it was a relief. Fallujah had happened two weeks before. He felt sick and numb because he knew in his gut that the mother dying with that baby in her and them losing his baby were tied together.

That there was more to come, it occurred to Daniel as he stirred fully into consciousness. And no Poppa God or Sonny Jesus would hear his arguments. There wasn't a damn thing he could do about anything, so he shouldn't even pray about it. That's the way things were. And there wasn't anything that he'd learned, seen or found out that was going to help. The best he could do, in what now seemed like a haunted house of maddening sounds and lights, was raise the bottle, take a swig and close his eyes. Fonzo was right. They were all bastards now.

Back from Vegas, he settled into his routine. Checking his email in the library after the weekend, there were only two messages. The first was a mass email from Fonzo. He'd entered both of his infant daughters in the city-wide Beautiful Baby Contest. People were supposed to vote online, and the baby with the most votes got the crown. There was also a small cash prize, but it was mostly a vanity thing. Looking at the baby pictures, Daniel wondered about the logistics of showing up for the announcement the night of the pageant. Mexicans are a jealous people, and undoubtedly there would be an awful fight if one of the two babies won. Dutifully, he went to the site and voted for both of Fonzo's babies. They were both cute, and Fonzo was telling the truth, neither looked anything like him.

The other email had the subject line: "Saturnino. . . ." It read, "I don't know if you are the son of Saturnino. That would make you my brother? I found out that he's my father and I would like to meet him. Could you call me or meet me? Virginia. P.S. This isn't a hoax."

A hoax? Who would try to pull something like that off? Daniel felt sure that Tino would have told them if he had a daughter. Wouldn't he have? He remembered something about his taking a trip on his own early in the marriage and there having been tension about that between him and his mother. Teresa had made a number of scenes before Tino left. He remembered vaguely that Tino had tried a few times before he married Teresa to find out something about where his ex-wife lived. Why he wanted to find her was unclear. It hadn't mattered much to Daniel, but he did remember that it was a sore spot for Teresa.

He thought about what to write for a long time, staring at the computer screen, feeling nervous. Even if it were true, even if this girl wasn't mistaken, even if all was on the level, what good would it do now? Tino was dead. Had been for almost a year. Wouldn't this girl have to know this if she'd figured out how to get in contact with him? She'd had to have found him through one of the relatives, and they surely would have broken the bad news to her that he was dead. But who knew what she knew?

He couldn't very well tell her Tino was dead over email. Maybe she'd been searching for him a long time. Maybe she was trying to find a way to get some information before she came around for a visit. It seemed logical. Maybe Tino had searched for his long-lost daughter, and this girl had found out and wanted nothing more than to meet her father.

In the end, he decided to write as little as possible. "Hello," he wrote, "I'm Tino's stepson. Call me." He included his phone number and hit send without rereading the message. It was shortly afterward, on his walk back from the library, that he began to wonder how this would affect his mother. It was sure to rekindle her grief, perhaps even reveal things that were better left buried with Tino.

He tried to put himself in his mother's place. If he had a wife who had suddenly died and left no living being behind to carry on her memory, something of her essence, wouldn't he be happy to find out that there was something of her still alive? Or would it be painful because that long lost child represented some kind of betrayal. Daniel decided to keep a lid on things until he heard from the girl personally and found out her story. He had a few questions of his own.

~~~

At least Alena had a good friend. She'd never been able to talk to her mother, and the church was great for a lot of things, but there weren't many her age. Either they were teenagers or they were older women with kids in high school. Elvira was her age, a neighbor who'd moved in two years before. She didn't go to church, but she was funny and liked listening to Alena's complaints.

Elvira loved Tonia. She told Alena that it was a blessing to be able to come over and escape the boredom of keeping house just for herself. She was single, mostly because she'd spent a decade caring for a sick mother who'd gone and died and left her with little to do except troll the internet. That, and enough insurance money to keep her afloat for a few years. The lack of a schedule allowed her all the time in the world to be a dutiful friend, helpmate even, to Alena.

From time to time, Elvira thought aloud about getting a part-time job. Alena would say, "Why do you want to do that? If I could be the boss of myself like you? No one breathing down my neck about my break time, no grouchy customers waiting in line with dirty looks and stupid requests? You deserve your time after all you sacrificed for your mother."

Elvira would concede with a nod and a smile, assured once again of Alena's need for her.

Elvira was a telenovela addict, especially the one called *Rubia,* about this very beautiful, young, naive girl cast into the big city. Rubia was from a small village, but she was so pretty that she ran off to Mexico City in hopes of making it as a model. She fell in love with the wrong guy, a liar and a cheat who pulled the wool over her eyes. But the tragic thing was that there was a good guy with blue eyes and blond hair named Jorge, who was truly in love with her. He wasn't flashy and he was too honorable to pursue a woman who was in love with another man, even if he knew that man to be a cad.

Elvira worked hard to combine both her obsessions, *Rubia* and Alena. At first, Alena resisted watching the show. It was cheesy and full of scandalous behavior. But after watching it with Elvira a handful of times, she'd figured out the basic plot and gotten hooked on the twists. Pretty soon she knew all the back stories and learned to recognize the real rats. She knew she was addicted when she began to hope for good things for the decent characters, especially Rubia. Rubia had made a big mistake taking up with a photographer who only wanted her body. She'd made powerful enemies intent on destroying her because of the threat her beauty presented. All this took place in the first week they'd watched the show together. Alena justified watching the show by telling herself that it was helping her Spanish and, in point of fact, her Spanish was improving with the help of *Rubia* and her new friend, Elvira.

The problem was that the show came on at six, and that was about the time that Richard came home. At first, he was fine with Elvira being over, but *Rubia* came on five days a week, and he wasn't crazy about having Elvira over every evening. It wasn't as if Elvira was a burden. She was a great cook and half the time, she put something together for dinner. It was a treat because Alena was a terrible cook, and it saved Richard the effort of making dinner at the end of a hard work-day. Alena thought Richard should be grateful. Instead of accepting their invitation to watch the show with them, however, he stayed in the bedroom and played video games. Alena wished he'd get some friends of his own. She would tell him, "Why don't you call Daniel and go bowling or something?"

She didn't want him to be out every night, but she did want him to do something that would take him out of the house. Richard didn't want to spend more time with Daniel, whom he saw at work. In any case, Alena was hooked on

Rubia and she was not about to give it up. Her most vital friendship and the show were intertwined, and Alena enjoyed having a confidante.

One morning, Cristina called her. Alena didn't pick up. She knew that she probably should have. After the baby had died, Alena was glad to give her sister-in-law a shoulder. Alena felt real empathy for her, especially since she herself had suffered a miscarriage early on in her marriage. Cristina's calls were inevitably about what a louse her brother was. Just before the split, she'd insisted on calling every other day and trying to persuade Alena to intervene on her behalf. Alena got tired of Cristina's pleading and anger. Finally, she told Cristina, "I'll pray for you and Daniel, but don't expect me to harass him. Pressure's not good for making babies." Cristina hadn't liked that, but too bad. Alena thought that her sister-in-law would have made a great *telenovela* villain.

Elvira told Alena that she looked like Rubia. If she'd only dye her hair blond, she'd be a dead ringer. Alena didn't know if she was a dead ringer for the heroine, but she did bear at least a passing resemblance. She could relate to getting into situations that she couldn't see coming. As silly as *Rubia* was, there was a lot of truth in the soap. It just told that truth in a melodramatic fashion. Bad choices and good choices were always presenting themselves, and most people, maybe all people, were usually caught flat-footed between what they wanted to do and what they should do. It was much like being a mother. Alena loved Tonia like nothing else, but that didn't change the fact that having a child narrowed possibilities.

Alena wasn't even thirty, and more and more frequently she was questioning whether she'd already reached the apex of her life. Was *this* her life? Stranded in San Antonio for-ever, doomed to housewifery and a feeble sex life? *Pues*, for-get about it. How about a little traveling, Paris, Rome, Venice? Don't think so, life was saying. Perhaps there'd be a trip to Israel if the church could raise the funds, but even that seemed like a pipe dream.

Then there was Richard. She didn't like to think directly about the possibility of leaving, but it did enter her mind more than casually. Locked into a boring, lifeless marriage, she could indulge in a little harmless fantasy. What would life be like if she didn't have to look after both of them? There, she'd thought it, and God hadn't struck her dead.

She wanted to grab Daniel and tell him, "Big brother, you are a true fool! You shouldn't be moping about divorce. You should be turning cartwheels in the street. You should be yelling from the housetop proclaiming freedom."

When she'd hinted at this recently, he'd grown serious and told her that she didn't know anything about it. But she knew much more than he gave her credit for.

Rubia lived in danger and sometimes she thought about giving up and going back to her little village, her dreams in Mexico City left to shrivel and die. But Alena envied her the danger, the risk, the intrigue of her love. As doomed as Rubia's adventure would turn out to be, it had romance and mystery. Elvira and Alena watched gleefully as Rubia kissed the evil lover, Jesse, who told her vacuous lies about his love for her. They envied her the fancy restaurants, the gourmet dinners, the designer clothes, the fantastic trips. It looked like such fun. Not to mention that poor, handsome Jorge was waiting in the wings to catch Rubia when she finally fell from the heights of her love affair with the wrong man.

And then, Elvira started internet dating. She showed Alena the website "Plenty of Fish." All you had to do was post your picture and write a few things about yourself, and then any man who was interested sent a note. You could look up their profiles and see if you liked them enough to respond. It seemed a little risky, even desperate to Alena, but in a short time, Elvira already had six or seven men writing to her. One or two were even cute. The most interesting thing about the dating was that many of the men didn't live in San Antonio. One of the online beaus was from Los Angeles. There was something alluring about that, an unknown quantity, a mystery man all the way in Los Angeles who'd reached out with a romantic message.

Elvira was saving up her money to go meet him.

"But what if he's a psycho," Alena asked her.

She only laughed and said, "C'mon, why would a psycho need to pick on me?"

Alena guessed she was right. After all, Elvira wasn't particularly attractive, and there were plenty of loose women a pervert could find in LA without having to resort to finding prey in another state. More than likely, these men were just lonely. The LA guy's profile seemed like he should be flush with women. He was handsome, tall, in good shape, and he worked for an advertising company. Why couldn't he meet women the regular way?

"He's no pervert," Elvira said. "He's had his heart broken and he is using 'Plenty of Fish' to make sure he finds a good one. Imagine the limits you place on yourself by choosing from people that you meet," she said. "The perfect person in the world could be out there, and you'd never meet because they live somewhere else. So, instead, you get stuck with the bore next door."

This made an impression on Alena. After all, she'd met Richard in high school.

After Elvira left that night, Alena went back to the website just to look. She perused both men and women in order to see what people said about themselves, what photos they chose to represent. She stayed on the site for a long time, too long, and before she knew it, she found herself looking through her own digital photos. She wondered which she'd choose for her profile. It was all hypothetical, of course. But it made for a compelling reason to pore through her pictures with a critical eye. Just what sort of man could she attract? Would she use an old photo, one from before she'd gotten pregnant, when she was much thinner and her hair was cut more stylishly? To her dismay, it was difficult to find a recent photo in which she looked alluring enough to attract the LA man.

After some patient digital excavation, she found an acceptable photo. It had been taken at Padre Island last summer. Richard was in it but standing far enough to the side to crop him out. She stared at the picture for a long time. She heard Tonia coughing, and just before shutting the computer down, she saved the cropped version.

∾∾∾

Her mother was over the next evening when Elvira showed up for *Rubia*. Richard was working late, and they'd decided to have a girl's night. It wasn't long before Elvira told Teresa about "Plenty of Fish." Her mother wanted to see the site, and Elvira was happy to oblige. She stood behind the two of them as they looked over Elvira's profile and the profiles of the men she was corresponding with. Teresa didn't have much of an interest in computers, but suddenly, the machine seemed like the most interesting device of all time. Alena could see her taking mental notes. Elvira was babbling about flirting.

"You see," she told Teresa, "if you see a profile you like, you send a smile, like this." She pushed a button on the screen. "Then he sees that and if he likes it, he'll look at your profile and if he's interested, he can either send you back a flower, a wink or a note."

Teresa was amazed. "So, you don't have to call them?"

"No, you just wait for them to contact you. They don't have your number or address. You don't put any of that information down. Just a picture and profile that tells what you're like, what you do, what movies you watch, what your religion is. Things like that."

"And men write you?" Teresa asked.

"I've got ten writing me right now," Elvira said through a big smile. "I'm going to travel to LA to meet one of them. He's going to pay for my flight!"

"My goodness," Teresa said. "Aren't you worried?"

"No, I talk to him on the phone all the time. He's very nice. It's just that his wife left him for someone else."

"*¡No me digas! Pobrecito*. He sounds like poor Daniel."

"He's got a little boy. I'm going to LA to meet them both. We're going to Disneyland, and then he says he'll take me to the beach."

Teresa's eyes grew big. "Well, how much does this 'Plenty of Fish' cost?"

"Nothing. It's free."

"Free?"

"Free."

"Oh, Elvira, you've got to help me get on the 'Fish.'"

Alena rolled her eyes in full view of her mother. "That's not something a woman like you should be doing."

At this, both Elvira and Teresa turned towards her. She'd managed to insult them both.

"Oh, am I too old?" Teresa said. "I'm a relic who should be in a rest home, is that it? No good for nothing?"

"Okay, Mother, don't get all dramatic. I just mean that you don't even have a computer and . . . well . . . Tino just died. I don't think you're ready."

"Oh, Alena," Elvira said, "Teresa has been mourning Tino for over a year. Anyway, this isn't a big deal. In fact, it's a great way to get back out there because you're not risking anything."

"Well, we'll talk about it some other time," Alena said. "*Rubia* is starting in five minutes."

"Oh, TiVo it," Teresa said. "Elvira, you've got to get me on the 'Fish' right now."

"You need a picture," Elvira said helpfully. "A good one so that people who see your profile will write you."

Teresa turned towards Alena. "You've got a bunch of pictures in your computer. You keep them all. I bet you have one of me that's nice." She turned towards Elvira with a small scowl. "*Ay, ay*, do you have to put how old you are?"

"No. They divide it into groups by decade."

"Who tells them what group you belong to?"

"You do."

"*Pues*, put me on the fifty-year-olds," she said. "I don't want any geezers."

"Mother," Alena said, "that's not honest."

"Honest? Who cares about honest? I want someone to write to me and I don't want some broken-down old man that I have to wheel around, *lavándole las nalgas* when he's pooped his diaper. Los Angeles . . ." she said to Elvira with a gleam in her eye. "What fun! I've never even been close to there."

Alena walked out while they scoured the database for a picture that would make her mother look like she was ten years younger. She didn't want any part of that. It wasn't right for her to be cruising the internet looking for strange men to take her to Los Angeles or anywhere else, for that matter. What ever happened to growing old gracefully? Her mother had been married twice. Fine, the first one was to a fink, but Tino was the best of the best. He'd only been dead fourteen months, and her mother was already going to shop around for the next one? It was depressing and unseemly at the same time. Whatever happened to true love? That reminded her that *Rubia* was on. She flipped the TV to the right station. She wasn't going to wait around for them to finish fooling around on the internet. She watched the show by herself as the idiotic giggling of her mother and her friend came from the other room. She didn't TiVo the show.

~~~

Teresa thought about Elvira. She really was a great girl. She'd helped Teresa set up her own "Plenty of Fish." They'd found a good picture of her for her profile. It was only about five years old, but Teresa looked good in it. Teresa tried to temper her expectations. It wasn't like she was going to meet anyone, anyhow. She was just going to spend a little time getting to meet some new friends. She didn't even need to talk to them on the phone. It was just a way to take her mind off things, depressing things. She couldn't spend all her time waiting for Alena to put her on the A-Team, sitting there in the house doing nothing but dancing around in front of the TV until Daniel woke up so she could make him lunch. Tino wouldn't have liked that. Teresa was sure that he would've approved of "Plenty of Fish."

Elvira helped her rewrite her profile. At first Teresa had written things about loving God and church and being a dancer in the troupe. She made up a little lie that she was on the A-team. She wrote that she was a widow who had a son living at home.

Elvira frowned at the description.

"What's wrong with that?" Teresa asked.

"That's not going to do," Elvira replied. "We've got to make this more interesting. It makes you sound old and depressed, and I don't think anyone is going to be anxious to get involved with a woman with a grown man living at home."

"Okay, well help me."

Profile: Beautiful lady who loves dancing, good conversation, mystery movies, long walks and traveling. I'm fit and funny and I'm looking for a friendship and maybe a little romance. If you've got a good story or seen a good movie or read a good book, I'd like to talk about it. Let's start a conversation.

Teresa liked that. It was a good description. Sometimes you needed someone else to point out your selling points. She'd only gotten home, and she was already itching to go back to Alena's house so that she could check the computer. She couldn't imagine why her daughter had been so silly about it. She almost seemed jealous, but jealous of what? Alena was the one who was young, still beautiful, still strong and healthy, with a handsome husband who loved her. Alena had everything a woman could want. And she? Was she supposed to be lonely for the rest of her life because her poor Tino had died?

That morning, she'd gotten out of bed and looked through her clothes.

What would she wear on a date?

Everything she had was so old and, besides, when Tino was alive, she stopped worrying about looking good. Tino wasn't picky so long as she kept her curly hair under control. All her clothes had grown frumpy and out of style. She would have to get something new if she went on a date. Also, she was out of shape. She had a *panzita* and a bit of a double-chin. At least she kept her hair colored, but she knew she had to get in better condition if she was going to start going on dates. Los Angeles. Imagine that!

She'd told Daniel earlier that after work she wanted him to take her to the library. She wanted to get a book on exercising. She also wanted to buy some tennis shoes. She needed to start walking again, and the dancing shoes that Alena had bought her were fine for dancing but not for real exercise. There was a nice track at the high school where Tino had walked when his legs would let him. She'd gone with him when she could, and there were always plenty of people walking around.

Teresa couldn't wait for Daniel to get home. She would go to the mall on her own and find tennis shoes. And although she wasn't ready to buy clothes before she got into better shape, she could look for good ideas. First, she'd check her "Fish" profile at Alena's house. She had Alena's house key and she could let herself in. What if she'd already received a message? Maybe there was more than one. Wouldn't that be something! But what if no one had written her? Ouch. That would be depressing. She liked this feeling of anticipation. It made her feel more alive than she'd felt in a very long time. It was exciting. That's what it was.

Inside, she turned on the computer and went to the "Fish" site. She'd paid close attention to Elvira's tutorial. No message. Just her picture and profile. She wondered if she was just a foolish old lady, too far gone to attract anyone in the fifties category. She browsed the pictures of men, finding a couple of good prospects who wore mustaches, real machos. She thought about, but dared not send them winks. She wished Elvira was there to coach her. After an hour, she gave up and flipped on the television and watched an old *Rubia*. She didn't feel like going to the mall anymore.

Alena was surprised to see her mother there when she got home. Tonia was happy and gave her a hug. She was a beautiful little girl with curly hair like her grandmother.

"Hi, Mother," Alena said a bit sourly.

Teresa thought that her daughter sometimes wished she'd go away forever. She was always using that tone with her, Mother, Mother, Mother, with the *th* growing longer and more impatient to demonstrate her growing frustration.

"I wanted to check the 'Fish.'"

"*Mothhher,* I don't know anything about that. 'Fish' is you and Elvira, and I don't want any part of it."

"I already checked," Teresa said wearily. "Nothing."

Alena made a cross face and huffed a time or two, then went to the bedroom. Teresa heard her bring the computer to life. She went in to join her daughter. On the screen was the big fish with all the little fish surrounding it. "Welcome to Plenty of Fish!" the screen said.

Teresa took a deep breath and logged on to her account for the second time that day. "What do you know!" There was a note from someone named Big Sam and two smiley faces and a flower! In just the time it had taken her to watch a *Rubia*! Even more exciting, it seemed that four men out there had looked at her profile and wanted to hear from her.

"Four bites altogether!" she told Alena, who stood over her shoulder still disapproving.

She'd been hoping that her mother would find that no one was interested.

"You've got to help me," Teresa exclaimed. "I don't know what to write back. I don't want to ruin it."

If only Elvira was there. She'd help her. She knew just what to write on her profile. She couldn't imagine what would have happened if she'd kept the stupid things she'd written at first.

"Alena, help me," she said again. She heard Alena sigh from above.

"Mother, this is creepy."

"Creepy my butt," she told her. "Sit down and help me come up with something clever. I don't want to sound like an old lady."

"You don't want to seem like an old lady on the make," Alena replied.

"Whatever," she said. "You need to help me write to this Sam fellow. I looked up his profile already. He's a little fat and bald, but he's not hideous."

"Hmph," Alena said. "How do you know that's even a recent picture. People do put up old pictures of themselves, Mother. He's probably as big as a house by now and as bald as a hard-boiled egg."

"I'm not planning on marrying him. I just want to write him a note and thank him for the flower. He looks nice. It says here that he has his own business and that he likes cars. Maybe he has money. I wonder if he likes to travel?"

"It sounds like you've got plenty enough to write, Mother. I've got dinner to get ready. Are you staying?"

"Not for dinner. I just want to do this thing on the computer. I told *m'ijo* that I'd cook him his favorite tonight. *El pobrecito* gets home tired from work."

Alena went off to cook dinner. What kind of dinner, Teresa couldn't imagine. Alena burned everything. Teresa didn't want to seem forward nor boring either. Oh, how she wished Elvira were there. Then she got the idea to go ask Alena for Elvira's phone number. Alena rolled her eyes, as she did most of the time when her mother asked her a question she found impertinent or irrelevant, but she gave her the number.

"Thank you, *m'ija*. Mmm, it smells good in here."

Back in the bedroom, she got a hold of Elvira. "I've got a bite on 'Plenty of Fish,'" she said immediately.

Elvira sounded more excited than Teresa. "What are you going to write back?"

"That's why I called you. Remember the awful things I was going to write in my profile? And you stopped me. So, help me again."

"Okay, hang on, let me get on the computer so I can see his profile too." After a couple of minutes, she came back on the line. "Hmmm," she said, "he looks nice."

"Well," Teresa said, "okay, he's not much of a looker, but I don't care. I probably won't meet him."

"Think of him as practice for a real catch, Teresa. With this one you don't have to worry if you make a few mistakes. He's lucky someone as beautiful as you will write him back. You'll make his day."

"Elvira, you're sweet. Do you really think so?"

"Of course. Before you know it, there'll be plenty of men, and you'll have your pick. This guy is perfect for working on your technique."

"Technique?"

"Yes, of course. You have to figure out how to keep them interested. All they get to see is your picture. There's a skill to keeping them coming back. You also can tell how interested you're making them by the gifts they send you."

"The gifts? Tell me more."

"The 'wink' is a flirt and that's free. But other things like a flower, or a song, or candy, or a glass of wine, those cost points. You only get 100 points a month, so if he's sending you a gift, it means he likes you enough to use points."

"Well, he already sent me a flower!"

"That's very good. A flower costs ten points. A song is the most expensive: fifty points. It's all there in the rules. Anyway, if he already sent you a flower, it means he really wants you to write him. Don't give away too much on the first emails. It makes you seem too interested. What did he write?"

"It says, 'Hello, Pretty Lady. I read your profile and thanked my lucky stars I ran across it. Write back. We could have fun getting to know each other.'"

"Hmm. Fresh."

"Do you think it's too fresh? Maybe I shouldn't write him back."

"No, no, Teresa, I was just joking. That's the way you do it. You have to make yourself sound interesting and exciting. You want *some* of your personality to come out. Let's think of something clever and see if we can't get Sam to send you a glass of wine or a song."

The two of them sat on the phone thinking out loud. Every once in a while, Teresa heard Alena walk past the room, clomping loudly to show that she wasn't happy. She was even cross with Tonia, telling her sharply that she needed to clean her room and take her bath. Alena got on Teresa's nerves sometimes, but now she ignored her daughter and concentrated.

Finally, they came up with this: "Hi Sam, I like having fun. What's your idea of fun? I like dancing. Let me know and we'll talk about your stars later."

"That's pretty good, Teresa. I bet he'll write you back tonight."

Tonight? How would she know what he'd written? She'd have to wait until the next day, and Alena was being a big brat about this. Then she remembered that Daniel was always going to the library to check his email. She was going to get him to show her how to use the computers there so that she could check "Plenty of Fish" whenever she wanted. She was betting that he would also help her write good messages. He was a good writer.

"What do the other three men who sent you winks look like?"

The other three men! She had forgotten about them. She didn't want to look at them with Elvira on the line. She told her she had to help Alena with dinner and hung up. Now Teresa could take her time. She looked at the first one. He was a disappointment. He was worse than fat, bald Sam. He must have been seventy. He certainly didn't look like he belonged in the fifty-sixty group. The *mentiroso* had one foot in the grave and the other on a banana peel. "Uh-uh, Charlie," she said.

It felt good to be able to throw a fish back into the sea. Teresa didn't delete his smiley wink face because she wanted to keep track of how many men wrote her. She went on to the next one. It was a pervert! He wasn't wearing a shirt and he had tattoos all over his chest and stomach. He was wearing a bandana like a dirty *pachuco*. As luck would have it, Alena had walked back into the room and was looking over her mother's shoulder before she could change the screen.

"Oh my God, Mother. That is bordering on the obscene. Ugh, he's disgusting! Is he in his underwear?"

"No, it's a bathing suit," she said.

"Some bathing suit! You can see his *pipi*. It's disgusting. Is this the kind of man you want to be meeting? He looks like a jailbird or a psycho rapist. What makes him think anyone wants to see him there standing in his dingy *chones* with his filthy tattoos? You ought to call the police."

"He looks nice," Teresa said trying now to upset Alena even more. "You know Tino had a tattoo and he was once in jail."

"Don't even joke that way, Mother. I really hope you're not going to answer that creep. . . . And really, I think you should just give up this 'Plenty of Fish' website. It's not safe or dignified."

"Well, we'll see," she said shutting the computer down after she'd sent her message to Sam. "We'll see."

CHAPTER 5
Saturnino's Daughter

Daniel was sweating bullets when his cell phone went off. It was hot in the truck, and he was loading up without much help from Richard, who was in slow motion that morning. He almost ignored the call because he didn't recognize the number. The last thing he needed was to spend the next ten minutes putting off another of Cristina's goddamned bill collectors.

It was the girl, Virginia. She was nervous, her voice quivery in a way that made Daniel feel sorry for her, even though he couldn't picture her. She told him that she'd been looking for Saturnino "all her life." She said that there was a reason for her renewed urgency but didn't want to discuss it over the phone.

"All the stories my mother told me were bad ones. I want more than that. It's important. Maybe you can help introduce us?"

"Well, we'll talk about that when we meet, okay?"

"Oh, yeah, I can't wait."

"What about your mom?" he asked.

"She's dead." Her voice sounded steady.

Daniel thought quickly. Who was this girl and what were her plans? Was she going to show up on the doorstep and make wild claims that would distress his mother? He could be useful now. He could check this Virginia out, see if she was legit and then guide the situation so as not to upend his family.

Daniel suggested he meet her in Houston. "I can help you find his brother, Leo. Show you around the neighborhood. It's been a long while since I was there, but it'd be good to re-connect with Tino's family."

They were to meet at a café close to the old Houston neighborhood called Magnolia by Tino since Daniel could remember.

After he hung up, Richard was in the truck asking him what woman he was planning to meet in Houston.

"Just a college friend," Daniel said.

Richard gave him a sly "fo sho" smile.

Daniel thought about the logistics as he and Richard made their stops. He needed to rent a car, maybe get a motel for the night. What if this was some kind of scam? It didn't seem like much of a scam, if scam it was. But what did he know about scams, anyway? He didn't have the scammer mental-ity. Whenever he tried to do something even mildly nefarious, he got busted at the beginning of the first act.

Even if this was Tino's long lost daughter, what did she want exactly? What if the girl wanted more? Maybe she wanted revenge. Maybe she blamed his mother for Tino's ab-sence. What did he know about what the girl's mother had told her growing up. From the stories Tino spun, Celia seemed like she'd been a beast of a woman. A souse, a slob, a brawler, and those were her *good* points. What sort of child had this Mother of the Year managed to raise? Maybe the girl was a drug addict looking for a score, a shakedown artist looking to cause him and his mother trouble. Teresa didn't need any more grief than she already had, and Daniel sure as hell didn't need yet one more woman breathing down his back.

Then Daniel thought about how much Tino had wanted to find Celia. Maybe what he really wanted was to find his daughter. Even if the poor girl was raised by a spider, this girl might have Tino's blood running through her veins. The Tino Daniel had known would have gone to Houston to meet her, only the poor guy didn't have a heartbeat. It fell to Daniel to be that heartbeat. He had to put aside his doubts, his paranoia, his self-obsessed mopery and try to solve this for Tino.

After work, he went home, packed a night bag and made the calls to rent a car and get a cheap room to stay if need be. When his mother got home, he expected a ton of questions, but instead she brushed his plans off with an, "Oh, that's fine." It didn't take long to find out what was on her mind.

"You have a good time, but before you leave, can you take me to the library? I want you to show me how to use the computer there."

Daniel was surprised, but he welcomed Teresa's lack of interest in his weekend plans. "Sure, but why? What do you want to do on the computer?"

"It's a big surprise. I'll tell you all about it on the way there."

"You're not getting ready to give some slimy televangelist the house, are you?"

"No," she said, "nothing like that. And don't talk like that about men of God. You know how much time I spent on my knees praying God would bring you home alive?" It was a sign of her unbounded interest in her mystery project that she stopped short of giving Daniel a full-throated reproach. "It's all very innocent."

This made Daniel even more curious. "Innocent? What are you up to, Mom?"

"I'm on 'Plenty of Fish!'" she said with a big smile. "Can you believe it?"

"What the hell is 'Plenty of Fish?'"

"It's for meeting people, silly! You should get on there, too. The sooner you forget that witch, the better."

"You're dating?"

"Yes!"

"Oh boy," he said. "You have to be careful out there. Lots of con artists and Sneaky Petes looking to capitalize on lonely women."

"Who's a lonely woman?" Teresa snapped back, offended. "Do I live alone with a houseful of cats? Am I an old widow waiting to die alone?"

"Nothing like that, Mom," Daniel said. He was blowing the opportunity to keep his mother occupied. "Just saying. . . . Look, it's fine. I think it's a great idea with a couple of caveats."

"What caviars?"

"Caveats, conditions. Make sure the site is reputable and that the people on there aren't Jack the Ripper."

"Well, you can tell me all about that," she said brightening. "You're going to take me to the library and show me how to work the computer. You can look at all those corvettes you're talking about. Let's hurry up before the library closes."

They got there an hour before it shut down, but it was the busy time of the evening and they had to wait to get on a computer. Daniel walked around browsing books. He didn't want to ask his mother a bunch of questions about Tino's past. Teresa was a curious cat, and he didn't want to poke her.

Finally, a machine opened up. His mother was all eyes and ears. She'd brought her notebook and pen where she'd had Elvira write full instructions in sequential order. They navigated to "Plenty of Fish," a cheesy dating site if ever there was one. Daniel scowled at the horde of losers lining its pages. But he didn't tell Teresa that. She needed the distraction. What was she supposed to do? Stand in front of the television wearing a hole in the carpet in the pathetic hopes of getting onto the A-team dancing squad of a tiny, westside church? It was too cruel.

"What does Alena think about this?" he asked.

"What do you think? She never likes anything I come up with. She's jealous."

"Don't be crazy," Daniel said. "She just worries about you, that's all. Me too. That's why I'm here, to make sure you don't get involved in some lonely-hearts ponzi scheme."

"What's that?"

"Nothing, Mom, just that I don't want you getting into anything too weird."

"Never mind, Fonzy," Teresa said, focusing on the computer screen. Her eyes gleamed at all the fish.

The site was a gallery of misfits, mopes, dead-enders, a trove of unloved losers at the end of their ropes. But it was free. The fatty his mother was waiting to hear from seemed harmless.

Teresa was disappointed because Sam hadn't responded to her post yet.

"Don't worry," Daniel told her. "This guy will write back. His silence is the least of your worries. Just make sure not to give him your credit card number."

She nodded solemnly as she combed through the photo galleries of "Plenty of Zeroes."

Daniel left her to wink and flirt. He picked up books mindlessly as scenarios played out in his head. Finally, the librarian made the closing announcement and Daniel went to his mom's side and pressured her to logout. She was all smiles.

"He wrote back."

"Son of Sam."

"Son of Sam? Are you making a joke? It doesn't matter, he wrote me back. He wants to meet me for coffee this weekend. What do you think of that? I can't believe it. It was so easy, and I owe it all to Elvira. She's so smart. When we get home, I want you to take a picture of me with the digital camera. I want to put a better picture of me up. Maybe I should wait to lose some weight. What do you think? Did you see the picture I'm using? Did you think it was good enough? It's a little old, but I don't think that it's too old. What do you think, *m'ijo?*" She gave Daniel a playful slap on the behind.

Daniel could hardly believe this was the same woman who'd been dragging her chin these past fourteen months. She was displaying an optimism that didn't come from a Paxil bottle. Maybe "Fish" wasn't so bad.

He didn't sleep that night. He slammed five oxys at once just to feel the warmth, but too many made him itchy, and that didn't help him sleep. He was anxious about the trip. He kept playing out the scenarios: the one where he had to warn the con artist to stay away from his family, the one where he and the girl had a tender moment of mutual recognition and closure, the one where something terrible was revealed. Before he knew it, it was four in the morning, and he was still wide awake. He tried thinking about something pleasant, something good, something still untouched from his old life.

He remembered when his mom and Tino had come to his college production of *Guys and Dolls*. Daniel played Tony. He did it well, sang well, danced well. It was a nice evening. Everyone was nervous, and Daniel calmed them down by telling everyone that no matter how much they stank, their parents would love the play. What a time! What a luxury to be nervous about a goddamn play.

Cristina and his parents were sitting front and center. Tino had never been to a play, let alone a musical. Tino's opinion mattered the most to him, and Daniel remembered feeling uneasy about whether his stepdad would think it was sissy stuff. But during the play, he could see him laughing at all the right places. Afterward, they'd all gone to dinner, and Tino had been proud of him. It had been a great evening.

The next morning, his mom was curious about the trip to Houston, but he put her off the trail by telling her it was an old college friend. He assured her that he'd be back by Sunday night.

The drive was murder. Now that he wanted to be awake and alert, he kept drifting off. He had to stop a couple of times for strong coffee. He smoked two packs of Camels, as many as he smoked per day in the Sandbox. That was the measure of things now.

Daniel disliked Houston. It was even hotter and stickier than San Antonio. The highways were labyrinthian and clogged. Everyone seemed ready to shoot everyone. He thought about how the confusion of the city was a kind of metaphor for his own situation. After making a couple of wrong turns, he ended up in Magnolia. Tino hadn't exaggerated its decrepit but lively state. It hummed with danger, sketchy dudes hanging out on the dingy sidewalks watching the lambs unaware of street risk. Fast food joints and raggedy bars lined otherwise vacant storefronts. The area had seen better days, but it was impossible to imagine what those days might have looked like.

Virginia took a long look as she walked up to Daniel. He was probably about twenty-eight, slender but muscular, nervous, maybe even a little unsure of himself. She could work with that. She had expected some westside barrio tough guy or a total square working in an accountant's office. He was neither. He looked like a normal dude in jeans and a blue T-shirt. Not dangerous.

He had gotten to the diner early and popped an oxy just to take the edge off. He killed some time by eavesdropping on inane conversations, petty dramas. He missed Virginia coming through the door.

She recognized him by what he said he'd be wearing. "Are you Daniel?" she asked him as he doodled abstractions on a napkin.

Standing in front of Daniel was a pretty young girl, maybe eighteen, thin, a bit plain in the face, although she had a strikingly long Spanish nose and pale blue eyes. There was no doubt about it: this was Tino's daughter.

Daniel put down the pen and stood up, banging his knee on the table hard enough to make him stifle a pained "fuck." Instead, he winced. "Virginia? Sit down, sit down," he said, taking in the full measure of Tino's daughter. "I'm Daniel," he said not sure if he should shake her hand or embrace her as a long-lost sister.

This guy was serious, Virginia thought. Maybe still nice. But serious.

He took her hand to shake it but shifted a bit to give her a loose, awkward hug. He quickly sat down facing her. "Yeah," he said nodding his head as he spoke. "Yeah. I see it. There's no doubt, you're Saturnino's daughter."

"I don't really know," she said. "I only have the one picture, and his face is kind of in the shadow. Sooo . . . maybe?"

"Oh yeah, no doubt in my mind. You look a lot like him. No mistaking."

They prepared to order, taking a few minutes for her to settle on what she wanted. She was suddenly hungry. Daniel was too nervous to eat anything. He ordered coffee.

"Man," she said, "I'm going to feel like a lardo with you sitting across from me watching me eat all that food while you drink coffee. Not cool."

"Oh, I'm sorry. I'm not a breakfast guy. I don't really eat, uh, in the morning."

"Well, you're going to help me with something, so I won't feel conspicuous."

"Okay," Daniel said.

He had questions, of course, but didn't know how to tell her the most pressing detail. She was too late. Tino was dead. He dreaded telling her, a weight dragging his tongue down, his stomach sick, the memory of having to tell others that loved ones were KIA. Get to the point, he thought. He did not want to be callous or abrupt. This was the daughter of his stepfather, a beloved and respected human being. It was remarkable, he kept thinking, how much she looked like Tino. It made him happy to see Tino alive in his daughter.

Before he could get it out, Virginia launched into her story, giving Daniel the basics without revealing everything up front. She'd learned this was a mistake, trusting too much too soon, if at all. Dead mother, long-gone stepfather, bullshit town, bullshit prospects, " . . . And so I left and now I'm here, looking for my real father."

The way she'd said "real father" sounded like the name of someone revered, not necessarily known, but revered all the same. Like God or a superhero. It was strange to him, such hope or faith too child-like for the girl who sat in front of him. She couldn't be that naive.

"His brother, Leo, I'm going to go see him this afternoon. I was hoping you'd come with me."

"I'm sorry," he started.

Virginia looked at him with some disappointment, believing that Daniel was going to decline the invitation.

"Don't you get along with him?" she asked.

"No, not that. It's that Tino is dead. He's been gone over a year now."

He watched her face, expecting her to break into tears, give some sort of emotional outburst. He wasn't good with that. But she didn't register much, just a sideways glance at something a hundred yards away.

"Dead?" she repeated to herself. "A year ago."

Daniel nodded solemnly. "Yeah. Real sudden. Massive heart attack, and then a few days in the hospital. I'm really sorry. I could've told you over the phone, but I thought you deserved to hear it in person." She turned her gaze to him. "Maybe I should have told you so you didn't make this trip. I thought that even though he was gone, that in a way you still found him," he stammered.

Her ability to recover from the shocking news was remarkable, Daniel thought, watching her. She swallowed hard a couple of times, gripping a napkin, her eyes suggesting someone who has just learned that their plans have gone awry and must be recalibrated. He admired her composure. It was as if she was practiced in calamity, not unlike a soldier on the chaotic battlefield taking measure of the damage and doing his best to push emotion to the side and find a way to proceed.

"Ever since I can remember, Celia would hint about me having a secret father. I knew it had to be true. That he was out there. It saved my frickin' life." She blushed, realizing that she'd sounded like a kid. "It kept me going. Everything has sped up for me since I found out about Saturnino. It's carried me here. So, I guess I have no choice but to follow through, right?" Her eyes watered a bit as she looked into Daniel's face, but no tears dropped.

Daniel took a sip of his coffee. "What can I do," he said thoughtfully, "to help you get what you're looking for?"

It was an awkward, startling offer.

Virginia looked up from her food, pausing a moment. "I'll let you know when I straighten that out." She looked back at the plate of eggs, waffles and bacon that the server had put down. "I was starving a minute ago. Now, this stuff doesn't look so good," she said. "You can have it, if you want."

~~~

Rubia had really done it. She'd gotten herself mixed up with a narco. That's all she needed. It was bad enough her fooling around with a weasel like Ernesto, but now this. Sometimes Alena wanted to smack Rubia in the face. What good would it have done? Rubia was going to do what Rubia was going to do. It was human nature, after all. Take her mother, Alena thought. For all the lists her mother liked to make, all the hemming and hawing, all the supposed appeals to common sense and rationality, her mother ultimately wound up going with her gut. Most of the time, she couldn't even begin to explain why she'd done what she'd done.

Alena would say, "Mother, I thought you'd agreed that it made more sense to tell your cousin that you couldn't go visit because you were sick." And Teresa would reply, "I know, I know, but I decided at the last minute to go." The last minute was how Alena's mother made most of her decisions. She hated that about her mother, but if she were going to be honest, she would have to admit that this was how she reached decisions in her own life: the last minute.

Alena and Elvira were watching Rubia get ready for a big party. She was wearing a flowing red dress with a brocade of black silk flowers. There was a diamond necklace, very, very expensive, a gift from the narco. He'd seduced her with good looks, honeyed words and an enormous bankroll. She was headed for disaster and couldn't see it.

Richard was in the bedroom playing his guitar. He was sulking because Elvira was visiting. It was a real drag, but at least he was in the bedroom instead of sitting with the women, ruining their show. He tried to watch a couple of times, but his constant eye-rolling and condescending snorting after every line of dialogue resulted in Elvira and Alena ordering him out of the living room. The last time he'd been kicked out, he'd said, "Okay, I'll go. But I can't believe you guys watch this horseshit."

"I'll remind you of that the next time you're sitting around all day screaming while you watch football," Alena told him.

Elvira had a good laugh at that one.

As soon as Elvira had left, Richard came out in his boxers, scratching his *huevos* and yawning. He barely looked at Alena as he walked into the kitchen. He opened the refrigerator and stood gawking at its contents. He pulled out a pudding cup and turned it around in his hands a couple of times, reading as if the decision to eat it was going to have anything to do with its nutritional value. He decided against it and put the pudding back into the refrigerator. He shut the door and walked to the living room doorway. He stood there, looking, his eyes going back and forth between the TV and Alena. He sighed.

"There's nothing good to eat," he said, finally going over to his Lazy Boy and plopping down. "You need to buy more fruit. There's nothing but junk for Tonia. It'd be better if she had fruit than all that pudding and jello and other shit."

Alena didn't say anything. He was spoiling for a fight. This happened every time after Elvira had left. Alena kept her mouth shut. It was an experiment to see if not feeding the beast could sidestep the argument. It wasn't as if she enjoyed arguing.

"Junk. It's all junk. Just like the TV crap you're watching, cramming garbage in your head. I wouldn't watch that shit if you paid me." Richard knew that bringing out the "S" word usually worked in drawing Alena into a fight.

"Are we going to do this again?" she asked him, knowing that they were already into it. "Just once, I'd like you to come out here and act like you're happy to be home."

He had an answer for that but was no longer sure that he was on solid ground. She might bring up sex or finances. He walked off to the bedroom, still feeling in the right. After a while, she heard him pull out the ironing board and start on his uniform for the next day. When he finished, he turned off the lights and went to bed without saying goodnight.

The phone rang, and Alena answered without looking. She was expecting a call from Elvira for the *Rubia* post-mortem. But it wasn't her. It was Cristina. Alena grimaced at her mistake of not looking to verify who the caller was before picking up. A call from Cristina was something to be avoided at all costs. There was a nagging feeling that she should probably try to be more understanding and give her sister-in-law a place to unburden herself in the hope that, given a chance to discuss things, Cristina might go a bit easier on Daniel. But Alena didn't like confrontation, and Cristina lived for it.

"Alena," she said in that fake cheery way of hers, like she was selling Mary Kay. "How are you? And Richard? And Tonia?" She was practiced in saying all the right things in all the right ways but still letting you know she didn't give a damn about how your life was really going. It was a formality. Cristina never called unless it was to complain about Daniel.

After the fakey preliminaries, Cristina got down to the real reason for the call. She was going to play the Victim, but Alena recognized from experience that she would soon move into attack mode. She wanted to chew Daniel's ass and wanted Alena to join in.

"I don't know what I'm going to do anymore. I think I'm going crazy. All I do is cry. I don't know who to talk to any-more. I can't call my family because all they do is tell me that I've done right in kicking Daniel out. They tell me to do what the lawyer wants, which is to take Daniel to the cleaners. My own mother, who *loves* Daniel, says, '*M'ija*, you've got to do what's right for you now. He misled you. He lied to you. He never meant to do what he promised before God and everybody. He should be ashamed, but he's not.' That's what my own mother tells me, Alena. And you know, as much as it kills me, I'm beginning to think that she's right. He *did* lie to me. You only know him as your brother, your big brother, your protector. For you and your mom, Daniel can do no wrong. I understand that. I do, Alena. I know the stories. I've heard them all since I came into the family, but Daniel isn't my big brother. He's my husband, or at least I thought he was. And he owed me that much, to treat me like his wife."

Alena listened to Cristina, her face getting more and more flushed as the anger and nausea grew in her stomach. Finally, she said, "What are you talking about? All I've ever heard or seen of the two of you is Daniel trying to keep you happy. So, unless he was beating you or having an affair, I don't have any reason to question what he tells me."

"Well, he's not telling you everything, Alena. Not the half of it."

She was goading Alena into asking for the other half, but Alena resisted. She wanted to know, but did she really need to know her brother's secrets?

"What has he told you about the baby, about giving me another baby?"

"Cristina, why don't you talk to him if you need to get something off your chest. I'm the wrong person to be giving you marriage advice."

"Hasn't he given you some explanation? You don't think he's just licking his wounds at his mommy's home?" There was real malice in her voice.

Alena didn't answer. As a matter of fact, Daniel had been pretty vague about why he was back at Teresa's house. He wasn't forthcoming about his problems, and she hadn't prodded. Alena assumed that he was sick from the war and from losing the baby. He had returned home, where he could get real love and care. It hadn't occurred to her to delve any deeper into his story. Daniel was the most responsible person she'd ever known, so why should she be getting into his private business?

Despite her instincts, Alena asked. "What is it he isn't telling me, Cristina?"

"I can't even say it." She went quiet, leaving dead air, waiting for the proper dramatic build up. She had the instincts of a soap opera actress.

"Well?" Alena said finally.

"He's been abusive to me," she responded in a tiny voice that held just enough vulnerability for Alena to feel compassion.

"That doesn't sound like Daniel," Alena said. "It just doesn't. He's the kind that would rather hurt himself. I've never seen him hurt anyone on purpose. My brother is kind. Too kind sometimes."

"You don't know him! It's been like living in a thunderstorm. Nothing but drinking all night, taking pills, acting like I'm a ghost in his life. And of course, no love, no sex. He promised me a baby after Pumpkin died," she blurted out, now crying into the phone so bluntly that Alena could almost feel the heat and humidity of her breath. "But he wouldn't even try. Nothing but horrible, drunken excuses. He wouldn't even hold a job. Just his puny money from the Army for being crazy! He's left me alone with nothing. I lost the house. Did you know? Does Saint. Daniel tell you what he did to me?"

"Jesus," Alena muttered, "I don't really . . . it's not my business, Cristina. He's got problems with . . . substances. But he's not violent. You said 'abusive.' You're the one who laid hands on him, right? You could've crippled him on those stairs."

Alena couldn't imagine the Daniel Cristina described. He was the injured party. She'd seen it firsthand, the effects of that terrible war compounded by this angry, mean woman. She felt sick.

"Spit it out," she finally said. "Just lay it out there, Cristina. What do you want from me?"

"I want you to know," she said, "that fag brother of yours, whining and hiding behind you mother's skirts so he doesn't have to face reality, has ruined my life!"

"Okay," she said, "enough!"

"Fuck that," Cristina yelled into the phone. "Your precious brother is a lying asshole, probably queer, who doesn't live up to his obligations. He's done bad things over there and over here. He's not what you think. He's a lying cruel bastard. And I'm going to make sure everyone knows it— you, your mom, everyone."

Alena hung up on her.

She sat there, everything in the room the same but not the same, like the room had been replaced by another room, other furniture, that looked exactly the same, only it wasn't the same and only Alena knew it. Could he be that different from the brother she loved and knew so well? She sat still in that foreign room for a good long time, when she felt her cell vibrating. It was Elvira but she didn't pick up.

~~~

Son of Sam was waiting for her at the coffee shop in the used bookstore that Daniel and Teresa frequently patronized. She recognized him, even though he was different from his picture: a little more balder and plenty, plenty fatter. But Teresa didn't care. After all, she was older-looking than her picture too. Anyway, she wasn't there to accept a marriage proposal. She was there to get a look at the man who had been writing her for six straight days. Each one of his notes got friendlier than the last, and he had indicated that he was a good Christian, although he didn't much like attending church. He said he was a dancer, although Teresa doubted this now. At least he'd been honest enough to tell her that he was a three-time loser in the marriage department. That's how he'd put it, "three-time loser."

He noticed her, looking up from his open newspaper, and he stood up right away, his pot belly making it a difficult maneuver at first and pulling him off balance. He recovered fast, smiling big enough to pull Teresa's view from his protruding belly. He walked the distance of the café, saying, "Hello, Teresa, hello," holding out his hand and all the time his big smile sitting on his face like yellow Christmas lights on a house.

"I knew it was you," he said guiding her to the table and pulling her chair out. "I knew it had to be the Angel Teresa. You're even more beautiful than your picture. What can I get you?"

"Some tea," Teresa said, the stocky figure turning for the counter before Teresa could thank him for the compliment.

"Decaf, right?" he said, his chubby legs propelling him.

A minute later he was back, talking before he got to the table. "You are the full package!" He set a tray down with the drinks.

The lights were bright, and there was nowhere to hide. Teresa was conscious that her wrinkles were probably on full display, even though good old Elvira had gone to the house to help her get ready for her big date. She didn't have much makeup of her own. Some lipstick was the only thing she kept. Tino didn't care one way or the other whether she made herself up. The makeup kit Elvira brought over was something else: two big boxes with all kinds of lipsticks and mascaras and cover-ups, lip and eyeliners, and a big hand-held mirror that magnified all her imperfections. There were four or five different perfumes. Teresa decided that if it took her spray painting her face in order to get some excitement, and maybe even a man, so be it. Elvira got a kick out of Teresa's boldness, something Alena did not find appealing.

In the café light, even though she was attempting to concentrate on what fat Sam was saying, she kept thinking about whether he could see her laugh lines. This caused her to smile tight little grins, very unlike the full-dimpled version truer to herself. What if he was taking note of the wrinkles around her mouth or her forehead? She tried to keep from making expressions that would make her lines deeper. With all the self-consciousness, who could really tell what poor, fat Sam was even saying? Something about his job, which sounded very boring. Something about auditing or something with numbers and some pizza restaurant whose finances he oversaw. Teresa wondered, unkindly, whether a fringe benefit of his work was eating his fill of double-stuffed pepperoni and mushroom pizza.

She managed to nod and keep a vacant, little smile to reward his efforts at charm. It was difficult for him to charm Teresa, because when he smiled, his fat cheeks got even rollier and pollier, and his eyes squinted up so that he looked piggier than ever. Yes, he had little piggy eyes with fat rolly-polly cheeks, and little teeth like pieces of yellow corn strung together carelessly and crookedly: a piggy, with corn cob teeth and little brutish eyes. Try as he might, he could never be charming, and especially when he could only talk about his boring job with numbers! All Teresa could think was that she shouldn't have come because fat, rolly-polly, corn-on-the-cob-teeth Son of Sam was much more charming on the computer when he was sending her a flower or a wink. And now it was ruined!

He talked about his wives and how one died and the other one was too young, and the other too picky, and she kept thinking, but what about your corn teeth? Or your rolly-polly belly and piggly-wiggly eyes, Son of Sam? And then it hit her that what kind of prize did she think she was, anyway? There in her borrowed makeup, anxious that the too-bright light would expose her horrible old, old, old age to Mr. Rolly-Polly-Corn-Teeth-Pig Eyes? And then she began to laugh because of how rotten and mean she could be, and how Elvira would laugh at her mean, rotten telling of this night.

She knew it was awful to giggle right in the middle of whatever solemn tale poor Son of Sam was spinning. He looked at her a bit confused, a strained smile still on his lips. He didn't know what he'd said to make her laugh. Teresa thought it better to shut up because she'd already made a lot of mistakes that night. Piggy Sam took a deep breath and went ahead with his futile, boring story.

If nothing else, it felt good to be on the market again.

#3

"Should we get a medevac up here?" Fonzo asks. "For the lady?"

"She's dead," Danny says maintaining his stare on the boy's face.

"You sure?" She looks like she might still be breathing.

Danny walks back to the mother's body.

She is young. Her eyes stare back at him: shiny, growing glassy as the blood running from her face and mouth and nose pools around her head. She is still alive somehow. Every few moments, she still tries to articulate something, a prayer perhaps. She is pleading. It is futile. And there is no mistaking that she is dying. Danny knows that there is a soul. He's seen souls leave bodies and the transformation is shattering. Something is instantaneously diminished, an unmistakable transformation from the dynamic, the human, to the inert, the object. From someone to be loved to a thing to be abhorred. He'd never seen it before the Sandbox. By now, he's seen it plenty, although he cannot get used to it. Partly, he doesn't want to. It will mean something too awful about himself. But mostly, it's that dying is the worst thing he has ever seen. It is shocking, always.

The young mother isn't there yet. Soon. Her dirty, bloody hands pull at the rags covering her stomach. Because her baby is dying inside her, she is trying to speak to it. Perhaps this is something she has been doing over the long, hard pregnancy. Perhaps she has made promises to her baby to protect her, despite the deprivation and danger. Maybe she is apologizing or offering a final blessing. Danny can't figure it out, although he is trying. From outside the house, Danny hears a helicopter blade chopping the air in rapid pulsations creating a vacuum inside. It is most likely evacuating a wounded soldier. Perhaps the young mother as she fades imagines that it is the angel of death come to take her and her baby. It is ghastly, her bluing lips moving ever more slightly. Silent, her throat too scorched to make a recognizable sound.

"Fuck," Sky says stepping over the boy's body as he approaches the woman. "Goddamn. Those motherfuckers are ruthless. Why fire from a house where you know you've got civilians hunkered down?"

"Fuck 'em," Fonzo says. "She mighta been the one shooting at us."

Danny looks on silently. The woman has stopped moving her lips. Her eyes glaze over quickly in the heat of the room. She is gone.

"Let's clear out," he says in a steady matter-of-fact way.

"Boogie," repeats Fonzo. "It ain't our funeral."

On the street, Danny spots a pack of wild dogs. They are everywhere in Fallujah, following the action, staying in the shadows, hiding under the husks of burned-out cars. Until the shooting stops. Then they come out. In fours and fives, as well-trained as any squad, sniffing at corpses and then digging in. It's a nauseating sight, but Danny keeps his eyes trained on them. They've found a fresh one, the body torn to pieces already, easy pickings. The alpha dog starts in on the corpse's throat, and the others join, one clever fellow taking the better part of a leg to another spot to gnaw on it without having to compete with the others.

"Motherfucking Muj," Sky says. He can't process the sight of the dead boy. He finds a spot next to the Abrams and collapses on his backside. He fumbles around for a cigarette. Danny turns from the dogs feasting on the dead Haji. He looks ahead at the destroyed street and crumbled house fronts. They unleashed the crazy shit on this block. He squints up at the blinding yellow sun. He'd knocked over a fishbowl once when he was a kid. Panicked, he'd stood there staring at the gasping goldfish as it died. Something about the blazing sun, the ghoulish dogs, the shattered buildings bring the clear memory of it. Then Danny pukes in front of his boys, wipes his mouth and orders them to move forward.

They continue their way up the street, house by house. Slowly now, not bull-rushing through, which is the prescribed method. The element of surprise. Don't let the bad guys get a bead on you. You get the jump. But that means a higher risk of tripping an IED. Danny doesn't feel much like taking risks. They fucked up with Scotty and Jaws. He's fucked-up big, blowing the shit out of that house and killing the family.

"Don't let that fuck with your head," Fonzo tells Danny, knowing what his buddy is thinking because he is thinking it too. It is fucking with his head as well. "No way of knowing what that broad was doing there. Most of the Hajis have cleared out. Anyone sticking around is on a grunt-killing agenda."

"Ain't nothing fucking with me," Danny says.

He wants to be telling the truth. He feels numb more than anything else now. He has time to wonder if this is now the new norm, the reality that the most violent, bloody, horrifying scenes to which he contributes as a matter of course have distorted his perception permanently, his psyche, into a diseased thing. He has time to conclude on that blazing white-hot day that he is now a monster. A fortunate one since he is the one doing the damage, the one walking away. Fonzo has got it right. It isn't his funeral.

There are doors to kick in, houses to clear, Muj to eliminate. The war is going on all around him. His training kicks in. That much has not been destroyed. It remains and reasserts itself.

Most every house they enter is empty or busted flat. They find a few AKs that have been abandoned. Some RPGs Fonzo detonates. Mostly they find debris and garbage. The whole country seems composed of nothing but debris and garbage. Garbage gardens piled high and deep. The Iraqis are left to do nothing but pile layers of putrid refuse over older, more putrid, more pungent layers of refuse. Garbage on garbage to be dealt with later or never.

The men hunker down for a few minutes and eat their rations quietly. They are too tired, too dirty, too banged up. The battle adrenaline has worn them down and left them exhausted. The doc moves around patching up cuts and gouges and burns. Hernandez, the gunner on the Bradley, has some nasty burns on his forearms from phosphorous he's come in contact with. The doc applies some medication to his oozing burns, wraps them, and now Hernandez is ready to go. They are always ready to go.

CHAPTER 6
Polaroid

Daniel suggested they go see Leo.

"I knew him a little bit. Mom and Tino took us kids to Astroworld back in the day, and Tino wanted to drop in on his big brother. It didn't go so well, to say the least." Daniel smiled although the memory wasn't particularly funny. "Tino called beforehand, and Leo invited us to stay with him and his wife—they were still together back then. It was a common-law thing, and Mom didn't approve from the get-go, but Tino really wanted to reconnect, and Mom agreed."

"What happened?"

"Shit, Leo was an all-pro alcoholic. That's what happened. He was a good drunk, though. Cheerful and funny. He welcomed us Tex-Mex style: barbecue grill going, *conjunto* music on the radio and about two cases of Lite beer. He'd probably already gone through half a case by the time we got there. Mom was vigilant about Tino drinking. She didn't want nothing to do with having a drunk for a husband."

"Was he an alcoholic?"

"Probably, I mean in the sense that once an alky always an alky. But I hadn't seen him touch a drink. That wasn't enough for Mom, though. 'I'd rather he be a cheater like your father,' she told me once. Long story short, Tino got shitfaced with his older brother. Nothing crazy. Just drunk, singing drunk. Mom acted like Tino and Leo were mainlining H. We had to leave that night. They got in a bad argument and, for the first time, I saw this side of Tino I never knew was there."

"Like what?" Virginia asked.

"He got scary, punched a hole in the wall at the motel because Mom had punked him in front of his brother. Real macho stuff. His eyes got small and hard. He yelled but in a way that got down into your stomach. Scary dude."

"What did your mom do?"

"After he sobered up, Mom hit him with the hardcore ultimatum. 'You ever get drunk in front of my kids or me again, it's over. I'll send you back to Houston with a paper bag full of your *chones* and nothing else!' It was a come-to-Jesus moment, and Tino, whatever you want to say about him, he loved my mother. He worshipped her. He stayed true to his promise. I don't ever remember him crossing the line again.

"Anyway, we should go see Leo. Maybe we can pry some decent information out of him. I'll bring a case of Lite. It'll get him talking. All you have to do is let me know what you really want to know."

Virginia pursed her lips a bit, thinking hard. She hadn't really thought in such concrete terms. Saturnino was abstract, an idea. It would have all come clear when she met him in person. Now he was dead. She had hoped he'd provide answers and a rescue. He couldn't do either.

"I'm not sure," she said finally. "This isn't what I thought would happen. He was going to be alive and embrace me. And just by being alive and loving me, the answers would come. The questions have always been physical. So I thought the answers would be too."

Daniel looked a bit embarrassed. "Okay," he said. "All right." He fidgeted with getting a cigarette. "So now, there's got to be a plan B, right? You want to find out all you can about Tino before he met my mom?" Lighting the cigarette, he inhaled slowly. "Who he was and why he didn't meet you sooner. Is that right?" he said exhaling quickly.

"Maybe," Virginia said. "This is all probably a waste of time."

"No," Daniel said. "I know about wasted time. This isn't a waste. It's a quest. It's a double quest. You got your reasons for wanting to find out some things, and I got my reasons for wanting to know some things. Look, maybe the questions aren't apparent yet. Maybe they'll come up naturally as we dig deeper. It's worth the chance."

"Okay," she said nodding her head slightly. She noted that Daniel had used the pronoun "we" and it lifted her. "Okay," she repeated, this time a more determined tone coming into her voice.

They called Leo. He was home. He was always home. He told them to come right over. Daniel stopped at a convenience store, bought a case of beer and a fifth of whisky. Then they stopped at Lennox Barbecue and bought two pounds of sausage and brisket.

"We're locked and loaded now," he told Virginia. "We'll get the family secrets out of him yet."

~~~

When they arrived at Leo's house, he greeted them cheerfully. Virginia was nervous, feeling like an intruder. Leo resembled her father's photo, an older, haggard, thinner version of Saturnino, but the eyes kindly, soft. There was compassion there. He was an alcoholic, this she could tell. His skin and eyes were yellow, obviously a sick old man. And here she and Daniel were, bringing some of the poison that was killing him. To find out what?

It was early but he was already drinking. He gave each of them a drunken hug.

"Daniel, how's the soldier boy? I heard tell you were over there fighting terrorists."

Daniel smiled a bit. "Something like that."

Virginia took the food to the kitchen while Daniel collected three glasses for the whisky.

"Your *papá* was proud of you fighting over there," Leo said, pouring three fingers of the liquor into his glass. "Thank you, *m'ija*," he said to Virginia as he took an enormous gulp of the top-shelf stuff Daniel had bought. "Join me," he said wiping his mouth with his sleeve. "It isn't often I get family visiting!"

"Those your kids?" Virginia asked her newfound uncle and pointed to a dusty 8x10 that sat on the cheap end table next to the threadbare sofa.

"Some of them," he said without looking back. "I don't see my kids so much. I wasn't such a good father. Maybe they'll come to my funeral," he said smiling.

His front left tooth was missing. The others were yellowed and rotting. She felt sad for him but alarmed also. Daniel poured himself a short one and began to pour one for Virginia.

"No thanks," she said quickly. "Too early for me. I'm doing water."

"Best thing for you," Leo said, refilling his glass with another three fingers.

Virginia wasn't sure if he was saying so about water or whisky.

"Yeah," he said to Daniel, "your *papá*, he sneaked a call or two to me when he could. Guess your *mamá* didn't approve of me too much, huh?"

Daniel nodded. "She wanted to keep Tino on the straight and narrow."

"Ahh, hell," Leo said, "it ain't none of it worth worrying about. Straight, crooked, *recto* or *chueco*, it all ends the same. You were in the war, right? You know this shit!"

Daniel didn't affirm or disagree. Instead, he took another drink, this one deeper and longer than the first.

"I was in a war too," Leo said finally. "Vietnam. I was in the Marines. Judge told me, you seem to like fighting, so you go fight or you go to jail. I'd been to jail, so I figured I'd go fight. Hell, I spent my whole life fighting on the streets, might as well do a little over there than spend more dead time in the *pinta*."

He showed his guests what looked like a homemade tattoo of the words "Semper Fi" on his forearm with the dates he'd served during the war. "Spent four years floating around. Want to hear the funny part? I got into more shit in the Marines than if I would've done some more time. I got hooked to my *huevos* on *chiva*. I used on the streets before I left for the war, but in the Nam, it was a helluva lot cheaper, stronger and easier to get. I came back a true-blue junky. Big monkey on my back, *sabes*?" He addressed this last line to Daniel alone.

Daniel nodded.

"Got that black tar from Afghanistan now," Leo said. "Back in the day, there was lots being trafficked from the Nam. I got back in '72, and there was more junkies than ever. Lots of soldiers bringing it in. Me too, a couple of times. Got caught once. Dude I knew smuggled some in a coffin. They used to do that back then. Anyway, that was it for me and the Marines. Did two years in Leavenworth. What did I care? Better than my chances in the jungle."

Virginia noticed that Daniel had filled his glass again.

"You see much fighting in Iraq?" the old man asked.

"My share," Daniel said.

"Me too," the old man said. "Course, I don't know what a share is. Seems like Mexicans get more than their share when it comes to shit."

Virginia excused herself and brought out the barbecue. She could see that Daniel and Leo were going to drink themselves into a stupor if they didn't slow down and eat something. When she came back with the plates and food, both men were sitting in silence, as if replaying private memories in their own heads.

"Here you go," she said handing them each a plate.

"Nice," Leo said. "I 'preciate the company, *hijos*."

Virginia and Daniel each took some meat and bread. Leo did not.

"I'll eat later when I get hungry," he said, pouring another glass of whisky.

"We wanted to talk about my pops with you," Daniel said, still chewing his brisket.

"Yeah," Leo said, "like I said, we talked less and less as time went by. That's okay. I get it. He had a good thing with your momma. Didn't want to fuck it up. 'Scuse my language, *m'ija*," he said to Virginia.

"Don't worry about me, Tío," she said. "I've heard a lot worse than that."

Leo laughed. "I bet you have, *m'ija*. I bet you have. That Benny-Boy, he was a real bad dude. I never liked him. Neither did your *papá*."

"They knew each other?" Daniel asked.

"Sure. Everyone in the barrio knows everybody. 'Specially when you grow up here. Benny-Boy was from the block. Far as I know, they never tangled, him and your daddy, but if Benny-Boy and Celia hadn't of been gone after Tino got out of the joint, there would've been some serious stress. Tino wasn't never someone to fuck around. 'Scuse me, *m'ija*. He was a warrior in the day. He never backed down from a fight. Never. That don't mean he didn't lose his share. But even when he lost, there wasn't no winner, I can tell you that much! You wanted to tangle with Tino, you was going to get bloody, dig? You practically had to kill him to win. I learned that the hard way a time or two growing up. He was the small one, but he didn't fight that way. Hell, no."

This was what they were here for. Both Daniel and Virginia let the old man keep talking.

"I deserved it," he said. "I was hard on your daddy. Had to be. Our old man, he was a useless drunk. Mean SOB. He only knew one way, and that was to kick your ass. Didn't matter if you had it coming either. Ass-kicking was the only way he knew to teach us."

"Teach you what?" Virginia asked.

"The only thing that matters, *m'ija*. Surviving. That's all I had for your daddy, too. I wasn't mean like our old man, though. I just never knew whether I was supposed to be a brother or father to Tino. It got mixed up." At this reminiscence, Leo teared up but did not allow a tear to roll down his face. He swallowed hard. "Your daddy was a real sweet kid. He didn't look for trouble. It always found him, though. 'Specially early on with our old man. He looked a lot like our *mamá*. *Papá* put her in the ground with his drinking and beating her. Not that we didn't try. There was seven of us boys. We tangled with the old man as we got older, but our momma, she didn't want even more trouble. Maybe she got to the point she thought she had it coming. It happens like that. It means your spirit is killed. It's a sad fucking thing. 'Scuse me, *m'ija*.

"Tino reminded him of what a bastard he was just by looking like our *mamá*. Anyway, the old man would beat him merciless, especially when there weren't none of us around to look out for him. All us brothers were either in the *pinta*, the service or out on the street slinging drugs. It wasn't long before he'd been kicked around enough that the meanness took over. Had to! Otherwise, the old man would've wound up killing him."

Virginia sat numbly.

Leo looked up at her. "You want to see some pictures, *m'ija?*"

She nodded, and Leo went into another room. Daniel and Virginia could hear him rummaging around. After a few minutes, he came out with three photo albums. They were dusty and worn, but Virginia could only anticipate the treasure they held inside their mismatched, deteriorating covers. There were hundreds of photos, mostly crimped black and white photos and a slew of dark Polaroids.

Leo placed the books in front of her on the table. Virginia began to turn the pages of the first one while Leo and Daniel continued to drink. A black and white and two Polaroids caught her attention not because they included Celia or anyone particularly recognizable, but because of the arc of innocence, pain and deep anger etched in each successive picture of Saturnino.

"That's us all, after my sister come along," Leo said, pointing at the picture Virginia was viewing.

Pictured were father, mother, seven boys and a baby girl, ranging from a tall, unsmiling Leo, who wore a slick-backed ducktail, to a small, slight three-year-old Saturnino, to a baby girl still in arms. Saturnino held a small hand out towards the camera as if pleading to be picked up.

"That was just before Momma died," Leo said. "I remember. You see her there? See how skinny she is? She was already sick. Even the *jefe* told her to go to the doctor. She didn't. She was dead by the end of the year. Cancer ate her bones. That's when I knew God was bullshit. She never hurt anybody, always taking up for us, taking the punches and kicks the old man meant for us. Wanna hear something stupid? The old man was real broken up over her. I never saw him cry, even when he was drunker than hell. But he cried for days after we buried her. Probably didn't mean shit, though. He was feeling sorry for himself. It wasn't no time before he was back to beating us up and drinking himself blind."

Leo took a long look at the picture, taking it from Virginia's hand before handing it back. "I was already using, so I don't remember it all so clear, but look at your *papá*," he said to Virginia. "He was nothing but a baby. The old man had no idea how to take care of him, or the baby, so he didn't. He sent my baby sister to my aunt, but Tino wasn't so lucky. He fed him, I guess. But it was a free for all till he found a cheap *ruca* at a bar. She lasted a few weeks. It was like that, a new *vieja* coming in like a parade of cheap drunks. Course, they were better than the old man. Most of them, anyway. One of them, Isla, she liked burning him with an iron when he messed up. That was even too much for *el jefe*. She burned Tino on his hands with the iron. God knows why. He must've been six or so. Anyway, the old man came home, saw the burns and kicked her out on her ass. He didn't bring any strange *viejas* home after that, at least as far as I can remember."

The first Polaroid was a shot of a ten- or eleven-year-old Saturnino standing next to his father. The old man towered over him. The boy's face was blank as a wall except for the dark eyes made even darker by the circles around them.

"Where are you guys?" asked Virginia.

"That was after the last of us hit the bricks. Lucio was the only one left, but he got in trouble and ended up in juvie. He was fifteen or so. Tino was left with the old man after that."

"How come . . ." Virginia said fading out.

"How come I didn't take him in?"

"Yeah. Why not?"

"*M'ija*, I was a stone-cold junkie dealing *chiva*, getting into all sorts of stupid shit. 'Scuse my language. Half the time, I didn't know where I was going to sleep. Course, that didn't stop Tino from trying to escape. The old man would kick his ass, and Tino would go sleep under a bridge or in the park. Now, none of us, including Tino, was innocent. We got into all sorts of trouble. Once, I remember, Tino must've been twelve, he decided to take a brick and break all the windows he could reach at the school. The old man was a drunk and a shit-for-nuts, but he wasn't a criminal.

"Thing is, I never met my *abuelo*, but I bet you dollars to donuts he beat the shit out of my old man when he was a kid. It goes like that, *m'ija*. It's a chain. Can't none of us break it. Your *papá* is a doctor? You probably be a doctor, too. Your old man is a good-for-nothing drunk who gets off on proving his manhood on your body, well, that's how you end up too."

Virginia looked over at the picture of Leo with his family. Two boys who looked uncannily like their father. Saturnino's family shared the same face. Where were those boys now?

"This last picture," Virginia said handing the Polaroid to Leo. "Saturnino looks bad. He looks. . . ."

"*Feo*. Mean. Hard. Whatever you wanna call it," Leo said looking at the picture. "Hard times. That was just before he got sent up for the manslaughter rap."

"Mean, hard, *feo*," Virginia heard, and then "manslaughter." The word "slaughter" imposed itself on her eyes even as she looked away.

~~~

Was she a bad sister? Alena loved Daniel. He was her big brother, her protector since she could remember. Why would that witch Cristina tell her such awful things about Daniel?

She'd made it sound like Daniel was dangerous, not just self-destructive. Alena had seen plenty of the latter since he'd come back from that horrible place, but never the former. In an involuntary shudder of a thought, she pictured Daniel with a gun to his head. He sat on the bed in their mother's garage, alone, looking down, gun raised, and then lifting his line of sight to meet hers, the watcher in the dark. And she could do nothing.

And then, because Alena was a dutiful mother, she thought, should she be trusting him with her daughter? A spasm of guilt. She immediately chastised herself for entertaining such awful doubts about Daniel. He was still the boy who went to work at twelve-years-old to help their mother, to buy a Christmas tree, to buy her a doll when there was no money and no father to give a damn. . . . When she'd been bullied by some bad girls, he'd picked her up at school and faced down the girls for her, telling them to leave her alone. And they had.

Daniel was no wife-beater, no crazy soldier ready to explode. Anyway, Cristina was full of pain, but the kind of pain that turned outward in rage. This was her attempt at revenge by seeding more heartache in the family. It wasn't enough for her to break her poor brother's heart. Daniel spent all his days thinking about his failure. Failure at what, exactly? Failure to make a chronically miserable woman happy. An impossible task.

What if it were true? Did she have to protect Tonia from Daniel now? Were there any signs of abuse? No. It was ridiculous. Who could think that anyone needed protecting from her sweet, handsome, loving brother? Only a witch like Cristina.

And then a terrifying idea: Daniel hanging himself, of blowing his brains out in her mother's garage, of him flipping out and killing Mother and then shooting a bunch of people at the HEB or the school. It did happen, and people always said, yeah, he was a bit troubled, but he was nice, quiet, friendly even.

The phone rang. It was Daniel. "I've got something important to tell you," he said. "I'm in Houston, but it's important." He waited for her to respond. "Well, aren't you going to ask me what it is?" He sounded drunk.

"I don't know," Alena said. "Do I want to hear it?"

"Since when does your nosiness have any limits? Of course, you want to hear it! It concerns us all: me, you, Mom, everyone."

"Oh, Daniel," Alena pled, "maybe it can keep till you get back. I can't handle much more tonight."

"Well, I guess. Is everything all right? Is Tonia okay? Are you and Richard fighting?"

Alena almost jumped at the excuse, but there was a part of her that wanted to know. "Cristina called me today."

"What'd she want?" The energy in his voice changed into something more anxious. "Why are you so fidgety?"

"Nothing. She upsets me."

"Well, for once, I don't want to talk about her. This is more important. Look, I'll come over in a couple of days. You need to hear what I have to tell you."

"Okay," Alena said. She hung up.

~~~

This current message on "Plenty of Fish" was interesting. Very interesting. It was like something out of the books Teresa read when she was a girl. She remembered one she'd read when she was ten, about an orphan girl who was a nanny or something like that, and she lived in a house of a rich man tutoring his daughter. The house was in the middle of nowhere, maybe close to the woods. The man was handsome but very mysterious, and he was always traveling off to some place and leaving them alone. So, this nanny, who was very beautiful and knew nothing of the world, fell in love with him. The interesting part was that she would hear bumps in the night and weeping, like the sounds a ghost would make. Well, what did you think happened? It turned out that the mysterious man's crazy wife was locked in the attic! That was a good one, that book. Teresa made a note to see if Daniel could help her remember the title. She'd like to read it again. They probably had it at the library.

The man writing her on "Plenty of Fish" was something like the mystery man of the book she remembered. His first note read,

> *To Beautiful Teresa,*
>
> *I hope my note reaches you in good health and well-being. I am most taken with your photograph and the charm you have revealed to me. I write in the hope of beginning a meaningful correspondence. Please allow me to introduce myself.*
>
> *My name is Terrence and I am currently residing in the Congo. I am a Canadian by birth, a British gentleman by education, and a self-made African entrepreneur by dint of my hard work and sober wit.*

"*Ay, qué* fancy," Elvira said over the phone as Teresa read. "An African explorer," she said giggling. "Does he plan to take you away to the jungle?"

Teresa continued reading,

> *I have been living in South Africa for the better part of ten years now. My wife died of a fever five years ago, and the product of our happy, but too brief marriage is a seven-year-old daughter who lives at a*

boarding school in Capetown. My business ventures take me all over the continent, but during the past two years, most of my time has been spent traveling between Brazaville and Kinshasa.

Lately, however, my attention has been given almost purely to my daughter, Eva, who has been ill.

"*Qué triste*," Elvira said.

In any case, I am reaching out to you because, as you may imagine, my life necessitates a solitary existence. I hope that you will consider writing me back so that we may get to know each other as well as this medium can afford.

"What do you think that means?" Teresa asked Elvira. "What's all this about 'afford?'"

"Don't give anyone money," Elvira warned.

"He sent his picture," Teresa told her. "He is very handsome. He looks like that actor, you know, the one who played the father on *Diana* back in the seventies. You know who I mean?"

"No," Elvira said. "I was just a kid, but I think my mother watched that one." She logged on to Teresa's "Plenty of Fish" account. "Okay, um-hum, I see his picture. *Muy chulito*, Teresa, *muy chulito*."

"He looks young, doesn't he?" Teresa asked. "Maybe too young. He's no more than forty."

"Maybe it's an old picture. You should ask him to send you some more pictures with his daughter in them, that way you can tell how old he is. What does his profile say?"

"It doesn't say anything about age. What's the Congo? It sounds like something from Tarzan."

"*El Congo, El Chango*, I don't know from which is which," Elvira said. "Let's google it." She grew quiet for a few moments. "Okay, it doesn't look like any place I'd like to go. There's a war and they are killing each other like flies. Yikes, the things going on there are too horrible for me to tell you. You'll get nightmares."

"Well, what do you think he has to do with it?" Elvira didn't know, so they wrote him another note asking for more details.

Who would have ever thought that Teresa, the moldering widow from San Antonio, would be writing to someone in the deepest part of Africa!

My Dearest Teresa,

Thank you for your quick reply. I am sending you a picture of my daughter on her horse, Cleo, which I gave her on the occasion of her fifth birthday. The two are growing up together and have shared many lovely days at our Capetown house. One of the hardest parts for her was leaving Cleo behind. As for my line of work, I cannot give much away, and in any case, it would only bore you. I am attaching a photo of myself scaling Mount Kilimanjaro last year. It was a grueling climb, but one that meant very much to me. If only you could see the vista from the peak! I very much wish to show you the whole of Africa, a misunderstood and wonderful place!

"Sounds like a ton of baloney to me," Alena told Teresa after she read the message.

"No, I don't think so. He's sent me pictures, one of them from Mount Kikkomanjelly."

"Mr. ManJelly is writing you from the dizzying heights of Mount Horseshit."

"Look, he's even sent me a picture, a photo of his little girl. She's sick. She lives at a school, and he doesn't get to see her much. He's lonely."

"C'mon, Mother," Alena said, "the internet is made for liars. It's the easiest thing to put up a BS profile with BS pictures and a BS story."

Teresa watched as she typed something, and a dozen pictures of an old man with a beard came up on the computer screen. She did something fancy, and one of the pictures showed up on a blank page. Underneath, Alena wrote, "The Baron Von Bull-Meister." She then sent an email to Teresa with a note and picture from the Baron: "Dear Teresa, I pine for you dearly. I'm miserable without you. I sit in my Romanian castle overlooking the Danube in despair waiting for word from you. Kindly send me $100 to get my pike out of layaway."

"By the way," Alena told her, "that's a picture of Walt Whitman, whose been dead about a hundred years. This Man-Jelly sounds like a scammer. Watch out, Mother. Next thing you know, he's gonna want your social security number so he can put his millions in your account because his government is collapsing."

Teresa looked wounded. "Can you look up his face? Take his picture and Hulahoop it for me."

"You mean google."

"Yes, hulagoogle. Whatever it's called, *m'ija*. Check him out for me."

"You can't google a face. Just use some common sense, okay?"

What did Alena know? Teresa thought. Alena would say anything to rain on her little parade. Terrence hadn't asked for anything but the company of her letters. What could that hurt? Besides, one's story was always a bit mysterious. Teresa's story might not be as strange as his, but damn close.

My Dearest Teresa,

I realize that we have only been corresponding two weeks, but I feel a growing affection for you, one that I did not think possible only a short while ago. As I write, I am traveling by train to Capetown to see my Eva, who has taken a turn for the worse. Unfortunately, I had to leave in haste. I received a telegram in the middle of the night. As you can imagine, there aren't ATM machines in the jungle. In fact, getting funds in the middle of the day is an exacting process. I am going to be making a stop in a small town along the banks of the Congo where there will be some access to Western Union. I won't go into the complexities, but I am writing to see if I can secure a small and very temporary loan until I am back in Capetown. Perhaps, you could wire me a small sum. I need only a few hundred to get back to my sick Eva.

Can you help me, my dearest Teresa?

Yours, Terrence

CHAPTER 7
Profile

Daniel sat silently for a beat or two. "Manslaughter?"

"Could've been worse," Leo continued. "Am I telling you something you don't know?"

"Tino killed someone?" Daniel asked.

"That's right. Pretty heavy stuff," Leo said.

"Tino told us about being in prison, but he never spent much time saying why, just that it was due to drugs. Mostly talked how he later cleaned up, found Jesus, then my mom."

"Your mom is a fine lady," Leo said looking Daniel in the eye somewhat unsteadily, drunk as he was. "She probably had her limits. Everyone does, *m'ijo*. She got mad just meeting me!" Leo laughed. He poured another whisky. "Imagine if your daddy would've told her all of it."

Virginia sat next to Daniel silently. These revelations were more than she'd wanted. But they were about someone named Tino, not her Saturnino. She needed to keep her real father in a separate, untouchable realm. This other man, Tino, he wasn't her concern. He hadn't molested her, beat her, called her a liar to her face.

Daniel looked stricken. He rubbed his face, stroked his chin, squirmed in his seat. He too poured another glass of whisky. The two men seemed immune to alcohol. Leo lit a cigarette. The smell of the whisky and cigarettes was nauseating. "So, tell us," Daniel finally said. "What did Tino do?"

"It was a war, *m'ijo*. Just like the wars me and you fought in. Least he didn't kill any civvies. He shot someone trying to rip him off. That's a death sentence in the drug business. Tino's boss wasn't going to let him off the hook, 'specially him letting some punk get the drop on him."

"What happened?"

"Some stupid sumbitch, probably wouldn't have lived much longer as big a *pendejo* as he was, owed for *chiva*, a small-time dealer. I didn't know him. A youngster, more balls than brains."

"Who though?"

"Some dumbass kid. Young, though. Tino went to collect. In those days, your daddy was scary. Probably got rough with him. The kid fought back, pulled a knife, cut Tino on his face and ran off. Tino was probably dusted to the gills. You gotta be to do muscle work like that. So, he shot the motherfucker. 'Scuse my language, *m'ija*," he said turning to Virginia, who looked as if she were somewhere far away. "Your old man was doing everything back then. Heroin, coke, whatever it took."

"How'd he duck a murder charge?"

"That five-inch gash on his face, plus the kid had a rap sheet. He was no goddamn angel. He'd done a couple of stretches for dealing and assault, from what I remember. Still, though, a dime is hard time. Your old man had a couple of cousins with him. Saved him a couple of times. Look, you don't spend ten in *la pinta* and come out straight. You ain't never the same again. You can smell the death on them. Ruined for good, you know?"

"No," Daniel said pointedly. "That doesn't sound like Tino."

"Afraid of everything. Crushed and ground up. No future, no hope, no nothing 'cept living like a ghost. Maybe you move in with your *mamá* if you're lucky, drink yourself into an early grave. Your daddy was one of the lucky ones. I never did put nothing into the church thing, but I guess Tino found him some real Jesus, eh?"

Daniel said nothing.

"I'm really tired," Virginia said suddenly. "We should go, Daniel."

"Where y'all going?" Leo said. "You don't have to spend money on a motel. You can stay right here. I got two bedrooms. I even got pretty clean sheets. It's late. Why you want to go driving around these streets this time of night?"

Daniel looked at Virginia. She nodded slightly.

"Sure," Daniel said. "That'll work."

Virginia readied herself for bed. The room looked like it hadn't been used in years. There was dust on everything and the room smelled of mothballs, but the bed was comfortable and clean enough. There was a picture of Leo and a woman who must have been his wife. She was holding a child in her arms. Leo was smiling. She and the baby were not. Perhaps it was the heat, since the picture had been taken outdoors somewhere. There were plenty of trees, a pecan grove, but the grass was brown and dead. She wondered if Leo had hung the picture there because he couldn't bear to look at it, but also couldn't bear to store it unseen.

His drunken conversation, often rambling, nevertheless had an underlying philosophy that was cogent. Don't look back. It doesn't do anybody any good, he insisted in his kind way. Kind enough, except that underneath his presentation there was a deep well of sadness and regret. It was solemn and tragic. And all the tragedy and solemnity were written on his sad, wrinkled face, like the old, faded mono-hued prison tattoos covering his arms with the names of his wife and kids.

Well, maybe that was the way one had to survive in prison, Virginia thought. She gazed at her face and body in the mirror that hung on the wall. There was a rice-sized creature embedded in her uterus. Did that grain of rice have a future? Did *she* have a future? How could one imagine a future if one was unable or unwilling to consider the past?

She knew all too well where she'd been, and she didn't want to forget any of it. A man named Saturnino was a previously unknown part of her past and represented her hope for the future. And now, that future may have been corrupted and ruined.

As she gazed at the mirror, she contemplated what it would mean to keep that grain of rice just where it was. Dressed for bed, she laid down in the dark and tried to connect to the creature. Was there already a bond? If there was, she felt as if she had to let it know that it was safe, that it had nothing to fear. But she couldn't do that yet.

Sometime later, Virginia woke up. She didn't know exactly what had made her stir. She lay in the bed, the A/C window unit humming so loudly it drowned out everything else. Something had awakened her. She got up and crept to the door, opening it as quietly as she could. Out in the hall, as her eyes adjusted to the dark, she saw the dull-yellow L-strip of light coming from behind the bathroom door. It wasn't closed all the way. Daniel's bedroom door was open, so he wasn't in bed. She wondered if he was still drinking or taking one of his pills. She'd only been with him a day but knew he popped pills constantly.

There was a flickering of shadow moving to and fro behind the door. She grew apprehensive and half-whispered, "Daniel, are you okay?"

There was no chance of her words being heard above the steady, soothing clamor of the window A/C units. She tiptoed to the door of the bathroom, intending to knock or call out. Instead, she peered through the opening. Daniel was sitting on the toilet, fully clothed, his head thrown back, eyes closed but aimed at the ceiling. He was shaking. At first somewhat mildly, his hands on his knees, knees jittering, elbows swaying. And then a more violent shake, his hands now off his knees, shivering violently, knees bouncing, his bare feet jumping off the floor. Now his shoulders shuddered so hard, his head vibrated as if he was operating a jackhammer. Daniel kept his eyes shut, his face maintaining a ninety-degree angle pointed to the ceiling. For all the shaking, he didn't utter a sound except for his breathing, which throbbed along with his trembling body. She thought that he was having some kind of seizure, but he hadn't fallen and didn't seem in danger of falling. It was as if he were in the midst of some kind of religious hysteria, as if he might start speaking in tongues the way the people at her cousin's church did when the loud music and thundering hellfire sermon hit the mark.

She knew she was intruding, spying even. This was something Daniel wouldn't want witnessed, yet she couldn't look away. It was shocking, frightening. The manic energy was hypnotic and terrible at once, as if Daniel was trying desperately to shake something loose, not from his body, but from inside his body, as if something inside him had taken over, was throttling him from somewhere so deep, so closeted, that it meant to rip him apart. It meant to vomit itself from deep within, no matter what Daniel did to repress it. Was this unfettered seizing, this private shaking, the only reprieve Daniel would allow his tormented inner self?

She looked on, lost in trepidation, and then, it stopped, suddenly, without warning. Daniel was still and his eyes were open. He was looking back at her through the crack in the door. Virginia stepped back suddenly, embarrassed, frightened and, closing her robe protectively, retreated quickly to her bedroom. She lay there, eyes open, staring at the dark ceiling until the bathroom light was turned off. She heard Daniel walk back to his bedroom and quietly close his door. The next morning, each pretended that nothing had happened, that nothing had been witnessed or endured.

As they set to leave Leo's house, the old man, now more familiar in Virginia's eyes, almost the shadow of her dead real father, took her by the elbow as he leaned in to say his goodbye. "I'm your *tío*, right? Let me give you some advice. I don't know a lot of things they teach in school. I know everything from hard knocks, the streets. So, here's one of the things I've learned the hard way, *m'ija*. You don't go asking questions you don't want the answers to. All this," he waved his swollen right hand in a circle, "isn't going to give you any real answers."

"Why is that?" she asked him.

"Because, *m'ija*, there ain't no real answers to anything that men do. They might think they know, might even convince the ones around them that they know. But they don't. No sir."

~~~

Daniel and Virginia were sitting at a Denny's outside Houston. They had said their goodbyes to Leo, promising to visit again. Virginia hated Denny's, where she had waitressed for a summer and learned food work wasn't for her. Griping managers with grabby hands had wanted to fuck her and they gave her shit schedules when she didn't accept their offers.

It was Memorial Day, when Denny's offered vets free meals. Daniel never celebrated Memorial Day or Veterans Day, but free food was free food. There was a table next to them with Airmen, who from the looks of them had just gotten out of boot camp. They were joshing around, giving the server a gaggle of leers. She was cool, though. She knew how to handle herself, and they wound up leaving her a twenty, a sizable tip for Denny's.

As the Airmen ambled out, Virginia couldn't resist delving into Daniel's war experience. "Why'd you join up?"

He had not mentioned his service until their conversation with Leo. "That's out of nowhere."

"It is Veteran's Day, and you're having a Moons Over My Hammy on the house. You and Leo seemed to bond over your service. Why did you go over there?"

"Over where?"

"The war," she said. "Iraq or Afghanistan . . . wherever."

"Long, long, boring story," he said, making a show of looking for the server. "Tea?" he mouthed when he got her attention.

Virginia kept her eyes on him. His aversion to speaking about his service made her all the more curious. More than that, she'd come to realize how important it was.

"I got my degree in English and Drama," he said smiling. "I like acting. It's why my sis won't let me alone about her stupid church production. Caught some shit for it on campus. My pals were all business majors, finance, engineering. They were going to make big dough, marry the blonde, big house, all that stuff. Me, not so much. They called me 'Danny College' in the Sandbox."

Virginia wrinkled her nose, took a sip of the empty glass sitting in front of her. "Yeah, but why did you join? Didn't you know they'd send you there?"

"That was the plan," he said, this time waving his hand at the server. "Can I get a refill to go? One for the lady, too. Check, also. Thanks." He smiled kindly.

"Oh, it's like that. Okay, I respect your silence. None of my business, right?"

Daniel kept his unassuming smile but looked away. "Not anything like that," he said. "Just boring stuff. The usual bullshit. Why does anyone join up? They either don't have other options or they want to prove something to themselves or someone else. That's it."

"How long were you there?"

Daniel took the check from the server. "Too long. Not long enough. One of these days if I'm drunk enough, I'll tell you about it."

Virginia left it at that.

~~~

Alena was tired of worrying about everyone and everything. She worried about her mother, about her brother, about her husband, her daughter. She worried about getting fat, that her life was passing her by. She worried that her friends and family would not like the Easter play.

Lately, she had taken to worrying that she was pregnant. It mattered not that she was on the pill. In the middle of the night, the idea would come to her, like a whisper: "You are pregnant again." She would get up and pray that she wasn't pregnant. Did she want to stay with Richard? How long had she been fooling herself?

She considered Daniel. Sad as his predicament was, he was better off than she. At least he was facing the truth head-on. She was tired of worrying. What would happen if she left Richard? She only had Tonia. That wasn't too much to ask another man to take on. She was still attractive, young. If only she could lose those fifteen pounds and start paying a little more attention to herself. The mirror didn't lie: she could see crow's feet, the smile lines, the spider veins in her thighs. She was twenty-eight. Too soon she'd be thirty and, if she didn't act quickly, she'd get pregnant again and then she'd be stuck. Life seemed easier if you didn't have a conscience.

Take "Plenty of Fish." It had only taken her mother a few weeks to meet someone she liked. She went through Teresa's profile and surveyed the men writing to her, flirting, asking if she'd like to meet them for dancing or a movie, for a romantic dinner, a nice walk in the park and some ice cream. They flattered her and told her she was beautiful, how she had lovely eyes, lovely skin, lovely dark hair. And her mother was old. She dyed her hair and wore clothes that were too young for her.

Alena was a younger version of Teresa, at least as far as looks were concerned. People always told her that she looked just like her mother when she was young. Now, in terms of personality, Alena wasn't silly or capricious, which her mother certainly was. She didn't flirt or bat her eyes. Alena wasn't good at making the man she was with feel like a million bucks. She didn't use flattery or cajolery or a little-girl pout to get what she wanted. Alena had two expressive modes: direct or quietly disapproving. That was her way. But maybe she could be more like her mother. More carefree, more confident in her feminine wiles. Maybe she could even recover some of the joy of living that had been bled from her in the recent years.

Alena stopped waiting for something to happen and put her picture up on "Plenty of Fish." She'd had the picture ready for a while. It was the one she'd cropped Richard out of, the one where she was at the beach, before Tonia. She made up a name, Filomena Descarre, and a fake profile that fit the kind of woman she might have been if she'd made different choices.

Filomena had roots in Peru, the daughter of an engineer who had to flee Lima due to the revolution. He'd come to the US with nothing but his powerful mind, his utter sincerity and fiery drive. He met Josefina, his wife, at the Saturday market in San Antonio, and it was love at first sight. Filomena was born a year later, but poor Josefina died from complications of childbirth.

Filomena was an artist, a dancer, and she had traveled far and wide, even attending an art institute in Mexico City for two years. She had no husband, no children. She was all spirit and grace. Filomena was everything Alena was not. She was brave, free, creative, unafraid to take chances. She said what she wanted, loved as she willed. As Alena wrote her profile, she started to feel almost drunk, like she was swimming in a cool lake, the weight of her body melting away.

Maybe it wasn't real. Maybe it was just a version of *Rubia*. But so what? Maybe on "Plenty of Fish" she could find an escape. That was it: pure escape, like a long daydream during a nice, warm bath. And if something should happen, well, *nothing would happen,* but if something *should* happen, well, she didn't know exactly what.

It was three in the morning when she was sure everyone was sound asleep. She went to the computer and found seven invitations. Seven. That was even better than her mother had done! She was sure it was way better than Elvira, who was a sweet girl but not much to look at. So how many fish could she catch? Twenty? Fifty? One hundred? How many fish equaled self-confidence, feeling sexy, feeling desired?

Giorgio was Italian. He was writing from Italy, or so he said. He had curly dark hair and sensual lips. His smile was a little on the wicked side, but he seemed to have a kind of open sweetness to him. No perverse suggestions or over-the-top flirtations. He worked at a bank in Sicily. Alena looked up Sicily. It was an island. She'd vaguely remembered that. It had a beautiful opera house. He wrote to her about it. His English was good, and she asked him about it.

"I don't think I would speak well if you were here. I would be too nervous to talk to you."

This made Alena smile, because it was a long time since anyone had been concerned with impressing her. He asked her about her dancing.

"I choreograph and perform modern dance." It was a bit of a stretch, but only a bit.

Giorgio wrote, "Send me a picture of you dancing."

She searched through the digital photos of dances she'd performed through the years and found one taken before Tonia, where she was still lithe and not at all like a mommy. She cropped it carefully so that it wasn't obvious it had been taken at a small church. She posted it.

He wrote back, "*Bella ragazza.*"

Bella Ragazza!

Of course, he might not be who he was claiming to be. And then a perverse idea crossed her mind. What if this Giorgio was a faker? What if he was really Richard? There was a song about that, something about *piña coladas* and the rain. Alena had an anxiety attack. She could feel her chest contracting, her breathing growing shallow, the fear creeping up her spine. What if this wasn't some innocent game like she was telling herself? What if it were all real? Perhaps in some alternate universe where she was setting things in motion, an alternate existence, but not necessarily a parallel universe? One that it might at some time intersect with her reality? And then what?

Tino used to say, "You can make a decision to do something, but you can't choose what will come of it."

What if Giorgio was just some slob with a forty-pound beer gut, sitting in his mother's basement hoping to get some sex talk out of this thing? Well, Alena considered, she would just have to decide to remain none the wiser. Yes. That was enough for now.

It was the way her mother was playing it. Teresa ignored the fact that all her contacts were losers, including the Illustrated Man, an ex-con, if ever Alena had seen one. He was covered in cheap tattoos that looked like they'd been made in prison with a rusty paper clip in the dark. In his picture he wore nothing but a dirty loincloth. He flexed his stringy muscles, giving the viewer the reverse look, with his skinny butt looking like two peach pits in a rusty-white handkerchief. He stood on a cinder block so that he could flex his calves. He wore his blue bandana to keep his greasy grey hair out of his eyes. He'd written the "pretty lady" to find out what she was "into." Then there was the Lonely Oaf, out of work, recently divorced, trying to figure out what to do now that everything was lost. He was horny but wouldn't admit it directly. He was discouraged, tentative, wimpy. The Smoker wanted everyone to know that he was a troubled loner. He was living in Caldwell on what he called his "ranch." He was interested in nature, horses and perhaps a little sodomy. He recently crossed into stage four emphysema. Teresa, liking macho types, had written him. The Retard was agog in his profile picture, his eyes half-closed, an empty expression for all to see. Alena guessed that his mother, whom he freely admitted he lived with, had probably set the "Plento of Fish" account up for him. He'd written to ask if Teresa would be his "girlfriend." Pathetic.

Then there was the Pervert. What a piece of work. He was twenty years younger than Teresa and he wrote that he enjoyed the company of "mature women." He wanted to suckle her *chichis* and have her powder his hairy *nalgas*. He included pictures of himself with his shirt off, a filthy, deranged smirk on his face. His invitation was followed by the Drunkard's, whose interests included cheap whiskey, partying, having a good time, letting it all "hang loose" and not being tied down. There wasn't a single photo of him in which he didn't appear fall-down drunk, his stupid mouth hanging in idiotic revelry.

Finally, there was the Muscle Head, the one her mother had been carrying on about. He wore a silly leather jacket that said Road Toad on it and sat on an oversized, ostentatious motorcycle. His gang, the Road Toads, was made up of old fogies like him. He was patriotic and had been in the Marines but hadn't gotten over it. The last thing Alena's mother needed was for him to wake up in the middle of the night yelling about the "gooks" and splitting her head open with a lamp.

Looking at her mother's pictures made her feel sick, as if she were trolling the internet like a desperate old woman, like some dissatisfied housewife. She swore she'd get off the site but neglected to erase Filomena's profile. When curiosity got the best of her, she had to check if Giorgio had written back. It was like tuning into *Rubia* to see what was happening to this other woman, this fictional character she'd invented.

Giorgio had written back. And not just him. Apparently, he had some compatriots who were also on the site and were writing her as well. Sergio, Alfredo, Sebastiano, Manolo. They asked her questions no one had ever asked her, like had she been to Italy? They promised to show her Rome and Florence, if she traveled there. They wanted to know why she'd chosen dancing to express herself. They asked about her aspirations.

None of them asked about her family, her unadventurous, boring marriage or her church life. She didn't have to discuss the day-to-day drudgery, the unexciting sex (when there was sex), the clothes-washing, the picking of healthy cereals at the grocery store. There were no arguments about petty finances or how much gas was in the car, whether Tonia had done her homework, when he was going to mow the lawn or why he should put the toilet seat up so as not to get piss sprinkles on it. Not one of them cared about folding clothes, dusting or who would wash the tub.

They wanted to know the mysterious and beautiful dancing Filomena.

"I'm on," she told Elvira.

"On what?"

"Plenty of Fish."

"I thought so."

"Do you think it's wrong," Alena asked her friend.

"Who is it hurting?" Elvira said. "It's just harmless fun."

That was what Alena wanted to hear.

~~~

One of the men who contacted Teresa had big muscles.
Big muscles. He wrote that he was a personal trainer and had
his own gym. He looked young, almost as young as the picture of the African Explorer, only he was her age. She told
Elvira she was afraid to write him back. He had to have all
sorts of younger girls sending him messages. Why would he
choose to send her a wink?

"Oh, please," Elvira said laughing. She was always
laughing. "He's *okay*. But he's not in your league. You're
beautiful."

This guy was a hunk, but she felt like a lump. How was that
for a happy couple, the Hunk and the Lump? She'd been watching her weight since joining "Plenty of Fish." She was walking
every morning now, got up at eight and grabbed the metal water
bottle Daniel had bought her. She'd drive to the track at the high
school and walk for an hour before the heat made it miserable.

Daniel had given her his old CD player on she listened to
her Joyce Meyer tapes. They were very inspiring. She walked
as fast as she could while Joyce told her that she shouldn't
give into stinking thinking, that the devil was at the root of
her low self-esteem. If that was true, then the devil's name
was Henry, her first husband who was always going after any

young girlie that gave him half a smile. Tino hadn't been that way. He was good for her self-esteem. He never looked at other women. It was like the others didn't even exist in his world. Just her, *"Teresa, mi tesoro."* She'd become used to that sort of adulation, and it had caused her to ignore the mirror. But now she was looking at herself without pretense. She saw a flabby old woman with wrinkles and a nice smile. Okay, she had high cheekbones. And her green eyes were still shiny. That was as far as she was willing to go.

A few days ago, she'd gone shopping with Alena and Tonia. It had been a miserable experience. No matter what Teresa picked up, Alena would wrinkle her nose like she was smelling a rotten turnip, her little brow all furrowed with a look somewhere between disbelief and disgust.

"If you're not going to be a good sport, why did you come with me?"

"I have to be honest, Mother. You can't expect me to tell you to buy clothes that even for someone my age would be too young. Wear appropriate clothes and let your natural beauty speak for you."

"Are you Oprah, now? Natural beauty means old, it means wrinkles and drooping *chichis*. My *abuelita* had natural beauty, but for her grandchildren. Not for a lover."

"Mother, not in front of Tonia."

Why didn't Alena understand? Why did she resent her so much?

Then it occurred to Teresa that Alena treated her this way because she was like the mirror in *Snow White* who told the vein queen that she was no longer the fairest of them all. Teresa was her future in living color. Maybe her daughter saw her own future in Teresa's face. Beauty fades. Lines deepen. Teresa was the embodiment of these terrible truths. How depressing!

The next day, Teresa went back to the mall with only Elvira, who was much more fun. The poor girl had no figure.

She was the shape of a cantaloupe, with chubby cheeks that always looked like she'd been out in a cold wind. She didn't have a boyfriend, although she was trying on "Plenty of Fish" without much luck.

The trip to California never materialized. Teresa didn't know if Elvira had been fibbing or if the man who'd offered to fly Elvira out there had seen her real picture. But what she lacked in looks and feminine grace, she made up for in pluck and sense of humor.

Teresa would ask her, "How do you do it, Elvira? How do you stay so happy?"

The girl had no answers, just more of her silly laughing. Perhaps she was a simpleton. No, that was mean. She just had a good spirit. Take Joyce Meyer. Teresa was sure that she got depressed once in a while. Joyce talked about it all the time, but her faith and self-confidence carried her through. Teresa wished she could be more like that. But even more than that, she wanted to be beautiful. And more than that, she wanted a boyfriend.

At the mall, they went back to all the same stores where Alena had insulted Teresa, and she bought most of the clothes Alena had made her put back.

Elvira was a great encouragement. "I wish I could wear clothes like you do. You have such a beautiful figure."

Teresa suspected that Elvira lied, but she decided to believe her nonetheless.

Teresa's favorite purchase was a black dress. It was kind of short, but her legs looked good in it because of all the walking she'd been doing. She'd always had pretty legs. They were clear and tan without any of those ugly blue veins that some women got.

The Body Builder was taking her out dancing that weekend. She told him a little fib that she was on the A-team at church and that she was a terrific dancer. Of course, she'd never been dancing at filthy bars or nightclubs. Tino had tried to get her out on the dance floor at her cousin's wedding, but she didn't even let him pull her out of her chair. Teresa had been raised to see dancing as a sin. Everything was a sin, everything pleasurable, anything to do with the body, evil, sinful. It led to spiritual death. Now, she looked back and thought, for what? Now, she was old and she wanted to be young again so that she could do the things she'd never done. Perhaps undo the things she'd done. What was the saying? Where there was life, there was hope. She wasn't dead yet. Now the past was dead, just like her poor Tino.

The Body Builder sure seemed like he wanted to have fun, and she was going to play her role. If she played the role convincingly enough, who knew, maybe she'd be able to get some of it back, some of the lost time.

Teresa hadn't let anyone but Elvira see her Body Builder. Daniel would worry. He'd warn her that the Body Builder wanted to steal from her or that he was a rapist or serial killer. That he was married. Okay, maybe Daniel had been right about the African Explorer. But that didn't mean he was right about everything.

She decided she wasn't going to show Alena the Body Builder's picture. Her head would explode. And Teresa wasn't going to make any of her pained positive/negative lists concerning the Body Builder. She was going to try to play it by ear from now on. This carefree attitude was part of the new Teresa.

They met at the coffee shop in the bookstore, where she'd met Son of Sam. She got there first and browsed the bookshelves instead of sitting. She didn't want him getting the idea that she was too eager. Besides, she wanted to get a good look at him before he got a look at her.

He came in wearing a leather jacket with some sort of military emblem on it, an angry eagle festooning the back.

He was handsome, just like his pictures showed. He wore a long mullet and carried a large manila envelope.

Teresa was nervous and thought about walking out. But Joyce Meyer would be disappointed, so she sucked in her breath and approached the table.

The Body Builder smiled and asked, "Terry?"

It confused her, being addressed as Terry. It was the name she used on her profile, but she had yet to hear it out loud. It made her feel giddy and new.

"Eric?"

"In the flesh, finally. Sit down, sit down. It's a pleasure. You're a heap prettier than your picture, if you don't mind me saying. And I'm not saying your picture isn't pretty, only that you're a beautiful woman."

He pulled the chair out for her. She smiled from a place she hadn't smiled in a long time.

He was a serious man, not much laughing, although he smiled enough, but a half-smile, a soft bending of the lips. He looked her in the eye, never dropped his gaze. Only somewhat rapid blinking gave away that he was a bit nervous.

"What do you have in the envelope?"

"Some pictures of my motorcycle gang, the Road Toads. We ride every weekend, mostly around the Hill Country or out to Canyon Lake. This one here," he said pointing at a man wearing big goggles and a leather vest with a big frog painted on the front, "is Big George Cray. He's got a hitch on his cycle and he pulls our grub. We get to one of the big parks and grill out, listen to some good music and then head back. No drinking. We ride safe."

Teresa wasn't quite sure what he was talking about but smiled just the same.

"You ought to come out with us next weekend. I think you'd like it. You could meet some of the gals that come along."

"That sounds fun," Teresa said. She had never been on a motorcycle. She'd never even considered it.

"The gals are called the Toadettes."

"Do you have one of those vests, too?"

"I mostly wear this jacket. My boots say Road Toads on them, though. That's good enough. On occasion, I'll wear the official gear, but it's got to be a big deal like the Texas Bluegrass Festival. Otherwise, I'm proud to let 'em know there's a veteran rolling with the Toads. Vietnam."

"You were a soldier in the war? You seem too young."

"I was young, all right. Too young to know better. I volunteered mostly so I could get out of Waupaca, Wisconsin. Pretty country, lakes as far as you can see, but there was more lakes than people. The Marines was my ticket out. Of course, the war came with it."

The conversation was lively and interesting. Most of all, it was entertaining. It wasn't long before he suggested a big steak at a place he knew. They left for a truck stop close to where he lived. Teresa enjoyed the food. More than that, she enjoyed Eric's company. She felt positively elated.

~~~

Alena couldn't believe that her mother was considering riding on the back of a motorcycle. "You threw a fit when Tino mentioned a motorcycle. Those things are dangerous. And what's this about a Vietnam veteran? They can be wackos."

Although Teresa had her own misgivings, hated motorcycles and thought that Road Hogs or Road Toads were stupid, nothing was going to keep her from being behind hunky Eric that weekend.

"He calls me Terry. I want you to call me Terry, too," she told Alena, who stared at her mother as if she had been replaced by a body snatching pod.

CHAPTER 8
Standard Beatdown

Daniel wanted to walk the neighborhood. Leo had given them the address and name of Tino's crime partner, a small-timer who'd run the streets with their father back in the day. They walked for blocks, feeling conspicuous. Daniel wasn't afraid. He'd walked blighted, dangerous blocks by the thousands in Iraq. It was the sense that he and she did not belong, despite speaking Spanish and wearing the right skin shade. It was as if they were visiting the homeland of their ancestors, places and sights remembered only through the memory of their parents and grandparents.

"This place is rough," Daniel said, looking up and down the street where Raúl Azarola had once, and might still, live. For April, it was already getting hot in Houston and, this close to the port, the air was miserably humid. The neighborhood was quiet, riddled with pot-holed streets and cracked asphalt. There were no sidewalks, and numerous railroad tracks cut through the streets. The small houses were imprisoned behind chain-linked fences, patrolled and guarded by fierce mutts.

"Maybe we shouldn't be here," Virginia said.

"Nah. These dogs are sweethearts. They wouldn't make it a day in the Sandbox. Iraqi dogs are for real vicious. These little fellas only want to get into your ass. They don't want to actually eat you."

After a few blocks of depressed houses and vacant streets, they happened on a game of football. Brown kids, adolescents, clowning around with each other in Spanglish. "You suck, *puto* face. Your *pinche abuela* coulda caught that."

Daniel and Virginia watched for a minute or two until there was a lull in the game.

"Any of you know a dude named Raúl Azarola?" he asked.

Most of the kids looked on vacantly, although one of the boys, the leader, sized up the couple curiously.

"You mean, old man Rolly?" He was wiry thin but athletic, a good-looking kid with self-confidence not yet blunted.

"Could be," Daniel said.

"He's down the block in that green house with the broke Chevy out front. He's mean, man," he said. "Old *vato*. . . . Every day he comes out to water his *matas* and poke his nose in everybody's business. My *abuelo* had a beef with him a few months back. They did a lot of yelling over that fence about Naco, my *abuelo's* dog."

"Yeah?" said Daniel. "What Naco do?"

Two of the other boys joined the group.

"Naco gets loose . . . wants some poonie, you know?"

Daniel nodded. "Yeah, dogs in heat, what can you do? That green house over there?" he said pointing.

"Yeah," the leader said.

"You a baller?" Daniel asked him.

"Andrés is gonna be a pro," one of the other boys said.

"Let's see what you can do," Daniel said.

The boy who'd asserted Naco's supremacy took off loping down the street. Andrés gave him a few seconds to run thirty yards and uncorked a clean, arcing spiral. The boy caught it on the run.

"Nice," Daniel said. "Gonna catch you on ESPN one of these days, homie."

Andrés smiled at the compliment. "Fo sho. Watch out for Rolly, though."

"*Ahi te watcho*," Daniel said, nodding his head, and gave Virginia a let's go gesture.

The two headed for Old Man Rolly's house.

"That was pretty good," Virginia said appreciatively. "I thought those kids were going to ask you to join in the game."

"Played a lot of touch football in the Sandbox," Daniel said, smiling. "Kids not much older than that boy."

"Why'd you ask him to throw the ball?" Virginia asked.

"Don't know," Daniel said, eyes trained on the green house. "The kid reminded me of someone."

"You?"

"Hah," Daniel said with a tight smile. "Not me. A buddy. He's dead now."

"I'm sorry," Virginia said.

"Me too," Daniel replied as the two stopped in front of the green house.

The fencing was newish, still shiny, not rusted brown like most of the other fences. The yard was neat, the cement porch crowded with large potted plants, smaller flowering ones hanging low above them. There was an old pecan tree that was tended well. The front door was wrought iron with a rectangular pattern. The gate to the house was padlocked. The windows were secured behind old painted iron bars.

"Looks like the joint," Daniel said.

"How are we going to knock on his door if we can't get into the yard?" Virginia asked.

"I thought you were from the hood," Daniel said. "Old school, Virginia."

He put two fingers to his mouth and made the loudest whistle Virginia had ever heard. "*¡Señor Azarola!*" he yelled in as friendly and respectful a manner as he could muster. "*¡Señor Azarola! ¿Podemos hablar con usted?*"

After a few moments, they saw a curtain move. And few moments after that, the door cracked open and an old man with a headful of white hair looked out.

Unsmiling, he asked, "*¿Quién es?*"

"*¿Tiene unos momentos para hablar de Tino Fuentes?*"

The old man scrunched his face, squinting his eyes in an attempt to focus on the faces standing at his front gate.

"Tino Fuentes?"

Virginia spoke up. "*Sí. ¡Mi papá!*"

The old man stepped out on the porch. "Tino Fuentes?"

"*Si tiene unos momentos . . .*" Daniel answered.

"The gate's not locked," the old man said.

Daniel looked down at the padlock and saw that it was unfastened. He pulled the lock out of the gate's u-hinge.

"*Gracias,*" Daniel said entering the yard with Virginia at his side.

They walked to the steps leading to the porch and stood waiting. Virginia imagined that they looked like Jehovah Witnesses visiting the unsaved.

The old man pulled a cigarette from a pack lying next to the window by the door. There was a large aluminum coffee tin serving as an ashtray. It was full of yellowed butts. The old man took a deep, long drag, expelling the smoke with a vicious cough. He pulled a red bandana from his back pocket and wiped his mouth, taking a second to look at the sputum.

"You kin of Tino's?" he asked with interest. "I haven't heard that name in a long time."

"Yessir," Daniel said respectfully. "I'm his stepson. This here is his daughter, Virginia."

Still unsmiling, the old man looked at Virginia carefully. "You look like 'im," he said. "I ain't heard that name in a long time." He took another drag, coughed again, wiped his mouth clean again, a lingering look at the sputum this time. "Who told you where to find me?"

"Leo, his brother," Virginia offered. "He told us you two were good friends when you were young." She smiled.

"Tino must be dead," the old man said.

"Yes," Daniel answered. He made a show of looking at the dozens of potted plants. "You have a lot of nice plants. If Leo would've told us you were a gardener, it would have made it a lot easier to find your house."

"I ain't a gardener," he said flatly. "*Mi jefa*, she was the gardener. I just look after them. All they need is a little water. Make sure the goddamned bugs don't eat them. No big deal."

He pulled another cigarette free, lit it. This time he didn't cough. "Sit down," he said, gesturing at an old beat-up yellow aluminum porch swing.

"So Tino's dead," he said in the same flat voice. "Everyone is dying."

"It happens," Daniel said in the same tone.

"Me, too," Azarola said.

He sat on a solid oakwood garden chair. "Cancer," he said blankly. "You want some water?" he asked Virginia.

"I'm okay. I don't want to trouble you."

The old man looked on, still unsmiling, his face not as unapproachable, but still reserved. He looked off to the side as he placed the fresh cigarette butt in the coffee can.

"What do you want to know about Tino?"

"Anything," Virginia said interrupting Daniel, who had thought to say something about prison. "I never knew him. I was raised by another man. A bad man, but I always hoped I'd meet Saturnino, that is, get to know him. I met him once, but I was a kid and didn't know he was my real father."

"Good, bad, worth knowing," he said lighting the final cigarette. He crushed the empty pack and placed it in the coffee can. "It all depends on who's telling the story. Sounds like your stepfather probably hurt you. Sounds like a sonofabitch. But others might have thought he was all right. Like I said, it depends on who's telling the story.

"The Tino I knew back in the day, everybody liked him. His old man used to kick his ass all the time, but he didn't let it make him mean, at least at first. He hung around us older *vatos*. Leo would bring him along, you know, doing stupid shit. Leo was a cold *vato*. Not Tino, though. Actually, he was too soft for the game. At least at first. I always thought Leo shouldn't be bringing him around. But you know, it wasn't my business. Until it was."

"What business?" Daniel asked. The old man looked at him detachedly. "Street business," he said coldly. "I think Tino was about fourteen or fifteen when Leo brought him around the first time. He was a talker. He was funny. Next time I saw him, he had a busted face. His old man. It was like that with him. Always some new bruise, a black eye, scratched up neck or arms. I felt bad for the kid. Like I said, I was older than him, like ten years. Finally, I told him right in front of Leo, 'You two ought to kick your old man's ass before he kills you.' Leo didn't like that, being told how to handle his pops or how to protect his *'manito*. But you know, I tell it like it is. Always have."

At this, Azarola felt around his pockets for a fresh pack of cigarettes. "I'm gonna get some more smokes. You sure you don't want any water?" he asked Virginia, as he entered his house.

"Okay," Virginia said. "If it's no trouble."

The old man made his way in.

"He doesn't want to talk about drugs or that kind of stuff," Virginia said to Daniel. "Don't bring it up unless he does."

"Old *cabrón*," Daniel said, "he knows what happened with Tino because he had a hand in it happening."

"I don't care about that," Virginia said as Azarola came back out.

He had a glass of water in one hand and an unopened pack of cigarettes in the other. He handed the glass to Virginia, sat back down, expertly opened the pack and drew out another cigarette.

"I don't know what Leo told you about me. I wasn't no angel. But I liked Tino. I felt bad for him. Leo was too fucked up to do any good for him. Tino needed money, so I gave him some jobs. Nothing serious. A delivery boy. Things didn't get heavy until I helped him stomp his old man one night. I'd driven down to pick him up to do some partying on a Saturday night. His old man was drunk, giving him shit outside the door. He didn't want him leaving, I guess. I never asked. All I remember is his *jefe* cranking back and giving him a punch to the face, hard enough it dropped Tino. Blap. Right in the mouth so square I felt it. I seen a lot of shit back in the day, but I never saw a pops hit his kid that hard before. Tino came up spitting blood and a tooth or two.

"I came out my car, saying whatever . . . I don't remember. The old man tried to talk smack, and I hopped the fence, and the *chingazos* started. The old man was too drunk to lay a finger on me, but before I knew it, Tino is in on it. He's kickin' the shit out of his pops. Me too. We went beyond, you know? The old man had pissed his pants by the time we done stompin' him. Far as I remember, that was the last time Tino ever went back home. Even when the old man died, Tino didn't want nothin' to do with it.

"I let him stay with me a while. Gave him some more work. Heavier stuff. He turned out to be my best man. *Firme*, you know what that means, right? A slugger. Didn't take shit no more from no one. He always delivered, never complained, never bragged. Just did what needed to be done. To me, that was a good dude. *¿Saben?*"

"How could he have been a slugger only sixteen years old?" Daniel said, his voice beginning to charge.

"I've known younger hard as stones. It is what it is. You be surprised, *a lo mejor*, what a person no matter what age can and will do when they got to."

The old man's face stayed in place, somber, detached as if barely aware that Virginia and Daniel were there. He took a deep drag of the cigarette and stubbed it out carefully in the coffee can so as not to drop ash on the porch. He liked starting cigarettes more than finishing them, Daniel noticed.

Virginia moved her arm over to Daniel's, slightly squeezing his wrist. Daniel knew she wanted him to stay calm. He knew that he needed to, so that both he and Virginia might understand. But it was hard with a bastard like this. He knew that what the old man said was true, that pushed, starved, scared, desperate people were capable of terrible things. He also had seen some pushed to heroic strength, physical or emotional, that they didn't know was inside them. After all, he'd been pushed. He was a killer of women and children. Why did he expect that Tino had somehow risen above the standard of cruelty and evil? Why did he want that so desperately to be the case?

"You do me a favor?" the old man asked Virginia. "If you don't mind, grab me some water. I get a little tired around this time."

Virginia stood up and nodded. "Sure. Daniel, you want some water too?"

Daniel shook his head.

The old man looked at Daniel, turning his gaze to his right forearm. "You Army?"

Daniel nodded. "You?"

"Navy . . . during Nam. Two years. I tell you, there's a lot of people out there that can rightly call me a bastard, but ain't no one can say I wasn't a good sailor. That's the thing about us Mexicans. . . . When duty calls, its balls to the walls. Call you a Mexican to take the fall. And we did. None of that mattered coming back stateside. We were still *pinches mojados* to the *bolillos*. You can't wear your uniform everywhere you go, *¿sabes?* I came back thinking I'd get a fair shake, but I was stupid to think that. I shoulda known. But that's the last time I got fooled."

"That right?" Daniel said.

"Goddamn right," the old man said.

Daniel turned to watch Virginia walk out of the house, water glass in hand.

Virginia took her seat on the swing next to Daniel. Daniel seemed totally disengaged, almost as if he was lost in a daydream. He didn't take a look at her as she sat down.

"Señor Azarola, thank you for talking with us . . . for your hospitality." And then turning to her left to acknowledge the greenery, "I love your plants. How many different ones are there?"

"More than fifty types," he said, his voice registering a note of pride. "Yeah, my wife, Hilda, she had a green thumb. Her father was a gardener. Taught her a lot. She passed it on to our daughter, Brenda."

"Looks like she passed it on to you, too," Virginia said approvingly.

"You could say that," Azarola said, nodding slightly in appreciation. "She got sick, so I'd bring her out, and she'd sit on the porch watching me water the plants. More than watching. Ordering. She kept it up to the end. I kept them up for her. She didn't ask me to promise, but I told her I'd keep them for her. I been mindin' 'em more than ten years now. I lost a couple right after she died, like they knew. But after that, none. I kept them alive. Healthy too. Like I said, it depends on who's saying what when it comes to bein' good or bad. My plants, they don't have any complaints."

"I can see that," Virginia said. "You said your daughter gardens, too?"

"She don't live around here," the old man said. "She moved to Minnesota after her *mamá* died. Got married to a *güero*. She met him in college. He makes a good living doin' computers. He's from there."

"Do you visit?" Virginia asked.

"Too far, too cold."

Virginia could tell that it was a subject Azarola did not want to talk about.

"About Saturnino, I really appreciate you telling us about him. I want to know all I can. It doesn't matter if it's good or bad. Just so I know."

"It don't matter to me," he said, lighting another cigarette. "I got a lotta memories. I don't forget nothin'. Everyone knows that about me. I remember everything." He drew another lungful of smoke and, upon releasing the smoke, coughed deeply and painfully, bringing his fist to his mouth. He took a drink of water. His legs shook to the point of convulsion as the hacking wracked his body. "Everything," his voice strained.

"My uncle said that Saturnino went to jail for killing someone," Virginia said finally. "Was he working for you?"

"Sure," he said after a moment. "He was workin' for me. But that kind of work, you always got to be ready for anythin' to happen, to fuck up, *¿sabes?*"

"No," Virginia said. "I don't know."

"Well, you do or you go down quick. Jail or dead or wish you were dead. Only three choices if you don't pay attention every minute. Truth is, even as ready as you can be, you still go down sooner or later. Lot of it is luck, who dies, who gets sent up, who skates through without major time."

"Are you that one, the one gets through without no major fuckups," Daniel asked.

Azarola kept his eyes on Virginia as he answered. "I wouldn't say that. I got my share of licks."

Virginia ignored the exchange. "How'd Saturnino go from being an abused boy to being, you know?" she asked Azarola.

"A killer? Guess he had it in him all the time, *m'ija*. Some do, some don't. Everyone on the street that does their thing has it in them. Tino took a lot of beatings. That anger don't go away. You just save it up. Some let it eat them, others use it for other things. Like me. Like your father. Probably like your stepfather."

"Tino wasn't like you," Daniel said. "I knew him. He was a good man, took care of my mom and me and my sister. He did everything he could to raise us right and keep food in the house and a roof over our heads. He loved my mom, respected her, too. He spent all his spare time talking to dudes whose lives had been wrecked by men like you. If sixteen-year-old Tino killed someone, it was you who pulled the trigger."

"Could be," the old man said, unmoved, still detached and calm. "But that's somethin' only a kid believes. . . . It's you believin' that someone else is responsible for what you do and what you put out there. I got my peace with what I've done in my life. I ain't never lied to myself about it."

Virginia was growing impatient with Daniel's line of questioning. He seemed determined to put the old man on the defensive. Seeing the conversation about to break off, she tried to bring the old man and Daniel to heed.

"I just want to know," she said as solemnly and kindly as possible. "I'm not here to find blame. I just want to know who the man was, maybe because I'm afraid that who I want him to be will take over and it'll all be a lie. I know the worst he did. I do. At least some of it. He never did come back for me."

Daniel turned towards her, surprised and slightly embarrassed. She was admitting something very private in front of them. He wanted to tell her to stop. It wasn't right that she do this in front of the old criminal who'd manipulated a young, homeless kid into harnessing pain and rage for his crimes.

"Tell me what you remember," she asked. "Please."

The old man stared at her, dragging deeply, exhaling slowly, watching her through the smoke he expelled. "If you want . . . I'm dyin' anyway. Got nobody comin' round these days. I might as well keep talkin'." Looking at Daniel, he said, "She looks just like her daddy. Same expressions even." Training his sight on Virginia again, he said, "Longer I talk to you, the more I remember about your daddy. That's how much you look like him."

He looked her in the eyes a long time and took the almost dreamy voice of reminiscence. "First of all, I don't care if it's yesterday, today or tomorrow, the cops don't change in the barrio. They always ready to throw a beatdown when it's good for them and throw a blind eye when they don't have time for problems. My instructions was keep it low-key. We doin' business. Don't act up unless you have to. But Tino, he had a bad temper on him. Worse than most. There was a long while there, you didn't want to mess with him. He didn't give a fuck. He was lookin' to throw *chingazos* or worse. You beat somebody's ass long enough, bad enough, it's gonna come out, *¿sabes?*

"But this one night, he was more edgy than most. He was doin' a lot of drugs. Pills, coke, H. And you could tell he'd been up a couple of nights, the way he looked. Eyes red as a baboon's ass. He stank from booze and cigarettes. I had this kid who hadn't paid and I needed him rounded up. That's all. Bring him to me, and I'll take care of the discipline."

Virginia became aware that she might not want to hear this. It was going to be ugly, as ugly as the retelling of her rape might have sounded to someone who'd never witnessed the savagery of it. She could sense that Daniel was watching her sideways, taking her measure. Virginia kept her eyes firmly on Azarola's face. Mercifully he'd paused to light another cigarette.

"I was just going to kick his ass some. Standard beatdown, ¿*sabes?*" he said glancing over at Daniel.

In his eyes, Virginia saw a shadow, dark and growing like a vulture taking flight. This troubled her as much as the old man's story.

"But before I know it—I think I'm just turning around for something—just in time to see your crazy daddy hit the kid in the back with a piece of pipe. It put the kid on the ground. Kid's cryin' by then. Probably pissed himself. I don't remember. But Tino looks at me, and he sees that I'm gonna let him handle it now. Then he hits the kid again, this time on his hand, because the kid's holding it up trying to protect his face. Broke fingers. You can hear it.

"Then the kid gets his ass in gear. Being scared for your life gives you a burst. Just starts runnin'. He's hurt, so he's not runnin' real fast. Fast for him, though. I'm telling your daddy, '*Chingao, vato*, go get his ass before he leads pigs back to us.' Tino is not fuckin' around. He isn't about to chase after this punk. He didn't look at me or nothin'. Just pulled out his *quete*, and bang! Hit that kid right in the back. 'Fuck, *vato*,' I said. 'You crazy.' He'd blown his lungs out.

"Anyways, me and your old man run over to the kid. He's not dead yet. Long as I'd been in business, I never seen shit like that. That's sayin' a lot. He was face down, still tryin' to get on a knee, even though he couldn't bring his leg up. Squirming in his own shit, man. Wheezin', coughin' like he's gonna throw up a lung. We were freaked out, I'm not gonna lie. Cops were gonna come. So, I got my pickup and drove up to the kid. Tino was jumpy as hell. Me too. By the time I got to the kid, he was dead. I don't know if he just went or if your daddy played him out. Shut him up, you know?"

Virginia felt numb.

"Like I said, bad, good, good-bad . . . it depends on who's doin' the countin'. What you need at that moment. Only you can know what's in your head. Maybe not even that."

"That's pretty fucked up," Virginia said.

"Very fucked up," Azarola said, lighting yet another cigarette, nodding, a plume of dirty smoke pouring from his mouth and nostrils. "That's what I'm saying. I never knew the Tino that raised you kids, but that wasn't him that night."

"He didn't raise me," Virginia said.

"So why are we talking, then? Because he was still your daddy, right?" Azarola said.

"That's some bullshit there. You let him take the rap? You were there and you let it happen. You could've stopped it," Daniel said.

The old man surveyed Daniel, as if he were recalibrating his first assessment. "Come on, you smarter than that. You don't stop shit that's already rollin'. Things happen fast in life. All you can do is roll with the punches and be smart, at least smarter than the other guy."

"That's what you say to let yourself off the hook," Daniel said.

"That's what I tell myself 'cause it's the truth. You don't stay in business long if you carryin' baggage. Don't be stupid.

You don't like me. So what? Doesn't mean you can't learn somethin'?"

"Let other people take the fall. Forget you're a piece of shit."

"Doesn't change what Tino did. He pulled the trigger, *vato*. So he did the time. He did his time like a man, too. He was good that way. Maybe you're good that way, too. I bet Tino taught you that much."

With that, Azarola stood up, took a moment to survey his yard and its plants, nodded at Virginia, and without another word walked into his house, letting the heavy screen door shut loudly and definitively.

"Is that it?" Virginia asked, looking at Daniel.

"Isn't that enough?" he said, standing up, still staring at the door the old man had disappeared behind.

On the way back to the car, Virginia expected the young men to still be in the street playing football. They were gone. It was growing dark. Neither spoke until they'd gotten into the car.

"I was worried he wasn't going to tell us much," she said as Daniel headed out of the neighborhood.

"It was just what I thought it'd be," he said, "a bunch of bullshit where he comes off like he was just there. An observer. No responsibility for anything."

"Taking responsibility is in short supply," she said finally.

"Got that right. It's different than in the field. There's no do-overs, no hiding when you screw up."

"Why are you so angry?" Virginia asked. "You already knew most of this stuff. Why's it bothering you more than it bothers me?"

"I thought Tino was a standup guy. He was solid, honest. Not a liar. That, I could count on. But all this, you, the killing, him not being honest with my mom. All of it . . . makes me think there's isn't anything true or honest out there."

Virginia considered him in profile as he drove. He seemed on the verge of a breakdown. "Guess we both want some things to be true."

"It's important I know what kind of man Tino was. I want the truth. That's it."

"I'm pregnant," Virginia said suddenly.

Daniel turned towards her as he slowed for a red light.

"I don't know why I'm telling you. But you're the first." He looked over at her.

"I don't think I have anyone else to tell."

Daniel turned his attention back to the road.

∼∼∼

Teresa called to Alena from the room they used as an office. She'd been invited to dinner. Teresa was lonely with Daniel having taken off on his trip.

"Come back here. I've got something I want to show you."

Alena had a crushing headache, but she knew that tone of voice. Her mother was excited about something and wasn't going to be held off. She walked back to the office, chewing two Tylenols as she made her way across the threshold.

Teresa was on the computer, "Plenty of Fish" on the screen. "I've got a couple of things I want your advice on. Now, sit down. No, not on the bed, over here next to me so you can see the computer. Now, this one is Eric. I've seen him three times. Three. And each has been better than the last. He's too good-looking for me, isn't he? Tell me the truth."

"He's okay," Alena said without conviction. "He looks like a muscle-head. He's probably 'roided up to the gills."

"Roided?"

"Steroids. He's too old to have muscles like that."

"What do I care about his hemorrhoids? *¿A mí qué me importa?* All I care about is that he's a good man. That, and that I'm not too old for him. So, what do you think? Give me your real opinion."

"Ugh," Alena said feeling desperate, "I'm giving you my real opinion. I'm telling you, this guy isn't even in your league." She made a move to leave.

"No, no. Just listen to this." Teresa put a cassette in the small boombox that she'd had for twenty years. "I made a tape of me and Eric on our date the other night. It's only about twenty minutes long. Listen to what a good time we're having!"

"Mother, there's no way I can listen to twenty minutes of the two of you goofing around on a date right now. My head's killing me."

"*Qué* goofing? No one is goofing. It was on the car ride back from the restaurant. We were singing songs and joking around. He doesn't seem very funny at first, but when he loosens up, he's very funny. Just listen for a minute, okay?"

Teresa looked at Alena with her most pleading smile. It was full of weird hope. Alena rubbed her face tiredly. The headache was threatening to turn into a full-blown migraine. Teresa patted the top of Alena's head as she sat down on the floor next to her. Teresa's scalp massages were soothing.

Teresa hit the play button, and a badly warbled version of some ancient Everly Brothers tune began to play. It went on and on as the two singers broke in and out of tune, forgetting words, making them up as they went along, peppering the gleeful but bad singing with adolescent peals of laughter from her mother and bark-like guffaws from the muscle-head. Alena opened her eyes to see her mother smiling, reliving the moment, waiting for her to smile as she recognized what Teresa wanted her to recognize. That she was in love.

"Don't we sound like we're having a ball? Huh? Can you hear how we're getting along? Can you, *m'ija?*"

She nodded her head and closed her eyes again.

"Just a few more minutes. It's getting to the part that I have a question about. Hold on, hold on," she said messing with the buttons of the boombox, fast-forwarding the hell out of the tape, the laughter racing back and forth through the speakers like a screaming lunatic duet. "I've been listening to this all day. Okay, okay, here's the part. Listen carefully."

"Yeah, I love camping," the muscle-head was saying. "I go all the time. Growing up in Wisconsin, you learn to love the outdoors. It's the only place I can relax anymore. Me and my ex used to go camping all the time."

Teresa clicked the recorder off. "Right there," she said. "Right there. What do you think?"

"About what? That he likes camping? Camping is horrible. The last person in the world I can imagine camping is you. You'd hate it. You have a heart attack every time if you see a bug in the bathroom. Imagine a snake? He wouldn't be able to get you out of the tree you'd jump onto."

"No, not the camping. The 'ex.' Why is he bringing her up? No one mentioned his 'ex.' Maybe he's still in love with his ex-wife. Maybe he's just using me as a rebound."

"I'm sure it's no big deal. Haven't you brought up Tino or Dad?"

"No. I don't want to spoil the mood when we're together. Anyway, why would I want to bring up the past? Married once is bad enough. But twice? It will get him to wondering just how old I am. I want to concentrate on the future."

"Fine, I guess" Alena said. "Enjoy the ride and see where it takes you."

Her mother nodded her head with a big smile. "Thanks for listening to my tape. It makes me feel better."

Teresa was finally moving out of the darkness of Tino's death, and here Alena was dampening her mother's spirits. But she couldn't help it. It was jealousy, a mind bending, petty, silly, unbecoming jealousy.

She sat rubbing her temples, the throbbing emanating from her right eye socket so that she squinted on one side like Popeye. The phone rang. It was Richard picking up a second shift. Some second shift, Alena thought. Probably going to hang out with his drunkard buddies for a Spurs game. It was a relief, actually.

~~~

Alena was right. Teresa hated camping, but she went along because she didn't want Eric to get the impression that she was an old lady who didn't like a little fun or a risk from time to time.

She prized the look she saw on Alena's face when she told her the next day that she was going on a motorcycle trip. And not just around San Antonio, but all the way to the Hill Country, where they were going to camp and attend the "Oldie's Rock Reunion," with songs Teresa remembered from her teen years.

Eric looked like a hunk on his motorcycle, Teresa thought. But the three-hour ride was tiring and made her *nalgas* hurt so much, she almost couldn't get off the cycle. And she hated the noise it made. There was no way to talk. And it was hot, like opening the oven door and sticking your head in while a chicken baked. She also hated camping. The tents were small and cold in the night and sweltering during the day. Everyone walked around with a beer in their hand and talked loudly. Those were the exact type of *viejos* that she'd told Tino she would not abide. But she couldn't tell Eric any of this. He'd dump her quicker than a hot potato. Even if they were doing stupid things, it was a sight better than staying home every night alone.

At Eric's house, he had a home karaoke machine with all sorts of CDs: oldies, country, gospel and Elvis. He turned the machine on almost every night, and the two would sing together. Sometimes she watched him sing. She liked Patsy Cline, so he bought her a karaoke cd featuring her songs. She loved singing "Crazy" while he accompanied her on guitar. He was pretty good, and Teresa liked a man with musical talent, one talent Tino had lacked.

He started to train her in his gym. It was small, but it had a large selection of machines and weights.

"I can help you get into good shape," he volunteered.

"You don't like my shape?" Teresa asked him. She said it like she was joking, but there was more to it than that.

He smiled at her and told her that physical fitness was important, and that her shape was just fine. He was training for the Senior Olympics. He wanted to compete in strength events.

Just six minutes into their first session, she thought she was going to pass out. She didn't like doing strenuous things. When she was young, only the boys played sports. Girls didn't get noticed for running around like *zonzas*. But she didn't want to disappoint Eric. She lifted weights and did crazy stretches until she thought she'd collapse. He would tell her, "Okay, take it easy for a few minutes and then back to work."

The next day she could barely brush her teeth. She was angry enough to tell him to stick his exercises. But she thought twice. He was good-looking and in shape. Where was she going to get herself another hunk like him? All these men wanted younger women, and she was sure that Eric did too. At least she'd get into good shape for other dates, other beaus.

Alena stopped calling Eric the "Muscle Head" after Teresa snapped at her. And Alena wouldn't help her write emails to Eric, no matter how much Teresa pleaded.

"Mother, if you don't want to mess up, the last person you should have helping you to craft love letters is me. I can't even make my husband happy."

It was good old Elvira who offered Teresa tips on keeping her man. "Don't pick up the phone when he calls. Make him call you at least two or three times before you answer. Never call him first. Make sure to keep your 'Plenty of Fish' profile up to date. Make sure that your profile is public so that he can see that there are other men competing for you. And for sure, don't tell him you like him."

"Why?"

"It gives him too much power. Oh, and uglify him."

"Uglify?"

"Whenever you get a chance, go shopping with him. Give him bad advice about what he should wear. Pick out the ugliest, least flattering shirts and the ugliest pants for him. Tell him he looks great in things that he looks stupid in. The best thing would be for you to go with him when he gets his haircut. If you can get him to wear his hair so that it looks bad, that's half the battle. You want to make sure that no one else thinks he's a catch."

Teresa listened carefully, taking notes. Elvira was very, very smart about men.

"You should keep your hair short in the front and long in the back," Teresa told Eric when he mentioned he needed a haircut. "It makes you look like Elvis."

"Elvis, huh?" he said as he looked in the mirror. "I don't look anything like the King, though."

"Oh, yes, you do," Teresa told him.

"I have red hair."

"It's the way you carry yourself, the way you walk and talk. Especially when you sing. If you cut your hair like I'm telling you, I think you would look even more like Elvis."

When he came back from the hair stylist, Eric had cut his hair the Elvis way. He looked like a red-headed parrot. Next, Teresa made sure that his shirts hid his muscles and accentuated his little pot belly. Teresa called it "Project Uglify." She wanted no competition. He was her dreamboat, and only she could know that under the bad haircut, the tacky clothes, the sometimes pungent B.O., the thick body hair and the countless T-shirts with the cutoff sleeves, she had herself a hunk.

Alena didn't like the ploy. Teresa was smug about her little *periquito*, her own red-headed parakeet. Alena, weighed down by Cristina's call, told Teresa that she had something very serious to discuss, something that might upset her.

"I don't like that kind of thing," Teresa told her. "If you've got bad news, keep it for a while, unless it's Tonia. Is it Tonia? I don't want to go around thinking the worst."

Teresa was very good at that, thinking the worst. Tino had said that she always put mustard on her ice cream. She didn't think it was a case of mere pessimism, just being ready for whatever was coming down the road. Of course, when the worst found you, it didn't matter whether you were ready or not, because, of course, you weren't ever really ready. Tino had always said that he wouldn't last past fifty. And Teresa had always told him not to talk that way. He'd smile like he was joking, but he'd known somehow. Probably because his brothers went so young. And when Tino died, Teresa froze. Parts of her were still frozen.

With Eric, she was always on guard, not that he would die or get sick, because he seemed as fit and strong as a bull. What she was on guard for was his finding another woman, one with fewer wrinkles, who didn't have liver spots, whose hair was still shiny.

"What I like best about you is how good I feel when I'm with you. I love spending time with you, Terry."

She told Elvira, "Hmph, why can't he tell me that he loves me? What am I, one of his road toad buddies?"

Then there was the other thing. Sex. She didn't care much for it, not even while Tino was alive. They fooled around from time to time, especially when they were first married, but then came the health issues, the day-to-day worries, the boredom. There were better things for her to occupy herself with. But Eric didn't find sex boring at all. He was starting to suggest strongly that he wanted intimacy.

Who could she discuss this matter with? Her children would be scandalized, and her church friends would disapprove. She'd tried Sister Gutiérrez, but she'd pretended not to understand what Teresa was driving at.

It was a sin, she knew, and not just because she'd been taught that since she was a little girl. She knew it firsthand: sexual sin brought heartache. She was no prude. No. It was that sexual sin brought misery. Her first husband had destroyed the family because he couldn't keep his thing in his pants.

It happened. She didn't resist. It would have been silly, a woman her age acting like a virgin. There was a part of her that wanted it to happen. It proved something about how Eric saw her. She didn't feel that she should ask for forgiveness for craving his attentions. Still, she felt guilty. But it was better than feeling lonely and old.

Teresa's uglifying campaign only worked so long as Eric was satisfied physically. Men needed sex more than women. It was a fact. Teresa had been married twice, had close relationships with several other men, and she knew what drove them. When they were young, they had to have it. It was all they thought about. It used to upset her, especially in her first marriage, but now she saw that it was a universal condition, as thoughtless an act for them as winning at some sport or game. A yearning that had no real connection to love or affection. As they grew older, it became a way of proving that they were still strong and powerful. It was no longer an impetuous act, but a drive, nonetheless.

So she'd given in. There was a short pretense that she was uncertain, hesitant, a calculation that this would make him feel all the more powerful. Guilty or not, it didn't matter, as long as she could hold onto him. She was determined to make him say those words: *I love you, Teresa*.

It was funny. Tino had been very sentimental. He'd tell her he loved her all the time. He called her his *reina*, his queen, his treasure. She was spoiled by his affection. She'd wrinkle her nose and play at being the *chiflada*, even though she was well-beyond those years. Tino enjoyed it.

With Eric, she was left waiting for the compliments, the doting. Instead, he was sweet, generous, protective. He was concerned about her health, her fitness, her state of mind, even her sleep.

"Who cares about all that," she told Elvira. "I want him to tell me I'm beautiful, desirable, that I'm the love of his life."

"But Teresa, you've only been seeing him a few weeks."

"Long enough that he's taken me to bed," she wanted to respond. Instead, she said, "Long enough to know how I feel about him."

#4

The sun sets on the first day but there is no rest. Night goggles are activated. More houses, more garbage, to the point where the squad might grow complacent if not for the constant barrage of armaments exploding and the clack-clack of automatic guns firing in the near distance. Danny fights to keep his men keen and alert. His fire team kicks in a door, a pitch-dark house that miraculously has escaped the opening barrage of artillery. As he, Fonzo and Fuentes move into position, Danny feels his gut do a flip.

"Watch your backside," he tells them.

Sure enough, as Fuentes kicks the door open, they catch fire from at least two fighters hiding in a side room to the large entryway.

"Stay on my wing," he says sharply to Fonzo. Then at Sky and Fuentes, "You two keep your shit together and fire steady once I'm exposed."

Danny moves forward in a crouch. His knees ache, everything aches, but his legs in particular feel heavy and rubbery, and his right knee is seizing up on him. It's on fire. He wonders if he'll be able to stand up when required. When he landed off-kilter earlier, he'd hardly noticed the painful snaps his ligaments made. Adrenaline and fear are effective painkillers. Now, as geeked as he is, he can't ignore it or the possibility that he might be frozen in a crouch when one of the Haji fuckers starts firing at him. He knows there are at least two in the stairwell, waiting for him to make his move. He can smell them just like they can smell him. Days of no showering, sweat, blood, all sorts of oozing stench combine to overwhelm the senses. No ordinary funk. This is the stench of rancid, unwashed humanity. It is the stink of killing, of burned flesh and decay. It is as thick in the air as the floury dust, eternal, overwhelming, the stink burrowing its way into memory and flesh combined that will stick with him until the end. War makes the ephemera of living dissipate quickly, giving way to the fundamental truths: humans are animals, in animal bodies, acting out as animals—snot, blood, sweat and spit, acute and immediate. Civilization works to dull the stink, to camouflage the reality of flesh against a background of deodorant, perfume, pleasant artificial smells that belie the strife and suffering of the flesh. This stench is not in any way pleasant, but it is real, overpowering, and demands the soldier be conscious of the concupiscence of flesh, the undeniable meatiness of the self. Beneath the rational self, the subjective me-ness, clean, untouchable as an idea or the moral, spiritual frame of consciousness, is always the urgent stench of Danny's body, more real, absolutely tangible and more pressingly indicative of his own fragile life force.

The pregnant woman—"mother"—comes back to him at that moment, inopportune but demanding. Her eyes glazing over as her fragile life force, the tiny but all-powerful life force of her unborn child, fade out all over again, leaving behind as the only witness of what had been the stench of the body, the undeniable this-ness of life absent except for the synaptic connections now firing through Danny's brain and nervous system, a vivid memory. His body understands what is happening, what has happened. This occurs in a few inarticulable moments in the language of distress and terror and horror in which Danny's body is hideously and increasingly fluent. When he wills his pained, frozen knees into action and springs forward into the dark stairwell, the conduit from one life, one consciousness, into another, he isn't thinking anything other than the hot rush of adrenaline, the age-old soldier's response to the violent all-demanding now. You can't fuck or fight your way outside of this narrow sliver of consciousness. Danny, his knees every bit as angry as he anticipated, the pain growing in intensity, steps forward.

"Fuck you, motherfucker, I'm coming!"

He bolts up the stairs, two at a time, the seventy pounds lbs. of equipment bouncing against his back. And yet, he might as well be naked. Like the chick-necked baby, his newborn son, reposing on his shoulder as they cross over the threshold of home in the fairytale he sometimes indulges when he feels most lonely and needs something to look forward to. All these ideas flood his system along with the adrenaline as he moves relentlessly forward in the dark. And then the unbelievably tall shadow of a Muj fighter leaps out at him as he reaches the top step. Suddenly, he is on his ass, a sharp grunt escaping as he goes flat on his back. No time to grab his knife or pistol, the rifle not useful in hand-to-hand combat. He has trained for this, over and over. He is good at grappling, at delivering the debilitating blow. But this big rancid motherfucker is not another grunt trying to immobilize him during a scrum to impress the drill. This motherfucker locks his huge hands over the top of his face, thumbs working their way towards his jelly-filled eyes. His breath, hot and smelling of rotten milk and an empty gut, become faster and deeper, so that drops of saliva paint Danny's face. He strikes out at the man's hands and face, his broken and torn nails finding their target, the Muj's eyes. The man's eyes shut automatically, but Danny forces his thumb into the left socket. The man grunts but doesn't scream as Danny pushes further into the gelatinous orb. The eyelid gives way, tearing slightly to accommodate the alien digit, the sharpened nail digging into the viscera. "You're going to die," he tells this wraith, whose face he still can't cogitate but whose eyes reflect the thinnest glint of light. He stinks, stinks as bad as Danny. At that moment, he turns his head suddenly and sinks his teeth into Danny's forearm. Danny feels the flesh tear in two, blood pouring from the ragged slit down his hand onto the fighter's face, mixing with the blood that oozes out of his eye. The pain of the teeth is unbearable. The worst thing Danny has ever felt. The man clamps down harder and harder until a hunk of skin rips away sharply. Then quickly, savagely, he reclamps his teeth down on the wound to rip away muscle and sinew. He is being eaten.

Danny lets go of the Muj's face, using his right elbow to box the man's nose and mouth again and again. He feels teeth give way, lips and gum mashing. But the Muj won't let go. He is grunting, as fevered as any starving dog on the street with a mouthful of stringy corpse. And then this second hunk of flesh in his mouth gives way and he pulls it away from Danny's arm, this time spitting it into his face. Danny has the chance to put his hands around his throat. He presses his thumbs as hard as he can into the fighter's Adams apple, but to no avail. He can't muster the strength to crush his throat anymore.

"No, no," the man says. Maybe it is the only word he knows. Perhaps he is not pleading with Danny. Perhaps he is screaming into the void, beseeching his coming fate to stop, to slow down. He pleads with his eyes and his guttural "nos" through blood-stained teeth, snot and blood running from his nose down his cheeks like thick, dark tears.

Danny realizes he doesn't want to kill him. Even as his grip tightens, he doesn't want to kill him. He wishes to be somewhere else, anywhere else. He can feel the Muj's breath on his face, the forced gasping, the humid living panting. This is an awful intimacy deeper than fucking. Danny's eyes, adjusted to the dark, recognize the panic and fear in the man's face. The two are mirrors, twin masks, more in common with each other right then than with blood kin. He is older than most of the Muj he's come into contact with, maybe forty or more. Whatever his commitment to the cause might have been, he, they, are now thinking about dying. It doesn't matter. Not anymore. Danny puts all his weight onto his hands and the man wriggles more desperately, more frantically, but can't manage even a gasp. His eyes bulge and turn upwards as he tries to mouth some kind of plea or admonition. Danny's wound continues to ooze fresh blood onto his victim's face, into his mouth. Not another breath escapes. Now only his tongue protrudes as his eyes go white, and he slowly stops struggling. Just then, a muzzle blast explodes to the right of his head. His ears ringing, he turns in time to see the barrel of an AK emerge just at the edge of his sight line. Fonzo runs into the stairwell, stops for a moment to see that Danny is alive, and ducks into the hallway. More fire, a few tracers illuminating the dead man's ghastly face. Danny gathers up his weapon and crawls behind Fonzo. The ghost isn't firing anymore. He is hiding in one of the bedrooms.

"Fuck that guy," Fonzo says, taking the pin from a grenade. He rolls it into the first bedroom. Shuffling from inside. Then a clatter, probably the rifle as the Haji jumps towards the grenade so as to toss it out. But too late. A blast sends the ceiling vaulting in the air, dust and granules of God knows what coming down in plumes of toxic air.

"One dead Muj," Fonzo says peering into the room. "That fucker's spread like cheap wallpaper." Then, turning towards his squad leader he asks, "You okay, Danny?"

"Good," is all Danny can manage. But he knows he will never be good again.

Outside, the boys congratulate Danny, Fonzo and Fuentes. Danny sits against a wall, the doc stuffing the gaping wound up, wrapping it tight. "You good?" he asks him. Everyone asks him if he is good. He drinks water, not having the energy to nod. He watches the dogs. In spite of the explosions and rapid fire, they have gone nowhere. They smell the meat. Slowly but deliberately, they make their way inside, smelling out the generous dead.

CHAPTER 9
Choreography

"You're pregnant?" he asked stupidly.

"Preggers. Knocked-up. In a family way. Bun in the oven."

They were headed for San Antonio. They'd found part of the story in Houston, but there was more to be discovered, and Teresa needed to be a part of that.

"Okay. I don't have any business asking, so you can tell me to fuck off. But what's the story?"

"Don't know yet," Virginia said. "I'm trying to weave it together. Nothing makes a lot of sense right now. Everything is a surprise, like I'm in a whatchamacallit, a maze, and every turn presents something different and unexpected. The day before I met you, I was ready to end it. Now . . ."

"You mean the pregnancy? You're not so sure now?"

"Right. Not so sure."

"What's the thing that's gonna make it sure?"

"Don't know, Daniel. All my life, I've just floated to the next thing and the next thing. No plans, no control. Just waiting. And now . . ."

"Fucking 'now,'" Daniel repeated. "Used to be that's all I could think about. You lose track of that, you're dead.

'Now.' It's different these days. It's the past I'm looking at now."

"What about the future?" she asked.

"What's that?"

"I'm tired," Virginia said as she turned her face towards the front window.

"That happens when you're pregnant, right?" Daniel offered.

"Don't know," Virginia said. "All I know is that I'm tired. All the way tired, like my mom used to say."

"I know that feeling," Daniel said after some silence. "Like I just want to go to sleep, fast forward the bullshit. Dream myself to death."

Virginia turned towards him, a puzzled scowl on her face. "It's not that grim!" She waited for Daniel to revise his sentiment, make a dark joke, at least. "You wouldn't be here if you really felt that way."

Daniel resisted looking at Virginia. He kept his eyes on the road instead. "No one really wants to die. Goddamn war showed me that. You die whether you fuckin' like it or not, whether you are ready or not, whether you are even aware of it or not. Just a pop in the head, your head snapping like a neck in a hangman's noose."

Virginia kept her eyes on the landscape running across the side window.

Daniel felt embarrassed. "I forget it's not that grim for everybody. I'm good for ruining your day."

"Nah," Virginia said. "You try your damnedest, but I owe you. You've come all this way to help me. I appreciate that."

Daniel felt his face flush. It had been a long time since someone had thanked him for anything.

"I'm not Mother Teresa," he said. "I have questions too. Questions I need answers to. I keep wondering why I'm on this quest. Is it for you, me or Tino? I don't know. But it's getting me off my ass. That's something."

"Why did you get so mad at the old man?" she said, changing tack.

"He was nothing but a ghost. Can't be mad at a ghost. I kept thinking about an abused kid with no one to give a damn about him, and how it was his sad luck to run into a manipulative drug dealer who gave him a semblance of care and acceptance."

"I have to pee," Virginia said suddenly. "Let's stop asap."

They pulled over at a gas station, one of the huge hundred-pump places popping up like pimples on Texas highways. Daniel didn't want to go in, but he got out of the car and had a smoke while Virginia went in to relieve herself. While he watched the dozens of cars gassing up, he drifted into a daydream. It was a sunny day, like that day, but in San Antonio, his mom's house, the two of them, he and Virginia, exiting the car, Virginia much further along in the pregnancy, big belly waddle, and Teresa at the door with a big welcoming smile. He couldn't quite see himself, but he knew he was walking tall like in the old days.

"What you doing?" Virginia asked, breaking the vision. "You zoning out? Your cigarette is long gone."

Daniel looked at the dead cig between his fingers, the filter blackened. "What you got there?" he asked her without answering her question.

"Peanut brittle," she said, holding it out. "They've got a ton of stuff in there, like a literal ton of stuff. I can't resist peanut brittle. I bought a bag."

"That's a big goddamn bag," Daniel acknowledged.

"I'm eating for two, plus I figured you'd want some. Who doesn't want brittle?"

"I'm allergic to peanuts," Daniel said.

"Jesus, my big old soldier is allergic to peanuts! What's next? Don't tell me you're a vegetarian."

Daniel smiled. "Thinking about it."

They made their way back to the car, Daniel walking slightly behind Virginia. He watched her walk as he contemplated the meaning of his daydream. Why had he gotten involved to this degree? Tino was dead, hadn't intended to meet his daughter or his grandkid. Maybe it was his mother's influence. He needed to know more about Tino, who had provided him his image of manhood, but thus far had only netted a darker vision of his stepfather. And what about Virginia? She was no blood to him, and she'd only just told him that she was pregnant. The idea "I could save her . . ." floated above his conscious thought like a wispy cloud.

"You're awful quiet over there," Virginia said.

"Just driving," Daniel said, his eyes focused on the road ahead.

~~~

"Leo said Saturnino's sister is living in Schulenburg. Can we stop there? Maybe she'll be around to talk to us."

"Lucia," Daniel said. "She's always been solid. When Tino died, she was there every day during the aftermath. Gave my mom a lot of help."

"Wonder if she knew about me," Virginia asked out loud.

Daniel shrugged.

"Can you call her, see if she'll see us for a minute?"

Daniel made the call. His aunt was home. He told her he had Virginia with him. Lucia didn't hesitate. She invited them over.

Schulenburg was little more than the town halfway between Houston and San Antonio. It was an old, German-settled area, a few pretty churches, only a couple of thousand people. But it had retained its character, with well-tended houses, a Teutonic commitment to orderliness. To both Daniel and Victoria, it seemed safe and peaceful, although neither said so out loud. Time, seemingly, had skipped over Schulenburg. They both felt it as they drove the uncrowded streets to Lucia's home.

She lived in a well-kept double-wide she shared with her husband, Dixon, whom she called Dexy. He had suffered a terrible stroke that left him speechless and paralyzed on the left side. He sat on the small porch by the front door, silent, slightly dazed, much like an old, languorous cat. Virginia smiled at the old man. His eyes followed her to the door but made no other acknowledgment that he was aware of her presence.

Daniel paused briefly by the sick man, patted his shoulder and said, "How are you, Uncle Dexy?"

Dexy murmured unintelligibly, gesturing towards the front door.

Just then, Lucia opened the screen and said, "Daniel, our soldier-boy Daniel!" She stepped out and gave him a long tight hug. "Look who's here to visit, Dexy," she said to the old man, who watched without expression.

Lucia then turned her attention to Virginia. "You look so much like your father," she said, raising both her hands in an invitation to her long-lost niece.

Virginia returned the gesture, and the two embraced in a long hug. Virginia felt a surge of emotion, much more than she had felt in Leo's presence. Perhaps it was the maternal nature of Lucia's response and being held, which she'd almost never experienced. Her own mother had shown her so little physical affection that she couldn't recollect a single hug. Virginia feared she might break down and weep in front of the strangers, Daniel included. She pulled away after a few seconds.

Lucia ushered the two inside, leaving Dexy in the sun.

"Should I bring Uncle in," Daniel offered.

"No, he's fine out there. The only thing he has these days that he can enjoy is sitting out there looking out on the world."

They sat down on a simple green couch.

"I knew this day would come. I hoped it wouldn't be too late. Before your father died, he wanted to find you, he did," Lucia insisted.

"He did?" Virginia said.

"Yes, *m'ija*, he did."

"Why didn't he then?"

"I don't know exactly."

Lucia poured the three of them coffee, settling back in her chair with a cup. "He went to see you after your mother had moved away with you. Something happened. He wouldn't say much about it. Tino didn't talk much, to start with. If it was his concern, it stayed his concern only."

Daniel pushed forward. "But you must know something, Tía. Anything. We need some answers."

The use of "we" did not escape Virginia.

"There were two letters," she told Lucia. "One's dated from when I was just a kid, after Saturnino got out of prison. It's about wanting to see me. The second is about meeting in Houston, about wanting me . . . " She stopped short of finishing the sentence, surprised again by the emotion rising inside, ready to breach the dam if she persisted too quickly. "There's a bus ticket to Houston."

"*Ay, m'ija*," Lucia said with compassion, "I wish I could help more with that. There's a hard story to all of this. I loved my brothers, but I had to get out of all that mess. When Dexy took me out of that life, I didn't want to go back. For so long, Tino and the rest just couldn't keep from hurting everyone around them. That's what happens when all you know is hurt.

Anyway, I turned away from all of it, most of it anyway," Lucia said in almost a pleading away, as if wanting the younger woman to give her a dispensation.

"I just want to know if my father cared. If he would've . . ." Again, she stopped.

"I don't know, *m'ija*. Not for sure. Mostly it's better to believe the best. I know who Tino was as a child, what he became after years of beatings and living on the streets. My father never touched me, but it seemed like he was always hitting those boys. I was just a little girl watching it all. When my mother died, my aunt, down the street, raised me. It was only a couple of houses over but it was as far as the moon, it was so different. I couldn't go back there. It was like a house of horrors, haunted and dark and ugly."

"But Saturnino . . ." Virginia said trying to direct the woman back to her father.

"Like I was saying, prison changed him. Getting clean and finding the Lord, that changed him even more. After he married Teresa, the change was complete."

"I remember you and Uncle Dexy visiting plenty of times. We'd go out to Victoria, when you lived there, and Dexy would take us camping. Plenty of times," Daniel said. "That's when he was so strong and able, he built you that cabin you lived in."

"Didn't Tino ever say anything to you about me?" Virginia asked.

"No," Lucia said after some thought.

"And you never asked?"

"*M'ija*, he had this new life. It was like the past was something too dangerous to go looking through. It wasn't going to do anyone any good to poke the wounds that were, well, maybe not healed, but contained. We never talked about the old days or my father, or even my mother. We pretended that it was a previous life. And it was, really. A previous life full of garbage."

"Garbage?" Virginia said looking at her aunt.

"I don't mean you, *m'ija*."

"I'm full with the stink of it, though," Virginia said, looking away momentarily at the realization.

Daniel reached for her hand, and she let him take it.

They didn't stay much longer. As they left, Daniel put his hand again on Dexy's shoulder. The old man had nodded off and didn't stir. Sorrowfully, Lucia looked back as the two got into the car and drove off.

"I just want to know," Virginia said, "if he gave a damn about me. I can deal with it if he wanted me, but Celia stopped him and lied. Even if Benny-Boy threatened him. But I don't think I can handle him just giving me up as part of some sick past, like the stink of garbage, like she said."

"She didn't mean that," Daniel said as he steered the car west towards San Antonio. "There's just some things . . . " he said carefully, the broken fishbowl flashing in his mind. He could not talk about that. "Some things stay stuck inside you and won't come out, like my Uncle Dexy sitting out on that porch. Things stuck inside him forever, things he's probably desperate to let out, only he can't. Sometimes, it's not a choice."

"I don't know what you're talking about," Virginia said, anger seeping into her words. "Seems like bullshit. Everyone seems to want to keep things shut up, wrapped! Fuck that. I'm not here for that. I want answers. I want to know. I don't care if it hurts or not. At least I'll know the truth. Doesn't that fucking matter? To anyone?"

"Sure," Daniel said. "That's why I'm here with you."

"Why do you care? What's your skin in the game? You're not actually related to me, although that wouldn't mean anything, anyway. My mom hated me, and it looks like my father didn't give a shit either. So why do you care?"

"Not sure," Daniel said. "Been thinking it over myself."

"Maybe it's to protect your mom," Virginia said. "It makes sense."

"Could be," Daniel said. "A recon mission, check out the enemy before engagement."

"Not funny," Virginia said.

"Sorry. Sometimes I say things the wrong way. You're not the enemy. Not to me. Maybe to yourself. One thing I've figured out is that's usually the case."

"Are you your own enemy?"

"Could be."

"Jesus. How about a straight answer? You keep the truth pretty guarded, you know that?"

"So I've been told."

"Fuck you," Virginia said turning away from him and looking out the window at the multitude of cars jamming I-10.

Daniel smiled and then gave a sharp laugh. "You are a straight-shooter, I'll say that for you."

"Yeah, well, I already told you that, soldier boy."

~~~

Sitting in front of her "Plenty of Fish" profile, Alena felt confident for the first time about the alter ego she had constructed, named Filomena. Filomena existed in another place and time and was not bound by anything but imagination and verve. Even gravity could not touch her as she danced to her own choreography. Nor church rules nor inbred guilt which could tie her down, as they did Alena.

Tomás Escassi had true feelings for Filomena. They'd been writing each other for weeks. He was an engineer in Mexico City. His profile pictures promised a man who was sensitive, kind, with intelligent eyes, a sweet smile. And he was tall and thin with the body of a graceful man, a man who could dance.

He was funny. He wrote about his small adventures in the city, about the people he worked with. His notes revealed a man who wasn't afraid to laugh at himself, even as he described the foibles of his co-workers and friends. He wrote about his shyness with women, even giving an amusing account of his first marriage, which had only lasted a few months. His wife had been older, dissatisfied with her life with the young brash Tomás. She'd left him for a restauranteur. Tomás was not bitter, though. He took it with a bemused, philosophical outlook.

Filomena asked him, "How did you find the courage to face the end of your marriage. Weren't you scared of being alone?"

He wrote back that being in a bad marriage was lonelier than anything he'd experienced as a single man.

Alena understood even better than Filomena the truth of Tomás' words. What did Filomena know about loneliness? That was Alena's domain. She looked longingly at the photos of Mexico City. She pictured herself there with Tomás. She went so far as to field airline ticket prices, which were much cheaper than she'd expected. It was all fantasy, of course. But what would it take to make it real?

If Alena were going to make one of her mother's incessant lists, she would have titled it, "What Would I Lose?" She scribbled: "protection, companionship, shared sacrifice, a helpmate, my best friend, security." But these were just words that she loosely associated with marriage in general. It was a modest list of core elements, nothing that she understood through experience.

She considered each word more closely. Protection? Would Richard risk his life to save hers? Yes. Probably. But that wasn't the kind of protection she was interested in. Richard had no clue about the things that threatened Alena. Companionship? Like two old maids sitting in a parlor knitting or playing cards, secure that the other is there, even though there isn't much to say. Sex? Non-existent. She didn't guess that Richard found her all that attractive anymore. A woman knew when a man wanted her. To be fair, she didn't exactly want him either. Sex was overrated, anyway. Shared sacrifice? There she supposed that both had given up more than they even suspected. Certainly, Richard wasn't aware of what she had sacrificed. What she was sacrificing. She saw herself on that airplane, taking her away. There she would find the mystery and excitement that was missing in the mound of dirty socks and underwear, the decade of not so furtive farting, of the horrific snoring that woke her several times a night.

There was no way that Filomena would have fallen for Richard. Filomena was meant for a bigger man, a more adventurous man, a writer or photographer, a world traveling man, at home with the exotic. A man of such depth that it would take a lifetime of digging to get to the bottom of him, and not even then. A man like Tomás Escassi.

Filomena had no siblings, no mother, no bland connections to anything. She traveled widely, had just danced the lead role in a big production in Chicago. Alena had never been to Chicago. She googled it. It was there that Filomena received rave reviews. Her fellow dancers were jealous but were bound to respect her.

Alena found the show on YouTube and closed her eyes, imagining Filomena jumping through the air into the strong arms of her partner, who lifted her up, one-handed, so that she was horizontal, like superman, her face up like that, the air brushing her flushed cheeks.

Filomena looked a lot like Alena, only she was thinner, more muscular, her hair was longer and shinier, and on her face you could read confidence and joy.

Alena googled modern dance and a million threads popped up. She combed through the pictures, finding one with shadowy faces. She sent it to Tomás. He wrote back approvingly about her grace and beauty on the stage. She didn't feel guilty because she was choreographing her own dance now. Filomena, Dancer in Shadow; Tomás, the Mexican engineer— a romance in the making. It existed in the copious ether.

"But what if he wants to meet you," Elvira asked Alena.

"That's not allowed," she answered. "It would ruin it all, meeting."

"I understand," Elvira said. It was like *Rubia*, she thought. Who would want to meet the actress who played her? Would you really want to see the sets, their unreal flimsiness dispelling the magical illusion?

"I want you to link to Filomena's page. Write regularly. You'll be her best friend who is in a sad and desperate situation, a bad marriage, something like that."

"What should my name be?" Elvira asked.

"Something rare, interesting. *Graciela*."

Elvira loved the name. "Oh, that's good."

"You're my best friend, a fellow dancer who gave up her career to marry. And now you're in a fix after finding out that your husband is deceitful, a real jerk. You've just left him and need my, I mean Filomena's, advice and comfort."

"Yeah," she said. "Yeah. And the evil husband will come looking for Graciela! Yes, what an adventure. And I get to be a dancer, too!" Graciela was not to be a lonely, bored, boyfriend-less loser, Elvira decided. She was an artist. Graciela wouldn't be chunky with heavy legs and a big nose and flabby cheeks, like Elvira.

They spent the next hour combing the internet for Graciela's face. She had to bear a resemblance, but just a passing one, to Elvira. The important thing was for her to be a worthy, beautiful avatar.

"Her, that's her," Elvira said.

It was a dark girl, as dark as Elvira, only younger, thinner, piercing eyes, clear skin and taut, wavy hair that shined. Alena worried the girl in the picture was too pretty.

"Too pretty for what?" Elvira asked.

"Graciela is supposed to be Filomena's friend, a supporting character. You should use your own face, like I'm doing."

"I'm not like you," Elvira said.

That made Alena feel a little good and a little sad. They planned a riveting story in which Graciela was busy making her comeback to dance after a serious knee injury.

"I like it," Elvira said as Alena typed her new profile. "Maybe Tomás has a friend that Graciela can get to know!"

~~~

I Love You. Three little words. A short declaration that had become a cliché. Or so Alena had told Teresa to keep her from fixating on why Eric hadn't uttered them yet. Those three little words, eight little letters, meant everything. Out of the mouth speaks the heart. The Bible said so.

Teresa called Alena at work. "Eric told me that he will never marry again. Why would he say such a terrible thing? Just to hurt me?"

But Alena scoffed at the idea that her mother should desire to ever marry again. "At your age?"

It was a mean thing to say, Teresa thought.

The past weekend, Eric had taken Teresa on a long drive to an estate sale. He loved them. He loved walking around dead people's houses, looking for interesting objects, for bargains. His taste was bizarre: porcelain clowns, military figures made of iron, small, faded wool rugs, books that weren't in the least interesting (stamp collecting, old grammar books), stuffed animals. Not the cute stuffed animals, the real animals stuffed after death: a raccoon, a bobcat, an eagle, an armadillo. He hung all this stuff in his living room, except for the bobcat, which he placed in the gym. The big cat peered down from its perch as Teresa and Eric worked out.

At first, she pouted because she shouldn't be expected to do such terrible exercises, especially if Eric was going to persist in yelling at her to "Do one more."

"You'll be in prime condition if you stick with me," he told Teresa.

She realized that this was a sweet thing for him to want to help her with, but it was also very insulting. Was she chopped liver in her current condition? She played along, nevertheless, and worked out hard. She was going to do everything in her power to get in the best shape of her life. There were too many younger girls out there ready to get their conniving hands on her man.

He made her warmup on the treadmill for twenty minutes. And then the monkey machine, an intimidating contraption on which Teresa knelt and then pulled herself up as if she were a man. There were weights too. One day upper body, the next, lower body. There was a decree that no more snacks or sweets would be eaten. This was hard for Teresa. She had a sweet tooth.

Eric didn't have to give up what he liked. He drank beer, ate all the meat he could: hamburgers, steaks, hotdogs, pork chops. "Protein, protein, protein," he would repeat as he gorged.

Teresa didn't care what he ate. His stuffed animals, his clowns, his nonsensical books, his mullet, his crush on Elvis, none of it mattered so long as he would tell her that he loved her. Three little words.

Alena said, "Mother, if Eric told you he loved you, it wouldn't satisfy you. You'd want a proposal next. And you'd get married and get even more jealous, dressing him like a child and making him grow that ridiculous mullet even longer. He already looks like a deranged professional wrestler."

Teresa liked this description. That's exactly what she wanted her little parakeet to look like. Why should she feel bad because her daughter didn't approve? Alena wasn't even able to keep a very simple man like Richard satisfied. Her advice was no good.

"Enjoy what you've got," Alena told Teresa. "Doesn't he take you all over the place? Doesn't he buy you things? He fixed your truck the other day, didn't he? He's taking you camping for a week. If he didn't like you, he wouldn't want to spend so much time with you."

Teresa tried to tell Alena that she suspected Eric wanted her only for the convenient sex. Alena refused to talk about sex.

"Come on," Teresa said, "let's pretend we're friends for a while. Let me ask you some questions, and you tell me your feelings. You're a big girl now."

"No," Alena said, "I draw the line at the sexual business."

No wonder the girl was frustrated, Teresa thought.

Alena didn't know how much Teresa needed to hear the three little words. How happy it would make her. Sure, Eric did all sorts of things for her. He complimented her constantly. He refused to let her go to the grocery store at night by herself, always accompanying her. He never failed to walk her to the door after dates. He'd even made some space for her in his bathroom and had given her a closet for when she spent the night with him.

They sang on the karaoke machine every evening, sometimes love songs, but more often, heartbreak songs, like "Your Cheating Heart."

Did Eric love her? Henry had told her that he loved her. So had Tino. He'd proven it by giving up his past life. His daughter . . . Teresa, didn't like to think about that. "You'll have to stop with Celia and with the girl," she had told him. "She probably doesn't belong to you, anyway. I need you here, with us, walking with the Lord."

Now, Teresa had more to worry about than she had with Tino. Eric was always talking about how he would move to

Montana before long. "A nice parcel of land where you can see the mountains and stars."

She'd get angry when he talked about leaving, because he always implied that he would go alone, that he could leave her behind and disappear into his little mountain fantasy. She would snap at him when she thought about this. "Well, why don't I just get out of your hair now?"

After she pressed the issue several times, Eric gave in, although giving her only small consolation. "Okay, Terry, I do love you. You gotta know that, right? It's just that I'm not *in love* with you. I'm not capable of that. I only got so much to give in that way."

Of course, this was not satisfactory in the least. "I'd rather he wouldn't have said anything," she told Elvira.

"At least you know he won't lie to you."

"Hmph. A little lying can go a long way."

"He'll come around," Elvira said. "You hang in there. You're a catch, a good woman, beautiful. You're the best thing that's happened to him."

This was true, Teresa thought, but why not admit it? Was there something wrong with him?

Eric's friends were mostly poor, damaged old men with something sad in them that never went away. Even when they were singing or laughing, one of them was sure to bring up the war, and the rest would follow suit. Before Teresa even knew it, they were all grim. They were unable to cut ties to the past. They were like ghosts in the present. She feared that this too was the case with Daniel. She looked for signs, comparisons, between those sad men and her son.

Among the cast of characters that Eric called "friends," was George, who was always unkempt, so hairy, like a hippie, and always smoking. He'd get up every twenty minutes to smoke outside by himself. There was Bobby, who liked to sing with Eric, and who was warm and friendly, but couldn't stay employed or find himself a good, caring woman. The saddest case was Albert, a huge man, maybe six and a half feet and carrying an enormous belly, his hands the size of baseball mitts. He didn't talk much. He went around in an old beat-up van, beige except where it was rusted through. Sometimes he dropped by unexpectedly, but Eric would always open the door for him. "We're brothers," he told Teresa.

Eric had a tattoo of a woman's name on his arm, Delilah. An exotic name for a man who prided himself on being a Midwesterner. "I'm just a midwestern boy, not used to all this hullabaloo," he'd say to Teresa when she was spoiling for a fight. "C'mon, Terry," he'd say, and the way he said her name would make her forget why she was mad at him.

She liked this "Terry." A new name for a new her! This Terry was a fun-lover. She did things Teresa would never have done. Terry went camping, motorcycling. She hiked. Went antique shopping. She worked out and lifted weights. She danced at the VA dances Eric took her too.

Of course, Eric didn't like to dance much. That was okay with her because she liked to make him a little jealous. Albert would take her out on the dance floor. He might have been fat and a bit smelly, but he danced with grace. One would never have known it just by looking at him. Teresa supposed that was true of everyone, a secret talent or desire, a gift that didn't seem to match them. Before Tino's death, Teresa had never known she was a dancer.

Three little words. Three little words she was sure he'd told Delilah. He'd loved her enough to tattoo her name on his shoulder. She didn't think that he would tattoo "Terry" on his other shoulder.

CHAPTER 10
Make Your Bed

Virginia had been asleep awhile, nodding off in the slow-moving traffic, early spring heat emanating through the car windows. As the mile signposts showed them getting closer to San Antonio, the pressure inside Daniel's gut grew. He felt the muscles in his neck and back tightening into a migraine headache. From his shirt pocket, he took three oxys and chewed them without water. They weren't enough to kill an anxiety attack, but they'd keep him from wigging out for a while. He had no plan. This was not the Danny from the Sandbox. This wasn't even druggie shit-for-brains PTSD Daniel. This was pre-Army Daniel. The inexperienced cat who let things happen to him rather than trying to manage the situation, to plan for the unexpected. Here he was with a pregnant girl claiming to be his dead stepdad's daughter, a girl who was surely going to cause a shitload of problems for him, his mom, his family. He had met the issue with no fore-thought, just goddamn gut reaction.

He couldn't very well show up at Teresa's house with Virginia. He'd either have to spill the entire story or lie his ass off. Neither was a viable option. He could put her up in some shitty hotel near the airport (he had very little money—his vet check wasn't coming for another three weeks). That was also not an option. He didn't want to leave Virginia alone. Really, the only thing to do was to call Alena and play on her good Christian nature to help the girl out. Excepting of course, that Alena had been unusually scattered the past few months.

He pulled over at a gas station outside Seguin, less than an hour from Alena's house. Virginia was dead asleep.

"Gonna hit the bathroom," he said softly.

She didn't stir.

Getting out gently, he closed the door as silently as possible, leaving the car and its AC running. He lit a cigarette and stood under the awning of the station entrance, dialing Alena.

No answer. The cell went directly to voicemail. "Hey, sis, I gotta situation and I need a favor, kind of a big one. Lots to discuss. I'm in New Braunfels and I'll be getting to your house in like an hour or less. I need you to put up somebody for a few days. A girl. I'll explain. Call me back."

No sooner had he hung up than Alena phoned him. "What's up?"

"I need a favor. Actually, we need a favor."

"What're you talking about, Daniel?"

"I've been in Houston. Look, it's complicated."

"How complicated?"

"I've got Tino's daughter with me."

"Tino didn't have a daughter."

"Yeah, he did. I'm looking at her right now. She's sitting in my rental, head conked over, drooling a little."

Daniel told her about the trip to Houston, about Virginia getting caught throwing her dead mother's bedclothes and sheets and belongings into a dumpster.

"It seems Tino lied to Mom and planned to meet Celia in Houston. I think he wanted to sort out something about seeing his daughter, maybe even bring her to live with us. He didn't show. Maybe Mom found out. Do you think Mom knew?"

"It would explain why she made him get fixed. Anyway, why are you getting involved with this?"

"What do you mean? I'm not *getting* involved. I am involved. We're all involved. Don't you care that you have a stepsister out there? She's pregnant, you know."

"Jesus, this keeps getting better all the time, Daniel. What in the world are you getting us involved in? Celia was a major tramp. Maybe this girl is in denial that that jerk stepfather you mentioned was her real father. Tino's dead, even if this is his daughter. The only person who is going to get hurt is Mother. Is that what you want?"

"You don't get it," he said. He lit another cigarette. "I need more time to explain. I've got her in the goddamned car. I need you to put her up for a few days. That's all. I'll straighten it all out."

"You'll straighten it all out," Alena said more stringently than she'd aimed for. "You? Will straighten all this out? Daniel, you can't even straighten yourself out! Your crazy ex is calling me, and who knows who else and telling them you're an alcoholic, that you're abusive, that you're using drugs! Who knows when she'll drop this on Mother's doorstep. How about you straighten that out?"

Daniel felt his chest constricting, his hands beginning to shake. "Look, I need a few days. This is important. I'm going to save her life!"

"What? Who? This girl or your ex? I just told you; she's calling people saying things about you that are shameful. What about that?"

"Look, it's probably all true, okay? That's only part of it. But I can't explain it all right now. There's too much. I've done terrible things. I can't make it up to Cristina. But this girl, I can help her, make things right."

"Cristina says you walked out on her when the baby died. Just left without so much as a goodbye. That's not true, right?"

"Look, I'm going to make it all right. I'm going to save her and her kid. I'm going to make it right this time. You have to help me."

"You sound crazy right now, Daniel. You can't even save yourself."

"Thanks for the vote of confidence. I mean, 'help her,'" he added.

"Only God can save anyone."

"Um, okay, sis. But I'm on my way. She needs a place to sleep. That's all. She's harmless. A sweet girl. You'll like her. I'm on my way."

"Don't—"

Daniel hung up.

Alena would relent. She loved him. She would help him. Back in the car, he cracked a couple of windows so that the still sleeping Virginia wouldn't be exposed to his chain-smoking. He had no choice. Cristina set him off. Most of the time it was a sinking into sadness that only the oxy could relieve. That wasn't an option now, and besides, he wasn't feeling sad. He was feeling anxious, restive. The traffic was moving too fast for him, the bright sunlight overexposing the concrete and the flashing bursts of light strobing off the hundreds of oncoming windshields. He needed to pullover, hypersensitive to the dozens of cars boxing him into the fast lane. Moving over seemed an impossibly dangerous maneuver, the act of driving breaking into discrete, increasingly disconnected actions. He fought the fear that he'd forgotten how to drive as he drifted into a lane. The car he moved towards honked and the driver gave him an angry look, his contorted face communicating that Daniel was an incompetent boob.

On the heels of panic, intense anger flooded Daniel's body, and he thought briefly about plowing into the car, forcing it off the road and bashing the punk's face into his steering wheel until his nose was paste. A small miracle gave Daniel the chance to move in behind the offending driver and edge off into the broad shoulder of the highway. At this Virginia, stirred.

"Everything okay?" she asked. She was groggy but alarmed as she noted that they were on the side of a busy highway. "What's wrong? You okay? Need me to take over?"

"Yeah, probably. I'm, uh, having a bit of trouble," he said, fingers gripped around the steering wheel, his face grown sweaty despite the blasting air condition. "Feels like everything is moving too fast."

"Here," she said opening her door, "let's switch. This traffic is nuts. It makes everyone crazy."

She stepped out and walked around to the driver's side. Daniel still sat, fingers gripping the steering wheel. Virginia knocked on the window and Daniel opened the door almost reluctantly. He scooted out as Virginia looked at him with some curiosity, partly amused, partly concerned.

"Let's pull into a parking lot somewhere so I can smoke a couple of cigarettes without hurting your baby," Daniel said.

"Sure," she said.

They'd only broken into the traffic, when Virginia spotted a rest stop. Pulling into a spot, Daniel opened the door and hopped out before the car was still. He lit up and walked to the bathroom. Inside, he set the cig on the washbasin edge and splashed his flushed face without looking at himself in the mirror. "Fuck," he said loudly.

Another traveler arrived and stood next to him. He commiserated politely. "Traffic's a bitch today," he said empathetically.

Daniel didn't look over or vocalize agreement. The other man dried his hands and walked out saying, "Take-r easy."

Daniel wished he could. He stood upright, this time looking at his reflection. He hardened his eyes, shook his head vigorously, his hands stretching, fingers splayed: open shut, open shut. He picked up the cig and inhaled. He finished it off and lit another. He had no intention of walking back out to the car until he could get a grip on himself. He couldn't have Virginia see him like this. If it had been an option, he would've taken a powder, leaving Virginia to wonder what the hell happened. It would be better than her seeing him crumble.

He thought about Cristina telling Alena that he'd left her after the baby died. It was true. But not true in the way Cristina saw it. She'd *wanted* him gone, maybe dead. She'd poured her grief and anger all over him like hot tar. He couldn't do a goddamn thing there. Her sadness was endless, depthless, and all he did was act as the living embodiment of their child's death. Night after night, he lay next to her, but she wouldn't let him comfort her, not that he would have been much comfort. He felt like an alien, disembodied one moment, as if he were simply watching it unfold feeling nothing, the other moment immersed in the sensory of his body, grotesque and overwhelming, as if he were wearing sandpaper, as if his touch would scour Cristina or anyone or anything within his reach. So, he fucking left. He made the call, got permission to return, took a cab, gear stowed, shame-filled, waited for the airplane that would take him back to the Sandbox, a relief, really. There he could do something about circumstances, could rely on training and experience to guide him, or at least he'd thought that.

He flicked the still lit butt at his reflection and, shaking his head vigorously one last time, walked back to the car where Virginia was waiting. Virginia watched him walk back to the car. He was shaken up, spooked even. She hardly knew him, but it didn't seem in character for him. He seemed mostly self-assured, maybe given to some bouts of emotion, but self-controlled and confident. She'd heard the term before, "military bearing," never really thinking about it, but Daniel seemed to be possessed by it. And yet, right then he looked unsteady, anxious, the cigarette in his mouth more for affect, for cover, part of a mask that without the butt would have made him look like a lost, scared child playing at being a man. Daniel walked to the driver's side and tapped on the window. "I'm cool now, I can drive."

Virginia shook her head smiling. "Nah, I feel like driving. That way I get to pick the jams. You ride. You deserve a break."

Daniel seemed relieved and walked to the opposite side of the car, opened the door, tossed the cigarette and got in. Virginia pulled out of the rest stop and onto the highway.

"You okay?" she asked him.

"Yeah. Fine. Too many smokes get me overhyped sometimes. That's all."

"Okay. But then why are you still smoking? Not that it's my business."

"Habit. Got lots of 'em. Some good, some bad."

"What's a good one?"

Daniel was staring out the passenger window. He was seemingly distracted but answered after a few seconds. He'd been thinking about the answer. "Making my bed. I always make my bed. Didn't used to. But I had this drill who told us, 'Make your goddamned bunk first thing and no matter what sort of shit day you have, you come back to a made bed. You can count on that, soldier.' It's one of the surest things I've learned."

"I'll keep that in mind," Virginia said. "I gotta admit, I don't ever make my bed. Seems pointless."

"Well, it's not," Daniel said. "Make your bed."

Virginia laughed. "You've convinced me, soldier."

She glanced at Daniel. He seemed a bit calmer, his posture relaxed as he continued to stare out the window at the billboards announcing someplace called Cascade Caverns.
"What had you spooked back there?" she asked.
"Did I look spooked? I wasn't spooked, just a little anxious. I get that way sometimes."
"Yeah, me too, I guess. But I hadn't seen you like that is all."
"Well, hang around. It's just, things close in on me from time to time."
"Because of the war?"
"Sure," he said rolling the window down and lighting another cigarette. "Because of the war. That and a lot of other things."
"I guess I'm one of those other things," Virginia said.
"You aren't a thing. You're a person. Things don't mean shit to me. People do."
"You learn that in the war, too?"
"Yeah," Daniel said. "Learned that the hard way."
"Why did you want to drive, back at the rest stop?"
"Just did."
"Was it because you always gotta feel like you're in control of the situation? I get it. Don't get me wrong. I'm like that too. The way I grew up, my mom being drunk all the time, my stepfather being an SOB all the time, I couldn't let my guard down, at least not in front of them. Only with my friend, Carmen, could I be easy. And even her, I didn't tell her about Saturnino."
"I don't know about all that," Daniel said. "Honestly, I'm always feeling out of control. It's been like that a long time. I came back from the war, my ex was a basket case, my head wasn't right, my old life didn't fit anymore. So, I unplugged everything."
"How do you do that?"

"Drinking mostly. Painkillers. Whatever gets me through."

"I see you taking those pills all the time. Lots of them. What are they?"

"Head shit the docs prescribe. Painkillers I prescribe. Like I said, whatever gets me through."

"Helping me out doesn't make a lot of sense, Daniel," Virginia said somewhat reluctantly. "And I'm not saying that so you'll disagree! So don't."

"I've got my own reasons, Virginia," Daniel said. "I'm no knight in shining armor. Not even close. I've done things in my life that I don't like to think about."

"Tell me about it," Virginia said.

Daniel smiled with an almost silent snort. "You have no idea, little girl."

"I think I do," Virginia said. "And I'm nobody's little girl. And I don't need a knight in shining armor either. So don't let that bother you. You aren't responsible for anything that happens to me."

"I left my wife alone after our kid died."

"You had a kid that died?"

"Premature. Never met him. I was overseas when it happened. My ex was seven months pregnant but something happened. When they're that little, their lungs aren't ready. Couldn't breathe without a machine. He died."

"That's terrible," Virginia managed. "Why did you leave?"

"Coward, I guess. Didn't want to face up to what I'd done."

"What you'd done? How's that figure? Wasn't your fault you were overseas, wasn't your fault the baby came early."

In his mind's eye, he saw Pumpkin and Goldfish, together, both struggling for breath, both gasping, tiny mouths moving, chests rising and falling quickly, no oxygen, hearts pumping in vain, tiny fists waving frantically until they didn't.

"Lots of times you don't know what you're responsible for until later. You do something wrong, something really terrible, and that's hard to own, but that's only the beginning. Because then there comes the results that you didn't see coming. Unintentional as may be, they come, the dues."

"I'm not following you," Virginia said. "What could you have done that was so bad that it somehow affected your baby?"

"Let's just leave it at that," Daniel said. "You're not my shrink. You don't get paid to listen to my bullshit. Let's just say, I'm trying to do better."

Now on the outskirts of San Antonio, Virginia turned her attention to the road. "Where are we headed?"

"Not far now. My sister lives on this side of town."

He pointed her in the right direction, and ten minutes later they pulled up to a small ranch-style house with a fairly big yard that contained three large, twisted live oaks.

"I'm kind of scared," Virginia admitted after she'd turned the ignition off but remained in the seat without moving to open the car door.

"Me too," Daniel said smiling. "Nah, Alena's a good person. She can be a little serious sometimes, but she's solid. I can count on her."

A slight smile playing on her lips, Virginia shrugged and moved to open the door.

～～～

Filomena and Graciela had many suiters. They lined up to talk to them, to court them, to tell them that they were beautiful and alluring, lithe, sexy even. Elvira had bought herself a nice little laptop, which she brought over to Alena's house a couple of hours before Richard got home.

The two would sit side by side on their respective computers, answering queries, chatting live with male friends. There were Italians, Greeks, a couple English blokes and an assortment of men from different places in South America. Filomena and Graciela had been invited to travel to many places, some exotic, all of them romantic.

Nicolo was concerned about Graciela's estranged husband, Serapio, and his growing hostility. Serapio had even threatened Nicolo from his own account. It was fun to bring people to life.

The suiters jostled for attention, sending silly poems, songs. They used all their monthly points to buy the two women virtual flowers and glasses of fine wine.

The fun stopped when Richard got home. Even though Elvira was a thoughtful guest, who often cooked dinner for the family, Richard made it a point to be sullen and even rude. He'd eat and not thank her and then go off to the bedroom to watch television. This was fine by Alena. It meant that the adventures of Filomena and Graciela could continue late into the night, the intrigue growing quieter.

Otherwise: life was boring. Alena's house, with its real smells, its crowded space, the snagged carpet, the grimy sofa growing even grimier, was boring. The sports fanatic husband who rarely left the couch on weekends was more than boring.

That snagged rug had cost $79 at Lowes. It was nothing like the oriental rug Filomena was presented with when she danced in Istanbul. Filomena was entranced by the architecture, the history of the city, its energy, its intricate complications, a city which was more a living being than a place, with fault lines of cultures and times past, that made the city seem incongruous, like a waking dream, but still coming together. Filomena and Alena were very similar in that way.

Alena was keeping a diary for Filomena. She wrote about her lovers, her adventures, her love for her father, an honorable man who'd given her all the love she needed, but who'd died young. Since then, Filomena had struggled to achieve her dream, and yet, now achieved, something was still lacking. That's why she frequented "Plenty of Fish."

Richard came into the room and looked around. He sniffed the air, looked a bit curious, a bit guarded. "So where's your shadow," he asked Alena. "Is *la Sombra* in her own house, for once?"

"She has a cold. She's resting today."

He smiled. "That's good," he said. "Real good. Maybe we can get out and do something?"

"Don't count on anything elaborate. I'm tired, and Daniel is acting crazier than usual. He's bringing over our long-lost, wayward stepsister. It's a real mess."

"Why haven't you mentioned this before? Seems like a big deal. You don't seem very happy about it."

"We've got full plates already, and Mother is flipping out."

"Doesn't seem too hard. Just meet her and be friendly. After all, what could she want?"

Richard was naive. People always wanted something. Money, some kind of claim on the pennies Tino had left Teresa? Maybe she wanted a place to live, free of charge. Who was to say that she was even Tino's real daughter.

"She's preggo, Richard, knocked up. A family is at a premium."

"I don't get why you're so riled up about this, especially when you bring up Daniel."

"Let's not," Alena said, still looking at the computer screen.

"Let's not *what*? What's the deal?"

"You don't want to know, and I don't want to talk about it."

"Sure. We won't talk about it. We won't talk about a fucking thing. Have a hell of a time on that fuckin' computer."

"You don't need to use vile language," Alena said.

Richard was halfway out the door when he heard her admonish him. He turned around, stepped between Alena and the computer, and ripped the monitor from the desk. He flung it into the wall, demolishing the screen. Alena was speechless. The act was violent and pathetic. In a rage that came from her stomach, she called him an idiot.

Richard stood there feeling like one.

~~~

Terry didn't like Vivian's long hair, her toothy smile and the flirtatious way she put her hands on Eric's motorcycle. The woman had accompanied Roger, another of Eric's good friends. He was fatter and older than Eric, but he was a lot of fun. He played the guitar and accompanied everyone singing around the campfire.

The woman that he brought was too pretty for him. Even though Vivian stayed on her side of the campfire and acted like she had no intentions on her Eric, Terry knew what she was up to. The eyes don't lie. She spent the night laughing too easily at Eric's jokes. He was many things, but he was not funny.

Of course, Terry laughed at all his jokes, but there wasn't any good reason for anyone else to laugh at them because they weren't remotely funny or even cute. Vivian laughed and batted her eyes, and for his part, Eric ate it all up. It was as if he liked making Teresa jealous. After a while, she dropped her hand from his arm. He should've noticed that as a major sign that she was unhappy.

Later, when she tried to tell Alena about the weekend, her daughter was unresponsive. Alena wanted her mother to feel guilty about her new love life. But Teresa did not feel guilty at all. Tino and she had lived their lives! Now that life was over, *had* been over, it seemed that neither of her children wanted her to start a new one.

Teresa tried to continue with her story. "Eric liked the attention. You should have seen him coming into the tent after I'd had enough. I thought he was there to apologize, but, no, he wanted his guitar. He was going to stay up all night singing to that *vieja*."

"It's so self-destructive. Why do you do that?" Alena was angry.

"He won't tell me he loves me, but he's proud of his tattoo with that woman's name on it."

"Is that it," Alena said. "Does it all boil down to that? Your insecurity! Jealousy? That's it?"

Teresa said nothing. There was nothing to say. What did Alena know about how she felt? About what she'd had to contend with after the first husband left her and after the second died? What did she know about the days growing shorter? How much of her life had she spent considering only others, worrying about what they thought, how they felt, how they were going to react? Now, it was her turn, and everyone could just get used to it.

CHAPTER 11
Monster

Alena was so goddamned rude. She looked at Virginia and Daniel, gave the merest sign of a smile, told Virginia to take a load off and then asked Daniel pointedly to help her with some things in the back.

"And if he lied to Mother all these years? Mother might not have had anything to do with any of this. You want to make her face all these ugly things?"

"She's Tino's. It's written all over her face. Why would she pretend to be Tino's daughter? It wasn't as if he had some kind of unclaimed fortune. He was a poor, ex-con, ex-junkie who could barely walk, couldn't even do menial labor towards the end. What's the gain in that?"

To Alena, the pregnant girl was obviously running from something or someone. Who was the father of her baby? He could be a psycho or a druggie. It could even be that stepfather's child.

"It's not just yourself here. You're talking about Mother and me and Richard and Tonia."

"I know all that," he said. "That's why we're talking. I need your blessing on this."

"Blessing to do what, exactly?"

"I'm not sure."

Alena give him the look reserved for idiocy. Daniel needed to worry about his own wrecked life, not some con artist bent on revenge on a dead father who'd abandoned her.

"I can't give you that," she told Daniel.

Alena knew that he was disappointed in her. So what! She was a skeptic, had a nose for trouble. And her nose was telling her that something wasn't right about this long-lost daughter.

"Weren't you the one warning Mother about con artists on the internet? Even if this girl is on the level, it means heavy duty problems for us." She wanted to ask Daniel, and what about your doings in Iraq and Cristina? When will those come out and add to all the fun?

"Look," he told her, "this Virginia situation is part of a whole ton of things going on in my life. I can't explain it, but I've got the feeling that helping her is going to wind up helping me, all of us, in the end."

Alena had heard enough. She wanted Daniel to get the message that his problems were enough for the family. Why did he want to steer right into more disaster, more heartache? "I told you, your crazy ex called and accused you of being a drunken, junkie wife-beater. She called you crazy. This isn't helping!"

"Let me tell you," he said, "you should have seen Virginia when she was telling me, like someone finally getting to the center of the biggest mystery of their life. Looking at that picture hidden from her for so long, she was seeing her real father's face, her own face. It was a face she didn't remember but now was coming to life in her mirror, staring back at her. Those blue eyes."

"Good Lord, Daniel, do you have to be so melodramatic? You sound like a soap opera. What about our problems? Our dad wasn't around either. Remember that?"

"I feel sympathy for our family, for Mother, for you."

Alena looked toward the patio door. "Finish the story," she said impatiently. "Who knows what that girl is up to inside my house. Tonia will be home soon. I don't want her alone in there with a nut job."

"Like I said, she's pregnant, but she doesn't know the father very well."

"Oh my God," Alena said. "That's just perfect. A slut to boot."

"There are these letters. Two. Both from Tino. One from when he was in prison for something he did before the long one at Huntsville. There's a censor's stamp on it from jail. I'm not sure about the dates exactly, but it would be close to just after he'd been sent up. He asks Celia to wait for him. He apologizes for being a screw-up, begs her, really, to forgive him. He tells her that he knows she's pregnant. He says he wouldn't blame her if she went away and forgot him. He wants to take care of their kid. You can tell he's hurting."

"Clearly, Celia wasn't having it. Tino told a million stories about that vicious drunk idiot."

"When he got out, apparently, he tracked down her address . . . visited her and Virginia when she was little. Years later, he sent her a ticket to meet up in Houston, only he didn't show up."

"Why not?" Alena asked despite her irritation.

"I've got my theory. It's postmarked from San Antonio, after he'd met Mom. Tells her that he wants to meet at their old restaurant."

"Very romantic."

"No. There's nothing romantic in the letter. He'd married Mom. Maybe he wanted to be a part of Virginia's life."

"Oh my God," she said. "This is what you want to reveal? That Tino was going around planning a secret rendezvous. Mom's not suffered enough?"

"That's just it. There's nothing romantic there. It's his attempt to meet and talk about his daughter. But it never happened. He didn't show up. Though Celia did."

"Why?" she asked despite herself.

"I don't know. He never wrote her back. There's a letter Celia wrote Tino after he didn't show. She never mailed it, though. Sad shit."

"This is only going to hurt Mother and make her mull over every moment she had with Tino, wondering if he was sneaking off behind her back—which he was. It's going to set her back, just like he died all over again. Worse, because it's killing the memory she has of him."

"What if Mom knows more than we think? Even if she doesn't, Virginia is having Tino's grandkid. All this girl knows is the Tino who showed up at the doorstop only to never return . . . and the terrible stories of his that we used to shake our heads at . . . all the worse for her because that was the old Tino, and she's got no idea about the man he became."

"Wait, I thought he didn't show up in Houston?"

"Apparently, at some point, Virginia doesn't remember when, only that she was a kid, Tino showed up at their doorstep in Louisiana. It didn't go well. Celia threw him out. She was either pissed that he'd found them or that he hadn't come to claim her but only to connect with his kid. Anyway, it's just a fuzzy memory."

"What kind of man would give up on a daughter?" Alena said. "Maybe there never was a *new* Tino."

"That's the thing, why did Tino go? What did he expect? Did Mom know he had a kid? Maybe he kept it under wraps. What the hell happened? This trip we've been on, we're finding the key to Virginia's past and where she is now. It means something to me, too."

Alena could see in Daniel's face that he wasn't going to let it be. "You've got two nights. You tell Mother. You lay out this awful story. But when it blows up, you're picking up the pieces."

"You'll see," Daniel said. "Something is going to come out of this, something good."

His sister's irate skepticism gave him pause, however. He might be wrong. He was often wrong, misjudging situations and people since he'd returned from the Sandbox.

~~~

Virginia sat acutely aware that Daniel and his sister were discussing her. His sister's house was small and tidy, and it was obvious that she knew how to make the most without much money. She made her own things, little knickknacks hung on the wall with pictures of her little girl from birth to her current age. This jumped out at her. Celia never cared about pictures. Virginia didn't remember her ever having a camera in her hand. She faintly recalled having to sit on Santa's lap when she was little and how the camera caught her making a shitty face. She only remembered because Celia brought the picture out once and told her, "This is what you look like when you cry! *Fea*, ugly."

Virginia felt uncomfortable, embarrassed. It was hot, and her legs and feet hurt. Waiting for a verdict from Alena made her feel like a poor slob, hat in hand, which is what she was, she guessed. She wanted something better for the tiny piece of rice floating around in her belly. But she wasn't even sure what "better" meant. A house? A good father? Something else that people talked about—success? She'd never known anyone "successful." When she thought of that word, she pictured old white men with lots of money, wearing fancy ties, going places no one else was allowed to visit or see.

A house like Alena's would be nice. Virginia didn't want or need anything big. Alena was successful. She had a husband and a house that smelled pleasant instead of like old, cooked food. A family. That was success. People who loved you and stuck around. She sat there like a small house inside another larger house, stuck, heavy, glued to the couch. She suddenly felt like running out of there as fast she could. She didn't know what she was doing there. What did she hope to find? These people were strangers, and here she was, butting in because she didn't belong anywhere.

Just then, Daniel stuck his head out of the kitchen. "Hey, Virginia, you need something to drink? We're almost done back here."

He ducked back and came out with a glass of water. He stood in front of her, offering the water, a smile on his face, only it was pained. It shook her out of her dark place, where there were nothing but questions. In that instant she had a totally messed up thought that Daniel was the kind to make a good husband.

Sure, he had problems. But he was sweet, not bad-looking, and he was the kind of man who would do whatever it took to keep his family fed and protected. That's the way her stupid brain worked. It made her sick to think that she needed someone to protect her, to shelter the baby she was sheltering in her belly.

"Thanks," she said, taking the glass. "How's it going out there? Tough, right? I'm sorry."

"Don't be. Everything is cool. It's just a lot to fill Alena in on and it's taking a minute. It's all good."

Daniel went back to the patio through the kitchen. Virginia heard the sliding door shut.

The couch she sat on was nice and soft, probably expensive. She looked at the picture of the three people who lived there. The man was good-looking. He seemed like a regular guy from his smile, which was more in his eyes than on his mouth. Alena seemed blithely unhappy, though. In fact, she

seemed like she might be a bit of a bitch. Part of this judgment was that Virginia could tell Alena didn't want her there.
But part of Virginia's assessment was based on her husband's
smile, which seemed a smile that only a long-suffering
human could manage. Of course, being a bit of a bitch was
necessary if you were going to survive. Virginia took pride in
being a bit of bitch herself.

Virginia wondered what they saw in her face. A slut, desperate, knocked-up. Well, she guessed it was true. But there
was a lot more they couldn't see. There was so much she
couldn't see herself. She felt like the baby, still developing,
still turning into something else. She could be anything, anyone, if. . . . What did she want? Just to make them like her?
Love her? Yuck. It sounded gross, pathetic even. The very
last thing she wanted to be. But everyone needed love, so
why was it yuck? Just basic love was all. Just then, a little
girl walked into the house.

"Mom," she called out, seeing Virginia on the couch.
"Are you home?"

She hung back near the doorway, not wanting to walk
through the living room where Virginia sat.

Alena came in right away. "It's okay, Tonia. I'm here. Me
and your uncle are talking a bit. Get yourself a snack." Alena
gave Virginia a look and quickly added, "This is Virginia, a
friend of your uncle's." With that she walked back to the
patio.

Rather than get a snack, the little girl gave a shy smile
and walked to her bedroom, leaving Virginia alone again.
After a few moments, she heard the bathroom door shut. The
sound of the door closing and the whine of the bathroom fan
made her feel even more lonely.

As Alena prepped dinner, she considered Virginia. The
girl was a little thing. She'd make for an odd sight once her
belly got big. She was barely 5'2". She didn't look like a con

artist, just young, a kid, maybe only a decade older than her seven-year-old Tonia. It made her wince for the both of them. Alena did feel bad for the girl but knew that she'd be trouble. Already, with all the stress over this Virginia person, she hadn't even thought to tell Daniel that Richard had thrown the computer into the wall. There was a time when she would've confided in Daniel immediately, but those days seemed gone.

During dinner, Alena went right to the baby talk, something easy for them to discuss. Virginia told her she'd only just found out. What more did the girl need to screw her up? And the father? Virginia told her right up front that she wasn't sure about his identity.

"It's probably this boy named Rick. But he's not in the picture anymore."

Probably? Alena had known the girl was trouble. "Well, it's very difficult raising a child, especially on your own. You better make sure he's in the picture."

She could tell Daniel didn't like her saying that, but if he wanted this girl in his life, in their lives, then Alena was going to speak her piece, and it was too bad if anyone didn't like it.

To her credit, Virginia didn't get smart with Alena. Nowadays, kids just gave you the finger or told you to stuff it.

Daniel began to fidget and so he brought up Saturnino. "So, what's your biggest question about your father," he asked her.

Virginia looked confused by the question, as if she hadn't thought about it or maybe didn't think someone would just up and ask her. She kept quiet for a minute and then said, "Did he ever mention me?"

Alena could tell that Daniel was ready to sugarcoat the answer, so she jumped in. "No."

Daniel gave her a look, a rare angry look, the one which showed that he meant business.

"I don't want to start off by us lying to each other," Alena said. "Something tells me you're not the type who wants to be told what she wants to hear. Neither was Tino. He called himself a straight shooter. I'm that way too. I don't want to hurt anyone's feelings, but sometimes there are tough things that need to be said."

"Did he care?"

"I don't know the answer to that," Alena answered.

"I'm sure he did," Daniel said quickly. "You told me how he went down there to find you when you were a kid. That wasn't a sign of someone who didn't care. In the end, it must've bothered my mom when he insisted on trying to find you. When things get confusing like that, it can cloud your judgment."

"Is that why he gave up? Because your mom didn't want him to make me part of his life?"

"I don't know," Daniel said.

"You want to know why?" Alena said. "Why did the things that happened happen? Somehow things got set into motion and messed up the plans. According to what Daniel has told me, you were supposed to end up in Houston, but instead you got taken somewhere else. And Tino, he wound up somewhere else, and your mother ran into someone else . . . and things got jumbled up, and bad things came to pass. . . . Now, you're here, but too late to catch up to him. Things have gotten all knotted up, and you want to un-knot them, see how things should've been. Only you probably won't."

"I'm here to find out, that's all."

Alena thought for a moment. Who was she to tell this girl such hard things? She remembered Tino and his commitment to the truth, or at least what she'd thought was his commitment to the truth.

"Nothing ever really gets un-knotted for anybody," Alena told them both.

Maybe she was telling herself too. Maybe even Tonia, who didn't understand any of it yet, but too soon would.

~~~

Elvira had come up with a good idea for them to use their made-up names when they were on "Fish" together. Alena loved the idea and suggested that they use their avatar names in conversation. She'd call her Graciela and Elvira would call her Filomena. It was a kind of a joke.

"Hello Graciela, you look wonderful this evening. Hahahaha."

Even though they laughed, it wasn't funny. More like they were conspiring to escape from prison and no one but they knew what was going on, not the guards nor the warden nor the other prisoners. They were going to dig their way out.

Alena had begun to see Richard charitably as a fellow prisoner, but one who could and would ruin her escape plan if allowed. He had to be kept in the dark.

It felt somewhat strange to Alena that she was wearing Filomena in front of others. It wasn't so much a disguise, more like a wonderful new wardrobe that she'd acquired that made her thinner and cuter and funnier and smarter. She wore Filomena when she went to the store or when she talked to the mothers at Tonia's school or the clients at the bank. Dressed as Filomena, she made out that she was there to cover for poor Alena, a friend in need. It was like the movie from when she was a kid, *Freaky Friday* where she was in someone else's body, or was it someone else's mind? It was getting a bit confusing. She wasn't confused about the feeling she got when she was Filomena. It was like she was Cinderella, a mistreated, misunderstood waif.

She surveyed the other mothers at the school: frumpy, trapped in their dreary lives, stuck with boring husbands in loveless marriages, raising entitled, snotty, dull children. Not that her Tonia was any of those.

She'd begun to exercise, stretching, practicing more explosive dance moves, even putting together a routine worthy of Filomena's talents. She watched dancers on YouTube and observed their strength and grace, their sensuality, a man with strong arms holding a lithe, powerful woman aloft. She pictured herself in the dancer's place. It added a dimension of tragic beauty to her movement. She was reconnecting to her body, her emotions, which had been neglected, and thus relegated to shows of anger and resentment. Alas, Filomena bore no relation to the stunted, one-dimensional woman that Alena had devolved into over the years married to Richard.

Alena put together a short dance sequence, a solo effort because she didn't have a partner. She'd never trained, never studied dance like she'd so desperately wanted to when she was young. She could have. She'd had talent, unrecognized and diminished by her mom and teachers, those who could have cultivated her ability and aspiration.

She'd never tried out for the dance team in high school. First of all, her mother would not permit it. The mere suggestion of auditioning had caused a commotion in the household, with Teresa shutting down Tino's advocacy on Alena's behalf. "I'm not going to have my daughter prancing around in a mini-skirt and pompoms!"

Alena had always been shy, but now had become more so. No—scared, Alena now realized. Shy was a lesser, inaccurate word for scared. The truth was she didn't think enough of herself to get out there and be seen. She blamed her mother for this. Never an encouraging word from her. Nothing but criticism, always telling her to cover up, to tone it down, to hush, to stop making a spectacle. Alena knew there was no question as to who was the true drama queen in the family.

Richard had played football, and she would go to his practice ostensibly to support him, but longingly, she'd watch the dancers the entire time. They seemed to have so much fun. They were confident and talked loud and fast with the self-assurance that came with acceptance. They were a crew with an identity. They were friends.

Trying again, Alena asked Teresa if she could join the pep squad. She explained that those girls didn't wear the same sort of skimpy outfits and didn't perform or march out there for the whole school to see. It was just a bunch of girls who sat in the bleachers cheering and waving pompoms. Being a member of something, anything, would have nurtured a bit of confidence. Who knew what could have happened? But her mother said no. It would interfere with Wednesday night church, where only the true believers could be found, mostly older people and a few kids dragged there by strict parents. Kids like her and Daniel and the Rodríguez girls, whose mom would make them sing a song every Wednesday night in front of the congregation. The Rodríguez girls wore baggy, home-made dresses and sang songs in Spanish that the rest of the kids mocked. Although Alena joined in the ridicule, she related to those poor girls and the silent shame forced upon them by an oblivious mother.

Elvira told her that she had some interest from a guy right there in San Antonio. He wanted to meet her for a drink, and she wanted to go. Alena reminded her that she looked nothing like "her" picture. But Elvira felt that she looked enough like Graciela that she could take the chance.

She had been dieting with Alena and lost even more weight than her. Of course, she had more to lose.

"Why do you want to go on this date anyway? Aren't we having fun enough?" Alena asked.

"I don't have a husband like you."

Alena considered that Elvira might be mocking her.

"Could you help fix me up? Like makeup and stuff," Elvira entreated.

For a second, Alena thought about telling her best friend that she could go straight to hell. If she wanted to ruin what they had going, then she could do it all on her own. But then Alena acted graciously and told her that she would do her makeup if the date happened.

They logged on from Alena's laptop and went to work sending each other messages. "I'm in California. I'm staying with friends in Napa."

"I'm in Miami visiting my beautiful sisters."

They played until Richard got home. As usual, he was in a foul mood, slamming things around in the kitchen, stomping up and down the hall, doing God only knew what until Filomena told Graciela she had to go.

The night Richard moved out, he had eavesdropped on their gameplay. "Who the hell is Graciela?"

"What?"

"Yeah, you called Elvira, Graciela."

"You made a mistake."

"No, I didn't," he said. "You called her Graciela, and she called you something like Filly."

"Since when do you care what I do or don't say to my friend? It's just girl talk."

"No, it's not. You're playing some weird game. You're always on that computer."

"Well, you've made that impossible. Are you going to break my laptop now?"

"You don't pay attention to Tonia or me."

"I don't want to argue. Do you want Tonia to hear?"

"You're cheating on me."

"Don't be crazy," she said.

She kept her eyes trained on the laptop but watched from the corner of her eye, lest Richard decide he needed to destroy her internet access.

"Things got to change around here," he said, standing behind her. "Did you hear me?"

She remained silent.

"No more of this computer shit. No more Elvira. No more of this fairytale make believe. You're my wife, supposed to be anyway."

"I'm your wife, not your daughter." She was still looking down at her laptop.

Richard snapped it shut from behind.

Now she turned to him. "What the hell do you think you're doing? Get out of this room! Don't you ever touch any of my things again!"

"I'll do a damned sight better than that," he said.

He spun around and headed for their bedroom. Alena could hear him pulling drawers open, pulling out socks and T-shirts. He had decided to play hardball. He was convinced she was going to come running in to tell him to put away his things. But he was wrong. After a few minutes, he went back to Alena's office.

"You really don't give a damn, huh? I'm going to stay with my brother. You can explain to Tonia. I can't stand living with you anymore."

Alena didn't even bother to turn. "Whatever."

Silently, he left the room, and a few moments later she heard him pick up the keys and leave the house. She listened to the sound of his truck rumbling away. For an instant, she felt a pang of overwhelming anxiety. But Filomena was there, too, and she wasn't scared or anxious at all.

The next day, Elvira came over early. She had a coffee date. Rather, Graciela had a date for coffee. She brought her makeup kit, which was all wrong for her. The palette didn't match her dark complexion. She'd brought two outfits, a cheap gown, tags still attached, ridiculously inappropriate for a first date, and something more casual, a short flowery skirt and a white blouse that she'd made herself.

She was ambitious: the blouse was still too tight despite her efforts at dropping weight. Filomena told her she looked good in it. There was no need to add to Graciela's nervousness. The two of them were best friends.

"Oh, Filomena," she said, "what should I talk about?"

"There's so much. There's your dancing and your recent trip to Miami."

"I looked it up like you said I should," Graciela said. "I know the names of beaches and some restaurants, like I've been there."

"You have been there, Graciela. Remember that."

"Okay, yes. But what did I see? What did I do?"

Filomena had her sit facing the mirror while she retrieved her much more extensive makeup kit. She turned on the mirror light, a fancy one she'd bought at Target.

"Now, Graciela, you tell me what you did."

"I spent time in the sun, a lot of time in the sun, and I met with my cousin and her two friends who moved to Miami to be models."

"Okay, but maybe only one model. Who were the other two?"

"Students?"

"That's good. Students at the school where these girls are studying to be doctors. They want to go back to Peru and specialize in tropical diseases."

"I don't know," Graciela said sounding far more like Elvira.

"Okay. What is it you like to do?"

"Me or her?"

"You."

"Hang out with you. Sew."

"That's good. You do know a lot about sewing. You made the skirt and blouse you're wearing. You talk tonight about how you've turned your sights on creating your own fashion line. You can show off your smart skirt. You'll be in your comfort zone. You do, after all, make clothes. Use the truth enough to hold the pattern together, to make it real."

"Like thread," Graciela said.

"Just like thread," Filomena agreed.

Tonia was full of questions about where her father had gone. Alena explained that he wanted to see his brother, Uncle Robert, for a few days. It satisfied her for the moment. She watched them dolling up Graciela and wanted to know why they'd made up names for each other.

Alena told her that they were pretending for a game. Tonia understood that. She and her friends did it every day on the playground, just like her mommy and Elvira did.

It made sense to all three of them now, the child and the two women. The idea of playing roles, of dressing up, of putting on makeup and finding a dreamboat. It was all nonsense, except when it wasn't. Because the pretense seemed deeper and more meaningful than the role that had been forced on them their entire humdrum lives.

Now that Graciela was having her night out with the mysterious Tony, Filomena wanted to get out there, too. All this computer stuff was only a long rehearsal. Alena owed it to Filomena to let her loose. *Us against the world*, she thought as she looked through messages from an admirer in Austin. He was just the sort of chap that Filomena might really like.

The real world was threatening. She had her marriage problems, then Daniel with his, and their mother and her romances. Filomena was such a wonderful alternative. Filomena had done such a good job that she was now inventing Alena. Filomena was not one to wait. Alena pictured Filo-

mena on a Saturday afternoon. It was a beautiful Spring day,
and she sat on a veranda, no, a porch . . . no, a balcony.
Watching from the heights of her Chicago apartment. She
was attempting to sort out her feelings about Tomás, who was
ardently demanding that she visit him in Mexico City.
He wrote that spring was the best time to visit. He'd take
her to Puebla. The cool evening breezes, the dramatic
churches and colorful squares, the trees glowing soft gold,
the smells of the bakeries and cafes radiating the romantic
warmth of two lovers' souls. He'd written that, "the romantic warmth of two lovers' souls."

Of course, Filomena could not go. She couldn't because
Alena could never go. The answer was to do away with
Alena, just drop her like an itchy, constricting suit of clothes.

With Richard's departure, Alena had a chance to figure it
out. What sort of reason could Filomena have to not take
Tomás up on his offer? Surely not the truth, that she was a liar
with a humdrum existence living in a small box house on the
westside of San Antonio with very little in the way of romance or intrigue or even talent.

This other life that she'd made? Now *that* was desire and
passion. She'd revived something dormant. She'd thought all
her life that a prince charming would do it for her. When
she'd first fallen in love with Richard, she'd thought that it
would lead to a rich inner life. This adventure of hers—and
who was it hurting anyway?—was what she'd longed for. She
was determined to accomplish it on her own.

Daniel called and asked for Alena to co-host a luncheon
to introduce Virginia to the family.

"Look," he said finally, "how about we do this at your
place? The dinner didn't go so bad, did it? It'll be small.
Mom, me, you, Richard, Tonia, a few of mom's cousins. It'll
be more comfortable at your house." He paused for a moment. "Help me," he said.

"No," Alena said forcefully. "Things are crazy for me personally. My marriage has flamed out. I bet Richard's told you."

"Not much more than that Elvira is there all the time."

"No, she's not."

"I'm not trying to make you angry with the poor guy, just trying to bring it to your attention."

"Graciela makes things easier around here. Richard doesn't understand how badly I need companionship, female companionship, a friend to talk to, share things."

"Who's Graciela," he asked her.

"Elvira," Alena corrected herself. "She loves Tonia and brings her toys. And we have fun. Is that so bad?"

"I guess not."

"I can't host the lunch," Alena said, "but I'll attend. That's all I can manage right now."

"Thanks," Daniel said.

She could hear the gratitude in his voice. She hung up. Now, she could go back to Filomena's complicated, urgent life.

~~~

Eric wouldn't tell Teresa that he loved her, but he gave her a dog instead. It was still a puppy, but already as big as a small horse. He was a black dog, some mix of two big dogs. He was stinky with a big tongue that hung out of his mouth. He slobbered all over the floor and then the couch that he obviously thought was his.

Eric seemed proud of his gift to Teresa. He'd brought in a big shiny chrome food bowl in one hand and in the other a sack of dog food the size of a forty-pound sack of potatoes.

"I haven't named him," he said. "I figured you'd want to name him."

"Why would I name him?"

"Because he's yours, Terry," he said putting the food bowl down in the kitchen. The big dumb dog followed him, expecting Eric to fill it up.

"Mine?"

"Yeah, that way you don't have to worry about someone breaking in. He'll be good company, too. Look at him," he said beaming at the slobbering black dog.

"He's too big. I don't want a dog. He scares me."

"He's a sweetheart. You'll see."

He walked over to the bag to fill the bowl, but the brainless dog got in between his feet and almost tripped him.

"You'll have to watch out you don't trip over him. Just give him a good nudge with your knee. He'll learn."

She didn't want a dog, especially this clumsy giant thing. But she could tell by the way that Eric was playing with him that he thought very highly of the dog.

"He'll protect you, Terry."

"I've got Daniel," she said, "and anyway, you and the dog really seem to like each other. Why don't you keep him?"

"You don't like him?" he asked.

The dog seemed to be wondering, too. They both looked at her expectantly, with big eyes, their hearts ready to break. She thought that she'd buy herself some time by taking the dog in until she could think of a good reason to give him back to Eric. Maybe Daniel was allergic to him. Yes, that would be plausible.

"Don't worry, I'm going to buy his food. I'll keep him fed. He's going to be big as a house. He's half Doberman and half German Shepard. You couldn't ask for a better guard or companion."

"I thought you were my perfect guard and companion," she said.

Eric knew what she was getting at. Even the dog seemed to know.

"Sure, Terry. He's just a sentry, my stand-in when I'm not around. You'll see. You're going to love this little guy. Any ideas on what to call him?"

"Big Ugly Dog?"

"Come on, Terry. You're going to hurt his feelings."

"Satan."

"That's not bad," Eric said.

"I was joking," Teresa said quickly. She wasn't about to invoke the devil a dozen times a day. She had enough problems.

"How about Adolf," Daniel said, coming out of his bedroom.

"Hi there, Daniel," Eric said. "What do you think of the new addition to the family?"

"He's really big."

"He'll get bigger," Eric said, petting the dog's belly.

"How about Cerberus?" Daniel suggested.

"What's that mean?" Eric asked.

"The three-headed dog that guards the entrance to the underworld. He makes sure no one gets out of Hades."

"What's all this about Hades," Teresa said.

Teresa watched Daniel walk to where the dog was still being scratched by Eric. He put his bare foot on the dog's tummy. She realized that if they named the animal, it would be that much more difficult to get rid of him.

"I don't want to name him now," she said. "I have to think about it, anyway. I don't know if he can stay. Daniel has allergies. Right, *m'ijo*?" She looked at her son, doing everything but winking at him.

He didn't get it. He liked the big vile thing. "Huh? Allergies. Nah, no allergies. Not to dogs. Peanuts and penicillin. You know that, Mom."

She rolled her eyes at him, but he didn't notice that either. He did like the big stupid thing. He'd always had a thing for strays. Too good a heart, Teresa thought. It got him into trouble.

"Monster," Teresa said.

"Monster?" Eric said.

"Monster?" Daniel repeated.

"Monster," Teresa said with finality. "His name is Monster."

"Well, he's one helluva lucky monster," Eric said. "They were going to kill the poor feller if it wasn't for me saving him in the nick of time. It's destiny!"

CHAPTER 12
Fairyland

After Eric left, Daniel knew it was time to talk to Teresa.

"Mom, a girl named Virginia, Celia's daughter . . . she says that she's Tino's," Daniel started.

It took her a moment to understand what he was talking about. Virginia? Tino?

"She's his daughter and she found me, us. And she's pregnant."

Teresa sat speechless. Tino's daughter? Now that he was dead and gone.

"How do you know that it's true?"

"Her story adds up. I know it's hard, but there's no other way. I need to tell you all of it."

"All of it?"

"He found them in Louisiana about four years after he got out of a short jail stint. Celia had left with this other guy. She'd gotten tired of Tino's criminal life. He went to visit once but never went back. It looks like Celia and him might have made plans to meet in Houston a few years later, but he didn't show up. Didn't he ever tell you anything about this?"

Teresa sat numbly, thinking and thinking. The girl had found them. It was an intrusion. It wasn't right that Tino's misdeeds should force her into the past, a past she didn't want to recover, a past that had died with Tino. How was this hers to deal with?

"She's a sweet girl," Daniel went on. "She's been through all kinds of hell. She's come all this way to find Tino. It's tragic, her having missed him by a year. That's why I'm helping her. I've brought her to San Antonio."

"What does she want?" Teresa asked him.

He looked at her with puzzlement. "What does she want? What sort of response is that? She wants answers about where she came from. She wants to know who her father was. I think she deserves to know the Tino we knew, and not just the guy her mother lied about. I don't know why Tino didn't stay in her life. It probably had a lot to do with Celia, but I think that we can help Tino by setting some things straight. Don't you want to do that? To see that Tino is still alive. He's got family and soon a grandkid. That kind of makes you a grandmother."

"What does she want?" Teresa asked again, just as coldly as the first time.

There was a ball of thick, dark mud in her belly. She didn't want this. She had finally let go of the past, let it disappear like the last point of a ship sinking deep into the ocean.

"You shouldn't have brought her here."

Daniel was looking at her with a deepening focus. "Mom," he said, "how much did you know about Virginia?"

"You never should have gone to find her," Teresa said.

"I told you, she found us," he said pointedly.

"Tino used to say, never ask a question you don't want the answer to."

"She's having your grandchild, yours and Tino's."

"Not mine," she told him. "I told him he had to leave his old life behind if he wanted to be part of our lives. No more dancing, no more drinking, no more drugs, no more connections to that ugly past of his."

"Did you tell Tino that he had to turn his back on his daughter?" Daniel said.

Teresa kept her eyes on his.

"You did," he said as if speaking to himself. "But why would you do that, Mom?"

She wouldn't defend herself to her son. It wasn't fair. None of it was fair.

"We all have our own problems. Tino had his. I have mine. God knows, you have yours. You do what you can handle. God gives you strength for that. This girl, she'll be all right, but it's not my duty to fix Tino's messes. Not anymore. He felt guilty about her, but I knew that if he went back to the past, it would suck him in."

Daniel shook his head.

"Don't shake your head at me," Teresa said with lacing anger. "You have no idea what it was like then, your father gone, me getting older with two young kids, and then a good man, yes, damaged, but still good, ready to love me and you kids! And then this horrible woman trying to tempt him back with a child that probably wasn't even his. 'It's us or her,' I told him. And although it hurt him, he didn't fight much because he knew it was true. Why do you want to bring this girl here after Tino is dead, only to find out what?"

With that, she stood up, walked to her bedroom and slammed the door after her.

Daniel looked after her in complete bewilderment.

~~~

"So, how did she take it?" Alena asked Daniel.

"Not well."

"What did you expect? How are you supposed to react when you find out your husband had a secret daughter and deceived you?"

Daniel didn't want to tell her the truth yet. He wasn't sure how to do it. "I was hoping for more. I wanted her to be happy, like she was getting a gift. I thought that Mom would feel like finding Tino's daughter was a miracle. Something to connect Mom to Tino. No use, she's rejecting everything outright."

"Good God," Alena said, "where is this magical fairyland you're living in? A 'miracle?' This ain't no miracle, Daniel. It's a nightmare where her dead husband was a louse, like the first one. You should've left well enough alone. She's trying to move on. You should let her."

"I thought you didn't want her moving on so fast," Daniel said.

"Well, I don't like everything she's up to these days—the serial dating, the ridiculous clothes, the exercise, the hair coloring. It's desperate. But at least it's not full-blown desperation."

"I can't let Virginia go," he said. "I still believe in the Tino I knew, that even if he turned his back on her, that he'd have done the right thing if he were alive today, that he'd have wanted her to find a place here with us."

"Maybe none of us knew Tino as well as we thought."

Daniel saw the shape of the secret, of the awful bargain his mother had put to his stepfather. If he wanted to be part of the family, he had to let go of the past, the past that was his daughter. Daniel felt implicated, and it made him feel sick.

"Look, I've invited Virginia to stay. I can't be part of denying her some kind of answers. She doesn't deserve it. She's not a 'problem.' She's family, damn it."

Alena looked at him with something that Daniel couldn't make out. This worried him. Usually, reading Alena wasn't a difficult task. She was either smiling or frowning. But what Daniel saw was something like disappointment, sorrow, fear and anger mixed in the witch's cauldron of his sister's eyes.

"What is it?" he finally said. "Whatever it is, you should spill it out. I'm not going to melt or anything."

"Nothing," she said. And then, "Cristina said all sorts of things. I didn't want to believe all the things, that you're a drug addict and that you've been going crazy. But now, with this girl? What's next? What're you trying to prove? Maybe you need to let go of the past, too, and start working your life out!"

"What? Come on, since when have you ever believed anything Cristina has to say about me?"

His sister looked on, a juror wanting answers.

"Jesus. Okay. It's true. Some of it, anyway. Most of it. I can only imagine what she told you, but the gist of it is true. I'm a fucking mess, all right? I turned my back on her, turned my back to my dead kid, and I've done a lot more. Things you don't want to know, things I gotta erase myself with painkillers to escape for even a few hours. But here's a chance for me, for us, for her. You have to see."

Alena looked at him with a mixture of pity and anger. Her eyes told him it was his pain to bear, not hers, not their mother's.

When Tino was dying, his mother was so lost. It was difficult to watch. Tino looked terrible in that hospital bed, like he had shrunk, the bed sucking him into its depths. He looked small. His face drawn, his eyes, already deeply set, sunk farther into his face. His breath so shallow, it was almost imperceptible. Above all, Daniel remembered the moments becoming excruciatingly slow. When Tino did open his eyes, they stared out at nothing, as if he were already looking into the Big Forever. And Daniel could tell that even his macho kick-ass stepfather was afraid. And that was scary shit.

The worst thing was that no one, not the steady stream of church people, or the relatives, or the neighborhood friends, could acknowledge the obvious truth that the Reaper was in the room. Everyone could smell death like a funky spoiled egg, but they weren't going to cop to it.

Everyone stayed busy instead. Alena and Daniel ran between the house and the hospital, the trips to the house filled with meaningless tasks designed to obviate the truth that there was not a goddamned thing to do. As Tino himself used to say, nothing left but the crying. The night he died, Daniel told Teresa that he would take the watch so that she could go home and get a little sleep. She was delirious with grief and exhaustion.

He didn't want to be there, in the presence of death so soon after he'd come back from the war. But it was his duty, to Tino, to his mother. So he'd sat six feet from Tino, listening carefully for a deep breath that might either signal the end or that he was coming to consciousness. Alena had brought over a bunch of framed pictures from Tino's years with them: wedding pictures, vacation shots, holiday pics, all happier, better times. Daniel realized there weren't going to be any more photos of better times.

Daniel called her when Tino went into the death throes, the raspy breathing. Teresa missed his death by minutes. She'd been awakened from a deep, restless sleep, muddled, and had to use precious minutes to get herself together for the drive to the hospital. The image of his Mom taking Tino's still warm hand and placing it on her face while she cried was still fresh, sharply focused. It was never going to fade. Teresa slammed her thigh with her free hand because she didn't have words for what she was feeling. Daniel remembered dead Tino's mouth slightly opened as if his stepfather was still fighting for one more breath. Tino's last breaths were so reminiscent, so familiar: the bloody cough of a Haji wraith spitting out a final curse as Daniel choked the life out of him. That deathbed scene had sent Daniel into a tailspin, a motherfucker of a panic attack. Then, like now, he'd chewed a handful of oxies.

The pills and his thinking about Virginia were the only makings of a bulwark against the incredible sadness working hard to overwhelm his soul.

≈≈≈

They'd be glad after they got to know Virginia. They'd understand the magnitude of bringing this young woman to them, when they realized that she was real, a vulnerable and honorable human, not just a threat creating divided loyalties. It had been so long since he'd felt hopeful about anything, so long since he'd been this nervous and excited at the same time. It was a good thing, what he was doing, even if Alena and his mother didn't see it yet.

His mother was a good woman. She was wise, kind, cheerful, sympathetic, fair. Most of the time. If, as it was becoming apparent, she had done wrong in keeping Tino from his daughter, she could still rectify the injury. Tino had done something grievous in acquiescing to the bargain of keeping his new wife and family in exchange for turning his back on Virginia. In one fell swoop, Daniel thought, these sins could be remedied. Perhaps even his own sins, more grievous, more injurious and abominable might be balanced. If not before God—for who knew what God considered or did not consider—then before the eyes of Virginia, perhaps even in his own tired soul. Maybe he might even be able to move forward instead of treading water, slowly succumbing, drowning.

What if Cristina should show up? Her emails grew more and more frantic, angrier, more threatening and desperate. Just that morning she's sent a note saying that she would unmask him as a liar and a pervert at his mother's church. "You killed our child and you left me alone, not just once, but again and again, you bastard!" He couldn't justify his cowardice, his abandonment, but maybe he could apologize in some way that would free her as well, if not from her grief and anger, at least enough so that she might see her way towards peace.

Maybe the girl . . . Maybe giving her back the family she might have had if Teresa hadn't been so afraid, if Tino hadn't been so afraid . . . If Celia hadn't failed her . . .

In his imagination, Daniel saw his mother and her cousins asking about the baby and giving Virginia advice about mothering. She probably hadn't had any of that, and he felt sure that she would appreciate the insights that these good women had for her. *Where is this magic fairyland*, the phrase floated in his mind.

Virginia didn't know the extent of Tino's betrayal, didn't know the role Teresa had played. The thought hit Daniel suddenly. This wasn't going to be a minor revelation. The girl was going to learn that her father and stepmother had agreed that disowning her was the best thing for their new family. She would learn that her fate was decided much like that of some poor pregnant woman and her son whose lives were collateral damage thousands of miles away. But goddamnit, he wouldn't let that happen. Not this time.

He would have to be the voice of reason. He, a drug-addled depressive killer. Daniel imagined what Cristina would say if she could only hear his thoughts. Once, she'd overheard him giving Alena advice over an issue she was having with Richard. He'd succeeded in calming Alena down and felt good about it until he hung up the phone. Cristina was sitting on the couch pretending to watch some dumb-ass show, one of those *Housewives of Whatever* shows. He was about to be deployed, and she'd been angry and anxious. Her pregnancy was at its start and had been deemed "high risk."

He went to sit with her, even though he hated those goddamned shows.

Just as his ass hit the couch, she'd turned to him and said, "What do you know about being a father, anyway? Or a husband, for that matter? You're about to leave! Got anything for me?" And then she snorted as he remained silent.

Maybe she was right.

He came to realize by then that he didn't like Cristina much. Not because he thought Cristina would make a rotten mother. She probably would have made sure Pumpkin was clean and fed, even loved. It had more to do with a revulsion at fathering a kid with a woman he didn't love. Even before the baby died, he'd been a shitty husband, which suggested he'd make a shitty father. All he knew was *his* shitty father, Henry, who'd never thrown a ball with him or taken him anywhere that he could remember, except for the couple of times that he'd dropped Daniel off at the movies alone while he went to jock his lovers. It occurred to him that even Tino, a man Daniel thought was different, had been a regular prick, too.

Daniel nodded off and dreamt that he was doing a waltz with someone clumsy. It was dark until he spun his partner under a spotlight to find, to his horror, that he was dancing with himself. He was disgusted, couldn't look at his other self in the face, much less in the eyes. He thought about choking this other self to death. But when he reached for its neck, it reached for his; his mirror-self who would take him out just as soon as be taken out. Who was who?

~~~

Virginia thought Daniel preferred the truth to come out a little at a time, dribbled out with a turkey baster. It was as if he were trying to keep the truth about her from his sister and mother at the same time as he was keeping her from a truth that would be devastating. She was tired of being lied to.

She'd lived with lies her whole life, and now it seemed as if the weight of the truth was hers, too.

She'd never fit in anywhere. Never even fit in her own body (although since she'd found out she was pregnant, something there was changing). She knew how people thought of her: a dumb little slut. Pregnant. Destined to suffer. They thought she was pathetic, sad, one of those dumb girls who thought she needed to have a baby in order to be something or someone.

Already the Baby Rice inside her was more her than she'd ever felt before. Virginia shifted in bed because her stomach was upset. Soon, she'd have a place to put her hands: a big pregnant belly. She'd never had that before. When she was a kid, her mom would slap her hard on the arm and say, "Quit fidgeting so damned much! Sit on those hands if you can't stop!" Virginia would get red in the face but wouldn't cry. It must have given Celia some sort of pleasure because she'd follow with, "Didn't you hear me tell you to sit on those *pinche* hands?" And Virginia would have to sit on them, feeling like a weird twitchy hen. Virginia saw herself in the near future, big belly and all, and thought, *I got a place for my hands now, Celia, what do you think about that?*

The thing was, she was tired. She wanted to fit in here, even though it didn't make sense. She was a stranger. Her father had been a stranger. These people were strangers. She'd been cheated her whole life. All sorts of cheated. Now, even her dead father had cheated her, too. It put her in the position of hoping that her mother had chased him away and told him never to come back. Even that was terrible, because what kind of man would accept that? Forget his child just as soon as he'd dropped off a stuffed dog, maybe even relieved that he didn't have to follow through on his meager obligations to her. Above all, she wanted to find that he had at least longed to take care of her, if only he'd been allowed.

Growing up with Benny-Boy and Celia, it had always
been cheat, cheat, cheat. Coming home and Benny-Boy's rig
parked out in front of the house, knowing he was back from
one of his hauls, knowing he'd be coming into her room, the
stink of his grimy old boots filling the room with the smell of
grease and fried food, and putting his finger on her lips, trying to slip it in her mouth in the dark, and her acting asleep,
and Benny-Boy feeling he was the one being cheated. Then,
she'd get to thinking, "There's my real father out there who'd
never cheat me." That there was this man who would've beat
the tar out of Benny-Boy, if only he knew. And now, only to
find that he was dead and that he'd known she was out there
but hadn't cared enough to rescue her.

So why was she there? What did she think she was going
to resolve or rescue? Her father wasn't there. He wasn't going
to tell her, "Misfit, you fit here." But there was Daniel. Maybe
he spoke for Saturnino. Maybe it was just him feeling sorry
for her. She'd accept the sympathy. She'd learned that something so elemental was hard to come by in this rotten, cold
world. Besides, maybe he was telling her what Saturnino
would have told her: that she could find a spot to rest there
where she didn't have to feel like she was a mistake, a nui-
sance who needed to be told to sit on her restless hands.

She kept wondering what it would take to make them
want her. Want her like she imagined a mother wanted her
daughter, or how a man wanted a woman he loved. Wanted
like she belonged proper. She remembered when she was still
a kid, not even out of first grade, and Celia and Benny-Boy
decided to take her on one of his long-hauls. Celia hadn't
been on the road with him since Virginia had been a baby.
Benny-Boy had taken advantage of this and had started
stringing out trips longer and longer, until Celia had finally
decided that she was going to come to the party uninvited, if
need be.

Celie tried to make it seem like fun. She bought Virginia some new jeans and T-shirts at the Goodwill. She packed her bags carefully, thinking about what she'd do in a place where there was a beach. Celia told her, "Virginia, we're going to a place that's named after you." She said "Virginia" like her daughter might be a little retarded and needed her to say it slow so that she'd understand. "We might even drive to where the President of the United States lives."

Benny-Boy didn't share her enthusiasm. He was glum the whole trip, silent, listening to the radio loud, so that Celia quit trying to talk to him just a few hours into the trip. After a while, she didn't even come to the front of the cab. She lay in the smelly bed that Benny-Boy used on his trips, an old itchy green wool blanket that smelled stale, like it had been crumpled under a damp rock since Creation.

Virginia liked riding in the front, the seat so wide she didn't have to sit close to Benny-Boy, the windshield so big it looked like the whole world was rushing toward them. She liked the mountains and how they swooped down the gray roads, all that weight behind them propelling them so fast, just barely under control. Benny-Boy even noticed how she liked the road and said, "You might just be a trucker yet, little girl." Little girl is what he called her happy or mad, the only difference being how he drew out "little" when he was happy. Celia hardly came out after that, only to eat when Benny-Boy pulled into a truck stop for a quick silent meal. Benny-Boy cleaning his plate fast and then moving to the counter to talk to some other trucker while her mother and she finished up. They didn't spend much time in Virginia. Just dropped off the trailer, hitched up another and high-tailed it back to Louisiana. Virginia never did see the ocean or where the president lived. They got back, and that's when Celia got fat: real fat.

~~~

Daniel called Virginia and said he was coming by Alena's to check on her. He asked if she was hungry. Being pregnant, it seemed like she was always hungry. He didn't even need an answer: "Of course, you're hungry. We'll go to lunch when I get there.

"Look, I've planned this thing on Sunday. A chance for you to meet my mom and some relatives. A welcome home for you."

The word "home" struck her, "home" like she was a part of something. She almost got teary-eyed but resisted. Being pregnant made her too emotional, and she didn't like that.

A little while later, they pulled into a taco place and had a good meal, although Daniel didn't eat much. He wanted to know how she was feeling. Finally, she got down to what was nagging at her.

"So, what's your mom think about all this?"

"Oh, she's looking forward to meeting you, everyone is." But he said it like he was unsure of his words.

"Who's coming," she asked him.

He drank from a huge glass of iced tea, big enough to hide behind. He sipped on it while he talked. "Oh, Alena and her family, maybe one of her friends, a neighbor she hangs out with a lot. Mom, of course, her boyfriend, Eric, who is a real character. A couple of mom's closest cousins. Don't take anything too personally, okay? My family can be a little flaky."

She smiled at that description. "Better than psychotic."

"My mom is hanging out with her boyfriend until Sunday. Why don't you come and spend the night at the house. It'll get you away from Alena. It's gotta be a pain right now. She and her husband are going through some things."

"Bad timing," she said.

She agreed and they picked up her small bag at Alena's and headed "home."

His mother's house was small, a ranch, pale yellow, with a chain link fence. A big dog was sitting on the porch, tired from the heat. He looked pretty interested when they pulled up.

"I'll put Monster in the house before I bring you out of the truck. He's not mean, but he can get rambunctious. He's practically knocked me down a couple of times."

The dog got on his hind legs when Daniel stood outside the truck. He licked his face and wagged his tail and generally spazzed until Daniel reached for the chain connected to his collar. He stood still while Daniel unhooked him. As soon as the chain fell, the dog went bonkers, running back and forth across the lawn, taking a leak on the one tree in the yard, running in circles. Daniel tried to chase him down. The dog thought he was playing and would stop just long enough for Daniel to get close before he burst out running again. The dog finally got curious about Virginia and came to the pickup, resting his big paws on the window and looking in at her, his black and pink tongue hanging out as he panted and slobbered on the truck.

"C'mere," Daniel said, using the dog's distraction to get him by the back of his collar. "You come in the house," he said like the dog understood.

He half-dragged him in, leaving the front door open. Virginia got out of the truck and grabbed her bag from the truck bed. It wasn't heavy. She was halfway up the driveway when Daniel came bounding out like the energy of the big dog had infected him.

"I got that, I got that," he said grabbing her bag. "Sorry about him. He's nuts."

The house was dark and cool from the air conditioning and the drawn curtains. It seemed like a great place for a nap. She felt tired and wired at the same time.

"Like I said, Mom's at Eric's," Daniel said. "She probably won't show up until tomorrow. Here's your room."

He led her back into the small room, painted bright pink for some reason, as if long ago it had belonged to a little girl. There was a full-sized bed, a small bureau and a closet with an open face, empty except for a dozen crooked wire hangers.

"You just make yourself comfortable," he said. "I cleaned out the dresser so you can put stuff away. Just make yourself at home. I'm going to put Monster back outside and get a few things ready."

He left her alone, which was nice because she wanted to take a few minutes to look things over and to feel something, make the four walls feel familiar, get used to the smell of the house, which was pleasant but different. There was a religious plaque hanging on the wall. It said, "You also, like living stones, are being built into a spiritual house." On a small shelf there were books with titles she didn't recognize, some of them religious and many others self-help.

Virginia pulled one out: "Raising the Godly Child." It was old, the spine worn out with spidery creases that no longer shared the title. She flipped through it, then tossed it on the bed for later, if she had trouble sleeping. On the way to the bathroom, she stopped in the hallway to view the line of pictures hanging there. A couple were older, black and white, of people probably dead by now. But there were a few of Daniel and his sister in grade school. Daniel looked happy, innocent, a little dorky. In the photo he wore a little orange belt that crossed his chest. There was a badge pinned to it. He must have been a crossing guard. He was wearing thick black glasses and smiling without showing any teeth. It made him look sweet, like the type of kid others picked on. There was a photo of Alena in her graduation camp and gown. She was all teeth, the smile seeming like it might be permanent, a mask to hide behind, because her eyes weren't smiling. There was no picture of Daniel's mother or Saturnino. She'd hoped there'd be a few pictures of him on display, but maybe Teresa had taken them down because they made her sad or because her boyfriend didn't like them.

A shadow moved in the corner of Virginia's eye as she realized that in the doorway, out of nowhere, the huge black dog was standing. He seemed cautious, like he wasn't sure what to make of Virginia, friend or foe? His head was hunched a little, as if he preferred to look at the ground, but didn't want to take his eyes off her for fear she'd whack him or something.

"You a good boy?" she asked him.

He looked around tentatively, backed up a couple of steps and looked into the kitchen, trying to see if his master was around, in case he needed him.

"You're a good boy, I can tell," she said to him.

She held her hand out to him; fingers outstretched. He took a look and moved forward a step and stretched his head out to smell her. Nothing there to eat, he figured out, but nothing out of the ordinary either. She took a half-step in his direction and he did too. Before long he'd gotten his head in her hands and she was petting him. Besides Daniel, he was the only one who seemed genuinely pleased to meet her.

"Monster," Daniel said, coming from a doorway at the end of the kitchen. "Is he bothering you? Did he try to jump on you?"

"No," she said, still petting the dog. "He's no monster. He's a sweet boy, right, Monster?"

"He's a chicken. Nothing to worry about. Let me put him back in my room. I left the door open. Sorry."

"He's not bothering me. Can he stay?"

"Sure. Rest up."

Monster decided to like her room. When she came out of the bathroom, freshly showered, he was on the bed.

"You like me, huh?" she asked him. "I like you too."

She sat down on the bed and, like the good boy he was, Monster got off and dropped to the floor, putting his big head over his big paws, looking up at her both winsome and wistful at the same time, as if he knew exactly how she felt. Virginia leaned over and again started petting him. His big brown eyes seemed to contain all the pain she felt but had no name for. She hadn't allowed herself to cry in front of anyone since the boy-cop. Crying didn't accomplish anything, didn't change a thing. Problems and sadness would still be there after the tears dried. She tried to force herself to be strong, not to give into emotions, but slowly, quietly, ever so softly, Virginia began to cry.

～～～

"Is this thing really going to happen on Sunday?" Alena asked Daniel on the phone.

"Yes," Daniel said with some exasperation. "Why wouldn't it? Are you and Richard coming?"

"I'll be there. Tonia too. Richard isn't coming, of course. I hope you didn't invite him."

"No, I didn't invite him. I told him, though. He probably wanted an invite, but I knew you'd be upset. I'm sorry about all that. How serious is this, anyway?"

"Very," Alena said.

"He says you're doing crazy stuff. That you're stuck in a fantasy."

"I'm no more stuck in a fantasy than you are with this Virginia girl, or than Mother with her telling everyone to call her 'Terry' and with her paranoia and insecurity about her Muscle Man."

"You have a kid," Daniel said. "You don't want her to wind up like Virginia, all screwed up, looking for answers no one can give."

"Look, I don't need lecturing. You solve your own problems. You've got enough of them, no need to worry about mine. Believe me. I have to save myself. Richard isn't going to do it. Mother or you can't do it."

"I don't know what's going on with you, sis. I really don't."

"I could say the same thing for you. Maybe it's my turn to be able to risk something instead of playing it safe and waiting to grow old and die. Ever think of that? I'm not living to *lose* anymore, Daniel," she said. "I'm going to live to get what I need. To win."

"I don't get it," he said. "What's winning?"

"You and Mother have always thought of me as being difficult, hard-headed, rigid. Don't deny it. It's true. I have been those things, always playing by the rules, always wearing the sensible shoes, doing the church girl thing, marrying when I was still a damned kid, giving up on my own dreams, always, always afraid of doing the wrong thing, committing the measly sin, getting caught, being found out, being thought a bad girl. Well, no more.

"It came to me a few weeks ago after you came here down in the dumps because of the emails that witch was sending you. I kept telling you that you should be happy to be rid of her. I was frustrated with you, but not because of you, but because of me. See, you've escaped. And I want to escape too."

"I've escaped?" Daniel asked. "Is that the way it seems to you?"

Alena wasn't listening. "And then I decided, screw it, maybe I have the same chance. If Mother can become 'Terry,' why can't I become someone else too? I've got dreams, aspirations, desires. I want to do some things, see some things. I'm not going to be left out of the makeover party." Alena could hear herself getting louder, becoming hysterical, but she didn't care. "No one's going to talk me out of this. I'm going to take my time and make sure that my next move will be the one *I* want to make, mistake or not."

≁≁≁

Terry resented Daniel trying to make her feel guilty, telling her that the girl being there was an opportunity to clear the air. But "clearing the air" meant taking responsibility for the suffering of the child Virginia had been. It would prove Tino had lived a lie. No, worse. It would make him into a liar, a man who could turn his back on his own flesh and blood. It would mean that she'd not only countenanced the abandonment, but also had forced the issue after Tino had married her. All she'd done was to save Tino from himself, from his own black past. So, "No more," she told him when she found out that he was planning on seeing his ex-wife to arrange bringing his daughter into his, their, lives. He could send money, if there was any left after their family's needs were met. But no more living in the past. In the end, truth be told, Tino hadn't needed all that much convincing. He knew the price of looking backwards.

In any case, those were *Teresa's* doings. She was *Terry* now. The past was dead and buried. What good would it do to confess? Tino was dead. He couldn't make amends for his sins anymore. The girl wouldn't gain anything from dredging up the past. Certainly not the lost years of Tino's love.

"Just a lunch, a nice talk," Daniel had said. He wanted the three of them to go to Tino's grave afterward.

Teresa didn't believe in cemeteries. There was nothing left at the cemetery. Everything of value had been taken up to

God—the soul, the person, the heart, all gone to God. The body? Nothing. Dust. Not worth visiting. Didn't he understand? This Virginia girl would drag the family through the mud.

Eric told her, "Look, Terry, facts are facts. Hiding from them is as useless as hiding from a bear when you're wearing hamburger undies. It'll sniff you out. Why don't you meet the girl? You'll know right away if she's his kin."

Eric didn't know the dark secrets of Tino and Teresa's bargain. His finding out was precisely what Terry feared. The more she thought about the situation, the angrier she got at Daniel and at the girl, who was probably nothing but a little lying, knocked-up slut.

Eric asked her, "Did you know he had a kid out there? Did he ever tell you?"

"I don't want to talk about it," she told him.

That night, Teresa dreamt that she was in a small brick room, shaped like a shoebox, windowless, but surely a sanctuary, although without any religious markings. She had her face to the back of the room, but she wouldn't turn around because she knew that at the front was a coffin. She hoped that if she didn't turn back, she could stay safe. But she couldn't manage it. It was just as frightening to not look. So, she turned and, sure enough, it was Tino's body in the coffin. Somehow, despite being terrified, she got the nerve to walk up to it. It was made of wood with the lid in two pieces so that she could lift the top half of it and look at the face. Slowly, she reached to open the top half of the casket and, just as the light began to fall on the dead face, she woke up.

It was a horrible dream, and she must have been moaning, because Eric stirred.

"Terry?"

"Go back to sleep," she said.

He turned back on his side and went right back to snoring. It was early morning. Terry could see the sky turning purple behind the thin curtain. She was sure Daniel was still awake. He was an insomniac. She called his phone. He didn't answer. Perhaps he was ignoring her. She left a message. "I'm not coming on Sunday. I'm not feeling well," and then she added, "and neither is Eric." She realized how silly it sounded, so she added to the message: "I don't want to give the girl my bug. Because she's pregnant. Okay?" She hung up and tried to go back to sleep.

#5

Danny's squad combines with Alpha and the platoon moves on to support Marines to the east of their position. It is mop up time at this point, but there are still days of fighting ahead for them. A week in their boots, in their filthy fatigues, bloodied, contaminated with germs, their own piss and shit. By the time they drag themselves to the FOB, they are glassy-eyed, too tired to do anything but climb out of the Brads and drop to the ground behind a concrete barrier that marks the perimeter of the compound. They are hungry for anything warm, but the mess hall seems miles away, so they sit against each other and that wall. Danny watches as one of his boys lets loose a stream of diarrhea, so tired he barely gets his britches down. There is a stream of FOBBITS walking to and fro, oblivious to their plight. It is time to eat, if they can make it to the mess.

Then some prick with a starched uni and a major's gold cluster comes up to the group. "We got *Stars and Stripes.* They want a story. You guys are it. The general will be here too. You ground pounders clean the hell up, for Christ's sake."

Danny stares. The boys all watch until the major walks away. This is the way it is, Danny realizes. Corporate bullshit, same as any in the real world. No one gives a damn about him or his men, except for him and his men.

"Hey," Danny calls after the major, who stops and turns. "You tell the general and those *Stars* guys to go fuck themselves."

"What was that, sergeant?" he says incredulously. "I know you boys just came off the line, but get your shit and gear together and be ready."

Without looking at him, Danny spits straight out in front of him, a loose tooth, from a blow he'd taken from the Haji, landing between his boots with the phlegm. It is almost worth losing the tooth, the wadded mess it makes in the sand.

Not wanting to respond, the major turns and makes his way back to his jeep.

"That was class-A," Fonzo says. "If that fobbit ever done anything worth a shit, it was an accident."

Danny shuts his eyes and falls asleep almost instantly. There is no Pumpkin to greet him in these tired dreams. Instead, there are flesh-eating dogs, dead mothers and the fading light of an enemy's eyes.

It isn't but two weeks later that Danny finds himself Stateside, a couple of pieces of chest salad announcing his valor, vials of oxycontin, a tormented wife mourning the death of their unborn child. Danny knows that this is God's way of punishing him for the mother and her unborn and born children, Goldfish and Broken Boy. And Danny, somehow, improbably, impossibly wants nothing more than to get back to the Sandbox to his squad.

CHAPTER 13
Balance the Scales

It was like the old days in the Sandbox, reconning, not Hajis, though. He was sitting in his car outside Cristina's apartment. Maybe it was just stalking. It had come to him in the middle of the night, as he shook like a motherfucking leaf in a windstorm, that he had to clear things up if he, they, were to move on. The truth was he'd left her behind, something he never would've done to an Army brother in the Sandbox. You didn't leave behind bodies, much less a wounded soldier. Danny wouldn't have left her behind. But Daniel had.

He couldn't tell anymore which one of his two selves was his true self. All he knew was that he was exhausted and half insane with carrying the weight of both. It was like one person forced to carry another person on their back, only maybe once in a while the other taking the weight for a while, then dropping it. Dead loads are heaviest.

She was home. Of course, she was. It was still dark, an hour before sunrise, but Daniel was taking no chances. He had to talk to her before bringing Virginia into the family. It didn't make any real sense. Cristina was no longer in the circle, hadn't been since she sent him tumbling down the stairs and he'd woken up in rehab. That had only been the fireworks finale, the one everyone acknowledged as The End. The real ending, however, had begun with the goddamned killings of Goldfish, Broken Boy and their mother. It was followed by Pumpkin's death. Last of all was the death of their marriage. That was Danny's weight, like carrying a dead soldier through the searing sands in Iraq. Now, how many corpses was he carrying around? Hell, pile on Tino's body as well.

He had to explain to Cristina, to let her know she didn't have to carry any of the weight. Daniel would do it. Was doing it. He was sorry that he'd left her alone. It was too late for anything like forgiveness, but at least he could try to help her out somehow. Release, maybe for both of them.

When the light in the apartment shone through the window, Daniel stepped out of the car. He lit a cigarette, gave her enough time to go to the bathroom, put her coffee on. He knew her routine. Routines didn't change.

Done with the cig, he tossed the butt and, donning a military bearing, marched to her front door and rang the bell. It was as scary as anything he'd faced in the Sandbox. And then she was standing in front of him at the threshold. She was in her robe, a white terrycloth deal that had seen better days. Her hair was ragged, something Cristina would be sure to rectify before she had her breakfast. She didn't say anything, her face was blank.

"Can I come in?" Daniel said after a couple of seconds.

"Don't know. Can you?" she said stepping slightly to the side.

Daniel moved into the apartment briskly. He needed a cigarette, but Cristina hated his smoking. He looked around the living room. It was decorated in a flowery ultra-feminine style, pictures straight out of some catalog, matching couches in pastels. There is no pain here, the décor insisted, only happy, gauzy feelings. Then his eyes fell on the shrine, a handblown glass pumpkin in violet, sitting next to a small framed colorized ultrasound of the baby, his tiny face clear as

day, a tiny fist in front of his mouth, eyes closed, incontro-
vertibly alive. A real little human, doing his little human
thing, getting ready for the outside world. In front of the as-
semblage sat an incense holder, half a stick waiting to burn,
grayed ashes powdering the shelf below.

"What do you want?" she said, now facing him.

"Dunno exactly," he said. "Thought we could talk for a
minute."

"Just a minute?"

"A little longer than that, I guess," he said.

He almost smiled but stopped. That would set her off. He
coughed, fighting the urge to tremble with all his might.

She nodded her head, turned and shut the door. She
walked to the kitchen to fix her coffee. Daniel followed.

"Want some," Cristina said without looking at him.

He was looking at her back now. He'd forgotten how
small she was, how delicate a frame she carried, everything
proportionate.

"No thanks," he said. "I try not to do caffeine."

"Well, that's one good thing, I guess," she said, stirring
her cup as she turned towards him.

She was still beautiful, although her eyes were tired-look-
ing, wrinkles forming, furrows in her brow.

"How about we sit down for a bit," he said.

He wanted to sit in the kitchen, away from the shrine, but
she walked back to the living room and he followed.

"That's nice, that memorial," he said.

"I won't forget," she said, taking a seat. "So? What do
you want?"

"I shouldn't have disappeared like I did," he said finally.

"Disappeared? More like faded away. You started to fade
before Pumpkin, but you finally just evaporated. Didn't have
the courage to say goodbye and fuck you very much."

"That sounds about right," Daniel said. "Never have thought about it that way."

"Lots of things you've never thought about," she said. She put her cup down. "If you're here to apologize, don't bother. That won't do either of us any good."

"You're right," he said. "It isn't apologies I'm here to give."

"Oh? You're here to give me something!" She gave a small hostile smile. Everything held a bitter double meaning.

"You know, I used to think about us when I was in the shit," he said, not sure of where he was going, fearful he was getting lost in the opiate haze. "I'd be on a cot or in a mummy sack, and I'd think about what it'd be like when I got home, and me and you and Pumpkin would be lying in bed together. I pictured it like a fox den, the three of us warm, underground, our smell, our little space, with me protecting us. Secure, you know?"

"No, I don't know. Never did know with you. I always thought that was the sickest part of this, that you're this soldier boy and you don't know anything about protecting anybody or anything. All I ever saw is you running away. I didn't even see that, actually. Just the space you left. So, why are you here?"

"I had to come," Daniel said.

He was finding it difficult to concentrate. The combination of painkillers, the vodka he'd swallowed them with, the lack of sleep despite enough downer in his system to knock out a horse.

"I know you're hurting," he said. "That's part of it."

"How would you know that?"

"I know. I've always known. I just never knew what to do about it."

"So, you helped yourself, and fuck me. I already know all that, Daniel. What is it you want?"

"I'm working on something, a plan kind of. It's more than that. It's tough to explain. Can't even really explain it to myself. Just kind of feeling it out as I go. Only so far, I'd only been thinking of myself, how I figured into it, not about you. Now, I finally get that the two of us are stuck in the same place, like a truck spinning its wheels in the sand. I want us to get out of there before we're both blown to bits."

"What the fuck are you talking about, Daniel? You sound high, like always. You look like shit, sound like shit and you make zero sense. I'm getting tired already. What do you want?"

Daniel stood up. He wanted to make it clear. This felt like the last time he was going to talk to Cristina, and he intended to make it count.

"I just want to release you. Let you know that Pumpkin wasn't your fault. It was me, my doing. Things I did over there . . . God decided to fuck me for. . . ." He stopped unable to hang a name on the sin.

"Yeah?" she said, the disdain fading for a moment, her thirst for some kind of answer to her pain more visible. "What did you do, Daniel?"

"I killed a woman and her kid. And she was pregnant. Watched her die. God took Pumpkin. He's not done yet, either. We're . . . you're . . . stuck. I have to balance the scales. Maybe then He'll let us . . . you . . . go."

"You just left me! Alone, again and again. You're a fucking coward!" The curiosity was gone. Her rage moved in closer to Daniel, threatening to engulf him.

"You want to hit me?" he said. "Would that. . . ."

Before he finished the sentence, she slapped him with all her might.

"Again," he said, holding his hands at his side.

She slapped him again, just as hard. His face burned, his left cheek beginning to numb. Still, he refused to raise a hand from his side.

"Again," he said.

She slapped him a third time, tears streaming down her face. This time the blow didn't even turn his face. Then he put his arms around her, and she begin to sob quietly into his shoulder.

"You left me alone," she said, the warmth of her breath and tears streaming down his neck. "You're not supposed to do that to someone you love. You didn't love me or Pumpkin."

"I'm gonna balance the scales," he said quietly but with determination. "I'm going to make Him set you free!"

"What're you talking about," she said, pulling away from his shoulder, her eyes red and swollen. "Are you going to kill yourself? That won't help."

"I've thought about it, but like you said, it won't help. God wants a fuckload more than that. I'm gonna help this girl, this pregnant girl. She's my stepsister. Then God is going to take one of those killings off the books. Pumpkin was the first, for the dead boy. Our marriage, that was for the mom. That leaves one for the unborn baby. I save the baby now, maybe God calls it even." He could tell that he was rambling.

Even so, Cristina was listening, trying to piece it together.

"You sad sonuvabitch," she said finally. "You don't choose a get-out-of-jail card!" She looked ready to slap him again. "I'm never getting out and neither are you!"

She turned suddenly and walked to a bedroom. Daniel could hear her opening drawers. After a few seconds, Cristina came back into the living room. She held a tiny camo T-shirt. Block letters spelled out "ARMY."

"You had daydreams about us sleeping like a good little family. Here's my dead daydream."

She tossed the T-shirt at him. He caught it, although his instincts told him to let it fall to the floor.

"Little Danny, not 'Pumpkin,' was supposed to wear this when you got back from your fucking war. Daddy's little boy waving a little fucking American flag for his hero. I'm tired of being the keeper of his memory. Now you can do it. You can take that fucking shirt and nail it to your wall. You can look at it, if you can muster the courage."

Daniel looked at the shirt, infant-sized, a fleeting image of a brown baby boy wearing it as Daniel came walking through the security gate at the San Antonio airport. But Pumpkin's face was no face, just a hazy brown oval, dimmed, unrecognizable. He rolled up the shirt and stuffed it into his back pocket like a bandana. He looked at Cristina, her eyes pooling with tears, eyes filled with pain, her mouth distorted by the combination of anger and profound sorrow.

"I'm sorry," he said.

"I can't have babies," she said. "When you left, I needed to have someone to fill the hole, someone to hang on to and love. I tried finding a donor but no go. My insides are fucked up. I guess you can feel better now. It's me that's broken."

"Cristina," Daniel said, "I'm sorry. I'm really sorry."

"You said you weren't here to apologize. So don't. It doesn't matter," she said. "Nothing will change it. Nothing will make me feel better, be better. God won't take notice of your balancing act, whatever you're calling it. This girl, you helping her? You can't and you won't. You'll fuck her up like you fucked me up. You're not capable of real love. You don't know what it is. You'll strand her in the muck and mire of your fucked-up dead soul. You never had what it took to be a real father, anyway."

Making a move towards her, Daniel extended his arms, knowing his touch would not be received. He tried anyway.

"Get away from me," she said, backing up a step. "I didn't tell you to come here. I don't want your comfort, your goddamn hugs! I hate you."

Daniel felt the urge to leave, to back up and run through the door, where he could have a smoke and drive fast, shaking or not shaking. But he couldn't. He was frozen in place as if his feet were magnetized to an iron floor. He was stuck. Just like Cristina was stuck. Like his Pumpkin was stuck in eternal limbo. As his mother and sister and poor Virginia were stuck.

"Get out!" Cristina finally yelled, a sickening weight slithering from chest to legs. She looked as if she were going to fall or faint.

Daniel watched her, his hands visibly shaking, waiting to see if he would need to catch her if she went down.

"I said, get out! Get out! Get out!"

She moved on him quickly as she gained her balance and, in a burst of energy, pushed him hard enough so that he lost his balance. He grabbed the arm of her flowery couch to keep from falling to the floor. It was a relief to be pushed. He didn't have a choice now. He had to leave. That's what Cristina wanted.

"Get out, you bastard," she said one last time before breaking into a pained, animal sob.

Standing uncertainly, Daniel backed up to the door as quickly as he could. Not wanting to turn his back on her, he found the doorknob. The sunlight flooded the room. It was a bright, spring day, already hot enough to raise goosebumps on his neck. He walked out, leaving the front door slightly open, as if closing it would signify something awful and permanent.

He walked to the car, got in, rolled the window down as he felt for his cigarettes. Finding the pack, he tried to pull one out, but his fingers wouldn't obey. His hands shook, and he cursed them. Finally, he flung a cigarette out of the box, bending to pick it off the car floor. Shifting in his seat, he felt the T-shirt still stuffed in his back pocket. He pulled it free and, looking at it, began to cry. He'd never held Pumpkin, never seen his body, never mourned him in tears. He'd felt nausea and sadness, which had morphed into a deadness necessary for him to leave Cristina and return to the Sandbox, where numbness was useful. Looking in the rearview mirror, he peered into his red, tear-stained eyes. Disgusted with himself for breaking down, he used the T-shirt to wipe his face. Unrolling it fully, he forced himself to see Pumpkin wearing it, reaching for him in some alternate universe, sun shining, Cristina happy, the three of them a family.

He draped the T-shirt carefully on the steering wheel and lit his cigarette. His tears continued to run despite his disgust, and he allowed himself to shake and moan as deeply as he had since he'd come back from Iraq.

"I'm sorry," he said finally to the T-shirt, as if he were speaking to his dead son. "I'm sorry . . . I'm sorry . . . I'm sorry," he continued tearfully.

Cristina was right. He couldn't even help himself, let alone Virginia. He was a goddamn fool, a coward, a monster playing games, a liar whose most pathetic victim was himself. He needed to leave, to get out before he destroyed anyone else. It was the only choice, the only thing he was capable of doing. He turned the car on, thinking about what to do. Virginia and his family would be congregating at Teresa's house in a couple of hours. He began driving, leaving the parking lot, entering the wide street in front of the apartment complex, the traffic nonexistent on an early Sunday morning. He reached for the glove box, fished for his bottle of oxy, shook three pills out and chewed them, the bitterness filling his mouth in what his body recognized as the signal that release was on its way.

Reaching the intersection at IH-35—south for his mother's house or north towards Dallas, with the vague promise of St. Louis and finally Chicago—he made his choice and gunned the motor as his left hand gripped the T-shirt-draped steering wheel and his right hand shook the pack of cigarettes for another smoke.

~~~

Virginia spent a long time contemplating what she had to wear. Small pickings. She'd brought only a small suitcase. Not that she had many choices in the first place. She'd brought only two dresses, a dark one that would be good for church or a funeral and a bright one with a colorful pattern of sunbursts and orange dollops that she had picked because the colors made her feel happy. On the hanger, it looked all wrong, too gaudy. She would look fake, a pathetic attempt to look cheerful and pleasant, a desirable, welcomed addition to the party. "I'll look like a big fat children's piñata," she thought. But the choice was that or the dark dress, which she imagined would make her look like a walking purple bruise. The inadequacy of her choices made her want to cry. She put off the decision for now and pulled out Celia's secret box that contained the picture of Saturnino. This was the truly important piece of the wardrobe. She was going to show it to Teresa and Alena at just the right time.

As quietly as possible, she opened the bedroom door to go into the bathroom and shower. The dog was lying in the hallway and he stood up immediately. Monster wagged his tail and looked at her with a good-natured desire to please. He wanted to be petted on the head and assured that he was a good little monster. But the girl looked at him with a blank expression. She brushed past him, carrying the box into the bathroom and closing the door in his face. He lay back down in the hallway. He could wait. Celia's box was the only important thing she'd brought to San Antonio. She reread the yellowed postcards and tattered letters and found the picture of Saturnino. She would show Teresa and Alena that Saturnino was hers, too. Although they'd got the better deal, with him being around, she'd gotten something too, something they didn't have. She had his blood running through her veins, in Rice's veins. They couldn't take that away. They couldn't deny the picture. They couldn't deny her, even if Saturnino hadn't come back for her.

She'd show them the picture, and she'd get answers. Did he care? Why didn't he come back? And then *she'd* decide what to do with those answers. She'd make the choice. "Am I in or am I out? Am I the grungy pregger slut or the long-lost daughter? Benny-Boy or Saturnino? Celia or Teresa? Who am I really?" she practiced by asking the mute, frozen face in the picture.

She showered and dressed. In the end, she chose the dark dress because at the very least it conveyed that she meant business. She then went to the kitchen and, not seeing Daniel, knocked on the door that connected to his bedroom. Nothing. Back in the living room, she peered out the window and saw that the car was gone. This gave her a sinking feeling. He hadn't gone out for supplies. He'd brought groceries home last night. It was only about an hour before lunch was to begin and nothing was being prepared. Monster scratched at the door, and she let him out. He ran out barking at a passerby.

~~~

"Alena doesn't know how to run a life," thought Filomena as she readied herself for Virginia's coming out event. "Not hers, and definitely not mine. I can't say I blame her.

She's got no social graces, no sense of self-control, no confidence. Inside she's made of jello, a scared little person who doesn't want anyone to see her for what she is."

As she slipped on sexy snake-skinned pumps, she remembered the time grade school Alena's friends were making fun of her old shoes, which were coming apart at the seams. She'd tried to glue the sole back, but even the glue was shabby, and when it came off, they made fun and called her Shabby Shoes. Alena didn't let them see her cry—Filomena gave her that much credit—but Alena never forgot, and every time she thought about trying something that required even the teensiest amount of risk, she recalled the incident so vividly that her stomach got quivery and she didn't try. Alena blamed her mother and her brother and her clod of a husband, Richard. But Filomena knew who was really to blame.

"That's why I'm here," Filomena told her reflection. "I don't regret anything. Regrets are for shabby, scared little people," she said out loud and then applied a thick layer of daringly red lipstick.

Filomena was a dancer, and good dancers, great dancers, were always ready to perform, to stand up and step up. You put the fear out of your head and you used the energy of the fear itself, like a shot of adrenaline, and you *danced*. Poor pathetic Alena had been born into a family of non-dancers, people who waited in the wings, in the shadows, scared to shine because they didn't know that they could. How could you know, if you'd never had the guts to even try?

Filomena had enough of the tiny corral Alena had boxed her in. A dancer without a real stage, without real shoes, without a spotlight, or decent backdrop. A paper doll.

"Well, Alena," Filomena said aloud, "I'm no paper doll. Today, I get to prove it. I'll tell them, 'Call me Filomena. That's my name. Now watch me dance.'"

~~~

Eric said she had to go. Daniel said she had to go. Tino's ghost said she had to go. He'd told her in a dream that morning. Teresa had to face the music for their bargain. Was it really a bargain? Tino had acted out of fear. She supposed she had, too.

Doing what had been commanded, Teresa got dressed and put on a happy face for a girl she'd "wronged." She could admit it.

It wasn't fair to the girl or to her. There was nothing that could be done or undone. Tino was dead, and the past should stay dead, too. But for some reason, for some damned reason, her son, her boyfriend, her dead husband, perhaps God himself, wanted her to face it. It wasn't fair.

Suddenly, she turned to Eric and said, "I'm not going."

"Of course you are, Terry."

"I'm not going."

He got up and puts his arm around her and said, "I'll be there with you. You can always turn right around and leave."

And with that, Terry let him lead her out.

CHAPTER 14
Juswannohome

Driving north, Daniel thought about where Pumpkin was now. Heaven, purgatory, hell? He wondered if his victims were with him, particularly Goldfish and Broken Boy. They were presumably Muslim. Pumpkin was buried as a Christian. It didn't really matter, he decided. He'd seen enough corpses to conclude that the end was all there was: ceaseless darkness. Where was he going? He should have killed himself by now. Turned himself into an object no longer placeable or knowable, beyond hell or purgatory. Until death, he could simply keep moving, keep circling, fluid and free from the choreography of guilt and memory, his being subsumed in the mindlessness of permanent movement. He opened the car window and threw out the Army T-shirt that Cristina had shoved in his face. He watched it flutter as it came to rest on the side of the road, next to Mile Marker 337.

~~~

Not knowing where Daniel was, Virginia decided she'd help out with the cooking. She stirred the beans, adding a half cup of water, a bit more salt. She tasted them. They were turning out well. That was huge. Good beans are the crux of a successful Mexican plate, covering a multitude of sins. Good beans, good meal. She was, however, worried about the rice. It was the most difficult dish. Every Mexican made it different. She'd watched her mother make it a million times. Virginia's rice always turned out bland, mushy, no zing whatsoever. Her mom's rice was altogether different. Always perfect, spicy with peppers, firm but fully cooked, effortless. She was a hell of a Spanish rice maker. No denying that. Just the right amount of cilantro, tomato sauce, garlic, chilis, chicken broth. Consistent and unsurprising.

Her thoughts turned to her own Baby Rice, now comfortably nestled in her womb. How would she turn out?

Terry and Eric parked in the driveway. Terry wasn't speaking to Eric. She was being petulant in a way that Eric associated with spoiled children, a behavior which he found cloying in Terry, unless she was trying to be cute. She was not trying to be cute now. He'd forced her into coming to the luncheon. She felt that she was being ambushed in her own house, her own home. That horrible dog would probably be waiting to jump on her from behind the couch, which he'd made filthy with his huge stinking paws.

Terry wanted to be angry. She wasn't about to cave to the pressure to be accommodating and sweet. Daniel and Eric thought that she'd melt like she always did when it came down to it. She wasn't going to do it. She had a secret strategy that she'd developed over the years to give her the added zing necessary to fuel righteous anger. And this was a justified case of righteous anger if ever there was one. So, she focused on something negative and found a way to relate it back to the reason for her anger. That odious Monster had shat all over the yard, and no one had picked it up. Huge piles of dog doo in every corner. The plants had been dug up (they were already dead due to the drought, but still). Torn dog toys and other weird items the animal had found were strewn all over. The Monster invasion was analogous to the invasion that was being engineered by those close to her. This girl, with her awful story, displayed Tino's deceitfulness and sin—the old Tino, the lost, pre-saved Tino. It wasn't fair to him. It certainly wasn't fair to her. She'd only found a way to help him put away the past decisively. It could be painful, closing the past, but it had to be done if he was going to move into the future a better man. She got angrier and angrier.

Eric opened his truck door and waited on Terry to open hers before he stepped out. She stayed still, turned as far away from him as possible as she looked out the window. The heat from the open door rushed into the truck cab like the opening of a kiln.

"Aren't you getting out, Terry?" he said.

She stayed silent, imagining that she could smell the dog doo wafting in with the waves of heat. "It smells horrible," she said finally. "That dog has really done a number on my house."

Eric thought better than to respond. He could smell the dog shit, too. He closed the truck door and turned the truck back on to get the air condition going. He knew he'd made a mistake because this would make Terry think that they were going to leave. Then he got an idea.

"We could just go," he said tentatively. He could feel mild confusion in her silence. He waited a few seconds. "Daniel can handle himself all right, I guess. No reason you should have to do something you really don't want to do. Let's just go. The boy will be all right."

"Just let me out," she said suddenly, as if Eric was keeping her locked in the truck.

She hated him in that moment because he'd managed to trick her into asking to stay. He came around the truck and opened the door for her.

"Be careful where you step," she said. "I don't want you tracking dog poop into the house. It already smells like a portable toilet, thanks to that filthy animal you brought here."

Eric felt the intense heat on the back of his neck as he watched her climb down from the truck.

Now back in the bedroom, Virginia looked at the purple ribbon that served as a belt for her black dress. It didn't look right. She pulled it out of the flimsy loops in which it drooped untied and held it in her hands. It might make a good tool for strangling someone. Monster raised his head as if sensing her murderous whim. She moved towards him, purple ribbon still in her hands, and wrapped it around his neck three times. She tied a flowing bow under his jaw. Monster looked dapper. She smiled. Accessorized as he was, he looked like her dog now. Monster wagged his tail, thump, thump, thump, against the bed.

She heard the front door open and close, the murmur of voices, one cold and cutting, the other lower, serious, without humor. The sounds made her stomach jump, or was it a cramp, a preggers cramp? She'd had them all morning: nervousness, she insisted. But for now, she put a smile on, making sure it wasn't too broad, not forced-looking, not prim nor silly. It was difficult because there was no mirror. She tried them out on Monster, who seemed to approve of them. This made her smile for a moment and then face the door, her true smile replaced by something else. Monster jumped from the bed and walked out before her. Thump, thump, thump, against the threshold. She loved Monster.

In the living room in hushed conversation stood the woman from the pictures and a strange looking white man with the longest mullet she'd ever seen. Eric turned towards her, hearing the dog, and gave her a nod and a small but sincere smile.

"Hi there," he said.

Terry pretended not to notice and walked into the kitchen and out of sight.

Eric looked after her, unsure, unsettled by her rudeness. He composed himself quickly but clumsily. "Looking for Daniel," he said, explaining Terry's abrupt departure. "She'll be right back." He nodded again. "I'm Eric Boone." He put out his right hand, looking down at Monster as he did so. "Guess Monster's gussied up for the big to-do," he said, looking at the purple bow.

"I'm Virginia," the girl said. She shook his hand as firmly as possible, despite not getting her fingers around the man's grip. "Daniel's not here. I think he must've gone to the store."

"Sure," he said straightening up. "Looks like you've got yourself a friend here."

Monster concurred. Thump, thump, thump against the sofa.

Terry scanned the backyard for Daniel. Also, for dog doo. Apparently, Monster only went out into the front yard. The damned dog couldn't even do her the small favor of taking a dump in the backyard when she needed it.

"The front yard looks terrible," she thought. "Daniel's got people visiting, and there's shit all over. Someone's going to step in it and bring it into the house. We'll never get it out of the carpet. He could have at least given the yard a once-over."

She went back into the house to find the girl sitting on the lounger, her hands resting on her small belly. Eric sat across from her on the lazy boy, reclining with his feet in the air. He had as much sense of inappropriateness as Monster. This was a blessing in its own way.

"Terry, this here's Virginia."

The girl stood up as quickly as possible, unsure what to do with her face, with her hands, holding her expression steady, her right hand out as if to shake, but the left at half-mast ready, should the surly-looking woman make an effort at a hug. Terry did nothing, her face frozen, except for her eyes, which scanned the girl from head to toe. Virginia felt every bit a bloated children's piñata. Just then a cramp hit her, an explosion of electricity running down her stomach to her thighs, everything tightening. She did her best to hide the jolt but couldn't. She grimaced and sat down on the couch faster and harder than she'd wanted too.

Terry had no choice but to sit down on the couch next to the girl. She was pregnant, Terry could tell, though she wasn't showing yet. She was so tiny that even a modest baby bump would soon be clear. For a moment, Terry softened with a combined pang of pity and shame. But she recovered by thinking, *dog poo, dog poo, dog poo*. She looked at the idiot dog.

"I hope he isn't bothering you. Daniel should know better. With a pregnant woman in the house, that filthy animal should be outside."

"It's okay," Virginia offered.

"Eric has no consideration, bringing that animal here, and Daniel was no help. They both made me keep him."

"He's sweet," Virginia said.

She had her hand over the pocket in which Saturnino's picture sat hidden for the moment. She wanted to bring it out, right then and there. But the moment wasn't right yet. The door swung open, the blinding outdoor light silhouetting Filomena as she stepped into the room with Tonia in tow.

"Hello, Mother. Hello, Virginia," she said.

She wore large black sunglasses and was holding a bag with two pies inside. The glasses obscured most of her face. Inside the house, she couldn't see very much because it had been so bright outside. Still, she didn't take off the shades. The little girl went to her grandmother. Terry greeted her warmly, giving her a tight squeeze, feeling that Tonia was her only ally in the world, the only person who wouldn't judge her.

"Where's Daniel?" Filomena asked.

"I don't know," Virginia and Terry said in unison.

"Maybe some last-minute stuff?" Virginia added.

"Have you called him?" Filomena asked.

Just then, Virginia felt another cramp run through her stomach, this one more painful than the last. She grimaced. Only the dog seemed to notice. He looked up at her for a moment and then put his face back in between his outstretched paws.

"Where's Richard?" Terry asked.

"I don't know," Filomena said nonchalantly.

"Isn't he coming?"

"I don't see why. I didn't invite him."

"Are you two fighting?"

"Not in front of T.O.N.I.A." Filomena said as if her exceedingly bright daughter couldn't spell her own name. Her eyes were scrunched intensely but her enormous sunglasses obscured them. Her tone was perfectly clear. "I've got some things to tell you, but not right now. After the party. When we can talk privately."

"Whatever," Terry said. She'd started to use this phrase frequently. She'd picked it up from Alena. "I'm going to make sure that boy's rice doesn't burn." She got up and went into the kitchen. Filomena followed, pies in hand, leaving Tonia alone with Virginia. Tonia edged up to Monster hesitantly, her hand held out for the dog to nuzzle. Monster sniffed her outstretched fingers, stuck his long tongue out and gave them a quick lick. There was nothing tasty there, so he went back to lying still.

"You can pet him," Virginia said. The cramp was receding. She liked Tonia, who was quiet and sweet.

"I like dogs," she said.

"Me too," Virginia answered. "Put your fingers on the top of his head like this."

She placed her fingertips on the top of Monster's skull and stroked his head lightly. Tonia followed suit. The two petted the animal together in the dark living room.

"How should I know? I just told you, Mother, that we're separated. I hope you didn't invite him."

"Uh, I think I mentioned the lunch to him."

"Why did you do that without asking me," Filomena said, taking her sunglasses off so that Terry could see the full extent of her displeasure. When she was satisfied that her mother had registered her anger, she put the sunglasses back on.

"If he shows up here, I'm leaving," she said. "I just want you to know that because I don't want you guilting me about leaving this coming-out party, or whatever this is. I'm not going to be in the same room as that man. Besides, it only confuses Tonia."

"You should have told me before today," Terry said.

Alena wasn't about to reply. Filomena wouldn't allow it. Filomena didn't answer questions that she didn't want to answer. Why should this old woman be demanding answers? Wasn't that her absurdly mulleted boyfriend out in the front yard picking up dog shit? She had more than enough on her plate, from the looks of him. Filomena looked at her watch. She wasn't going to stick around very long, especially if that dimwit Richard was going to show.

"Call me Filomena," she said.

"Filo-what?" Terry said.

"Mena," Filomena said. "If you can adopt a new name, *Terry*, then I can."

Virginia was back on the couch, Tonia on the floor petting Monster with no fear.

"How you doing?" Eric said, entering the room from outside, the glaring sunlight blinding Virginia.

"I'm feeling a little tired," Virginia admitted. "It's not anyone's fault. I'm just nervous."

She waited for Eric to say something. He seemed deep in thought. "I don't think people like me being here," she said through a small, sad smile.

"You just gotta give them time. They're good people. Terry just got hit about the D.I.V.O.R.C.E."

Tonia perked up her ears. She knew that spelling meant grown-up talk. Her mom and dad did it all the time now.

"I like his bow," Tonia said out loud.

Virginia looked at her. "If your momma gets me some scissors, I can make you a little bow for your wrist just like Monster's, and you'll both be in purple."

"Sure, scissors," Eric said and retrieved some sewing scissors from Terry's room.

The girl had already untied Monster's purple bow. Virginia measured out a short span of the ribbon and cut it with the scissors. She placed the piece on her lap while she re-tied Monster's bow. It was no longer quite as flowing as it had been before. Now, it made him look more like a present than a dapper dan. Tonia held out her wrist with anticipation. She wanted to look like Monster. Virginia wound the ribbon around her small wrist once and tied a small, but pretty bow.

"Say, that's pretty," Eric said.

Both girls smiled.

"Whatta you say, Tonia?"

"It's pretty, just like Monster's," she said.

"Say, I better take that dog outside to do his business," Eric said.

Outside, he waited on the dog and looked at clearing any Monster poo he might have missed. There was no shade. The only tree was long dead. He made a note to bring his chainsaw over and cut it down before it tumbled into the house and destroyed the roof. A car drove slowly down the street, as if trying to find an address. It slowed to a crawl and stopped in the middle of the road in front of the house. The window came down and an older woman with iron-gray curly hair stuck her face out.

"Is this Teresa's house?"

"Pardon?" Eric said walking to the fence.

"Is this the lunch?" the woman said louder.

"Yes, ma'am," he said. "Park it and come on in. There's no poo on the lawn."

The woman looked at him quizzically, then rolled the window up, backed the car up at an acute angle and parked awkwardly. The car was nowhere near the curb. This bothered Eric.

"I can re-park that for you," he told the two women exiting the car.

"It's fine like it is," the driver said pleasantly. "I've done a lot worse than that before!"

They walked through the gate and met Eric in the yard. "You have to be Eric, with all those big muscles," the driver said. "I'm Sister Gutiérrez, from Teresa's church. This is my daughter, Lizzy. We're here to meet Brother Tino's daughter."

"I'm Eric," he said. "I'm Terry's boyfriend."

"Oh, yes," Sister Gutiérrez said. "I thought we were lost. It's been such a long time since I've been to Sister Teresa's . . . Terry's . . . house. I don't drive too well anymore."

Eric noted her glasses. The lenses were so incredibly thick, they seemed like a novelty item, part of a nutty professor get-up.

The girl smiled. "Mom wouldn't let me drive. I don't know why. It's like riding with Mr. Magoo."

The two women laughed. "I sure wouldn't make much of a navigator," Sister Gutiérrez said. "Well, show us in. It's time to meet the prodigal daughter."

Once again the living room was flooded with bright sunlight. Monster jumped up and stared at the intruders. He recognized Eric and relaxed. The two women could be trusted. He sat back down at Tonia's feet.

"Church folk are here," Eric said.

Virginia tried to stand.

"Don't do that," Sister Gutierrez said. "You sit there just like you're doing! And look at you," she said to Tonia, "you're too cute and with that pretty bow!"

Tonia smiled and said, "Hello," too low for Sister Gutierrez to hear.

"And you have to be Tino's daughter!" She bent down and grabbed hold of Virginia's head, bringing it into her breasts in a tight embrace. "It couldn't be any more obvious. I wish your dad was here."

The smell of perfumed powder engulfed Virginia while she fought the instinct to squirm away.

"The best thing that ever happened to your stepmom's family!"

"I have a picture of him from when he visited me," Virginia said.

She pulled it out and handed it to Sister Gutierrez. She'd meant to show the picture at a more auspicious moment, but these two women were the first to seem interested. Sister Gutierrez and Lizzy looked at it closely.

"He was young back then," Sister Gutierrez said. "Has Teresa seen it?"

Just then, Terry came into the room. "Sister Gutierrez, I thought that was you. Hi, *m'ija*," she said, giving Lizzy a small hug.

"Just meeting your new friend and your stepdaughter," she said, letting go of Virginia and turning to embrace Teresa. "Have you seen the picture of Tino?"

"What picture," Terry asked.

"Virginia's picture," Sister Gutierrez answered. "Show it to her," she told the girl.

"It's so hot out there," Terry said, ignoring her remarks. "We could've done this at Alena's but Daniel wanted it here. So, we're stuck in the house."

Virginia pressed the picture to her tummy. Another spasm took hold of her stomach, muscles tightening their grip. She grimaced. Once again, only the dog seemed to notice. He turned towards her, watched for a moment and then turned back to Tonia. This time it was a prolonged cramp. Still, no one seemed to notice.

"I need to go to the bathroom," she said.

Eric moved in to offer his hand, and she took it, standing up a bit clumsily.

"Thank you," she said and made her way down the hall slowly.

"She's the spitting image of Tino," Sister Gutierrez told Terry.

"I don't see it," Terry said.

"You need to see the picture she brought. It's obvious. She's come all this way, and things are what they are, Sister, and you might as well accept it."

"I don't want to talk about that," Terry said. "Come help me look after the rice and beans. I don't know where that boy is. It's just like him to put together this thing and then forget he did it or to leave it to someone else to follow through. He didn't used to be this way. It's just like him now, after all that war stuff and the divorce. He hasn't been the same."

With Sister Gutierrez nodding sympathetically, the two women headed to the kitchen.

In the bathroom, Virginia suffered another cramp. It was like when she had a period, but different. She stood in front of the mirror, hands rubbing her lower belly, worrying. What if she were getting her period? What if she wasn't pregnant? Rather than relief, she was surprised at the pangs of anxiety and deep disappointment. She wanted this baby. Just then, someone knocked on the door. It was the only bathroom in the house. "I'll be right out," she said. She rubbed her tummy a few more times, flushed the empty toilet, counted to ten and opened the door. There was no one there.

Back in the living room, Eric was talking to Filomena in a soft tone. "Your mom's feeling a little bit uptight." Noticing Virginia, he stopped short of finishing the sentiment. "There she is," he said cheerfully.

As she sat down, there was a thunderous rapping at the front door. It startled everyone, especially Monster, who stood at full attention and gave a short bark. Again, someone pounded on the door heavily.

"You gonna get that?" Terry asked from the kitchen.

"Hold your fire," Eric shouted at the door banger.

He moved to the door, but before he could reach it, it flung open. Once again, the sunlight flooded the room. Richard stood in the doorway in silhouette.

Filomena peeked from behind her enormous sunglasses. "Richard?"

The shadow swayed, a mostly empty bottle of tequila in its right hand. Apparently, he'd used the heavy object to bang on the door.

"Hi there, Richie," Eric said as he positioned himself between Richard and the women sitting on the couch. He could see that the man's eyes were bloodshot and swollen.

Richard stepped into the house, raised the bottle as if giving some kind of drunken toast, or considering throwing the bottle at one of the room's occupants. He stood there, bottle raised, thinking and swaying.

"Daddy," Tonia said. She stood up and walked up to him. He didn't look down at her. He kept his eyes trained on the other people.

"Richard," Filomena said, "stop acting like an ass in front of your daughter. Put that bottle down." She looked at Terry.

"This is your fault. You shouldn't have told him anything about this."

Richard took a long final swig and then sent the bottle to the ground hard. The empty bottle bounced harmlessly on the carpeted floor. He then stumbled into the light of the room. Eric stepped towards him. "Hey, buddy, let's step out for a breather."

Richard just kept walking, brushing past him, his mouth beginning to quiver. "You made me do this," he said to Filomena. "Why're you blaming your poor momma?"

"Whoa, there, big fella," said Eric. He put his hand on his shoulder, but Richard shook it off and swooped with more agility than his drunken state should have afforded.

"You done this to me!" he yelled at Filomena.

This time, Eric got hold of him from behind. It was this that sent Richard over the edge, and he attempted a two-handed grab at his wife, who was still wearing her sunglasses.

"What do you think you're doing, you idiot!" she screamed at him.

Tonia started to whimper like an injured animal.

Richard took a swing at Eric, but held as he was from behind, the punch went nowhere.

"*Dios mío*," Terry said, "*Dios mío*. What's going on in my house!"

There was a short, clumsy scuffle that ended up with Richard pinned underneath Eric. Richard began to cry underneath the heavily muscled Eric.

"Look what you done, Alena. Look what you done."

Filomena took Tonia by the hand and rushed her into her old pink bedroom, slamming the door behind them.

"I'm sorry," Richard cried, Eric straddling him like a professional wrestler. "I'm sorry, Alena," he moaned. "I just want to come home. Justwantacome-ome. Juswannacomome."

"Get off the boy," Sister Gutierrez said. "You're not going to cause any more trouble. Right Richard?"

"No trouble," he said still sniffling. "Juswannohome."

Virginia, the cramp alleviated, watched numbly. She knew more about drunken domestic scenes than all the assembled people combined. A wave of nausea engulfed her, and she made her way to the bathroom once again. Sister Gutierrez went to the kitchen to find some coffee. Terry brushed past the pregnant girl and stood knocking softly on the bedroom door in which Filomena and Tonia had taken refuge.

"*M'ija*, open the door," she said softly but firmly. "Open the door." She jiggled the locked doorknob to no avail.

In the bathroom, Virginia took a deep breath and put the toilet seat down. She sat. She still had her father's picture in her hand. She gazed at it, wondering how long she might be able to stay there before someone came knocking. She considered praying. But she could think of nothing that Jesus might be willing to do at that moment. Nothing ever worked out, anyway. Just then, someone knocked on the door.

"You okay, Virginia?"

It was Daniel. He'd finally arrived.

"Never mind her," she heard Terry say. "Come over here and help me with your sister. She's got Tonia in there with her." Virginia heard the two shuffle to the bedroom door. "Go on, talk to her," said Terry.

"Hey, Alena," Daniel said as calmly as he could. "Hey, open the door. What the heck is going on?"

"It's your fault," Filomena said. "Now, you deal with it. You get him out of here. I'm not moving until he's gone."

"I juswancome-ome," Richard said. Somehow, he'd gotten away from his keeper and had made his way to the door. "Tell her I juswannacome-ome." He looked at Daniel expectantly, a pathetic look of hope resting in his eyes. "Tell 'er, pal," he said, gripping Daniel's arm.

"He just wants to come home, sis," Daniel said as he looked into his brother-in-law's drunken, childish face.

"Get him out of here!" Filomena said in a choppy, ragged tone.

Daniel knew this voice, knew she meant business. He shook his head at Richard. "Better call it a day," he told him. "C'mon, pal. Let's get you some coffee and get it together. It's best to give her some space right now."

At this, Richard stiffened. Daniel could see a stubborn look coming into his brother-in-law's face. He was about to engage in some drunken resistance.

"I'm naagonaneeeware," he slurred. "Imagonahome."

Eric came up behind Richard and put his hand on his shoulder. "You don't want this right now, buddy. You come with me. I'll help you straighten out and give you a ride where you're staying."

"She don kiss me no more," Richard said to no one in particular. "She didn't even kiss me on my birthday."

"Sometimes these things happen," Eric said. "You have to keep your chin up, fella."

"Come on, bro. Things'll be all right," Daniel said, despite knowing that they wouldn't be. "I'm going to talk to her. She'll come around. You just need to give her some real space right now. You're in no condition to win her over. You'll see. You give her some time."

Richard looked at Daniel and then turned his face down towards the floor. Daniel could see that last bit of piss and vinegar drain from his brother-in-law's face. He seemed to deflate in front of Daniel's eyes. He took Richard by the shoulder and led him back to the living room. Terry stayed at the door waiting for Filomena to open up.

"I'm sorry," Richard said to Daniel. "I didn't mean to call you fag."

He sat back down on the couch, and Sister Gutierrez brought him a cup of instant black coffee. She'd put three heaping tablespoons in the mixture, and it looked like tar. Richard drank it straight. He grimaced. "Thas horble."

"This is all your doing," Terry said angrily to Daniel. "This is no time to be bringing this girl around. Your sister is going through a terrible time. And now this!"

Inside the bathroom, Virginia felt her stomach tighten in a spasm. She took a deep breath, looked in the mirror and wiped her face. She was afraid to come out.

Daniel knocked on the door. "You okay, Virginia?"

"Yeah," she said.

"Do you want to come in?"

She opened the door but didn't step out.

Daniel stepped into the bathroom and shut the door behind him. He looked at Virginia, about to apologize for his absence. Her face was flushed, and he could tell she was struggling to keep from crying.

"You know what we should do?" he told her.

She shook her head, and suddenly felt unsteady, a sense of vertigo engulfing her.

"We ought to grab Monster and head for Colorado or Montana, somewhere that the bunch of them can't find us."

Virginia looked at Daniel with a flushed face, dizzy, even confused. He didn't seem to be joking. "What are you talking about?"

"Look, you're not going to find Saturnino here. All the Saturnino you have or are ever going to have is that little baby you're carrying. Fuck them all," he said evenly, a revelation striking him as he stood next to the toilet.

"I need to lie down," Virginia said. "I'm feeling dizzy, and my guts are cramping."

"You okay?" Daniel asked. "Come on," he said leading her to his room.

She sat down on the edge of the bed.

"Go on, lie down," Daniel said.

He grabbed a duffel bag from his closet and haphazardly began stuffing clothes into it. "You look like you're in pain," he said, grabbing things randomly. "You'll feel better when we get the fuck out of here."

"Where were you?" she asked. "I started to think you'd, you know, cut out."

"I'll tell you about it on the way."

"On the way where?"

"Like I said, Colorado or Montana or wherever. So long as it's a long way from here."

Just then, Terry burst into the room. "This is a disaster, Daniel. It's all wrong. Look, *m'ija*," she said to Virginia, who'd suddenly shot up from the bed. "There's nothing here for you. No one has any answers. Your father was a good man. He did bad things, but he became a very good man. I wish he'd been good to you. That's all there is."

Now, Eric was in the room. He put his hand to Terry's elbow. "Come on, Terry. Let's leave them alone. The girl's tired."

"Let go of me!" Terry said, pulling away from Eric. His touch opened the vault. "You've no right to come here opening old wounds, Virginia! And you, Daniel, what a way to repay me! Everyone suffers, not just you! You need to take this girl back home. She can't stay here. There's nothing here for you. Nothing."

Through the divider separating Daniel's room from the kitchen, they heard growing chaos now. The yelling came from Filomena. The four of them walked into the kitchen to find Filomena pushing her finger into Richard's chest.

"I'm Filomena, you son of a bitch. Filomena. Your good girl is gone!"

Richard grabbed her by the shoulders and quickly, for a drunk man, slapped her hard enough to send the sunglasses flying.

"You sonafabitch," he screamed when Monster bit him from out of nowhere.

Richard put his hand on his torn pants, his ass cheek bleeding through from the bite.

"You bastard," Filomena yelled and connected with the back of his head. "You bastard, you're such a bastard."

Eric stepped in between them and pulled her away. Richard slid to the floor and began crying again, this time holding his daughter, who'd grown hysterical, in his arms. There was now a circle of stunned relatives, some of whom had just arrived, filling the room.

"¡Dios mío, Dios mío!" Terry kept shouting.

Sister Gutierrez and Lizzy held each other's arms as if one of them was going to either faint or bounce off in hysterics. In response, Terry prayed loudly and desperately.

In all this noise, Daniel made his way to his room, grabbed his duffel bag and keys. "Can you walk," he asked Virginia.

"I can walk," she said.

They moved through the crowd of cousins, now silent. As they walked through the living room, Daniel noted Tino's picture on the floor. It had been bent and torn in the scuffle. He picked it up and handed it to Virginia.

"Thanks. Don't want to lose that," she said.

They opened the front door, the light flooding the interior with a shocking brightness, behind them a tableau of frozen relatives standing in the kitchen doorway. As they got into the car, Daniel saw his sister and mother come out of the house, hurrying, wanting to stop them.

"Daniel," they took turns imploring. "Come back here, now!"

Monster looked at Daniel and Virginia and approached the car with a pleading look.

"Your choice, boy," Daniel said and opened the back door. "Every living thing gets a choice."

Monster didn't hesitate and jumped in the car. Virginia looked at him as he wagged his tail. Daniel waved off the two women. Eric, now in the doorway, gave Daniel a casual salute. Daniel nodded, climbed into the driver's seat, turned on the engine and backed the car out of the driveway quickly. A car honked, a near-miss. Daniel shook it off and shifted into drive.

"Don't worry, I've got it," he assured her. "You okay?"

"I think so," she said. "I've been feeling the pains all day."

"You okay?" he asked her again now with more concern. "That was some crazy party you threw."

"I almost didn't make it," he said.

"Oh yeah?" Virginia said, looking at him as he stared at the road ahead.

"A soldier doesn't leave his partner behind," he said pointing the car north. "I almost forgot that."

Monster agreed by thumping his tail in the backseat.

"Is that what we are, partners?"

"If you want that."

"Partners in crime," she said, smiling now as she patted his hand.

"Hey," Daniel said, "look in the glovebox."

Virginia opened the compartment about to snag a cigarette for Daniel. Instead, she found a balled-up green T-shirt. She straightened it out. It was rumpled, somewhat dusty, infant-sized, with "ARMY" stenciled across the chest. She looked at Daniel quizzically.

"I thought your little baby can wear it. Consider it a first baby present."

"Yeah, okay," she said smiling. She stretched the T-shirt out and draped it over her belly. "Fits perfect."

Reaching the on-ramp, Daniel got onto I-35 north.

"I'm sorry about all that back there. I should've been there on time. I had to take care of something. But look, everything is gonna be fine."

He turned his palm over so as to hold her hand properly.

Virginia's last cramp now subsided, she laid her head back on the headrest and closed her eyes. She believed him.

Epilogue

Saturnino woke up on that sad morning. He slowly became aware that his eyes were open and that he was staring at a gray ceiling. He could not remember what he'd been dreaming. He turned his head and looked at his wife snoring softly, her mouth opened slightly, her hair bunched and resting under her head. He slipped out of bed, quietly found his *chanclas* by the side of the bed facing outward, ready to go. He liked things to be efficient, to be prepared for use. He stretched, raising his hands upward, and then twisted at the waist in both directions, exhaling deeply as he did. He walked to the kitchen and put a pot of coffee on, then took to the bathroom, shat, showered and shaved. He could smell his coffee now and he went to the kitchen and poured a cup. He stood at the kitchen window looking out at the still dark neighborhood. He would have been on the road if not for the conversation he'd had with his wife the night before. Already cars were backing out of driveways, moving outward, cautiously, as if their drivers were mindful of the risks the day would bring, the possible losses, the unexpected catastrophes. They were like new cons going out into the exercise yard for the first time, weighing the benefits of some fresh air versus the possibility of getting shanked or rolled.

Saturnino felt like a prisoner. He refilled his cup and headed for the back door. It was the middle of summer, and the sun had only begun to rise. So the heat was still holding back, but only for a few more moments. Saturnino could feel the heat waiting just beyond the horizon to begin its rush forward and make everyone angry at everyone else as the asphalt underfoot broiled their soles. For a few more moments, the pre-dawn cool held. He looked across the street for Menríquez. He'd be out on his lawn, coffee cup also in hand, ready to run down neighborhood business. He circled his house carefully surveying it, not for damage or wear, but like a man taking precise measure of where and how he lived.

Saturnino felt like nothing was his. It could be taken from him at any moment. Just like the dawn coolness would give way to the overbearing sun. Like a mirage, it would dissipate quickly. This he knew.

Saturnino, coffee cup in hand, mustache warm from his last drink, tried to pray. He asked God to forgive him this grave sin. His prayer slipped between supplication and memory, the wronged in his life coming forward to play out imagined fates on the dawning, purple sky. He prayed for the girl he'd never know, whose face he could barely fix in his mind, even with the help of his powerful imagination. She would never see this house, would never know it as home, or so he thought

He prayed, as he did every morning, that he still, by some miracle, might be able to see her again. He knew that a bus from Louisiana was driving into Houston. He'd made an appointment but wouldn't be keeping it. He prayed that the girl might someday understand that he loved her even though he'd abandoned her. The sun broke through the horizon, and Saturnino wiped his face at the sound of his old friend Menríquez calling his name, prompting him to walk into the new day, like all of God's fortunate monsters.